# TALL, DARK AND WOLFISH

# LYDIA DARE

sourcebooks
casablanca

Published by Sourcebooks Casablanca, an imprint of
Sourcebooks, Inc.
P.O. Box 4410, Naperville, Illinois 60567-4410
(630) 961-3900
FAX: (630) 961-2168
www.sourcebooks.com

Printed and bound in the United States of America.
RRD 10 9 8 7 6 5 4 3 2

*To Petrina and the ladies at the Historical Romance Critique Group on Yahoo!—Thank you for cheering me on, your wonderful friendship, an endless supply of smileys, and for catching all those pesky typos.*

# *One*

IF ELSPETH CAMPBELL REVEALED HOW MUCH SHE wanted to leave the cold, damp cave, her coven sisters would surely think she was mad. Her plaid slipped from her shoulders, and she fought the shiver that threatened, trying to close her eyes and mind to the chilly Scottish air. She couldn't pull the plaid back into place until the ceremony was over.

They were meeting earlier than scheduled, as Caitrin foresaw trouble on the horizon for the *Còig*, though she hadn't revealed her fears to them yet. Truthfully, Elspeth didn't think Caitrin was certain what threatened them. They all knew the visions were clearest for their seer when the five of them were together.

To her right, Rhiannon tightened her grasp on Elspeth's hand while Sorcha and Blaire closed the space between them, which tightened the ring of four around Caitrin. In the middle of their circle, the seer's eyes were closed, her hands stretched toward the heavens.

Caitrin hummed an ancient melody, passed from one generation of *Còig* witches to the next. Then she stopped and all was quiet in the cave—so quiet that Elspeth could only hear the drumming of her own heart and Sorcha's rapid breathing to her left.

"I see a handsome man," Caitrin began softly. Her lilting voice echoed off the dark cavern walls.

"I'd like ta see one of those," Sorcha giggled.

The murderous look Rhiannon shot the youngest witch prevented any further levity from entering their circle.

"He bears the mark of the beast," Caitrin continued as though she'd never been interrupted.

Chills shot down Elspeth's spine, which had nothing to do with the loss of her plaid or the cool air in the cave. *The mark of the beast.* She'd heard those words her entire life.

"He will disrupt us. He will try ta take Elspeth from our circle."

Suddenly Elspeth had three sets of eyes on her. It would have been four, but Caitrin's were still closed as the vision played out in her mind.

"The beast canna be allowed ta break our coven. Disaster will fall if he succeeds." Caitrin's haunting blue eyes opened and she focused them on Elspeth.

Sucking in a surprised breath, Elspeth tried to snatch her hands back from Rhiannon and Sorcha, but their hold tightened. Her heart pounded faster and she felt certain she would faint.

Caitrin stepped forward and touched her fingers to Elspeth's brow. "Do ye ken the man I speak of, El?"

A nervous laugh escaped Elspeth's throat and

she nodded. She had never thought he would actually come for her. After all, he'd abandoned her mother long before she was born. "My father," she whispered.

Though Elspeth had never met her sire, she knew he wore the mark of the beast. So it must be him. Who else would try to take her from her coven?

Caitrin's brow furrowed. "He felt younger than that."

Elspeth shook her head. "I doona ken another man with the mark, Cait."

Finally the seer nodded. "Very well. Ye must be diligent. He canna be allowed ta take ye from us. The future of the *Còig d*epends upon it."

Elspeth nodded. She'd never known Caitrin's visions to be wrong, but in her twenty-one years, her father had never even contacted her. It didn't seem likely he would suddenly show interest in her well-being. "I will be careful."

*At the same time in London…*

Rain poured over the brim of Lord Benjamin Westfield's beaver hat. He stepped out of the darkness and crossed the threshold of Canis House, the exclusive social club to which he belonged. He handed his drenched greatcoat and ruined hat to the awaiting footman and walked into the warm light of the drawing room.

Ben glanced around at the other members, searching the faces for his older brothers. They weren't there. Thank God! He didn't think he could put on a cheerful face tonight, and they would most certainly see through his dark mood.

"Is the Duke of Blackmoor here this evening?" he asked the footman just to be certain.

The man shook his head. "I have not seen His Grace. However, Lord William was here, my lord."

Ben looked around the room once more. He didn't see Will. If he was quick, he could leave before his brother ever knew he was here. "And Major Forster?"

The footman gestured toward the back of the drawing room. "At his usual table, my lord."

Ben took the first relieved breath he'd had in days, hopeful the major could help him. He thanked the footman and then crossed the room to where his father's oldest friend sat in a dark corner, sipping whisky. "Am I interrupting?"

Major Desmond Forster's dark eyes twinkled as he looked up from his drink. "Ah, Benjamin. It's been an age. Please, please." He gestured toward an empty chair at his table. "To what do I owe this honor?"

Ben swallowed. It wasn't something he could just blurt out. In fact, now that he was here, he didn't know what to say to Forster at all. "I, uh, could use your counsel, sir."

"*My* counsel?" The old man leaned back in his seat and grinned. "I am flattered. I thought you generally sought out Blackmoor."

Usually he did want his brother Simon's advice. But this wasn't something he could discuss with either of his brothers. In fact, keeping Simon and Will from learning his secret was of the utmost importance. Ben took a deep breath and leaned in close over the table. "I'm in trouble, Major."

The man's smile vanished instantly. "What sort of trouble, Benjamin?"

He held tightly to the table and willed the words out of his mouth. "I didn't change."

"You didn't change?" the officer echoed.

"With the full moon last night," he explained. "I. Didn't. Change."

For the first time in his life as a Lycan man, Benjamin Westfield hadn't sprouted a tail, long snout, or paws with the coming of the full moon. He'd sought the moon the same way he always did, this time in a clearing in the woods, for his transformation. But last night nothing had happened. A moonbeam touched him, but the change that was so much a part of him didn't come, and he'd stood there for an eternity waiting and wondering why he was broken.

Major Forster's face drained of its color and his mouth fell open. "You didn't *change*?" he repeated, this time in *sotto voce*, with a world of meaning in his words.

Ben shook his head. "Do you know why?"

"Benjamin, we always change."

"Well, not me. Not last night."

The major motioned for two more glasses. "What happened?"

"Nothing happened. The moon hit me like it always does. But I didn't feel the pain, nor the joy, of changing. Nothing happened at all."

Major Forster scratched his head. "Prior to last night, did you feel the same call of the moon in the days leading up to the moonful?" He pushed a glass of whisky toward Ben with the tips of his fingers.

Ben sighed. Now that he mentioned it, he hadn't felt the same call. He hadn't been lusty or angry or felt the need to withdraw. But he hadn't really paid it much attention. Changing was as natural to him as breathing. It had been a part of him for fourteen of his twenty-six years, since adolescence.

Ben could only shake his head in dismay as he slumped in his chair. "No. I don't believe I did."

"Do you believe this has anything to do with that little incident in Brighton last month?" Major Forster raised one eyebrow.

Ben's eyes shot up quickly to meet the major's. "How did you know about that?"

"News travels quickly in our circle, Benjamin."

"I didn't mean to hurt her," Ben mumbled.

"We never do," the major said as he clapped a hand to Ben's shoulder. "What did Blackmoor have to say about it?"

Ben exhaled loudly and shook his head. "What *didn't* he have to say about it?" he breathed.

"That bad, huh?"

"Worse," Ben admitted.

"Those of our kind have to be aware of our strength—and our lust—as the moon grows fuller." His eyes narrowed as he regarded Ben.

"I know. Believe me, I have heard it all from Simon. *'You can't be with a woman that close to the phase of the moon. You could get out of control. How many times do I have to tell you? Now look what happened!'*" He mocked his oldest brother's imperious tone.

Major Forster chuckled.

"The woman was just scared. Really scared. Who would have thought that a whore would have been so squeamish?"

"Blackmoor, obviously."

Ben finally took a sip of his whisky and appreciated the way it made his eyes water. At least he felt something then. "I went to see the woman after the full moon. She's doing just fine. *She* actually apologized to *me* for screaming loud enough to call the watch."

"What did you learn from that experience?" the major asked.

"That I can't control the beast when it's so close to the full moon. I thought I could." He waved a hand in the air. "Other Lycans control themselves with women. They get along beautifully together."

"You will learn more about the type of relationship they have when you meet your own mate, my boy."

"But what do I do about not changing? I think I'm broken. I need to go back."

"There's only one way to go back," Major Forster mumbled as he scrubbed a hand across his mouth.

"Pardon?"

The major coughed into his hand. "There's only one person who can help you." He stopped talking and fixed his stare on his glass of whisky. Ben watched him for a moment.

"Major?" he finally prompted him.

The man finally tore his gaze from the glass. "Yes?" he asked, obviously distracted by his own thoughts.

"You were going to tell me how to fix it."

"Oh, yes." The man sat forward. "You must find a healer."

"A what?"

"A healer," the major repeated.

"You mean a witch?" Ben fought back a hysterical laugh. He'd come to his father's old friend for guidance, and he was going to send him to find a fabled creature that didn't exist. Oh, life was not working in his favor.

"A witch. A healer. Call it what you will. But you must find one."

"Everyone knows that witches are the things of legends and myths."

"As are we, my boy. As are we. But you can take my word for it, Benjamin. They do exist."

# Two

ELSPETH BRUSHED HER HAIR FROM HER EYES AND SECURED
it with a pewter hair comb. Her fingertips lingered a
moment over the raised surface of the comb, which
was etched with the form of a large dog, his snout
raised in the air. It was one of the only things she had
left of her mother.

Despite the fact that it had been given to her
mother by the man who left her with child, Elspeth
adored the piece because her mother had never been
without it. It had held back Rosewyth Campbell's
flaming red hair every day that El could remember.
And now it held back hers.

The flyaway locks were quite a nuisance at times.
She never could quite keep the wayward tresses in a
tidy chignon at her neck like most girls. Her hair had
a mind of its own. And it didn't want to be tamed.
Much like Elspeth herself refused to be tamed.

Before her mother had died, El's lack of social graces
had been the cause of their most frequent arguments.

Elspeth smiled to herself as she thought of her
mother telling her to tie her hair back with a ribbon

to keep it out of her face. Or to tuck it under her bonnet so that no one would notice her constant state of dishabille.

Caitrin broke her from her memories. "I ken ye want ta meet him."

"Meet who?" Elspeth asked, her mind on other matters.

"The one who wears the mark of the beast."

Elspeth sighed. "Since ye can see the future, ye must ken I'm already curious."

"Curiosity is in yer soul, El. No' in yer future," the girl chuckled as she hooked her arm through Elspeth's and dragged her down the street.

"I canna help it if I've a naturally inquisitive mind."

Caitrin leaned close and whispered dramatically, "I believe the word is 'meddlesome.'"

"I am no' meddlesome." Elspeth spat it out like the vilest of curse words. Then she couldn't hold back her grin. "I just need ta ken everythin' about everyone and help out if needed."

"Exactly. Meddlesome," Caitrin laughed, but then she sobered. "What do ye think it means? The mark?"

Elspeth had really hoped they'd changed the subject. "Honestly, I have no idea."

"But that is what yer mother called the mark *you* have?"

Elspeth's fingers automatically slid over her left wrist, where her own moon-shaped mark marred her skin. "She did. My father was a beast. And he wore the mark. So *I* wear the mark. That's all she ever said about it."

"Ye doona ken more than that? Surely she said somethin' about the man who sired ye."

"Very little," Elspeth confessed. Whenever the

subject arose, her mother's eyes would fill with tears
and the conversation came to an end. El eventually
stopped asking questions. "All I ken is he was a large
man. He stood a head and shoulders taller than most
others, my grandfather says."

"And he just disappeared?" Caitrin asked, unable to
hide her scandalized tone.

Though they were members of a mystical coven,
none of whom followed social strictures, being the
bastard daughter of Rosewyth Campbell was still
offensive to propriety. "Aye. After he got what he
needed from my mother, he disappeared. I canna help
but wonder what he needs from me now."

Caitrin stopped in her tracks, drawing Elspeth to a
halt. "Ye canna go with him, El."

"Doona ye think I ken that?" She started walking
again toward the dress shop on Queen Street.

Caitrin chased after her. "Aye, but…"

"I have no intention of leavin' with him, Cait.
But I have ta meet him, especially if he's come for
me. He's part of me and… well, I doona expect ye ta
understand." She pushed open the door to the shop,
and a little bell tinkled as she stepped inside.

Almost at once she was nearly knocked to the ground
by the suffocating sandalwood scent that assaulted her.
Elspeth blinked back tears and stared up into the dark
brown eyes of Mr. Alec MacQuarrie. "My dear Miss
Campbell," he began smoothly in his cultured English
accent. When Caitrin entered the shop, his smile broad-
ened to that of a lovesick puppy. "And Miss Macleod. It
is truly a pleasure seeing you this fine morning."

Caitrin shot Elspeth her most exasperated look.

In the last few weeks, it had seemed as though they couldn't go anywhere that Mr. MacQuarrie didn't show up. There was nothing outwardly offensive about the fellow, other than his unwanted and pointed attention constantly focused on the pretty, blond Caitrin. Mr. MacQuarrie was quite handsome with burnished auburn hair, an athletic build, and a strong chin. However, he was well aware of his attributes and often appeared more vain than the silliest of debutantes. But, Elspeth supposed, a fine English education would probably have that effect on anyone.

"Mr. MacQuarrie," Elspeth replied with a fraudulent smile as Caitrin turned her attention to the young shop girl. "I certainly wouldna think the interior of Mairghread's dress shop would interest ye of all people."

His smile didn't falter. "I was hoping to find the perfect ribbon for the perfect girl." His eyes flashed to Caitrin. Then he whispered, "Might you take pity on me, lass? I think you know her tastes better than I."

Before she could respond, Caitrin cast him an irritated glare. "Alec MacQuarrie, have ye taken ta followin' me now? And pesterin' my friends ta help with yer suit?"

"Miss Macleod," he pressed, stepping around Elspeth. "You can't fault me for wanting to bask in your presence, can you?"

"I see no future for us, Mr. MacQuarrie."

Elspeth had to smother her laugh. Alec MacQuarrie would never get around *that* objection. Poor fellow just didn't know it.

Undeterred, Mr. MacQuarrie clasped Caitrin's

hands. "Let me escort you somewhere. Anywhere. If I can't turn your head, I'll leave you be."

Caitrin's frown darkened.

"Give me at least a chance."

"And then ye'll leave me be? No more followin' me in ta dress shops or ta the park or—"

"You have my word as a gentleman."

Elspeth turned away from the pair and smiled at the shop girl. "I doona suppose the muslin I ordered has come in?"

The young girl nodded, apparently relieved not to bear witness to Caitrin and Mr. MacQuarrie's exchange any longer. "Just this mornin', Miss Campbell. Would ye like me ta package it up for ye?"

"That would be wonderful. Thank ye."

Elspeth turned around to see Alec MacQuarrie escape back on to Queen Street. She glanced at Caitrin. "So?"

Her friend shrugged. "So I told him he could take me ta Sorcha's ball. That should put an end ta it."

"But that's a fortnight away. Ye doona want ta dispense with him earlier than that?"

A beautiful smile lit Caitrin's face. "He is rather handsome. And I'd prefer no' ta attend the Fergusons' ball without an escort."

"I see." More likely Caitrin didn't want to have to face Wallace Ferguson all alone. In addition to the gift of second sight, Caitrin Macleod had been gifted with the body and face of an angel, which most men found positively alluring. It was one thing to rebuff the attentions of Alec MacQuarrie, but more difficult to do so with the brother of one of her sister witches.

"Ye can wipe that smug look off yer face, Elspeth Campbell, I ken what ye're thinkin'. I'm no' afraid ta face Wallace Ferguson."

"Of course no'."

Her friend heaved a sigh. "We were talkin' about yer father before MacQuarrie stumbled upon us."

"So we were. But I believe we've finished that conversation."

The shop girl stepped back into the room with a brown wrapped package. "Here ye are, Miss Campbell."

"Thank ye," Elspeth replied and handed the girl a coin for her troubles. Then she turned to leave the store with Caitrin right on her heels.

"Just promise ye'll be careful."

Elspeth grinned her most charming smile. "I am always careful."

"Ha!" Caitrin replied, though Elspeth could barely hear her over the sounds of passing carriages.

❧

Ben crept down the stairs of his rented townhouse. He felt like the biggest of fools, sneaking from his own rooms. But he hoped he could escape London, find the healer in Edinburgh that Major Forster mentioned, and return without either of his brothers being the wiser. It was a ridiculous plan. One or both of them were certain to miss him for the month or longer the entire journey would most likely take.

A healer!

He'd gone and lost his bloody mind.

"Ah, there you are," came a booming voice behind

him. Ben cringed before turning around to face his brother Lord William Westfield.

"Morning, Will."

His brother's icy blue eyes raked across Ben and his portmanteau, and he had to keep himself from reacting.

"Going somewhere?"

"Uh," Ben began, searching for the right words. "Just an impromptu trip up north."

"An impromptu trip up north?" Will echoed. "That sounds rather nondescript."

Damn his irritating brother. Ben shrugged, hoping he projected the carefree man he'd been a sennight ago. "Just visiting a friend. Nothing much to tell."

Will leaned his large frame against the doorway leading to a parlor. "A *female* friend?"

The last bit of Ben's patience evaporated. "God damn it, Will! What are you after?" When a look of surprise flashed in his brother's eyes, a prickling of guilt washed over Ben. "Sorry. I didn't sleep well."

That at least was the truth. He kept hearing Major Forster's words about witches and healers every time he closed his eyes. It was no wonder he was jumpy this morning.

"You feeling all right?"

Ben nodded. "I, uh, got word from Alec MacQuarrie in Edinburgh. He's been bored out of his mind and asked me to visit." Thankfully he knew someone up north to pull off this ruse, at least temporarily. He hoped MacQuarrie was still in Scotland. It had been a month or two since he'd last heard from his old friend, which was unusual. Something must have captured his attention.

"Oh." Will frowned. "Well, I suppose, considering

what happened in Brighton, it's not such a bad idea for you to change your scenery for a while."

Ben closed his eyes. He didn't want to think about the incident in Brighton, and he hated that both his brothers knew about it. He hated that *everyone* seemed to know about it. "Well, there you are. If the inquisition is over, I'd like to start my journey."

Will pushed himself away from the door frame and smiled. "Are you sure you wouldn't rather stay here? I'm supposed to meet Simon for lunch today."

All he needed was for both of his brothers to hover and watch his every move. The image sealed his resolve to find the fabled healer the major spoke of, as ridiculous as it sounded. Ben shook his head. "And leave poor MacQuarrie to his own devices? I wouldn't be much of a friend to desert him in his time of need."

Will laughed. "Very well. Travel safe, will you?"

"I always do."

# Three

AFTER TRAVELING THE NORTH ROAD FOR NEARLY a fortnight, Ben was relieved when the city of Edinburgh finally came into view from his coach window. He'd sent a note to Alec, inviting himself to stay with his old Cambridge pal at his home, and he hoped his friend had received the missive. He would hate to show up unannounced.

However, Alec had dropped in on him in London more times than he could count. So he felt that turnabout was fair play. In fact, the last time Alec had paid him a visit, he'd left Ben in quite a mess. He could still hear the clipped tones of Simon's voice, which spoke of his disappointment in his youngest sibling.

Being the youngest was difficult. For Ben, it meant he was never fully alone. His two older siblings constantly watched everything he did. Simon, the Duke of Blackmoor, did so in a fatherly fashion. A very strict father, who lived by a certain moral code. And Will, the middle brother, had stood back and watched Ben make a fool of himself on more than one occasion. Then he swooped out of nowhere, laughed like he'd done when they'd both been in short pants, and dusted him off. Then he stood back and let him do it all over again.

This time Ben was bound and determined to solve his little problem himself. It really wasn't a little problem, though. Not being able to change with the fullness of the moon was a huge problem for someone like him. It threw his whole life out of kilter.

And that was exactly how he felt when he stopped at the home of his oldest and dearest friend, Alec. Out of kilter. The coach pulled to a stop in front of the mansion, and Ben took a deep breath before he reached for the handle. He could do this. He could be his normal happy-go-lucky self, find the fabled witch who could heal him, and go home. Or he would do the opposite and prove the witch didn't exist. Either way, he'd had an opportunity to escape London in the wake of his recent scandal. And that alone was worth the trip.

Ben stretched his legs when he stepped out of the coach; they had never made those things big enough for men like him. The butler met him at the door, took his hat, and left him waiting in the parlor while he went to find Alec. Ben heard the stomp of booted feet as someone moved at a hurried pace down the corridor. At least Ben hadn't lost his keen sense of hearing when he'd lost his beastliness.

Ben was surprised to see that Alec was dressed in his best evening clothes. In fact, his friend wore a devil-may-care grin that made him look like quite a rake. It was a reputation well earned, much of which they'd cultivated together.

"Benjamin Westfield, is that you?" Alec said as he turned the corner. "I thought your letter said you'd be a few more days, my friend." He held out a hand to Ben.

"So you did receive my note?" Ben asked, extending his hand to shake. "I'm quite glad. I was afraid it wouldn't reach you and I would arrive without warning."

"I believe I did that to you last time I visited London, so that would have been just fine as well. Come, come," he said, motioning toward his study. "I have a bottle of whisky you can help me sample."

"You know, you didn't have to get quite so dressed up for my arrival," Ben joked as he accepted a glass of amber liquid and settled into a comfortable chair.

"I wish I could say this was for you." Alec smiled. "Alas, this is for a lady."

"Just as I thought. You've planned a night of debauchery and drinking, I assume." He crossed one foot over his knee.

Alec colored slightly. "Actually, no. I have planned a night of dancing, and if I'm lucky, I'll get a walk in the garden while I hold the girl's hand."

"*That* kind of a girl, is she?" Ben was shocked. His friend had never looked quite so discomfited to discuss a member of the opposite sex.

"That kind, aye," Alec admitted. "The kind I'm not quite sure what to do with."

"I feel sure that you'll come up with something. Where are you going?"

"The Fergusons are hosting a ball." He pulled his pocket watch from his breast pocket by the chain and flipped it open. "I have an hour yet before I'm to arrive at Miss Macleod's."

Ben grimaced. "Please tell me you're not a man besotted. I don't know what I would do with myself if my best friend shackled himself with a wife." He shivered dramatically.

"Not besotted. Just a bit intrigued. She wants nothing to do with me." Alec frowned into his whisky glass.

"Oh," Ben laughed loudly. So loudly and so long that he clutched his stomach. "A woman who won't give *you* the time of day. What a novelty!"

"It has never happened to me before, I must admit. But I do so love a challenge. Speaking of which, you should come along. The Fergusons won't mind if I bring one more, especially the brother of a duke. In fact, I am to escort a friend of Miss Macleod's as well. You can ride along and accompany her."

"When did two women become too much for you, Alec?"

The man looked shocked. "Never. I just didn't want you to feel all alone." Alec frowned. "There's a bit of scandal attached to Miss Macleod's friend, however. I hope that's not a problem for you."

"What kind of scandal?" Ben was suddenly intrigued.

"A circumstance of her birth, unfortunately," Alec sighed. "She is a bit illegitimate."

"One can't be a *bit* illegitimate, my friend. She either is or she isn't."

"Well, then she is. But she's a splendid woman. Fiery red hair. Beautiful eyes."

"All the women in these parts have red hair, don't they?" Ben threw back the last of his whisky.

"It's not quite fair to lump all Scottish women into one basket, Westfield. Miss Campbell is a very nice woman," Alec admitted.

"Campbell, did you say?" Ben instantly sat forward.

"Aye. Miss Elspeth Campbell."

How many people in Edinburgh wore the surname of Campbell? Probably hundreds. Surely this one couldn't be related to the old witch he sought. That would seem much too easy. And nothing had ever been easy for Ben Westfield before. Why should it start now?

"I'm wearing a fortnight's worth of trail dust, but if you can lead me to a bath, I assume I could make myself presentable."

"I'm afraid I've nothing to offer you to wear, so I hope you have appropriate clothing. You're much too big to wear anything of mine."

"I think I brought something that will fit the occasion."

"Just don't outdress me, old friend," Alec smiled. "I plan to turn Miss Macleod's head in *my* direction."

Ben could honestly say that for once he was much more interested in meeting his own companion than trying to steal one out from under his old friend.

❧

"I do so hate to be a tagalong," Elspeth grumbled as she bustled about the busy bedroom. She turned to allow the maid to tie the laces of her gown.

"Ye canna be called a tagalong," Caitrin said. "I need ye. Ye have ta attend the ball, even if I have ta drag ye, kickin' and screamin'."

"Doona tempt me," Elspeth retorted as she settled

into a chair and allowed the maid to brush through her long hair. She remarked to the woman, "No matter how ye pin it, it'll all be down around my shoulders within minutes. It seems ta have a life of its own."

The maid turned to pick up hairpins from the table.

"Oh, no." Elspeth stopped her and passed her the two combs that belonged to her mother. "I willna go without these."

"Then that's probably why yer hair is always so out of control," Caitrin replied absently. "Allow Jeannie ta do it up properly, will ye?"

"Certainly I will. With *these* combs," she said as she pressed them into the maid's outstretched hands. Elspeth smiled at Caitrin, who scowled from across the room. "Nothin' about me has ever been proper. I doona ken why I would start with my hair."

"I think yer definition of 'proper' is quite skewed. Ye're proper enough for us."

Elspeth knew she meant the other members of the coven. But they had no choice but to accept her. They didn't have the privilege of choosing the members. They were born into it. Elspeth had inherited her gift of healing from her mother. Just as Caitrin had inherited her visions of the future from her mother.

"Aye, I ken, ye love me," Elspeth grumbled. "Ye really just want ta keep me between ye and Alec MacQuarrie."

Caitrin laughed. "I need to use ye like a windbreak, in case of an emergency."

"Happy ta be of service."

Once the maid had Elspeth's hair pinned atop her head, she stood and shook her gown. "I'm afraid I willna have time ta hem my gown before we leave. It's a bit long."

"I told ye that ye could wear somethin' of mine. But ye refused."

"I think my gown is passable."

"All in the village ken ye've a gift with a needle, Elspeth. Yer gown will be one of the best at the ball, even if it is a bit long."

"I'll just have ta work ta keep from steppin' on it."

"Ye'll do just fine," Caitrin remarked absently as she nodded to the maid, who announced, "The gentlemen have arrived."

Caitrin and Elspeth glanced at each other. "Gentlemen?" they both asked at once.

Caitrin colored slightly. "I did ask Mr. MacQuarrie ta see if he could find an escort for ye." When Elspeth opened her mouth to complain, Cait replied quickly with, "Ye can forgive me later."

Then she walked past Elspeth and out the door, leaving El no choice but to follow in her wake.

The two women stopped side by side at the top of the grand staircase, which led to the foyer. They stopped and looked down at the men who stood talking casually at the bottom of the stairs, completely unaware of their presence.

"Oh, my," Caitrin breathed. "He's quite somethin', isna he?"

"Somethin'?" Elspeth whispered back. "He's beautiful." And much more. She gaped at the stranger with Mr. MacQuarrie. She'd never seen a man quite so tall. His evening jacket fit snugly against the wide expanse of his shoulders. Light brown hair, a bit too long, touched the top of his collar. But it was the intensity of his eyes that caught her attention, a light color she couldn't quite make out from the distance.

Then she took a tentative step. Yet she was so enthralled by the man standing at the bottom of the staircase she forgot to lift the edge of her gown. Her foot caught in the material and she stumbled. She was able to do no more than flail her arms in the air and close her eyes tightly before she braced herself for the blow.

But no sooner did she stumble than she felt strong arms catch her in the air. She came to an immediate stop, safely and well caught within the grasp of the handsome stranger. How had he moved so fast?

Elspeth opened her eyes slowly and met the smile of the man who now clutched her so close. One hand was wrapped around her waist and the other pressed against her bottom. She gasped, far more discomfited by that hand than she had been by the fall in the first place.

The man spoke, a laugh coating his words. "'Beautiful,' you say?" he asked quietly.

# Four

OF COURSE HE'D HEARD HER. HE HAD HEARD THE footsteps down the corridor and smelled the beautiful scent of her long before she graced the top of the stairs. Somewhere in the back of his mind, he noted that another woman stood near. But he couldn't draw his eyes from the flame-haired beauty long enough to take the other in.

Then she nearly threw herself into his arms, right after she called him beautiful. It was times like this that he loved his beastliness. His heightened sense of smell and hearing had served him well in the past. And they served him well now. Well enough that he had a fiery redhead tucked in his arms, and he'd only just arrived in Edinburgh. And she thought he was beautiful.

"I-I," she stuttered. "Ye can let me go, sir."

The melodic lilt of her voice made Ben's mouth go dry. But she was gazing at him with the greenest eyes he'd ever seen, and he somehow found the strength to gently put her down. "Are you all right, miss?"

She blinked at him. "Ye're Sassenach?"

The derogatory term for English slipped easily from her lips. Oh, the Scots would never admit the word was derogatory, but it was the way they said it that gave them away. Ben grinned at her. Being English was the least of his sins. "My family has land in Dumfriesshire, if that makes the circumstances of my nationality more palatable for you."

Miss Campbell's cheeks flamed at his words and she looked away. It was always too easy to make a redhead blush. Alec stepped forward, concern etched across his brow. "Miss Campbell, are you all right?"

She nodded, but refused to look back at Ben. "I'm dreadfully clumsy, Mr. MacQuarrie. Perhaps I should stay here this evenin'."

Her friend, a slight blonde, gasped at the pronouncement. "Sorcha Ferguson would never forgive ye if ye missed her ball."

"Think nothing of it," Alec replied smoothly. "We all make a misstep one time or another. Miss Macleod, Miss Campbell, may I present my dear friend Lord Benjamin Westfield."

"Lord Benjamin." Miss Macleod curtsied. "It's so nice ta make yer acquaintance."

"The pleasure is all mine," Ben replied, though he kept his eyes focused on the flame-haired lass in front of him. "Shall we, Miss Campbell?" He offered her his arm.

Her green eyes flickered up to him as she nodded and placed her gloved hand on his forearm. Even through his sleeve her touch was cold, and Ben fought the urge to cover her hand with his to warm her up.

*To warm her up.* He nearly laughed at himself. He wanted to do a lot more than warm her up. Perhaps whatever was wrong with him had righted itself. He hadn't felt such pull, such lust, since the jaunt to Brighton, before he was broken.

Miss Campbell cleared her throat and looked up at him. "Lord Benjamin, aren't we ta follow Mr. MacQuarrie?"

Ben pulled himself from the spell of her eyes and noticed that his friend was halfway out the door with Miss Macleod at his side. "Yes, of course."

She looked away from him, tugging at her dress to pull the hem from the floor as they started for the doorway.

And that's when he saw it.

In her mass of red hair sat a pewter wolf disguised as a hair comb. He nearly stumbled. It was an unusual piece. Most women didn't wear wolf adornments, not unless her lover was a Lycan.

A wave of something akin to jealousy washed over him. Some other wolf had claimed her. Some other wolf that was *capable* of claiming had done so. He stopped in his tracks, unable to move.

Miss Campbell turned, confusion on her lovely face. "Lord Benjamin?"

He heard her words, but he couldn't take his eyes off her bare neck and shoulders. His gaze raked one side then the other. He didn't see any evidence that she'd been claimed. She had perfect alabaster skin without a blemish of any kind. Not even a freckle marred her skin. Had she been claimed, he would see evidence of it. He knew what to look for. There was nothing, and he breathed a sigh of relief.

"Sir," she pressed, "are ye all right?"

Ben nodded, forcing what he knew was a charming smile to his face. "My apologies, Miss Campbell. It was a long journey to Edinburgh, and I'm apparently more tired than I thought."

Compassion settled on her face. "Perhaps ye should rest, sir. I'm certain my friend will understand if I miss her ball."

"Elspeth Campbell!" Miss Macleod called over her shoulder. "Ye ken as well as I that Sorcha Ferguson would be put out for at least a fortnight. Stop tryin' ta wriggle out of attendin'."

A mischievous smile lit Elspeth's face and she shrugged. "Well," she whispered conspiratorially, "it was worth a try."

A laugh escaped Ben's throat. "Miss Campbell, I do believe you need close watching."

She pretended to pout as he led her out the front door. "That's a fine thing ta say ta me. I was only concerned for yer well-bein', my lord."

"I'm concerned enough for both of us, lass."

He helped her climb inside MacQuarrie's coach, and his eyes dropped to her perfect little bottom, which he'd already had the pleasure of squeezing. The men in Scotland were fools if they let a little thing like the circumstance of her birth keep them from her.

Ben settled himself next to Miss Campbell on the bench before a prune-faced Macleod maid squeezed herself inside the coach as well. Ah, a chaperone. Apparently Alec's reputation must have followed him north.

❧

Elspeth's eyes adjusted to the darkened coach quickly. She tried to steady her breathing, which was a difficult thing to do considering Lord Benjamin had pressed his leg against hers and rested his arm on the seat behind her head.

*Mo chreach*! He was like no one she'd ever encountered before. She would certainly have weathered Sorcha's ill temper for missing her ball if she could have kept herself from the handsome Sassenach at her side. There was something dangerous about him simmering beneath his surface. She could feel it. She felt the danger as clearly as she did the heat that radiated from him.

Caitrin managed to find idle things to chit-chat about until they reached the Fergusons, though Elspeth couldn't quite follow the conversation. She could do nothing but stare out the darkened window and wish the evening were already over.

She felt his scorching gaze on her. How she managed to keep from shivering she had no idea, but continuing an acquaintance with the man was to be avoided.

When the coach finally rumbled to a stop, she breathed a sigh of relief. She would find Sorcha as soon as she stepped inside the Fergusons' sprawling home, and then she'd make her excuses and return home to her grandfather. Caitrin had MacQuarrie well under control, so she wasn't truly needed. Besides, she abhorred societal functions. She was only marginally accepted at these sorts of events, and only because the Macleods and Fergusons were loyal to her.

Lord Benjamin climbed out of the coach then turned and offered his hand. She accepted his assistance and tried not to stare into the light hazel depths of his eyes. Dangerous. He was definitely dangerous.

"I do hope you'll save me a dance, Miss Campbell," his gravelly voice rumbled in her ear as they followed Caitrin and MacQuarrie toward the Fergusons' ballroom.

Elspeth forced a smile to her lips. "I never dance, my lord."

"Never?" he echoed, a wolfish grin on his face. "I have a hard time imagining that."

No one had ever asked her, though she'd rather not divulge that sort of information. "I'm terribly clumsy," she said instead. "Perhaps ye noticed."

He laughed. "I do believe I'll take my chances."

A squeal erupted once they entered the ballroom adorned in heather and white roses. Elspeth was glad for the interruption. She knew that squeal, and the faster she wished Sorcha a happy birthday, the faster she could leave this event altogether. She dropped Lord Benjamin's arm, spun on her heels, and smiled at the *Còig*'s youngest witch.

Dressed in a pretty rose silk, Sorcha's dark hair was piled high on her head, and her dark eyes danced as they swept over Elspeth. "Oh, El! Ye came! I thought for certain ye'd find an excuse."

So much for trying to leave early. Elspeth shook her head. "Sorcha, ye ken I'd be here ta wish ye the best on yer birthday."

The young witch squealed again as she threw her arms around El's neck. "Who's the handsome devil with ye?" she whispered in her ear.

Stepping away from her friend, Elspeth gestured to the strapping Sassenach. "Miss Sorcha Ferguson, this is Lord Benjamin. Sir, I'm afraid I've forgotten yer last name."

He smiled a dangerous smile. "Westfield."

Sorcha sucked in a breath. "As in the Duke of Blackmoor?"

Elspeth's eyes flashed to her escort. Even *she* had heard of Blackmoor's scandalous exploits. His brothers were rumored to be even more debauched. Lord Benjamin's smile faltered. "It seems my brother is known in every corner of Britain."

"*This* is Scotland," Sorcha informed him with an arrogant tilt of her head.

"So it is," he said quietly. Then, as the first strings of a waltz began, he squeezed Elspeth's shoulder. "I do believe this dance is mine, Miss Campbell."

Without a way out, she looked up at him and accepted his outstretched arm. Lord Benjamin led her to the middle of the floor and slid one arm around her waist. His light eyes twinkled in the chandelier light, and Elspeth suddenly found herself unable to look away from him. He was mesmerizing.

"You're light on your toes, Miss Campbell."

"Ye lead well, my lord."

His hand splayed against the small of her back, and he pulled her closer to him. "Your hair combs are unusual."

What an odd thing for a gentleman to notice. "Is that a compliment?"

"I find myself drawn to them."

"Ta my hair combs?" She couldn't help but giggle. "That has ta be the strangest thing a gentleman has ever said ta me."

He wasn't even fazed by her words. "Where did you get them?"

"They were a gift."

A muscle twitched in his jaw and Elspeth swallowed nervously. Why should he be so concerned with her hair combs? It didn't make one bit of sense.

"From whom?" he asked with a darkening frown.

She tilted her head back to see him better. "My mother."

# *Five*

BEN WAS SO TAKEN ABACK THAT HE COULDN'T AVOID a misstep. "Ouch!" Miss Campbell softly cried as he stepped on her toe. She stopped dancing long enough to wiggle her toes within her slipper. Her eyes met his. Was that a twinkle within the depths? "I think they're all still attached, thank goodness," she continued.

"My apologies, Miss Campbell. I don't usually clod upon the toes of my dance partners."

"Does that mean I should consider myself ta be special?" she asked as he led her back into the dance.

"Quite special," he admitted. Special enough to have wolf hair combs that had been passed to her from her mother.

"Where did your mother get the combs?" he asked, trying to keep his tone casual, yet aware that he probably was failing miserably.

Her brows knit together. "Why are my combs so important ta ye, Lord Benjamin?"

"My brothers tell me I'm a curious sort." He attempted a smile. He really wanted to pull the combs from her hair so that he could inspect them for a maker's mark. He might find their origin that way.

"My mother had a liking for dogs." She shrugged.

The hair on the back of his neck stood up. He had never been insulted so rudely. "I did you a good turn, yet you look me in the eye and insult me?"

"Pardon?"

"You don't pretend ignorance very well, Miss Campbell."

Ben fought the rage that suddenly built within him. Normally he only felt such tendencies at the moonful, in the days before the change happened. But tonight he was feeling it in full force. The intensity of it scared even him.

It was terribly bad form to leave a woman on the dance floor. But Ben felt a sudden and intense need to escape. He led Miss Campbell away and then dropped her hand and bowed respectfully to her. "Thank you for the dance. Regrettably, I must take my leave."

He didn't wait for a response, but turned and skirted quickly around the room. Fresh air. He needed fresh air. Quickly.

Ben's senses were in overload. He smelled the perfume of every woman he passed, the shaving lather of the men. He heard the whispers around him, most of which were normal fodder for the scandal pages. But they sounded like screaming to his ears. He burst through the terrace doors. Ben leaned as far as he could over the terrace wall as he looked down, gauging the distance between the terrace and the ground. Not too far to jump. He raised one leg over the wall.

"Did I say somethin' that offended ye?" Miss Campbell asked from behind him.

Ben stopped his climb and closed his eyes tightly, wishing she would disappear. Because if she didn't, she would be the most obvious source of release, the only outlet for his anger. For his beast. For himself.

He swung his leg back to the right side of the terrace wall. He was before her in seconds.

"You insult me and then seek me out?" he growled.

"I doona ken how I insulted ye," she breathed.

"Those aren't dogs," he growled.

This time it was Miss Campbell who faltered. She reached a hand to her hair to touch the rough surface of the comb. "Certainly they are."

"My dear Miss Campbell, there is no one who knows better than I. Those are *not* dogs."

"And what makes ye an expert on women's jewelry?"

"Not on jewelry," he said quietly. Her eyes rose slowly to meet his when she tipped her head back. "On beasts."

"Beasts?"

"Yes. Beasts," he snapped.

"Ye're certainly doin' a fine imitation of one now, are ye no'? So I assume ye're quite an expert."

A twinge of guilt nearly made him wince. How much more did he have to reveal before she admitted the true origin of the combs? He searched her face, looking for even a hint of subterfuge. He found none. "You truly thought they were dogs?"

"I've never been told differently," she said quietly.

"I'm telling you differently now."

"I doona ken what difference it makes. Beasts?

Dogs?" She tugged the combs from her hair and held them out to him. "Just what about them offends ye?"

❦

Her hands shook noticeably and she worked to steady them. His eyes narrowed when he noticed, but he took the combs from her and held them up to the lantern that lit the terrace.

"You speak of them like they're average creatures," he mumbled. "Like they're inconsequential."

"No' inconsequential," she denied. "They're beautiful." She raised her index finger and ran it over the snout of the beast. "Look at the way he raises his head. He calls ta the moon, as though it is part of his very soul."

"It is." He sighed. "Or it usually is." Was that sadness that entered his voice?

She took the combs from him and attempted to put her hair back to rights. Finally she gave up, allowing her shoulders to drop in defeat. She settled onto a bench in the shadows.

"I'm sorry I overreacted," he said softly.

"It's all right," she allowed. "I'm used ta it."

"Used to men who act like children?" he asked as he sat down beside her.

"No. Used ta bein' miserable at events like this." She leaned back and looked up at the stars. "I doona ken how I do it. I offend ye and I doona even know ye."

Lord Benjamin's finger surprised her when he touched her chin, gently forcing her to look up at him. Still, she avoided his gaze.

"I'm very sorry," he said quietly. "I mistook what you said. It's completely my fault. Not yours."

"I almost got one dance in this time, so it's better than usual," she admitted, the heat creeping up her cheeks when she realized what she'd said. "Thank ye for the opportunity."

"You said you normally don't dance. Why not?"

"I'm sure ye've heard the rumors." She looked up and caught his gaze. Of course, he'd heard. He was an English lord. People who walked in his world didn't accept people from hers.

"I heard rumors that there was a girl named Miss Elspeth Campbell who had flaming red hair and eyes that danced with laughter." His gaze lingered on her mouth. "And I am quite happy to find out the rumors are all true." He bumped her with his shoulder. "Now, tell me why you don't dance."

She sighed and admitted, "The only reason I'm invited ta these things is because I have a few friends. They feel like they have ta bring me in, despite the fact that I'm no' quite respectable."

"And just what about you is not respectable?" he asked, his eyebrows drawing together. "If you'll point out the people who said it, I'll go and have a discussion with them."

No one had ever attempted to stand up for her before, aside from her grandfather and her coven sisters. She found that it warmed her heart, more than a little.

"It's no' important," she whispered. "Do ye still want ta flee as fast as ye can over the wall?" she asked, pointing a thumb behind her.

"Only if I can take you with me," he said softly. He reached to cup her face, the pad of his thumb caressing the apple of her cheek. "Care to go and be really unrespectable with me?"

She couldn't help but laugh at him. "Ye would jump over the wall? How would I get over?"

"In my arms. How else?"

How else, indeed? It sounded like quite a feat. Before she could say it, he replied, "I'm not an average man."

"That much is obvious, Lord Benjamin. That much is quite obvious."

He stood and held a hand out to her. "Then if you won't go over the wall with me, I'll have to take you back to the party. It's either flee or dance. What'll it be?"

Oh, how she truly wanted to flee. She would be much more comfortable running away with him than returning to face the judgment of the party-goers.

But then all four of her coven sisters stepped out onto the terrace. Lord Benjamin's head swiveled around as they descended upon them.

Caitrin spoke first. "Are ye all right, Elspeth?" Her gaze shot to Westfield, the look scorching.

"Aye, I'm fine. Just takin' a little break from the party."

"Why did ye need a break?" Caitrin asked, her eyes never leaving Lord Benjamin. "And what happened ta yer hair?"

Westfield chuckled and said very quietly so that only she could hear. "I'll leave you to your friends so they can put you to rights. Then may I claim a dance when you return to the ballroom?"

Elspeth could only nod. She admired the swagger

in his walk as he went back to the party through the terrace doors.

They all descended upon her at once. "What happened? Why is yer hair all a mess? Did he take it down?" All their words ran together as one.

Elspeth just laughed and shook her head. She held up the pewter combs. "He was just admirin' my hair combs. I took them out so he could see. He dinna do a thing that was improper. I promise."

The group sighed with collective relief. But Elspeth couldn't help but wonder what it would be like if he did.

# *Six*

"So," ALEC BEGAN AS HE DRAPED HIS ARM AROUND Ben's shoulder. "You like the lass after all?"

He did. He liked her a lot, surprisingly. If nothing else, Elspeth Campbell kept his mind off his own problems. "She doesn't fit in here. I'm afraid she'll be eaten alive amongst the others in your ranks."

Alec sighed. "You do have the right of it. Half the people here wouldn't speak to her under normal circumstances if it weren't for a few powerful families she's attached to. But if they get a case of gout or a fever, you should see how fast they run to her. Hypocritical bastards, the lot of them."

Gout or a fever? Ben frowned at his friend. "What do you mean by that?"

Alec chuckled. "Superstitious Scots. When they've a need of her, they think she can cure the pox." His attention shot to the terrace doors, where five young women reentered the ballroom, Elspeth in the center of them all. "No matter how badly they treat her on the street, she never turns anyone away who needs her help. She's a saint, if you ask me."

Cure the pox? Ben's eyes lingered on the pretty lass. "They think she's a healer of sorts?"

Alec threw back his head and laughed. "A healer? She's good with herbs, is all. She learned it at her mother's knee. Honestly, Westfield, you sound as ridiculous as the unlearned masses that go to her for help."

Ben shook his head. It was ridiculous. He was looking for a healer, so he had jumped at the idea it could be Elspeth Campbell. It would certainly make his search easier. She might not be the woman he sought, but he wouldn't mind spending his spare time with the lass. She was more genuine than most people whose acquaintances he kept. Like a breath of fresh Scottish air.

He tried not to laugh at his foolish thoughts, but failed. The pretty girl across the room was *not* a Scottish witch. How many times had he seen *Macbeth*? Scottish witches looked like hags with hooked noses and spent their time around open cauldrons, stirring up trouble for nobles. No doubt Rosewyth Campbell, wherever she was, couldn't hold a candle to the beguiling Elspeth.

"What's so humorous?" Alec asked.

"I think I'm tired from my journey," Ben admitted. "My mind's playing tricks on me."

"Well, don't go around laughing to yourself. People will think you're daft."

"Thank you for your concern," Ben remarked drolly. "Excuse me, will you?" The lovely redhead still owed him a dance. He started toward the five women, but was stopped by Alec's hand on his arm.

"The lass doesn't receive much attention, Westfield. You've already danced with her once. Any more and ye'll have tongues a waggin'."

"Let them wag," Ben said, shaking out of Alec's hold.

The only brightness he'd experienced in weeks was in Elspeth Campbell's presence. Besides, the lass deserved attention. Perhaps he could make all the blind Scots realize what they had been missing on a regular basis.

He crossed the room, his eyes focused on Elspeth the entire way. The four girls who flanked her all seemed to take the same collective breath as he reached them, but his red-haired beauty's eyes dropped demurely. Ben couldn't hold back a smile.

He reached his hand out to her. "Miss Campbell," he said as a waltz began.

"I doona ken how things are in London, my lord," Miss Macleod said with a frown, "but two waltzes in a night isna proper here."

"Ah, but my first one was interrupted," he replied, his hand still outstretched.

"El," one of the brunettes hissed, the single syllable an unmistakable warning.

Elspeth turned her head. "'Tis all right, Rhiannon." Then she focused her startlingly green eyes on him. "Could we take a turn about the room instead, my lord?"

Ben nodded. "If that's what you'd like."

Elspeth would *like* to be wrapped in his arms again. But her sister witches were right. It wouldn't look proper, and she still had to face all these people after Lord Benjamin returned to his life in London. She didn't need to make things more difficult on herself.

She placed her hand in his and immediately felt a warmth envelop her entire being. He towed her to his side and placed her hand on his forearm. "Smile, Miss Campbell, or your countrymen will think I'm forcing you to spend time in my company."

A giggle escaped her and she looked up into his twinkling hazel eyes. "No one would ever believe that."

He bent his head toward her and whispered, "You know it's still not too late for us to make our escape."

She couldn't hide the smile that tugged at her lips. "I think ye're a bad influence on me, Lord Benjamin."

"Ah, I do tend to have that affect on women."

"I have no doubt."

He squeezed her hand and winked at her. "Most women don't complain."

"Ahem!" someone cleared his throat beside them. Elspeth pulled her gaze from Lord Benjamin's handsome face to find Wallace Ferguson, arms crossed in front of his massive chest, glaring at the Englishman.

"Friend of yours?" Lord Benjamin asked with a cheeky grin.

Elspeth sighed and she tipped her head back haughtily. "Wallace Ferguson, what is the matter with ye?"

The overgrown Scot shifted his weight from one foot to the other. "I, uh, wanted ta ask ye ta stand up with me, El." Something he'd never done in the past.

She looked over her shoulder to find Sorcha gesturing to her brother. Obviously Wallace had been put up to this by his sister.

*Havers!* She was simply walking about the room with Lord Benjamin. Did her coven think she couldn't take care of herself? It wasn't terribly complimentary. "Ye can thank Sorcha for her concern, Wallace. I'm perfectly fine with his lordship."

Wallace frowned. "Have a heart, El. She said she'd help me with Caitrin if I did this for her." Then he frowned at Lord Benjamin. "Besides, he's no' even one of us."

"Something in his favor." She narrowed her eyes on Wallace. "Yer services are no' needed, Mr. Ferguson."

The big Scot hung his head. "I never thought ye were a stubborn one."

"Well, now ye ken." Then she took pity on the man. "I'm certain ye'd rather dance with Caitrin anyway."

His eyes flashed to the dance floor, where Caitrin was in Alec MacQuarrie's arms. "Aye, but I'll have ta settle for just watchin' her."

"This song willna last forever, Wallace."

He shuffled his feet and shrugged. "Thanks anyway, El."

When Wallace ambled off, Elspeth looked up into Lord Benjamin's eyes. There was a warmth in his gaze that made her heart thump faster.

"Your friends think I'm dangerous," he said as they began walking again.

"Are they wrong?"

A charming grin spread across his lips. "They're more right than you can possibly imagine."

Elspeth didn't know what to make of that, so she said nothing and watched the spinning couples nearby. After all, she couldn't very well agree with him, because as a witch, she could imagine quite a lot.

"Alec says you're a talented herbalist," he said.

He had asked his friend about her? She almost tripped on her hem. "I suppose ye could say that."

"This will probably sound strange, Miss Campbell,

but maybe you can help me. I'm looking for a... healer of sorts."

That time she did stumble. A healer. It wasn't possible he knew, was it?

His arm snaked around her waist and steadied her. "I've got you," he said, his warm breath brushing her neck.

"I warned ye I was clumsy," she whispered back.

"So you did." He laughed. "But I don't scare so easily."

"Well," Alec MacQuarrie's voice halted them, "the two of you seem to have hit it off."

"El," Caitrin began, hanging on to her companion's arm, "I'm so tired and asked Mr. MacQuarrie ta return us home. Do ye mind leavin' early?"

Elspeth frowned. Caitrin and the others were so transparent. It was becoming a bit frustrating. "Actually, Cait, I'm havin' such a wonderful time, I think I'll stay."

"I'll see you returned safely home, Miss Campbell," Lord Benjamin promised.

Caitrin's creased brow was quite satisfying. Elspeth turned her attention to the Englishman and smiled, grateful for his assistance. "That's very kind of ye, sir."

"It'll be my pleasure."

"Ben," Alec MacQuarrie's voice held a warning.

But Lord Benjamin paid it no heed. "Miss Macleod is tired, Alec. You best be on your way." Then he guided Elspeth past them with just a bit of pressure on her back.

She heaved an irritated sigh as they moved past their respective friends. "It's so nice ta ken they doona think I can make wise choices," she muttered to herself.

Lord Benjamin laughed. "I can relate, Miss Campbell. My older brothers are inclined to behave the same way."

"How do ye handle it?"

"I escaped to Scotland."

# Seven

"ESCAPE SOUNDS HEAVENLY," SHE SAID QUIETLY. BEN studied the downcast sweep of her gaze and the slump of her shoulders.

He covered the hand that still held his arm with his own. Her gaze immediately rose to meet his. "I offered to take you over the wall, Miss Campbell." He nodded toward the terrace doors and waited for her to reply. He would still do it. At that moment, he wanted nothing more than to take her in his arms, jump the wall, and run away with her.

"There's enough scandal attached ta the Campbell name, Lord Benjamin. I could never subject my friends and family ta more."

"I have never fully understood the bounds of propriety, Miss Campbell. When one should be at ease and when one should not. I prefer studying *Latin* to studying human nature. And I truly abhor Latin."

Her green eyes flashed. "I would have ta disagree with ye there, Lord Benjamin."

"You enjoy Latin?"

Her tinkling laugh was music to his ears.

"No. I enjoy studyin' people quite a bit, though."

"Tell me something interesting about someone here," he said offhandedly. Perhaps she would feel more at ease if he encouraged her to talk.

"I could never share secrets that are no' mine," she sighed.

"As loyal as you are beautiful," he remarked. Her face colored prettily.

Ben glanced around the room, immediately noticing the couples who'd paired off. His keen sense of hearing allowed him to pick up bits and pieces of conversation.

He nodded toward a couple leaving the dance floor. "Those two have a romantic tryst planned in just a moment."

"That is no secret, Lord Benjamin. Everyone at the ball is privy ta that bit of information. Except her husband, of course," Miss Campbell said as she looked over her shoulder at a brooding hulk of a man who was much too busy entertaining his friends with tales of his importance while someone else entertained his wife.

"Poor bloke," Ben couldn't help but mumble.

He was surprised when she narrowed her eyes at him. "How did ye ken about them?"

"Just a guess," he lied smoothly. Truly, being a Lycan did allow him some freedom to listen to bits here and there that others missed. Of course, he couldn't tell her about that talent.

Ben turned her smoothly around a knot of people gathered in their path. As they passed, he heard a vile remark about Miss Campbell. "So much like her mother, isn't she?" The whisper came from a group of dowagers. Ben squelched the urge to bare his teeth and growl.

"Is somethin' wrong?" she asked, her hand tightening on his arm.

"No, nothing." He attempted a fake smile.

She stopped walking and pulled her hand from his. Her eyebrows drew together. *There* was that fiery redhead's temper he'd expected from the start.

"Then what's wrong with ye?" she asked.

"Why on earth would you think something is wrong with me?" Ben asked, feigning ignorance.

"Stupidity is no' an act ye portray well, Lord Benjamin."

"Well, I should hope not, Miss Campbell," Ben retorted, fighting hard to bite back a grin. It wasn't often that a woman called him stupid and made him like it. He ran through the events in his mind and wasn't entirely sure how she'd done it.

"What did they say?" she asked quietly as she gave up and tucked her hand back into his arm. "And doona tell me nothin'. Because we both ken that's no' true."

Ben debated for a moment before answering. "They were comparing you to your mother," he finally admitted. "Which can't possibly be a bad thing. I imagine that's where you inherited your beauty."

"I'm said ta resemble my mother much more than my father, aye."

"And he was?" Ben prodded when she stopped talking.

"I've no idea," she admitted.

"That's his loss, then, isn't it?"

"No. It was mine. Because he killed my mother."

This time it was Ben's turn to stumble. But before she could remark about his ability to put one foot in front of the other, they were interrupted.

⤲

"Miss Campbell," Caitrin's maid interrupted them and curtsied to Lord Benjamin. "Beg yer pardon, miss, but Miss Macleod sent me ta get ye."

"What's wrong?" Lord Benjamin barked before she could even squeak out a reply. She frowned at him. He showed no remorse.

"It's yer grandfather," the maid said. "He's taken a turn for the worse."

Elspeth quickly gauged the fastest way out of the room. Truly the quickest way to get to her grandfather was to cut through the woods. She knew the woods well and often traveled that route to visit Sorcha.

"Lord Benjamin, do ye still feel led ta climb the terrace wall?"

He blinked at her twice and nodded. "Lead the way, Miss Campbell."

Elspeth absently gnawed her bottom lip as she skirted the room, vaguely noting Lord Benjamin's presence beside her. She exited through the terrace doors, walked to the wall, and peered over into the darkness.

"I believe it's farther down than ye think. I should go out the front door." She fought the panic that threatened as she realized what valuable time she'd lost.

But before she could go back through the terrace doors, Lord Benjamin scooped her up in his arms. She lifted her face to rebuke him, but the intensity in his eyes stopped her. "Please put me down," she choked out as tears threatened to fall. "I have ta go."

"We'll go together," he said quickly. "Put your arms around my neck." When she didn't immediately respond, he sighed, "I've never had to beg a woman to put her arms around me. But I'll start with you. *Please* put your arms around my neck. Else there's a chance I could drop you."

Elspeth reached up to wrap one arm around his shoulders and clutched the lapel of his jacket with the other.

He walked closer to the wall and lifted one leg, then the other, until he sat on the edge. "Ready?" he asked, the intensity in his gaze alarming.

"Ready." She nodded as she closed her eyes tightly.

He slid off the wall. It seemed like hours but was only seconds before he landed solidly on his feet in the grass. He dropped her legs and allowed her to slide down his body. Thankfully, he didn't expect her to bear her full weight immediately.

"I could stand like this with you all night, love, but I feel sure you'd be mad with me later if we did."

Elspeth shook her head, trying to regain her senses. "How did ye do that?"

"I'll explain it to you some other time." He took her hand in his. "Which way?" he asked as his eyes searched the darkness.

"We've no light," she groaned.

"That's all right. We don't need one," he said as he tugged her fingertips. "I can see well in the dark."

Truth be told, he could follow the scent she'd

left on previous journeys down the path to get to her grandfather's, he was so in tune with her at that moment. She showed him the trail that led into the woods and raised one eyebrow at him. He immediately realized she had no plans to wait for him to lead.

She picked up her skirts and dashed ahead of him, leaving him to sputter to a start behind her. He did so with very little thought, except for how beautiful she looked with her skirts hiked up about her knees, her hair escaping its knot, which her friends had just restored for her. Her flaming locks caught the moonbeams that filtered through the tree branches and shimmered like fire.

Immediately, Ben felt the call of the moon. He felt the urgency and the intensity that normally presented itself to him in the days prior to the moonful.

Never before had he ever heard of anyone like him changing unless it was at the moonful, but he felt the rush of power. He tamped it down and took his gaze from Miss Campbell. His head spun as he wondered which was calling more powerfully, the lovely creature before him or the moon. He couldn't tell which led him. But he was forced to follow.

She broke from the forest and never slowed her pace as she crossed a meadow. He moved up to run at her side rather than behind her. He'd never met a female who could run so far or so fast, and he found a smile erupting as he realized how wonderful it was to run free with her.

Miss Campbell slowed as she approached a fence. But Ben did not. He vaulted over and then held out his arms to her. She climbed the fence and hopped into his waiting arms. He held back a laugh of sheer contentment as he caught her weight with ease.

The tiny cottage where she lived was located on the outskirts of town. She slowed only briefly as they neared her home. The MacQuarrie carriage sat in front. Alec paced outside the entrance.

Miss Campbell rushed past him and into the house, the door slamming hard behind her.

Ben bent at the waist as he worked to catch his breath. "The woman runs like a wolf. Never seen anything like it," he said to Alec.

"Like a what?" Alec scratched his head.

"Like a deer. The woman runs like a deer." Ben corrected himself.

"Did you just run—" He stopped and pointed toward the woods. Then his eyes opened wide as he realized the two of them must have run all the way from the Fergusons' to the Campbells'. "I've seen you do a lot of things to get a woman into bed, my friend, but this one has to be the best."

Alec didn't even finish the thought before he found himself pressed against the door, Ben's arm beneath his throat, his feet several inches off the ground.

"I'll not allow anyone to speak of Miss Campbell that way," Ben snarled.

Alec grunted and pulled against Ben's arm, but Ben ignored his struggle. "Put me down," he gasped.

Ben fought his conscience, unsure of how to respond. The wolf in him wanted to show his dominance, to make Alec come to heel. But the friend in him was ready to release the poor gent. The choice was taken from him when the door was flung open and they both fell inside in a heap.

# Eight

"Just what do ye think ye're doin', Lord Benjamin?" Miss Macleod asked, her hands upon her hips, standing above them.

Alec pushed him off and shrugged to his feet. "Protecting Miss Campbell's honor, I believe," he muttered as he held a hand out to Ben and pulled him up.

"From ye?" Miss Macleod asked. "Why in the world would he need ta do that?"

"Why, indeed?" Alec asked, his head cocked to one side as he regarded Ben with curiosity.

Ben dusted himself off and leveled Miss Macleod with his haughtiest look, the one only sons of dukes ever seemed to master. "What's the matter with Mr. Campbell?"

Her lip quivered and she blinked back tears. "He's dyin'. He has been for some time. El's done everythin' she can ta keep him alive."

Elspeth couldn't possibly have the funds to hire a decent physician. Ben took in the cottage. It was tidy and clean, but quite small. Different in every way from the Fergusons' mansion and the Macleods' impressive home. Paying for a physician wasn't, however, a problem for him.

He turned to Alec. "What are you waiting for, MacQuarrie? This is your city. Find your best doctor and bring him here."

Miss Macleod gasped. "Ye think a doctor can do better than Elspeth has?"

Ben frowned at the girl. Was Alec right? Were they all uneducated and superstitious? "Knowing herbs is one thing, Miss Macleod, but science is another. The finest medical school in Britain is here in your fair city."

She puffed herself up to her fullest height. "Thank ye for seein' her home, but I think ye should leave now, my lord."

If she'd punched him, he wouldn't have been more shocked. Alec clapped a hand to his back. "Come along, Westfield. I'll take ye home." Then he smiled at Miss Macleod. "Will you be all right here, lass?"

She nodded. "Thank ye, Mr. MacQuarrie, for everythin'."

Ben allowed himself to be dragged from the cottage. "There's nothing to be done, Westfield," Alec said.

"How can you say that? Are all you Scots completely mad?"

Alec pulled open the door to his coach. "You can call on her in the morning if you're of a mind."

Against his better judgment, Ben climbed inside the coach and settled against the leather squabs. "This feels wrong, Alec."

His friend sighed as the coach slowly rambled down the dark lane. "You know as well as I there's nothing to be done for a wasting disease, Westfield. Even London's most prestigious doctor wouldn't be able to save Mr. Campbell."

A wasting disease? Ben cringed as he realized Alec was right. Poor Elspeth.

❧

Elspeth clasped her grandfather's hand. It was clammy and she noticed his pulse had slowed dangerously. She shouldn't have left him to go to Sorcha's silly party. "Papa, can ye hear me?"

She felt a hand on her shoulder and looked back to see Caitrin swipe a tear from her eye.

"He'll be all right," Elspeth vowed.

But Caitrin shook her head. "Ah, sweetheart, I wish it were so."

She blinked at her friend. "What do ye mean by that?"

Caitrin smoothed Elspeth's wild hair and sniffed back more tears. "Mr. MacQuarrie was walkin' me ta my door when I saw yer grandfather, El, in my mind. He's no' goin' ta wake up. I sent for ye as soon as I realized."

Tears poured from Elspeth's eyes as she turned back to her grandfather. She clutched his hand tighter and willed him to wake. "Papa, I'm here. Doona leave me."

Caitrin squeezed her shoulders. "Ye should get some rest. Ye're goin' ta need it."

Elspeth shook her head. "Ye saw him die?"

"Aye."

"Then ye must've seen me stay with him until then." She'd never leave him. Not now. Not when he needed her the most.

"Aye," Caitrin whispered. "I saw that, too."

Elspeth barely noticed when the others arrived. But soon her grandfather's small room was filled with all the witches of the *Còig*.

Sorcha and Blaire lit candles in every corner. Then the five of them joined hands around Mr. Campbell's bed, Elspeth's sisters offering silent support.

Elspeth had never felt so helpless in all her life. What was the point of being able to heal others if she couldn't save her own grandfather?

In the dead of night, old Liam Campbell took a loud, deep breath and released it. His chest stopped rising and falling. Elspeth staggered to her feet and pulled the family plaid up under his chin. She kissed his cold cheek and stumbled from the room.

Caitrin stopped Sorcha from going after Elspeth. "She needs some time alone."

Sorcha bit her bottom lip but did as she was asked.

"There's somethin' ye're no' sayin'," Rhiannon whispered, successfully catching the others' attention.

Caitrin hated that she was so easy to read. Still, there was no point in denying the truth. She nodded. "It's the Sassenach, MacQuarrie's friend."

"Lord Benjamin?" Blaire asked.

"Aye. I've seen him before."

"When ye went ta London last year?" Sorcha reasoned.

"*Mo chreach*, ye're daft," Rhiannon complained. "He's the one, Cait? The one from yer vision?"

"Aye," Caitrin admitted. She hadn't been certain until after she and Alec MacQuarrie had left the ball. A vision flashed in her mind during the short journey home before she'd seen Mr. Campbell take his last breath. Westfield intended to take Elspeth from them; there was no doubt in her mind. He wore the mark she'd seen weeks earlier.

"I ken he was trouble," Rhiannon grumbled. "He had her hair undone. No gentleman does such a thing."

"But she said nothin' happened," Sorcha protested.

As the two of them argued, Blaire touched Caitrin's arm. "What're we ta do?"

"I doona see us keepin' her," Caitrin whispered, the words ripped from her soul. But it was true. She didn't see them winning.

"Well, we canna give her up. Ye say the man's a beast?"

Unable to speak, Caitrin only nodded.

"So we'll fight ta keep her. We'll move her ta yer house. She'll stay with ye and we'll outlast him. He canna get through all of us."

It was a losing battle. But Blaire was right, they couldn't just give up on Elspeth. She was part of them. She was their sister.

"Rhiannon, make the arrangements with the vicar, will ye?" Caitrin asked.

"Of course."

"And, Sorcha, ye and Blaire can help me pack up the house. The sooner we move Elspeth, the better."

❧

Elspeth sat in a small chair and stared off into her memories. She knew this day was coming, but it was still hard to believe. It didn't seem all that long ago that her grandfather had been a robust man, the strongest she knew.

Rhiannon explained before she left that she'd make the arrangements with the vicar, and Elspeth nodded silently. There wasn't much else she could do. Then she realized Caitrin and the others were packing up her herbs and oils.

She stood on shaky legs. "What do ye think ye're doin'?"

Caitrin rushed toward her. "Doona worry, dearest. We'll get yer stores settled right."

"Why do they need settlin'?"

Caitrin swallowed. "Well, ye're goin' ta come stay with me for a while."

Elspeth shook her head. "I'm no' goin' anywhere. This is my home, Cait."

"Ye shouldna be alone right now. Ye'll just stay with me for a little while."

"No. This was my grandfather's home. It's my home. I'm no' goin' anywhere."

Caitrin draped her arm around Elspeth's shoulders. "Be reasonable. Ye've been through so much."

"And there's the man with the mark," Sorcha added with a quiver to her voice.

Elspeth stepped out of Caitrin's hold. "I'll no' run from him. My father could knock down that door right there, and I'll no' leave with him. And I'll no' leave with ye. This is *my* home." It was filled with memories of her grandfather and she wasn't leaving. They couldn't make her.

"But Lord Benjamin," Sorcha began. "What about him?"

A hysterical laugh escaped Elspeth. "What about him, Sorcha? I ken ye doona like him, but he's a nice man. That's all. What do ye think the brother of a powerful English duke wants with me? Nothin', that's what. Now enough of this. I doona want ta hear any more."

"But what if he's the man?" Sorcha persisted. "The man with the mark?" The girl's eyes flashed to Caitrin.

Elspeth felt the last of her patience evaporate. "That's the most ridiculous thing I ever heard. I bear the mark myself. Doona ye think I'd feel it if another were near?"

"Do ye feel it?" Caitrin whispered.

She felt nothing now but emptiness. "Of course no'. This is foolishness. I appreciate all of ye bein' here for me, but I doona want ta hear any more of this nonsense. When my father arrives, I will speak ta him. I'll ask him a lifetime's worth of questions, I'll find out what he wants from me. But I'll no' go with him. Now I'd very much like ta be alone."

"Promise ye won't go off with Westfield, and we'll leave."

"Out!" Elspeth yelled. "All of ye!"

# Nine

BEN SAT BOLT UPRIGHT IN BED. WHAT AN AWFUL DREAM. Another moonful had come and gone without his changing. He heaved a sigh and fell back against the feather pillows. He would go in search of Rosewyth Campbell in the morning, just as soon as he checked in on Elspeth.

A wasting disease. He shivered at the thought. When his time came, he hoped it was quick and easy. He didn't want to wither away before the people who loved him. The poor girl. He hadn't even been able to wish her a good night, make sure she was all right.

Ben crossed his hands beneath his head and thought about how she had looked as she ran through the woods. He had never seen anyone so passionate or uninhibited. She'd lifted her skirts and run. *Run like a wolf.*

Ever since Ben was a boy, he'd loved to run. He'd far outdistanced his friends and his brothers. Even other Lycans could not match his speed or stealth. But he'd been matched by a mere slip of a girl.

Suddenly he knew what he had to do. He had to

see her. Ben rose and dressed in the dark of night. His purpose for coming to Scotland was to find the healer. But he'd found more than that. He'd found a fiery-haired beauty who was vulnerable. And she called to the wolf in him, unlike anything else had for quite a while. He walked quietly down the stairs and reached for the door handle. But Alec's voice stopped him.

"Where you off to, Westfield?"

"Why are you up?" Ben shot back.

"Messenger woke *me* an hour ago. Now it's your turn." He raised an eyebrow at Ben.

"I was going to see Miss Campbell. To see how her grandfather is doing."

"He didn't survive the night," Alec said as he shook his head.

"How do you know?" Ben spun to face him.

"Miss Macleod sent a messenger when he died. That's what woke me. I asked her to let me know when something happened. I am surprised she sent her man so late—or early, as the case may be."

"Why didn't you tell me?" Ben snapped.

"And what would you have done?" Alec narrowed his eyes. "You're nothing to the girl, Ben. You can't help her through this."

"I could try," he mumbled.

"You've never cared for anyone, aside from your brothers. You've been with more women than I can count on my fingers and toes. And never for more than a night." He advanced toward Ben. "You're not good for her."

"And who are you to decide that?" Ben felt a blinding rage. He pressed through it. During most of the time that he was tarnishing his name, Alec had been right beside him. "Who made you her guardian?"

"Not her guardian." His friend shook his head. "But I know she'll not be safe with you. You'll ruin her. Then you'll disappear, like you always do. She'll be left to pick up the pieces of her tattered reputation. Her mother had a hard life. I'd not want the same for her." He clasped Ben's shoulder. "You hear me? She's a *good* girl. Leave her be."

"She's all alone?"

"She has friends. They'll take care of her." He shot Ben a warning glance.

"Who's with her now?" he pressed. He needed to know she wasn't alone.

"I'm not sure anyone is at the moment. Miss Macleod's note said the lass kicked them all out."

Ben chuckled at the image of his fiery Elspeth doing just that.

"It's not funny," Alec reprimanded him with a scowl.

"No. It's not funny at all," he agreed. "It's sad." He turned and started back up the stairs.

"You're giving up so easily?" Alec asked.

"I'm not good for her. You said so yourself."

"Well, I never expected you to agree," Alec mumbled as he walked back toward his study. "But I'm glad you do. Rest easy, Westfield."

Ben tried to maintain a casual pace as he ascended the stairs. But as soon as he turned the corner out of sight, he sped up. He went back to his room and crossed to the window. Only two stories up. He'd jumped farther before.

Ben pushed the window up slowly, happy to hear that

it made little noise. He swung one leg over the side and then the other. He hung by his fingertips until he finally dropped, landing in a crouch in some soft moss. But he immediately rose and jogged across the back lawn and into the woods. Then he let his senses lead him to her.

He didn't stop until her cottage came into view, then he stopped and shook his head. It wasn't even dawn. What madness had come over him? In the back of his mind he could hear Simon lecture him for his reckless impulsiveness.

Not that it mattered. The pull Elspeth Campbell had over him was too strong, and he couldn't turn away if he wanted to. He continued toward the door.

Before he could knock, it opened and Elspeth gasped. "*Mo chreach*! Ye frightened me!" A pail dropped from her hands.

"My apologies, Miss Campbell." He reached out his hand to keep her from falling and grasped a handful of her skirts.

Her eyes widened and she backed away from him. "What do ye think ye're doin'?"

Ben heaved a sigh. This wasn't going at all the way he'd planned. Who was he kidding? He hadn't planned a bloody thing. "I just wanted to see you. MacQuarrie told me about your grandfather, and I wanted to make sure you were all right."

She looked into the darkened night. "No horse? Did ye walk all the way here, my lord?"

He took a step toward her, not even trying to hide the grin on his face. "I took the path you showed me. I didn't know another way."

❧

Elspeth stared at the handsome Englishman. It would be so easy to get lost in the depths of his eyes. How could Sorcha possibly believe *this* man wore the mark? She shook her head to dispel such foolish thoughts. "Ye shouldna be here. I have things ta do."

"What things could you possibly have to do in the middle of the night?"

Elspeth retrieved her pail of tar. "People will start comin' to see him in the mornin'. I need to blacken the door and—"

"Blacken the door?"

"'Tis tradition, Lord Benjamin."

"You Scots and your traditions," he said with a smile and reached out his hand toward her pail. "I'll do it."

She motioned toward the house with her hand. "I already stopped the clocks. But I havena covered the mirrors yet," she said absently, but she let him take the pail from her.

"You should rest."

Elspeth swiped a tear from her eye. "I'm tired of everyone tellin' me ta rest. I'm just fine."

"Yes," he said, his deep voice rumbling over her like a caress. "I can see you don't need anyone." Lord Benjamin closed the distance between them and wrapped his arms around her. Elspeth couldn't help but sag against him, even though she knew she shouldn't. It was heaven not to support her own weight, so she let him do it for her.

"I canna stop," she said, unable to keep her voice from cracking. "If I do, I'll no' be able ta start again."

"I know," he said softly. He didn't even pull away

when she began to sob against his chest. "It's all right," he crooned, his voice soft and melodic, and he rubbed her back with the flat of his palm.

Elspeth clutched the lapels of his coat in her hands as she pressed her forehead into his strong chest. "I'm sorry ta be such a bairn."

He tried to tip her chin with his finger so that she would look up at him, but she didn't move her head. By now her eyes were probably all red and her nose puffy. But he didn't give up. His hand cupped her face and tilted it toward him.

Her eyes met his with a jolt. "You're not a baby," he said softly. "You're human, that's all." The pad of his thumb stroked her cheek. "I'm sorry your grandfather died."

"I'm sorry I wasna here," she whispered.

"He wouldn't have wanted you to suffer, too, love. I'm sure of it."

She knew his words were meant to be comforting, but they simply started another storm of emotion. When he bent and slipped one arm beneath her legs to pick her up, she didn't argue. She just wrapped her arms around him. She couldn't even find the strength to protest when he sat down on the bench outside the front door and placed her on his lap.

His strong arms enfolded her and pulled her close as his hand pressed her head into his shoulder. He reached into his pocket with the other, retrieved his handkerchief, and handed it to her.

"Tired of me drownin' yer shirt, are ye, Lord Benjamin?" she asked quietly.

A chuckle rumbled through his body. She moved

to sit up, but his arms still enfolded her. "Not yet," he said. "I was just getting comfortable."

"My friends would say this is highly improper, what with me sittin' on yer lap and all."

"Then I'm really glad they're not here." Another laugh moved through his body. Then his lips touched her forehead.

"They're all angry with me anyway," she said as she blew the hair from her eyes.

"I'm sure they're not angry," he tried to assure her.

"Ye dinna see the look on Caitrin's face. Do ye ken she tried ta make me leave with her?"

"She wouldn't dare!" he cried in mock dismay.

Elspeth simply raised her head and swatted his chest with her fist. "Ye're no' so funny, ye know," she mumbled. "Ye're mighty handsome. But no' so funny."

"I can't be perfect," he said, his eyes dancing with mirth when they met hers. He brushed her hair back over her ear. "Your hair is beautiful down around your shoulders."

Elspeth's hands flew to the top of her head. "My combs!" she cried. "My combs are gone." She jumped to her feet. How could she have lost them? Tears stung her eyes again as they started to fall. How could she have lost her grandfather and all she had left of her mother in the same night?

She rushed into the house and spun around. Thankfully he hadn't followed her. Elspeth closed her eyes and opened her hand. "*Faigh, faigh, faigh. Còmhnadh.*"

Then she peeked open one eye. Nothing sat in her palm. Wherever the combs were, they were too far away for her summoning spell to work. Then again, she was distraught; perhaps her concentration was off.

Lord Benjamin stood in the doorway, watching her. She didn't have time to think about what he thought. She checked the floor and the small table. She searched beside her grandfather's bed, by the mirrors she'd covered, and by the windows she'd opened. But the combs were nowhere to be found. How could she have been so foolish?

"They're gone," she cried, as the last bit of hope escaped her.

"It's all right." He took her shoulders in his strong hands and forced her to look at him.

"It's no' all right. They're all I have of her."

Understanding dawned in his eyes. "I'll find them," he promised.

"The ball?" she asked as she motioned toward the door.

"You had them when we left the ball. I'll go back and find them." The strength in his gaze startled her, leaving her speechless. "I'll find them. No matter what."

All she could do was nod. Then he was gone.

# Ten

BEN RAN ACROSS THE MEADOW BEHIND HER HOUSE. He ran as fast as he could. The haunted look in her eyes was fresh in his mind. He knew it was the loss of her grandfather, not her hair combs, that she was truly concerned about. The trinkets were something for her to fret over, but he was bound and determined to find them anyway. They meant the world to her, and he'd make sure it was one less thing she had to worry about.

Ben followed his nose into the woods, tracking Miss Campbell's scent and his own, retracing their steps. The night closed around him like a shroud, the trees blocking all evidence of the moon. But he knew it was there. He finally *felt* it. He finally felt something.

He searched the darkness, looking for the glitter of the pewter combs, hoping they would present themselves. If not, he'd look all the way to the light of day. He wouldn't let her down. He simply could not.

He was a bit ashamed to admit how much he'd enjoyed holding her in his lap, feeling the soft angles of her body pressed against him. He'd tamped down his desire and simply allowed himself the pleasure of comforting her. She had needed him at that moment. But for some reason, he felt he needed her, too.

Then something caught his eye against a large moss-covered rock. He bent and picked up one pewter wolf. He smiled up at the crescent moon. One down. One to go. He pocketed the comb, then knelt beside the rock and patted the ground.

Nothing.

He finally stood and dusted the dirt from his knees. What were the odds that the two combs would have landed in the same place anyway? He went back to following their scent, heading in the direction of the Fergusons' mansion.

Just as the sun broke the horizon, he heard church bells ringing off in the distance. Then he spotted the second comb. It must have fallen from her hair as soon as they'd started to run. He picked it up with a smile and added it to his pocket with its mate. He was gratified to feel the heavy weight of the pewter wolves in his pocket.

He ran at a leisurely pace back to her home. The sun was up now, so he took in the tidy but small appearance of her cottage. But what caught his attention was the coach out front. He slowed to a walk and peered around the corner of the house.

The young dark-haired chit he'd met the night before, the one who didn't appreciate him lumping all of Scotland in as part of Britain, was just reaching the door. Her big lummox of a brother was at her side.

"I doona ken why *we* have ta sit here all day," the giant complained.

The girl turned an irritated gaze upon her brother. "We're here, Wallace, because El shouldna be alone. Someone has ta sit with Mr. Campbell. We'll all be takin' turns. And Caitrin specifically asked for yer assistance."

"She did?" He brightened just a bit. "Is Cait here, then?"

The girl let out an exasperated sigh. "*Mo chreach!* Does yer every thought have ta be about Cait? No, she's no' here. No' yet, anyhow."

The lummox's smile widened, completely unaffected by his sister's outrage. "But she'll be here later." He pounded on the door, nearly shaking the cottage to the ground.

Ben watched the pair enter the house, then he leaned against the wall. Poor Elspeth, if those two had been designated to keep her company. Still, they were her friends, and he was... nothing. Just a fellow passing through town. Dread washed over him.

He pushed himself off the wall and started for the door. He had hair combs to return. Then he would start his search for Rosewyth Campbell.

Ben ambled up the front step and knocked lightly. A moment later the dark-haired chit pulled the door open, and her jaw dropped. "What're... I mean, Lord Benjamin?"

As soon as his name fell from her lips, Elspeth came into view. Her green eyes sparkled in the early morning light, and Ben's heart leapt in his chest. It was ridiculous for the girl to have such an effect on him. Still, he couldn't look away from her beauty. She hadn't slept in more than a day, and yet she looked as radiant in her simple homespun as she had in her ball gown the night before. "Miss Campbell," he said softly.

A beaming smile spread across her face, making her even lovelier, which he hadn't thought was possible.

"My lord, I'm so sorry ta have sent ye on a wild goose chase last night. I wasna thinkin' clearly."

Ben stepped inside the cottage, which seemed much smaller in the light of day. Of course, the overgrown Wallace Ferguson took up a large amount of space.

He reached into his pocket and pulled out the two pewter hair combs. "I told you I'd find them."

Elspeth gasped as her eyes landed on the two wolves in the palm of his hand. Before Ben could say anything else, she threw her arms around his neck, nearly throwing him off balance. He wrapped his arms around her, keeping both of them from tumbling to the ground.

"I canna believe ye found them," she gushed. Her pretty green eyes glistened, and she looked at him as though he were her own personal hero.

If the Ferguson chit hadn't suddenly suffered from a fit of coughs, Ben was certain he would have kissed the beguiling girl he still held in his arms. As it was, doing so with an audience wasn't the best idea.

He smiled at Elspeth then drew back, though he wanted nothing more than to hold her even tighter to him. Ben opened his hand once more, revealing the pair of pewter wolves. She snatched them from him and clutched them close to her heart. "I canna ever thank ye enough, my lord."

"It was my pleasure, Miss Campbell."

"Doona go anywhere," she said. Then after one more beatific smile, she escaped into a room off the side of the main one.

Ben turned around to find the Ferguson siblings glaring at him. He lost his silly grin and then frowned when he realized the girl was raking her gaze over every bit of exposed skin he had—his face, his neck, his ears—as though she was looking for something on his person. Quite disconcerting. "Hello, again, Miss Ferguson," he said, hoping to embarrass her into looking away.

She folded her arms across her chest. "Am I ta take it ye were here last night, Lord Benjamin?"

"I—"

Before he could finish, Elspeth called from her room, "Sorcha Ferguson, I will throw ye out again if ye canna keep a civil tone in yer voice."

The girl clamped her mouth shut.

Ben bit back a smile. He turned to the hulking Scot. "Mr. Ferguson, have you lived in Edinburgh your whole life?"

"Aye," the man replied gruffly.

Well, that was a bit of luck. "Perhaps you can help me. I didn't set off for Scotland merely for holiday."

"No?" Ferguson's brow furrowed.

"I'm actually looking for someone who may be a bit hard to find."

"Who?" Sorcha interrupted.

Ben graced her with a smile. At least the irritated sound was gone from her voice.

"A woman. I was sent to find Rosewyth Campbell."

Wallace Ferguson's eyes went wide, while a frown

marred his sister's pretty face. "Well, my lord, I doona think ye'll have much luck with that endeavor."

⁓

"Why not?" he asked, his mouth agape.

Sorcha opened her mouth to reply, but Elspeth quickly strode out of the room and spoke over her. "Because she's no' acceptin' visitors, my lord." She shot a look at Sorcha, who bit her lips together so hard a line of white appeared around them. "What did ye want with her, Lord Benjamin?"

"I heard she was a healer," he said quietly.

"And are ye in need of a healin'?" Maybe he was ill. Maybe he needed her help.

"No…" he hedged. His eyes refused to meet hers. He looked at every surface in the room. "I just needed some information."

"What kind of information?" She faced him and placed her hands on her hips. She *would* find out why he was searching for her mother, what reason he had to be in Scotland.

"It's a bit private," he said quietly. His face colored. The man was blushing?

"Then let's step outside and discuss it, shall we?" She smiled an easy smile at him. He seemed a bit discomfited at that moment. So she hoped a friendly face would put him at ease. And maybe loosen his tongue a bit.

He walked to the door and ushered her through it with a hand at the small of her back. Then he closed the door soundly behind them.

"What is it I can do for ye, Lord Benjamin?"

"Ben." He began to pace across the lawn.

"Beggin' yer pardon?" she asked.

"Ben," he repeated. "That's my name. I give you leave to use it. I mean. I'm asking you to use it." His eyes met hers. "Please, call me Ben."

"Ben," she repeated.

A smile finally crossed his face. "That's better."

He would not lead her astray so easily. "Rosewyth Campbell?" she prodded. "Ye needed her healin'?"

"I'm not sure, but I'd heard she could fix things."

Things? "What sorts of things?" The man would wear her out with all the pacing in mere moments.

"I really just need to talk to *Rosewyth* Campbell. Can you tell me where I can find her?"

Oh, sure she could. Six feet under the ground. "Let's take a little walk and discuss yer concerns. I've a bit of a healin' touch, too, ye ken," she said as she motioned with her hand for him to follow.

He walked leisurely down the lane by her side. He was quiet and obviously preoccupied. "Yes, I'd heard you have a way with herbs, Miss Campbell."

"Elspeth." His glance rose to meet hers, finally. "My name is Elspeth. I grant ye leave ta use it." She couldn't contain the small smile that hovered around the corners of her lips.

"Elspeth," he repeated, as though tasting the name on his tongue. It was an old family name. Of which she was quite proud. "It suits you."

She simply inclined her head.

They walked leisurely down the lane until they reached the small church. Elspeth turned down the pea-gravel drive and motioned for him to follow.

"Are ye goin' ta tell me what's ailin' ye, Ben? Or will ye make me guess?"

"Nothing is ailing me." His eyes met hers and then danced away. "I would really rather talk with Rosewyth Campbell." He glanced around. "Does she live near here? Are we close?"

"Aye, Ben. She resides here." She pointed toward the tall stone monuments in the churchyard, each marking the graves of loved ones. "My mother died five years ago. She was Rosewyth Campbell."

# Eleven

BEN HEAVED A GREAT SIGH. HE STUDIED THE HEADSTONES in front of them. Of course the woman would be dead! What other luck would he have? First, he'd lost the ability to change with the moon. And now his only hope for salvation was dead. He'd been left with the mere slip of a girl who stood before him, her head tilted at an angle as she regarded him curiously.

"If ye'll do me the honor of tellin' me what's ailin' ye, I'll do my best ta help ye. I promise," she said, her green gaze dazzling him as she placed a hand on his arm. He had her full attention. That much was positive.

"It's not something I'm comfortable discussing…"

She simply tipped her head in the other direction, her gaze never breaking from his.

"It's fairly personal."

She blinked.

"I can't discuss it with you." The girl was probably still an innocent. He couldn't possibly tell her about the incident with the whore and that after that horrible night, he'd lost his ability to turn into a hairy, drooling wolf who howled at the moon.

"I have dealt with problems similar ta yers before, ye ken?" she smiled softly at him.

"You don't even know what the problem is," he gasped. Surely she didn't know. She couldn't possibly read minds as well as work with herbs.

"I can guess. Men like ye only get so squeamish about one thing." She laughed, a melodic little tune. "It's nothin' ta be ashamed of. Happens more than ye ken."

Men like him? Ben could only assume his mouth had fallen open in surprise, as he stared at her, completely dumbfounded. How many other Lycan men had lost the ability to change?

"I have just the thing for it." She nodded at him enthusiastically.

Ben scratched his head.

"But I have ta ken, does it work for ye?" Her face colored. "When ye're alone?"

"I *was* alone and it didn't work," he admitted. Perhaps she did know what she was talking about.

"Does it work when ye're with a lass?" She pointed to his thighs. What did his lap have to do with anything?

"I've never done it with a lass," he admitted. Simon had always beaten into him how dangerous it was to be with a woman when the moon was full. Pushing his luck was what had gotten him into this situation.

"At yer age?" Her hand fluttered to land on her chest. "That is surprisin'," she muttered.

"Why is it so surprising?" Now he was thoroughly confused.

"Forgive me for bein' so bold, but it's no' very often ye meet a man yer age who has never been with a lass." Again her gaze wandered down to his waist.

*Never been with a woman!* She thought he was talking about *that*? Ben buried his face in his hands and chuckled. He laughed so hard his shoulders shook.

"There, there, Ben. No need to cry over it. We'll get ye all fixed." Her hand touched his back, rubbing a light circle.

Ben finally raised his head and wiped the tears of mirth from his eyes.

She put her hands on her hips. "Were ye laughin' at me?" Indignation sparkled in her eyes.

"No, Elspeth." He held up both hands in surrender. "I promise," he chuckled. "I'm not laughing at you."

"Then what is so blasted funny?"

There was only one option. He'd have to show her.

Ben hauled her to him with one hand as he pushed the hair back from her face with his other.

Elspeth couldn't even sputter in surprise as he clutched her to him. He moved much too fast. One moment she was standing several feet from him, and the next she was pressed along against his body.

"Ye don't have ta put on a grand show just ta prove ta me ye're a man," she scolded him.

Another chuckle rumbled through him. She raised her hands to his chest to push away from him, but she was well and truly caught within his arms. His chest flexed beneath her fingers. She tested the hard wall with her fingertips.

"I *am* a man," he said quietly. Then his lips touched hers.

The first taste of him was heavenly. His lips pressed softly against hers, no more than a whisper against her skin. Elspeth had been kissed before. Once by a clumsy stable boy at a church picnic and once by Alec MacQuarrie, who had quickly decided that Caitrin was more to his liking. It hadn't bothered her, though, as kissing him could be compared to kissing her brother, if she'd had one.

But kissing Ben was nothing like that. Ben's lips slid across hers. His hand lifted to brush the hair back at her temple. She sighed against him, and he took the opportunity to touch her lips with his tongue. She gasped and then he took full advantage of her mouth.

His tongue slid against hers, and she had no choice but to reach and meet him with her own. They played a game of catch and retreat, neither losing. This was a winning game for both of them.

Elspeth's heart beat so hard she feared it would clamor so loudly he could hear it. His hand wrapped tighter around her waist, drawing her even closer. The length of him pressed against her belly.

She broke their kiss. "Ye *have* been with a lass, I'd wager." Breaths heaved from her in gasps.

"What makes you think that?" he chuckled.

"Ye doona kiss like ye have problems with *things* workin'." She glanced down his body.

He tugged her closer to him, if that was possible, and growled closer to her ear. "You make things work just fine." His lips pressed against the sensitive skin beneath her ear just before he cupped her bottom and pulled her against his hardness. She yelped and swatted at his chest.

A loud cough drew her attention. It actually sounded more like someone was strangling Caitrin, but she assumed her friend meant for it to be a cough.

Ben allowed her to step back and turned to face the churchyard. "You go. I'll follow along in a moment. I think we have some things to discuss."

They certainly did.

Elspeth was sure her blush matched her hair, if the scandalized look on Caitrin's face was any indication. Her friend hooked her arm with Elspeth's and practically dragged her back toward the cottage. "Have ye gone and lost yer fool mind?" she hissed.

That was a distinct possibility. She thought she'd been in control of the situation, right up until his lips touched hers. "It was just a kiss, Cait."

"Ha! And I'm Mary Queen of Scots."

"Ye look rather good for yer age, and with the missin' of yer head," she countered. Though she knew Caitrin had a point. It was more than just a kiss. Not that Elspeth regretted it for one moment. The feel of his hands, of his body pressed so close to hers, made her shiver at the thought.

"I dinna tell ye this last night, what with yer grandfather, El, but Westfield's the one. He's the one from my vision."

Elspeth shook her head as they neared the cottage. "Do ye think I'm daft? I saw the looks between ye and Sorcha. But ye're wrong, Cait. He just has an ailment. He was lookin' for my mother—"

"Aye, Sorcha told me. Doona ye think it strange that he came lookin' for Rosewyth Campbell? The last beast that came ta these parts left her with a bairn ta raise and no proper name ta give either of ye."

Elspeth ripped her arm from Caitrin's. Never in all the years of their friendship had Cait spoken so vilely of the circumstances of her birth. If her friend had struck her across the face, she would have been less stunned. "I suppose I should thank ye for puttin' me back in my place, Cait. I nearly forgot ye were higher born than me."

Her friend closed her blue eyes and sighed. "I dinna mean it the way it sounded. I'm just trying ta get ye ta see reason." She opened her eyes and pierced Elspeth with the intensity of her stare. "He is the one from my vision, El. He bears the mark. He will try ta take ye from us. And from what I've seen, he's done a mighty fine job of that so far."

The mark? Was it possible? Elspeth felt a connection to Ben Westfield, but she didn't think it was the mark. It didn't feel like she expected it to. But mark or no mark, he'd come for her help—actually her mother's help, but it was the same power. If he thought Rosewyth could heal him, she was certain she could. She probably should have asked the extent of his ailment, however.

It was hard to imagine that he had anything wrong with him. She'd never met a more virile man. He'd searched the countryside all night looking for her hair combs. How many ailing men could do that? How many healthy ones could?

She leveled her dearest friend with a furious glare. "We each have our roles, Caitrin. You're a seer and I'm a healer. If Benjamin Westfield needs me ta heal him, I'll do so. I doona expect ye ta understand, but I do expect ye ta respect my decision."

"Ladies," Ben's deep voice came from behind them.

Elspeth nearly jumped out of her skin. "Heavens, Ben! I dinna hear ye."

A wolfish grin spread across his face. "I do tend to move quietly. Am I interrupting?"

Elspeth turned back to Caitrin to find her glowering. "Ye're no' the only one this affects, El. Bear that in mind."

Then her dearest friend in the world stomped off through the trees.

# Twelve

AT FIRST BEN DIDN'T BELIEVE HIS EARS, THOUGH THEY'D never failed him in the past. Caitrin Macleod was a seer? The image of five beautiful women standing together at the Fergusons' flashed in his eyes. A seer. A healer. A coven. Not the hooked-nose witches from *Macbeth,* but a coven just the same.

Did the good people of Edinburgh know who resided right under their noses? And what powers did the other three women possess?

Not that it mattered overmuch. He'd come for a healer, and he heard Elspeth vow to help him. Whatever Caitrin Macleod thought he was after, she was wrong. He wanted only to return to his Lycan self, then he'd leave them in peace.

Leave *her.* Elspeth. He'd only known the woman a day, but the thought of leaving her pained him. He shook the thought from his head. Major Forster had said a Lycan bonds with his healer. That's all it was. Though the pull the lass had on him was stronger than any he could ever remember. He'd have to take special care not to let things progress to where they shouldn't.

He didn't think Elspeth could handle it. Who was he kidding? He didn't think *he* could handle it.

God, but she felt good in his arms.

"Ye look a million miles away, Ben." Her lilting voice brought him back to the present.

"I suppose I was in a way. Are you really a... healer, Elspeth?" *A witch,* he wanted to ask, but thought better of it.

"Aye. As was my mother before me, and her mother before her, and on and on."

Ben smiled. His family's heritage was much the same. All Lycan males, until him. Until this.

"What exactly is yer ailment? I've never seen a healthier man."

Healthy, at least, in all the ways anyone could see. It was inside where he was broken. Ben stared at her. To get her help he'd have to be honest. How was she to fix him otherwise? He'd left his home and come all this way to find her. Well, to find Rosewyth.

Still, being a Lycan wasn't something one openly admitted. In London he'd be locked in Bedlam if he even thought of telling anyone. Or Newgate. He wasn't sure which was worse. Creatures like him usually only confessed all to their intended mates.

An image of mating with Elspeth flashed in his mind, and he couldn't shake it away. Bonding. It was just bonding with his healer. He could tell her. He had to.

"I'm a Lycan," he blurted out before he came to his senses. "Do you know what that is?"

She shook her head, though he noticed she rubbed the skin of her wrist beneath her gloves.

"A werewolf, in layman's terms."

He half expected her to run through the woods, screaming like a banshee, but she simply tilted her head to one side and waited for him to continue.

"You have nothing to say to that?"

She shrugged. "What would ye like me ta say?"

"I don't know. Maybe run in fear, at least."

Her beautiful smile returned. "I doona believe there is a thing about ye I should fear, Ben." Her gaze moved from the top of his head to the bottoms of his feet, lingering as though she'd find the secret of his creation somewhere upon his person. "What does all of this mean? What does bein' a Lycan entail? Do ye change ta a wolf every night?"

He shook his head. "No. We change only when the light of a full moon touches us. The rest of the month we look like any other man, but beneath the surface the beast inside struggles to be released, stronger in the days surrounding moonful."

"I see," she said looking up into the forest canopy above them, though the sun was high in the sky. "The moon is but a sliver now."

Ben heaved a sigh. It was easier to talk about this with her than he had expected. "I left almost immediately after the last moonful."

"Why?"

"I didn't transform."

"And ye *want* ta transform?" she asked with a frown.

"Of course I want to change," he barked. When her green eyes grew round, he shuffled his feet. "Sorry. I suppose I'm not explaining this well after all. The *change* is part of me, Elspeth, who I am. I need to fix whatever is wrong with me."

Elspeth stared at the man in front of her. A Lycan. A werewolf. A beast. Caitrin had been right about that. Is that what the mark indicated? Again she rubbed the mark on her wrist. Was that what her father was? Was that why he'd sought out her mother?

"Do ye have a mark, Ben?"

"A mark?"

"On yer skin?"

He smiled. "How did you know?"

Elspeth shrugged. "Lucky guess. Where is it? Can I see it?" Did it look like hers?

His grin widened. "Only if I remove all my clothes." He glanced around the woods. "I don't think this would be the place to show you."

Shivers danced across her skin at the thought of Ben Westfield without a stitch of clothing. As a healer, she'd seen men unclothed before, though she'd thought nothing of it. Somehow she didn't think that would be the case with this man. "I'll, um, need ta see it. But no' here, no' now." Then she straightened her shoulders and looked him square in the eye. "I'll need time ta figure out what ta do with ye. Can ye give me a few days?"

"You can have all the days you need, lass. Do you think you can heal me?"

"I've never encountered a case like yers before, but I'll do everythin' in my power." And she would try to locate any notes her mother may have left about Lycans. Why hadn't her mother told her more?

Caitrin threw open the door to her father's study. She didn't know who else to turn to, and she was furious. Angus Macleod looked up from the papers on his desk and regarded her with a look of amusement. "*Havers*, Cait! Ye look like a cat whose tail's been set aflame."

She glared at her father. "How flatterin'."

He chuckled and leaned back in his chair. "I'm glad ye're here, lass. A gentleman came ta see me today about ye."

Caitrin shook her head. Nothing he had to say could be more important than her current predicament. "Papa, did ye ever meet Elspeth's sire?"

Her father frowned and tapped his chin. "No, but yer mother did."

"Did she say anythin' about him?"

His laugh warmed the room. "A thing or two. Nothin' I'll repeat in yer presence, lass. Yer mother wasna one for cursin', but she made an exception for Rosie's beast."

Caitrin rubbed her hands across her face. Could the man never be serious? "Oh, Papa!" she groaned. "I've seen a man, a beast," she clarified. "It's all comin' ta pass. He'll take Elspeth from us and—"

"Now ye sound like my Fiona."

"Why?"

"Doona work yerself up, Cait. The visions are no' always accurate."

She blinked at her father. What was he talking about? Her visions had always been accurate. She'd never once been wrong. "Papa, ye doona seem ta understand—"

"I lived with Fiona for a quarter of a century, Cait. I understand perfectly. She was right most of the time, I'll grant ye. But she wasna right about Rosewyth. Maybe it's somethin' in the nature of these beasts; they mess with yer powers."

"What do ye mean she wasna right about Rosewyth?"

Her father sighed and sat forward in his seat. "I'd never seen Fiona more upset than she was when she received the first vision about the beast. She kept rantin' and ravin'. The man was goin' ta take Rosie from the coven. The *Còig* would fall apart…"

Just like what she'd seen with Elspeth. Caitrin's heart began to race. She had no idea her mother had seen something similar.

"… turn out that way. So ye see, lass, yer mother wasna always correct—"

"Papa, I missed what ye said. Go back. Mama thought the *Còig* would fall apart," she prompted.

"Aye. Fiona said the man would come for Rosie and take her away. Then the man did come, but Rosie dinna go with him. She chose ta stay with the coven instead. Just because ye can see what is supposed ta happen doesna mean that people canna change the course of the future."

It should have been good news that Rosewyth Campbell chose another path. It meant Elspeth could do the same. Yet it was troubling that her mother had been wrong. Caitrin hadn't known that was possible.

"And speakin' of the future, Cait. The fellow today, Mr. MacQuarrie, he stopped by early this mornin', wantin' ta speak with me."

Caitrin shook her head. "MacQuarrie is

inconsequential, Papa." Though she wished he weren't. She'd seen such strength in him the night before, and he made her warm and tingly all over. But his future lay along a different path.

"I'd hardly say that, Caitrin. The lad asked me for yer hand."

She gasped. She hadn't seen that coming either. Why not? Her mind was a jumble.

"I told him he had my blessin' but that ye made yer own decisions. Just like yer mother."

# Thirteen

BEN AMBLED UP THE STEPS OF ALEC MACQUARRIE'S stately home. Before he could knock, the butler opened the door with a frown. Ben sighed. Must all Scots frown at him? He was starting to take it personally.

Honestly, he really wasn't such a disagreeable fellow. Most people, most English people, found him a delight to be around. He generally attended the best parties, told the best stories, and spent the rest of his time with the best women. He couldn't understand why all of Scotland seemed to take umbrage with him. Well, all of Scotland except for Elspeth.

He'd left her in the care of the Fergusons and made her promise to get some rest, which was exactly what he planned to do once he reached MacQuarrie's.

"My lord," the butler began with a bow, "Mr. MacQuarrie would like a word with ye."

Ben resisted the urge to groan. After their conversation last night, he wasn't looking forward to another interview. Besides he was nearly dead on his feet. "Do tell Mr. MacQuarrie that I'll see him at dinner." If he was awake by then.

He turned his back on the dour Scot and climbed the stairs to the next floor. He made his way to his chambers and collapsed, facedown, onto the bed, leaving his boots dangling over the edge. His feet were heavy, and he wished he had someone here who would pull them off for him.

Elspeth.

He'd love for her to pull off his boots and then his trousers. He smiled into the pillow as an image of his lovely witch entered his mind, thankful again she wasn't of the *Macbeth* variety.

Most men of his acquaintance would run in fear from a witch. But Ben wasn't most men, and he did need her help. He thought again about how her wild red hair hung about her shoulders and the way she'd thrown herself in his—

Something cracked him on the back of his head. "Ow!" He rolled over, prepared to fight, only to find Alec standing over him brandishing a rolled-up periodical.

"That's the thanks I get? You come to my home uninvited, and I let you stay as a guest. I ask you to leave Miss Campbell be, but the legendary Lord Benjamin Westfield can't possibly do so. And when my man tells you I want to speak with you, you ignore him completely and pass out across your bed?"

"I didn't ignore him," Ben complained as he rubbed the back of his head. "I told the man I'd see you at dinner. I'm a bit tired, Alec."

"Aye, from staying out all night, like I asked you not to."

Ben pushed himself to a sitting position. Now he could take off his own bloody boots. "I'm a bit tired of the sanctimonious Alec MacQuarrie, to be honest. We both know I'm far from a saint, and we both know it, you Scottish hypocrite, because you've been with me every step of the way. And *now* you decide to tell me which females I can and cannot spend my time with?"

Alec heaved a sigh and dropped into a chair just a few feet from the bed. "I didn't want to speak to you about Miss Campbell."

The fight instantly evaporated from Ben. "Oh. Well, I was just trying to catch a bit of sleep. I was up all night searching the woods for hair combs, if you can believe it."

Alec gaped at him. Then his lips broke into a smile. He threw his head back and laughed.

"I can't imagine what you find so humorous about the situation," Ben grumbled.

Alec wiped a tear from his eye and brought his levity back under control. "And I thought I had it bad. You really must care for the lass."

"I didn't want her to worry about them." Ben shrugged, suddenly feeling uncomfortable with his friend's all-knowing eyes focused on him.

"Ah, of course not. Heaven forbid she get herself all worked up over a pair of hair combs."

"What do you want, Alec?"

Immediately his friend sobered and sat forward in his chair. "I wanted to ask your advice about Miss Macleod."

The pretty blond harridan who hated him? Ben had some advice concerning Miss Macleod. "Run the other direction."

"I don't think I can do that." Alec frowned. "I

spoke to the lass' father this morning, and I asked for her hand."

Ben nearly choked on his own tongue. He knew Alec was entranced by the girl... by the witch. Did his friend know that little detail? "How much do you really know about her?"

"I'd say a bit more than you know about Miss Campbell," Alec shot back.

"Touché." But did he know the girl was a witch, a seer? Not that he could tell him. Ben needed Elspeth's help, and bringing attention to her coven wasn't the best idea. "If you've already asked for the girl's hand, what do you want to ask me?"

Alec grimaced. "Well, I'd hoped Mr. Macleod would accept my offer—"

"He didn't?" Ben's mouth fell open. MacQuarrie had more money than most Scots. He'd been well sought after in London by marriage-minded mamas and their daughters. He couldn't imagine Mr. Macleod had received a better offer for his daughter.

"He gave me his blessing but said Caitrin herself would have to accept me."

Understanding dawned on Ben. "She won't give you the time of day." She was too busy interrupting Ben's affairs.

Alec grinned, but only for a moment. "Well, I did win a kiss from her last night, quite a nice one actually; but she's a stubborn lass, and I'm not quite sure how to convince her."

"Quite a nice one? Please don't tell me that you saw sparks when your lips touched hers. Because that would quite turn my stomach, old friend." Ben lay back on the bed and put his forearm over his eyes. He raised his head when Alec groaned and swatted him again. "Seduce her, MacQuarrie," he finally said.

"*Seduce* her?" The man looked slightly ill.

"You've done it before. This time, do it with marriage in mind."

"Seduce her. I might just give that a try," Alec muttered as he stepped from the room and closed the door. Then he opened the door again. Ben didn't bother to raise his head.

"Don't go and get similar ideas about Miss Campbell, Ben. Mark my words. Seducing that one is not in her best interest. Or yours." The door clicked shut.

Ben turned his head in his pillow and closed his eyes while he worked to get a girl with hair the color of fire and fury off his mind. But even in repose she met him in his dreams.

❧

Elspeth dropped her head in her hands and groaned. "I canna take one more day of this, Rhiannon. No' one more day. If another person comes ta the door with well wishes, I might just lose my temper."

"I honestly dinna ken ye had so many friends, El. It's pretty nice ta see them all comin' together for ye."

El pushed the corners of her mouth up and glared at Rhiannon. "But my face is goin' ta freeze like this if I have ta smile at one more person."

"Only one more day. The burial will be tomorrow and then ye can start fresh."

*Only one more day.* Elspeth repeated the phrase over and over in her mind.

"Uh-oh," Rhiannon said as she removed her feet from the settee where she reclined. She crossed quickly to the window. "Ye've company, El."

Elspeth rose and raised the drapes to peer out. She quickly threw open the door when she saw the man approaching. He met her with a smile.

"Lord Benjamin," she said.

His eyes twinkled. "I thought I gave you leave to use my given name, Miss Campbell."

The door opened farther and Rhiannon spoke over her. "'Tis no' proper, and ye ken it," she whispered vehemently.

"Shush yer mouth, Rhiannon. His lordship is here to see *me*. No' ye." She very nearly stuck out her tongue. "Stay with my grandfather, will ye?" Then she turned and closed the door behind her. "What can I do for ye, Ben?"

"To be quite honest, I wanted to see if you have any ideas for how to heal my little..." He grimaced. "Affliction."

"I do have quite a few questions on the topic. I suppose I could take a walk with ye." She looked over her shoulder and saw Rhiannon staring daggers at her from behind the window glass. This time she did stick out her tongue. Ben chuckled at her.

"Lead the way, and I will follow." He motioned toward the lane.

"No' that way," she said, motioning over her shoulder. "The best views can be found in the other direction."

As they started down a well-worn path, Elspeth began her line of questioning.

"How long have ye been a Lycan, Ben?"

"Since birth, Elspeth. It's a family trait, passed from one male to another. One cannot choose to be Lycan or not. It just is. I find that I miss it quite a bit, now that I no longer have it."

"Did ye lose it because of illness? Were ye sick? Or did ye suddenly just lose the ability ta change?"

"There was an incident," he said as he glanced at her out the corner of his eye.

"What sort of incident?"

"The sort that I can't explain to a woman of your standing." Color crept up his face.

"Beggin' yer pardon? Ye canna tell someone who's illegitimate about yer incident?"

"Oh, no, no!" He stopped walking and turned to face her. "I truly don't care if you had one parent or two. You could be born of a gypsy tribe and I wouldn't feel differently about you."

"Just how *do* ye feel about me, Ben?"

# *Fourteen*

How *did* he feel about her? Good question. It was one thing he needed to think about. She was more of a distraction than any woman he'd met in quite some time. She was the only woman he still thought about when he walked away from her. But he couldn't possibly tell her that. Because very soon he would be on his way back to London.

"I have great trust in your ability to heal me." He hoped she didn't realize what effort it took to hedge around her question.

"Then ye have more trust than I do, Ben. Because I've no idea if I can help ye or no'. Why did ye come all the way ta Scotland ta find help? There are no healers in London?"

"There are doctors, yes." He nodded his head as he absently plucked a piece of tall, dry grass and rolled it between his fingertips. *No mythical healers, however. No one like her.*

"But no one ye could tell about yer Lycan side, I assume?" She raised her face to his. Her hair shone like fire, and he wanted nothing more than to put his hands in it. He coughed to cover his moment of discomfort.

"It's a bit difficult to talk about," he admitted. And it was forbidden. "If any of my Lycan brethren knew I'd revealed any of this to you, they would feel terribly betrayed."

"No' ta fear, Ben. I can keep a secret when it's needed." Her smile was all the reassurance he needed. "May I see yer mark?" she asked.

"The mark of the beast?"

"Aye, the mark of the beast. I'm simply curious." She shrugged her shoulders and suddenly looked vulnerable.

Ben looked around. The area was secluded. No one would see, and there wasn't anywhere else they could be alone. One of her coven or another was always there, sitting watch.

He tugged his shirt from his trousers and slid the top button of his waistband through its buttonhole.

She gasped slightly, her hand fluttered to her pinkened cheek. There was no doubt in his mind she was an innocent.

Ben took her hand in his and gave it an affectionate squeeze. "I don't have to show you."

Elspeth shook her head. "I forgot ye said ye'd have ta remove yer clothes."

Ben chuckled. "Not completely." He lifted his shirt and pointed to a spot just below his waistband. "It's here."

Elspeth leaned over to get closer to the mark. He immediately felt the warm touch of her breath against the tender skin of his abdomen and stepped away from her.

"I canna see it if ye move, Ben."

"This might not be such a good idea," he said, fully prepared to tuck his shirt back in, just so she would step back. He was already hardening under her gaze.

Elspeth dropped to her knees in front of him and tugged off one of her gloves. "Doona be so daft, Ben. It's a strip of skin and nothin' more."

But it was quite a bit more than a strip of skin. And if he didn't take her attention from the area, it would soon be even more.

She smoothed the pad of her thumb across his birthmark. "Heavens, ye are warm."

"It's a trait," he grumbled. And getting warmer every second.

"Hmm." Her finger caressed him. "It's no' so much, is it? Small thing, it is."

Ben felt the tender swipe of her thumb all the way to his core. He instantly felt the beast in him rise to the surface. He turned from her to face in the opposite direction.

Her delicate hand came to rest on his back. It was hot enough to brand his skin through his clothes.

"I have a fear greater than that of losing my ability to change with the moon. And it's that I'll hurt you, Elspeth." He wanted to drag her beneath him and toss her skirts up. He wanted to be inside her. And he wanted it right at that moment.

"Why?" she asked. Her eyes narrowed as they searched his face.

"Regrettably," he started, trying to remove the growl from his voice, but failing miserably. "I must go." Ben turned to jog away, but her hand on his arm stopped him. "Let me go, Elspeth," he barked.

"And if I do no'? Then what will ye do, Ben?"

❦

If her coven sisters could have seen her at that moment, they would have told her she was playing with fire. Yet she couldn't have walked away if she had wanted to.

Elspeth raised her hand to Ben's cheek. He immediately turned into it and nipped the center of her palm with his teeth.

"Ye do have a bit of the beast in ye, I'd wager," she said, feeling a tickle as it crawled up her spine.

"More than a bit, lass," he growled as his hand cupped her neck and pulled her to him. "When you touched my mark, I felt like I would shift into a wolf right here and now."

"Is it gettin' better, then?" She raised her hands to his chest.

"Not yet," he breathed as his lips hovered over hers. His exhale became her inhale.

"I like the beast," she said as her hand slipped down to his waistband. She felt an intense desire to stroke his mark again.

"Don't touch me there, lass," he said as he took her hands in his and raised them to his mouth. He nipped the pad of her finger between his teeth. "I'm already close enough to taking you now."

"Takin' me?" she asked.

"Taking you beneath me," he breathed. "Taking your clothes off. Taking your innocence." Moisture flooded her center as he said the last.

"And if I said yes, Ben?"

His hands fell to his waist and he took a step back from her, a strange look in his eyes.

"I'll assume that's a no," she mumbled as her eyes dropped to the path. She hadn't thought he'd reject her.

"What the devil?" he hissed.

Elspeth raised her eyes, this time taking his whole body in. His polished boots were wrapped in vines, anchoring him solidly to the forest floor. His wrists were bound in a similar fashion.

"Sorcha Ferguson!" Elspeth cried. "Call off yer vines. The man was only goin' ta kiss me!"

Sorcha stepped into view, an unrepentant tilt to her head. "He wanted much more than *that*, El."

Ben had never known ivy to be so strong. It was nearly impossible for him to move, and he was stronger than most. The vines tightened around his wrists, holding him, cutting into his skin. He felt the growl building in his chest as the wolf in him chafed at being held captive. He tamped down the rage and faced the little chit who'd done this to him.

Apparently he'd stumbled upon Sorcha Ferguson's power. He'd never heard of one using botanical manipulation as a weapon before, and he was a little surprised that the lass had used her ability in front of him. Wasn't she afraid of exposing the coven?

Elspeth closed the distance between them and tugged on one of the vines binding his wrists. "I'm so sorry," she whispered.

Then she turned her gaze to the young dark-haired witch. "Ye ken the rules, Sorcha."

The girl shrugged. "Cait said the rules doona apply ta him."

"What are ye talkin' about?" Elspeth's gaze danced from person to person.

"He's no' a real man. If he says anythin' about us, we'll tell everyone what he is."

Ben gasped. "You told them?" She'd just finished promising him that she could keep a secret.

Elspeth looked back at Ben, worry on her lovely face. "No, I swear no'. Though I suppose I do owe ye an explanation."

He would have gestured for her to continue, but he still couldn't move his arms. "I'm waiting."

She bit her bottom lip and took a step away from him. "Sorcha, if ye doona release him, I'll take an ax and hack them away from him."

In the next instant, Ben felt the vines loosen then fall away from his arms and legs. He stepped away from the ivy, toward Elspeth. "An explanation," he reminded her, though he had a fairly good idea what she would say.

She sighed deeply and flushed red. "Sorcha, a moment if ye doona mind."

The dark-haired lass shook her head. "I'll no' leave ye alone with the likes of him."

Elspeth raised herself high and glared at the younger witch. "It's no' yer decision. Now, be off."

After one more pointed glare in his direction, the girl vanished back into the foliage. Ben rubbed his wrists. Damn if they weren't sore. "The chit can make vines do her bidding?"

Elspeth's eyes fell to his feet, and she winced. "I had hoped I wouldna have ta tell ye this, Ben. I'm no' just a healer who works with herbs."

"You're a witch," he finished for her.

Her gaze shot to his. "How do ye ken that?"

# Fifteen

ELSPETH WAS CERTAIN HER FACE WAS AFLAME. How did the man know she was a witch? Other than the fact that Sorcha had just used her vines to tie him up?

It was something no one spoke of outside of the *Còig*—well, other than within their families. After all, it wasn't all that long ago that witch hunts in Scotland had decimated the population, though not everyone put to death had been guilty of the *crime*. Still, generation after generation had protected the members of the coven. Yet Benjamin Westfield somehow knew she was a witch?

He took a step toward her. "That's why I was looking for Rosewyth. She wasn't just a healer; she was a witch with mystical healing powers. The only one who could help me."

Elspeth felt the air whoosh out of her lungs. "Ye knew this the entire time, and ye dinna say anythin'?"

"What was there to say, lass? Besides I didn't know until I realized you were Rosewyth's daughter that you'd inherited her abilities."

She frowned at him. How could he possibly have deduced that?

Ben looked away and shrugged. "And... I *might* have overheard Miss Macleod talking about a vision. She's a seer, isn't she?"

Elspeth stumbled back a bit. He knew about *all* of them? "How...?"

One corner of his mouth lifted. "I have excellent hearing. It's another Lycan trait. Though..." His smile faded as if he'd just sorted something out.

"Though what?"

He shook his head and began to pace in circles. Elspeth thought he would never answer her. So she asked again, "What are ye no' tellin' me, Ben?"

"You first," he hedged. "The others... What sort of powers do they have? Miss Ferguson, I gather, is in touch with botanical arts of some sort."

Elspeth had never discussed what powers the others had with outsiders. But Sorcha *had* revealed herself. "She does have a bit of a green thumb," she admitted. "Sometimes she talks ta the plants. They do her biddin'. It's always come in handy durin' the harvest season."

"And the others?" he prompted.

Rhiannon and Blaire hadn't done anything that warranted her revealing information about them. She shrugged.

"It's no secret that your friends, the members of your coven, don't care for me, Elspeth. I'd just like to know what I'm up against."

She rushed forward. "Ben, they would never hurt ye. Please believe me."

He offered his arms as evidence otherwise, revealing where Sorcha's vines had cut into his skin. "Normally my body would heal itself. But I seem to have lost that talent when I lost the ability to change."

Elspeth's breath caught in her throat. She tore off her second glove and placed one hand on each of his wrists. She closed her eyes and visualized him whole and hale until she felt the power leave her fingertips and fuse with him.

When she opened her eyes, she found his hazel ones boring into her.

"You have the mark, Elspeth." His voice sounded strangled.

She glanced down where her hands still grasped his wrists. Her moon-shaped mark seemed to glow red in the light. She dropped her hold on him, as though she'd been burned.

"Why didn't you tell me?"

Why didn't she tell him? Speaking about her sire wasn't something she ever did. Neither had her mother. "I dinna think it mattered."

"Ah," he said with a frown, "but you were terribly interested in mine. What else are you keeping from me, Elspeth?"

She shook her head. "I dinna realize I owed ye an explanation about anythin' else, Ben. Ye're the one who sought *me* out."

He stomped away from her. "When you're ready to be honest with me, I'll be at MacQuarrie's."

❦

Ben had to get away from her. His mind was a mess. He hadn't realized that his Lycan abilities only seemed to work when he was with *her*. He'd heard *her* call him beautiful at the Macleods'. He'd been able to sniff out the hair combs only because he was following *her* scent. He'd felt the change come over him only because of *her* touch to his skin. He hadn't experienced his normal abilities at Alec's. He hadn't experienced them his entire time in Scotland. Only with her.

What did that mean?

Would she have to be present during the moonful for him to transform?

He couldn't do that. It was too dangerous. He'd never put her at risk like that. Simon's voice echoed a warning in his mind.

There had to be another way. Some spell she could cast on him. Some potion she could make him drink. Something that wouldn't place her in peril.

And the mark? Why hadn't she told him her father was a Lycan? She had to know it. Why else did she want to see his mark? *A lucky guess.* He snorted as he tore through the woods. What a fool he was to have believed her.

Ben stomped up the steps of Alec's home. Before he could even toss his hat to the waiting butler, his friend was ready to interrogate him.

"Where have you been?" Alec snapped.

"Out," Ben said, his gaze meeting his friend's. Alec may be a bit smaller than him, but they'd had more than one altercation through the years. He was a force to be reckoned with when he was angry.

"Please don't tell me that you have taken to bothering Elspeth Campbell." He arched one eyebrow.

"I wouldn't call it *bothering*."

"Then what would you call it?" The man really needed to mind his own matters.

"We went for a walk, that's all." Ben shrugged, hoping Alec would approve of his nonchalant attitude.

"Then why did Caitrin take off like a feline with her tail on fire?"

"If the lovely woman is running from you, perhaps it's *you* who did something to make her retreat?" Ben pinched the bridge of his nose between his thumb and forefinger. It had been a really long day.

"Oh, no. It wasn't me. I was spending quite a lovely day in her company. Then she suddenly stared off in the distance. When I got her attention back, she started mumbling something about Elspeth and 'that beast.' Then she ran off." He slapped the flat of his hand on the wall. "I will know what that was all about, Westfield."

"You won't know anything until you speak with Miss Macleod." His eyes met Alec's. "Because that group of women is a mess that even *I* can't figure out. You've known them much longer than me. You probably have a better idea of what's going on than I ever would." *Please forgive me if you ever find out about my lies.*

"There has always been something mystical about the five of them. But I've never been able to figure out what brings them all together."

"Mystical?" Ben asked. How much did Alec truly know?

"'Mystical' is probably not the right word." He scratched his head. "But there's a bond there that I can't understand. So when she ran off worried about Elspeth, I automatically assumed you were the beast she had in mind." He clapped Ben on the shoulder. "Sorry I assumed the worst of you."

If he only knew how bad the worst could be.

Elspeth walked toward her small cottage, her breath coming in small gasps. She flung the door open and walked inside, nearly startling Rhiannon. Then she turned and stuck her head back out the door. "Sorcha Ferguson, I ken ye're close by. So ye may as well show yerself!"

She turned and came to a complete halt when she saw that Caitrin was there as well. "If we had Blaire here, the whole coven would be present," she grumbled.

"I'm here," Blaire said as she stepped in the door with Sorcha. "Ye doona think she came up with the vine trick on her own, do ye? The battlefield is in my blood. And I doona really care if I have ta cheat ta win."

"I had ta heal him after yer little stunt." Her gaze flew back and forth between Sorcha and Blaire. Their eyes lowered to the floor. "Ye actually broke the skin. Ye *wounded* him. I canna believe ye did that. I dinna ken ye had the power to do that."

"Neither did we," Sorcha admitted, her gaze still lowered. "Truly, I had no idea the vines would break the skin."

"Now ye ken, so doona let it happen again." She shook her finger at the two younger girls.

"Caitrin said ta keep ye apart," Blaire mumbled.

"She did what?" Elspeth spun around quickly to glare at Caitrin.

Her friend didn't lower her gaze. She shrugged nonchalantly and said, "I was worried for ye. Ye'll have ta forgive me for carin'." Her words dripped with sarcasm. "And just what did ye think ye were doin', kneelin' in front of him with his pants unbuttoned?

Answer that question for us. It's no place for a lady ta be, Elspeth."

"I never professed ta be a lady! And I was just lookin' at his mark!" She pointed to the one on her own wrist. "He wears the mark of the beast. It's exactly like mine. Exactly! The shape is the same. The size is the same. And even the texture is the same."

"Ye touched him?" Caitrin looked scandalized. "Down there?"

Would this nightmare never end? "No, I never touched him *down there*. I touched his mark. And I felt it in my own when I did."

The other four girls stared at her with their mouths open. "Oh, and now when I need ye, ye decide ta shut yer mouths." Elspeth groaned as she dropped into a chair.

"Ye felt it in yer own mark? When ye touched his?"

"Aye, I felt it. I dinna feel a mere touch. I felt what *he* felt when I touched it, when I ran my thumb over it. At least I think it was what he felt. I've never experienced anythin' like it."

"What was it like?" All four girls sat forward.

"It was hot. And wild. And free. And... needy."

"Needy?" Rhiannon asked. "And just what would he be needin'?"

"Me."

"Ye?" Sorcha asked.

"At that moment, he needed me."

Caitrin broke in. "He needed ta get ye flat on yer back, El. Doona ye see?"

"No, I doona see." She gave the seer in their midst a hard stare. "But obviously, ye *did* see somethin'. So out with it."

"I saw him ruin ye," she finally admitted, her eyes filling with tears.

"Thanks for believin' in me," Elspeth ground out. Caitrin colored brightly under her stare.

"I could be wrong," Caitrin said quietly.

"Ye've never been wrong before," Rhiannon reminded her, coming forward to stroke her hair.

"No. But my mother was."

Elspeth spun quickly to face her. "What do ye mean?"

"Yesterday my father told me that mama had a vision about yer parents. She saw that yer mother would leave ta go with yer father."

"But she never did," Elspeth's voice trailed off quietly.

"No. She chose ta stay and keep the coven together."

"Doona look at me like I've left ye already!" Elspeth snapped. "I'm no' goin' anywhere."

"In some ways, maybe ye have," Blaire said softly.

All four girls turned to leave. "We'll see ye tomorrow at the funeral," Rhiannon threw over her shoulder.

"I havena gone anywhere!" she cried from behind them. But they didn't look back. Not a single one of them.

# *Sixteen*

BEN LAY ON HIS BACK IN THE BIG BED, HIS HANDS behind his head as he stared up at the ceiling. He'd spent the entire night thinking about Elspeth. She wore the mark of the beast. Her father obviously was one of them. But who was her father? And why was her very existence shrouded in mystery?

He probably shouldn't have barked at her the way he had that afternoon. He'd just been so stunned to see the mark on her wrist.

He supposed he should be thankful she'd agreed to help him. After all, he was at a loss for what to do. So he'd have to apologize in the morning for his abrupt behavior and hope for success with whichever method she chose.

Ben closed his eyes tightly and worked to push all thoughts from his mind so that he could get to sleep. But then he felt a touch. He opened his eyes quickly. He could have sworn Elspeth had just laid her hands on him. But no one was there.

He closed his eyes again and tried to clear his head. But then her fingertips grazed his abdomen. His eyes flew open. "What was that?" he whispered.

The touch moved across his belly, a flat palm sliding across his chest.

"Elspeth?" he whispered. Surely the little witch didn't have that kind of power.

Ben rose and dressed quickly. He raised the window to his room and dropped down to the spongy turf below. He stood still and closed his eyes. The touch lingered, soft and hot, but no longer overwhelmed him. But then heat enveloped his manhood. He drew in a quick breath. It was as though her delicate little hand was closed around his length.

It was nearly impossible to run with this heaviness between his legs. He was rock hard, but he pushed the thought to the back of his mind and ran as fast as he could toward her little cottage. He streaked through the woods like a predator hunting prey. Elspeth was speaking to him. He just didn't know how.

He saw her as soon as he crossed the meadow. She sat on a hill, limned by the sliver that was the waxing moon hanging over her head. She sat and absently stroked her fingertips down her forearm, her gaze far away.

"I wish you wouldn't do that, lass," he said, his breaths coming in great heaves.

Her head jerked around and she looked up at him. "What are ye doin' here?"

"I believe you called for me," he said quietly.

"I dinna call for ye." She shook her head.

Ben sat down beside her on the damp grass. He tugged his shirt from his trousers. She protested, "I doona think ye should be doin' that, Ben."

"I need to show you what you were doing to me," he mumbled. He lay back on the grass and covered his eyes with his forearm. Perhaps if he didn't look at her, he would be able to show her without devouring her.

He slowly trailed his fingers across the mark that was usually hidden beneath his clothes. She gasped. He did it again. She cried out.

"So it does work both ways, I see." He chuckled.

"How did ye do that?" she asked, her breaths coming in a quick pant.

"You started it," he laughed. "I was just lying in bed and then I felt you touch me."

"I touched ye? Where?" Elspeth pressed her hand to her heart.

"Where it hurts, love. You touched me where it hurts."

❧

"I dinna mean to hurt ye, Ben. I promise." Truly she would never do anything to hurt another human being. His eyes narrowed as his gaze searched her face.

"Does this hurt?" he asked quietly as he dragged his fingertips across his own mark.

Immediately Elspeth felt the rush of heat between her thighs and the thumping that was her heartbeat as it pulsed there. She breathed, "Hurt is no' quite the right word for it." Her nipples hardened as he stroked again. "What are ye doin' ta me?" she asked quietly as she sank back on the dewy grass.

"It appears as though we're tied together, love." He stroked again and laughed when she couldn't hold back a purr. "I do so like the noises you make when you're pleased."

"I doona think this is proper, Ben," she said quietly, the thump between her thighs still taking most of her attention.

"I would say it's quite improper," he said as he leaned over her. "I can smell how much you want me." Her heart skipped a beat. "I can smell your desire."

She stroked across the mark on her own arm. Two could play this game. "It does the same ta ye, Ben. So take care with how ye use that little tool." He groaned and lifted himself above her.

"I'll just ask for you to do it again," he said quietly against her mouth, before his lips touched hers briefly.

"Ye've no shame, do ye?"

"None at all," he confirmed as he untied the strings at the front of her blouse with his teeth. Never had there been such an enticing sight. She had no thoughts of stopping him. "I want to love you."

"Love me?" she gasped out as his teeth pulled her bodice lower to reveal the upper swell of her breast. His teeth nibbled gently along the ridge of flesh before he reached up and uncovered it completely. He immediately drew the peak into his mouth. Showers of sparks clouded her vision. He raised his head to look at her. "*Make* love to you," he corrected his earlier statement.

"We canna do that," she groaned. A cool breeze teased her ankles as he gathered her skirts in his hands and delved beneath. When she started to protest, he rubbed the mark on his lower belly once. She nearly melted there on the grass.

"Ye doona play fair," she choked out.

"And right now I don't plan to," he said as he stroked across the mark again. She cried out and clutched his shoulders. The thump of blood in her most secret places called out for something. What, she had no idea. But there had to be some end to the sweet torment.

"I ache," she moaned as she buried her face in his shoulder.

"I can fix it for you, lass." His hand slid up her thigh and walked around to her front. He quickly untied the laces of her drawers and pulled them down. She didn't bother to protest. She simply wanted to find some release from the sweet torment.

"Fix it," she begged. "Please, fix it."

His hands pushed her skirts up around her waist as he bent between her thighs.

"What are ye doin'?" she asked as his head disappeared beneath the folds of her skirt. She never once thought of stopping him when she felt the warm insistence of his fingers as they spread her. And his tongue as it speared her slick folds. She clutched wildly at the grass.

He licked quickly across the nub that was her center. Pleasure poured through her, suffusing her limbs with liquid heat.

"Doona stop," she whispered as she arched her hips to meet him.

She felt the movement of his head as he nodded and sucked her pliant flesh into his mouth. That was all it took to make her shatter into a million pieces. His fingers stroked as his tongue licked across her, drawing every bit of release from her body. He worked until she stilled.

Ben pushed her skirts down and looked into her dazed face.

"What was that?" she muttered. He simply chuckled in response and pulled her into his side. Suddenly she lifted her head. "Ye dinna find the same pleasure."

"I do not have to…" he started. But Elspeth saw the look on his face. He longed for sweet release the same way she had.

"What can I do ta help ye?"

With a sheepish grin, he unbuttoned his trousers and pulled a handkerchief from his pocket. He quite effectively blocked her view by pressing himself against her, under her skirts. When he was settled, he lifted her arm to her own mouth and growled. "Lick me." Immediately, she knew what he wanted. She stuck out her tongue and licked once across her own mark. He moaned and pressed his face into her shoulder. "Oh, Elspeth," he ground out.

With a small smile on her face, she lapped at the mark again. And a third time. That was all it took. He followed her into bliss.

# *Seventeen*

ELSPETH RESTED HER HEAD ON BEN'S CHEST AND HE stared up at the night sky above them. He'd never felt so wild yet content at the same time. Whatever this power was she held over him, he liked it. He held her close and brushed his lips in her hair. How nice it would be to stay curled up with her like this forever.

Then suddenly she sat up. "Oh, I've got ta get back."

"Tell me you don't have somewhere else to be." He groaned.

Elspeth tapped his chest. "Wallace Ferguson has been keepin' watch over my grandfather. I told him I wouldna be gone long."

She scrambled to her feet and Ben tried to tug her skirts, but she was too quick for him. "Wait," he called.

She looked back over her shoulder. "I'm sorry. I've been gone too long."

Ben leapt from his spot and chased after her. He always seemed to be chasing her, he realized, which was never the case with most women. Of course, no other woman could make him climax by licking her wrist either. If there was a woman worth catching, it was Elspeth Campbell.

He caught up to her at the base of the hill and wrapped his arms around her waist, pulling her against his chest. "One more moment won't hurt, Elspeth."

She sighed and leaned her head against his shoulder. "Ben, I have ta go."

He nuzzled against her neck. "I just wanted to apologize for earlier. I shouldn't have barked at you."

Elspeth turned in his arms, her emerald eyes glistening under the crescent moon. "Ye did nothin' wrong. I should have told ye about my mark, but it's hard for me. I doona ken anythin' about my father except that he gave me that."

He brushed his lips across her cheek. "You can tell me anything, Ellie."

She wrapped her arms around his neck, and Ben tightened his hold on her. "Do ye mind waitin', then? Let me dispatch with Wallace. Then ye can come in for tea."

"Of course."

Elspeth stepped away from him and hurried along the path to her cottage. Ben watched her go, the delicate sway of her hips, quiet as a wolf. He'd been a fool not to see it earlier.

Elspeth rushed in through the door to find Wallace sitting vigil by her grandfather. He barely looked up when she entered, as he seemed lost in thought. She cleared her throat and he nearly leapt from his seat. "Oh, El, I dinna see ye there."

"No worries, Wallace. I'm sorry I was gone so long. I hate ta keep ye waitin'."

He shook his head as he started for the door. "Doona worry yerself, lass. Tomorrow it will all be over with."

She walked him toward the door. "I canna thank ye enough for everythin', Wallace."

He reached for the handle and then stopped and looked at her. "Are ye goin' ta be all right? Ye ken ye can always come and stay with us. I hate for ye ta be all alone."

Elspeth sighed. "I'm no' all alone, Wallace. I have all of ye. Thank ye again, for everythin'."

Wallace nodded, then opened the door and disappeared into the night.

Elspeth went to the stove in the middle of the room and put some water on to boil. Chamomile with a hint of blueberry ought to do nicely. Then she went to her grandfather's doorway. If she didn't know better, she'd think he was sleeping peacefully. She quietly shut the door and returned to the stove to pour the water for tea.

Just as she finished, she heard a light rap at the front door. Her heart sped up at the thought of Ben on the other side, and she rushed to answer it. Instead she found Caitrin with the Macleod plaid covering her hair. She resisted the urge to groan. All she needed was for her friend to see Ben.

"It's late, Caitrin."

Cait pulled the plaid from her head and gestured to the settee in the small room. "I ken. I willna stay long, I promise."

Elspeth opened the door wide. As Caitrin stepped over the threshold, she looked past her in the darkness. But she couldn't see Ben anywhere. She closed the door a little harder than was necessary.

Caitrin flopped down onto the settee and wiped a tear from her eye. Elspeth rushed toward her friend, awash in guilt. She should have realized the girl was upset. "What is it, Cait?"

Her friend clasped Elspeth's hands in her own. "I hate this, El. I hate all of it. Ye're my dearest friend, and I hate bein' on opposite sides."

So did Elspeth. She smiled sadly. "Then stop."

Caitrin shook her head. "I canna stop. I doona want ta lose ye. None of us do."

"Cait, I'm no' goin' anywhere. I doona ken how many times I have ta tell ye."

"But I've seen it, El. And if ye go off with him, back ta England, the *Còig* will fall apart. We have ta have all of us."

Elspeth sighed. "I think ye're puttin' the cart before the horse. He hasna asked me ta go ta England with him. He's just lookin' ta be healed. After that, he'll go back ta where he's from." She glanced down at her mark. She was connected to him, though. Would distance matter? A year from now if he touched his mark, would she feel it?

"He will ask ye, El."

Even if he did, she couldn't go. She wouldn't fit into his world. "Cait, this is my home. It's all I ken. Ye've known me my whole life. Do ye honestly think I'd run off ta London?"

Caitrin looked over El's shoulder toward the window. "Aye. I've seen it." Then she focused her eyes on Elspeth. "Ye ken I love ye and I want the best for ye?"

"Aye."

Her friend smiled wistfully. "Good. Because I'm no' givin' up on ye. If yer mother stayed with the coven despite mama's vision, I'll fight 'til the end of time for ye."

"Cait—"

She waved her hand as she rose from her seat. "Doona even think ta stop me. Ye're the closest thing I have ta a sister."

The others would probably have been offended if they'd heard that, but Elspeth knew the words were true. From their youngest of years, the two of them had been closer than the others. Caitrin threw her arms around Elspeth's neck. Then she stepped away. "He's been outside ever since I arrived. I suppose I should leave ye."

Elspeth gaped at her friend. She was just going to leave her with Ben after all this? "What happened ta fightin' for me 'til the end of time?"

"Oh, if he tries anythin', I'll ken it. Then I'll ask Alec MacQuarrie ta toss him out on his ear." With that Caitrin walked across the room, opened the door, and strode out into the night. "I ken ye're out here, Westfield," she called. "No need to hide like a dog."

Ben stepped out of the shadows, a look of boredom pasted on his face. "Ah, Miss Macleod, what a pleasure it is to see you again."

"Just so we're clear, Westfield, if ye do anythin' ta hurt Elspeth, I'll see ye boiled in a cauldron of oil."

"With your scintillating personality, Miss Macleod, it is easy to see how you've charmed so many admirers," he responded drolly.

She tipped her nose high in the air with a wicked smile. "Just remember what I said."

❧

Ben didn't even watch the haughty chit disappear into the darkness, as his eyes were focused on Elspeth. Her hair hung wildly about her shoulders, and the fire from the hearth inside gave her a radiant glow. She stepped toward him, a pretty blush staining her cheeks.

"I'm sorry about that."

Ben smiled in return. "Not to worry, love. Miss Macleod doesn't bother me." Then he ushered her back inside the cottage.

She gestured for him to sit on the worn settee, then vanished into the kitchen area. "Good, the tea is still warm," she called.

Ben looked around the small room. Again it struck him that she deserved more. Before he could expound on that thought, Elspeth turned the corner with two mugs of tea, offering him the unchipped one. "Chamomile and blueberry," she said.

"Blueberry?" Ben echoed. It smelled delicious.

"Aye, blueberries encompass the aura of the moon. Ye should eat some the night it's full."

Ben chuckled. "You think blueberries can heal me?"

Elspeth took a sip of hers. "I doona think it can hurt."

She did have a point. He took a swallow and closed his eyes, savoring the flavor in his mouth. He'd never had more delicious tea. "So," he finally said, "are you going to tell me why Miss Macleod despises me?"

Elspeth shrugged and dropped her eyes to her lap. "Cait thinks ye're goin' ta whisk me off ta London and they'll never see me again."

The wind rushed out of him. That's exactly what he should do. Why hadn't he thought of it himself? The moon did call to him when he was with Elspeth. He should have her with him always. Then there was the little matter that he *liked* having her around. He could just imagine her waking up in his arms every morning. "And what do you think about that?" he asked.

He could offer her much more than this cottage. Her grandfather was gone. No one needed her like Ben did. This was perfect.

"I think I hardly ken ye."

Ben smiled. "Ah, you know me better than most women, Elspeth. No one else knows what I am. No one else can touch me the way you do." No one else made him burn for her the way she did either.

She shook her head. "I'll tell ye what I told Caitrin. This is my home. I willna leave it."

He blinked at her. Didn't she know who he was? What he could offer her? If he could get her away from the other four, maybe he could convince her to stay with him. "Not even to find your father?" he suggested.

Her emerald eyes grew round with surprise. "That's impossible."

"Not necessarily," he informed her. "I've been thinking about it, wondering who he is. I should take you to see Major Forster—"

"Major *Forster*? He's Scottish?"

Ben frowned. "I suppose he is." He'd never thought much about that before. He sounded nearly as English as the next fellow after his many years in the army. "He runs the Lycanian Society in London—"

"The Lycanian Society?"

"Hmm. It's an organization for my kind. Most of us are registered. About ninety, ninety-five percent. The Society knows about each of us. Who we are. Where we've been. That sort of thing. And we take care of our own. Orphaned boys, those who need medical care. With a little research, we can probably find the Lycan who—"

"—is my father," she finished. "I never thought ta find him. It never seemed a possibility."

Perhaps it was a bad idea. She looked so sad, Ben wanted to envelop her in his arms and make her forget he mentioned it. "If you don't want to look for him, that's understandable, too."

Elspeth placed her tea on the small table in front of them and looked down at the mark on her wrist. "If he's still alive, I would like ta find him. I have many questions. A lifetime's worth."

Ben brushed his knuckles across her cheek. "Then I'll help you find him, Ellie."

Her smile lit up the small room. "Like ye found my hair combs?"

Her hair combs. They had to have been a gift from the girl's sire to her mother. "Exactly."

They could leave tomorrow after the funeral. The sooner he got her away from the others, the better.

"But no' until I heal ye."

"Can't you do that in London?"

She giggled. "Everythin' I need is here, Ben. Ye came ta me ta be healed. I canna let ye leave until then."

# Eighteen

ELSPETH WATCHED BEN OVER THE RIM OF HER TEACUP.
He'd settled into the settee and looked more than
comfortable with himself, his light hair hanging
rakishly across his brow. She could watch him forever
and never tire of it.

After a moment, Ben sat forward. "I should probably
go. I would hate for anyone to find out you were alone
with me after dark." His hazel eyes twinkled at her.

*But she didn't want him to leave. Not yet.* "It's rare ta
have visitors this late at night. I'm sure we're safe for at
least a while." His head tipped to the side. "So doona
go," she mumbled.

"We have excellent hearing, you know?" The
corners of his mouth tilted into a grin.

Elspeth bit back a curse. "Of course ye can hear me.
Ye can probably hear my thoughts as well."

"No. Your thoughts are safe. But I do have fun
trying to read your mind."

"How successful are ye at that?"

"Not very, actually." He scratched his chin. "Why don't
you make it easy for me and tell me what you're thinking?"

"Because then there would be no challenge and you would lose interest completely." And she did *so* want to challenge him.

"Very true." He nodded his agreement before his eyes roamed across her body. El crossed her arms over her chest when she felt her nipples harden. He chuckled.

She gasped, "Ye *can* read my mind!"

"No, lass, I promise you." He held up one hand to silence her protest. "Your body speaks to me much more clearly than your mind does." He adjusted his trousers. "And I really should go, because sitting here makes me want you again." His eyes darkened a shade, but he made no move to leave.

Her heart skipped a beat. "But we just—" She motioned toward the door and then glanced at the mark on her wrist.

"That was nothing, love. A bit of pleasure. But it can be better." His gaze went from warm to smoldering.

"I doona ken if I can survive better," she whispered to herself.

"Of course you can," he chuckled. He flashed a wolfish smile at her discomfort and pointed to his ear, relaxing again against the settee. "Excellent hearing, remember?"

"What other gifts do ye have?"

"Aside from being able to bring you pleasure?" His grin widened.

"Aye, aside from that," she sighed. The time for games was over. Because Elspeth suddenly had the feeling she was outmatched.

❧

Ben enjoyed teasing her. He enjoyed it more than anything he'd done in a long time. But he kept forgetting she was an innocent. She wasn't a whore or a widow, or even a tavern wench. She was a good girl. And he'd do well to remember that.

She rubbed her hands together nervously.

"Sorry, lass, I'll be on my best behavior. Ask me anything you want to know about Lycans," he prompted, sitting forward with his elbows on his knees, prepared to give her his full attention.

"Anythin'?"

He winked at her.

Elspeth sat forward, too, her inquisitive smile warming his heart. "Will ye tell me more about the change?"

"What would you like to know?"

"What's it like for ye? Changin'?"

"It's hard to explain," he started.

"Give it a try."

He took a deep breath. Where would be the best starting point? "When Lycans come into maturity, we grow bigger, stronger, and faster than others. We need this strength on our wolf side in order to compete with predators who might destroy us when we are in our wolf form. It can be a bit scary at first."

"In what way?"

"You start to feel the pull of the moon. As it waxes, the call is stronger and stronger. We become more aggressive as our bodies prepare for the change." He narrowed his eyes and watched her closely so that he could gauge her reaction to his next revelation. "We become more lusty, too. Which is how I got into this mess."

"Ye know what caused ye ta stop changin'?" she asked.

If he told her about that, she could probably guide him better. But he was so hesitant to reveal that aspect of his life to her.

"Out with it. Tell me what happened." She didn't appear to be willing to take no for an answer.

"I can't." Heat crept up his face.

"Are ye blushin', Ben?"

"I suppose I am," he said quietly.

"Tell me more," she prompted.

"I was with a…" He stopped and tugged at his cravat. This was harder than telling her he was a Lycan.

"A person?" She motioned with her hands for him to continue.

"Yes, a person. A woman, actually." He stood up to pace. If he kept moving, kept talking, he could tell her. "You see, Lycans cannot be with women in the days prior to the moonful, because we get a bit lusty and that lust can cause us to hurt someone." He stopped pacing and stared at her.

She gasped. "Please tell me ye dinna hit a woman, Ben." She stood up and shook her head.

"I never hit her," he started. "But I was a bit too forceful with her. I lost control."

"I still doona understand." This was growing more and more frustrating. "What did ye do ta her?"

"I bit her," he snapped quietly, and was immediately sorry for his tone.

"I'm afraid my hearin' is no' as keen as yers." Although Ben would bet it was better than most. "Will ye repeat that?"

"I said, I *bit* her," he repeated with more force.

"Well, why in the world would ye do that?"

"I couldn't help it."

She closed her eyes and breathed deeply. She was obviously frustrated with him.

"Lycans mark their mate."

Her eyes flew open. "Mark? As in *bite*?"

He nodded. "Although she wasn't my intended mate, I lost control and bit her. I knew she wasn't mine. And if I hadn't been in the wrong place at the wrong time, I wouldn't have lost control. And I would still be able to change."

He walked closer to her and lifted the fiery tresses from her shoulders, revealing her neck. He lowered his head to where her neck met her shoulder. He breathed in her scent for a moment. "This is where a Lycan marks his mate," he said before he very gently nipped her skin with his teeth.

Immediately the scent of desire engulfed him. Her body warmed beneath his touch and reflected off her in waves.

"That dinna hurt," she whispered, clutching his jacket.

"I didn't mark you." His fingers brushed over the spot he'd nipped. "I just showed you where a mark would be."

"Would ye want ta mark me?" she asked, refusing to meet his gaze.

He tipped her chin up with his finger. "More than anything, Elspeth."

"Oh," she breathed. Her heart was beating so fast he could hear it.

"But I cannot," he said, taking a step backward. "I wouldn't take the risk of hurting you." He tried not to let disappointment cloud his words, but it was difficult.

"Ye lost control with this woman? Who was she ta ye? Yer intended?"

"Not exactly," he hedged.

"No?" She smiled brightly. "Then who was she?"

"Elspeth." He sighed her name and rolled his eyes away from her, trying to buy some time. But she just glared at him with those beautiful green eyes. So he told her the truth. "She was nobody, just a whore."

He closed his eyes and waited for her reaction. But she slung her fist and hit him in the jaw before he even felt the rush of wind that was her setup.

# Nineteen

"WHAT WAS THAT FOR?" BEN BLINKED AT HER.

Elspeth had never hit another human being in her life. But a blinding rage overcame her when he'd said the word "whore." It was a word she'd heard her whole life, usually in reference to her mother. And it would not be tolerated in her home.

"I'd appreciate it if ye'd go, Lord Benjamin." She walked to the door and held it open without even looking in his direction.

"Elspeth," he began, walking toward her. "Please let me explain."

"No explanations needed, Lord Benjamin." She pushed his shoulder to get him through the door, though it would have been easier to move a boulder. "I would suggest ye go, or I'll summon Caitrin and have her bring that cauldron of oil." Her gaze met his, finally.

He looked tortured, but she refused to budge. "Ye've no idea what damage a few witches can do with a cauldron of oil."

"I'll leave," he whispered, then soundlessly he left her cottage and disappeared into the darkness.

Numb, Elspeth stared into the chilly night before finally closing the door. *Nobody, just a whore.* Anger engulfed every part of her. How dare he say something like that? That woman, whoever she was, wasn't nobody. She was a person. Maybe she had children to feed and clothe. Maybe she'd stumbled on hard times. Maybe she'd fallen in love with the wrong man, who'd used her then abandoned her.

*Nobody, just a whore.* She'd never get to sleep with this fury pounding through her. Elspeth looked about the room. There was plenty to do to keep her busy.

She could tidy up before tomorrow. She could use a spell and be done in an instant, but that wouldn't help her get rid of her irritated energy. She picked up the teacups and spoons before sweeping the floor and scrubbing the table. It didn't matter, however. Nothing helped her forget Ben's cruel words.

Once the cottage sparkled and she couldn't find anything else to occupy her, Elspeth finally stumbled into bed and slid beneath her counterpane. Breathing in the calming scent of heather by her bed, she closed her eyes and willed herself to sleep.

Ben thrashed his way through the woods. He could just kick himself for being so goddamned stupid, for being so dicked in the nob. He knew telling her about the lightskirt in Brighton was a mistake. But he'd gone and done it anyway. He was being honest with her. Telling her what happened. He was baring his soul, for God's sake—and she'd thrown him out.

Had he learned *nothing* from Will's mistakes? Women didn't understand men's baser needs, and Ben's needs were more base than most men's. So what if he employed the use of whores from time to time? It wasn't something he was ashamed of. Most men of his station did so. And he wasn't married.

But she just kept pressuring him. *Tell me, Ben. Tell me what happened. Who was the woman?* Well, women shouldn't go around asking questions if they don't want to know the answers.

He'd so hoped Elspeth was different than that. There was something between them. A connection he didn't know how to explain. A connection he didn't *want* to explain—he just wanted to enjoy it.

And now she was furious with him, for something he'd done before he even knew her. He was a bloody idiot.

Ben stopped in his tracks when he noticed a light in one of the front windows of MacQuarrie's home. Damn! All he needed was another conversation with Alec. He was not in the mood to hear more warnings about spending time with Elspeth Campbell. Perhaps he could stay the night in the stables.

Perhaps he should just pack up and go back to London.

Before the thought had time to take root in his mind, he shook it away. He still needed Elspeth to heal him. God damn it, he simply needed Elspeth.

Nothing had ever been easy for him. He somehow always picked the toughest path. One would think he'd learn after a lifetime's worth of mistakes. So what did he have to do to get back in her good graces? Flowers? Jewelry? An apology? Though what would he apologize for? *I'm sorry I've bedded other women before I met you?* He'd be a pretty sad man at six and twenty not to have done so. He'd be the laughingstock of the Lycan world.

"Are you going to stand there all night?" Alec's voice called from the front door.

Damn! Ben's shoulders slumped as he started toward his friend's house.

"You look like a man who could use a drink."

That was probably true. He ambled up the steps. "What are you doing up so late?"

Alec shrugged and opened the door wide for Ben to pass. "Couldn't sleep. I thought some whisky would do the trick."

Whisky sounded wonderful. Numbing his brain was preferable to trying to sort out the way of women. "Lead the way, *mon ami.*"

Inside Alec's study he poured two generous tumblers and handed one to Ben. "So I take it from your down expression that things aren't going well with Miss Campbell?"

Ben took a sip and welcomed the smoky burn down his throat. "Please don't start, Alec."

His friend laughed. "I'm not one to kick a man when he's down, Westfield. You look as if you're in enough misery without me adding to it."

Ben raised his tumbler in a mock toast. "Many thanks."

They sat in companionable silence for some time, which was nice. After a few more rounds of whisky, Ben leaned back in his chair and stared up at Alec's ceiling. "Do you ever think you'll understand the workings of the female mind?"

Alec sighed. "Not if I live ta be a hundred. I'm beginning to think it would be easier to perform Hercules' twelve labors than to court Caitrin Macleod."

"Perhaps you should take that as a sign from the gods." Ben couldn't imagine a worse fate than being leg-shackled to that haughty witch.

"Now, now," Alec began good-naturedly, "if I'm keeping my mouth shut about Miss Campbell, you can at least return the favor where Miss Macleod is concerned."

That did seem fair. "All right, what's the problem?"

"You'd think I was daft."

"Who says I don't already?" Ben chided him.

Alec sighed. "I'd rather not confirm your suspicions, then. You want to tell me what Miss Campbell said to get you looking like a lost puppy dog?"

"She wasn't happy to learn I've had relations with whores."

Alec choked and Ben sat forward to pound on his friend's back. "Are you all right?"

"Good God, Westfield! I don't even want to know how you ended up discussing that."

Feeling like the biggest of fools, Ben slunk back into his seat. "She made me tell her."

Alec roared with laughter. "I can't imagine why you would do such a featherbrained, idiotic thing."

Ben glowered at him. "I don't want to talk about it."

"Do you tell the duchess of your exploits as well?"

*Mother.* He hadn't written her in weeks. She was probably worried about him, but she'd be more so if he put pen to foolscap. After all, he'd never been able to fool her when something was wrong. Now he didn't even bother. Besides, if Elspeth could heal him, there was no reason to get his mother upset in the first place.

Alec laughed even harder. "Please tell me you haven't."

"Of course, I don't tell my mother everything." Who would need to? She could read about it in the society rags. "I'm going to bed."

The sound of Alec's laughter followed him up the stairs.

# Twenty

ELSPETH WOKE TO THE SOUND OF A GENTLE KNOCK ON her door. She pulled a wrapper over her nightrail, lifted her hair over the lace collar, and opened the door a crack.

Caitrin's blue eyes flashed at her. "We ken ye're angry at us, but we're here ta support ye today, no matter what." Caitrin, Rhiannon, Blaire, and Sorcha brushed past Elspeth into the room. "Ye bury yer grandfather today, and we'll be here with ye whether ye want us or no'." She brushed a tear back from her cheek.

"Cait, of course I want ye," Elspeth said as she fell into the huddle of girls. "Ye're my family, and I canna do without ye."

When they finally separated, Caitrin looked down at her friend's wrapper. "Is that what ye plan ta wear today?"

"Of course, it's no'," Elspeth said. "Doona be daft."

"Then ye better hurry, because the vicar already rang the death bell in the square. People will be arrivin' shortly." She clapped her hands together sharply. "Let's get ye movin'."

"I overslept?" Surely she hadn't stayed in bed that long. Although it *had* been late when she'd finally fallen asleep.

Caitrin smoothed Elspeth's wild hair with her hand. "Ye deserve ta rest more than anyone I ken. Ye've been dealin' with a lot." Then she moved to the window and raised the curtain. "The first of the mourners are walkin' this way. Unless ye plan ta greet them in yer nightrail, ye need ta dress."

Elspeth spun into action. She disappeared into her room and changed clothes after washing quickly. Then she combed through her unruly locks. They had a mind of their own, no matter what she did. She secured the flyaway tendrils with her mother's hair combs, knowing all the while that her hair would be down around her shoulders before the hour had passed.

She bustled around the kitchen, started a pot of water for tea, and rushed out the front door. As soon as she stepped through the opening, she ran into the broad chest of a man.

"Whoa, there," a deep voice said as strong arms steadied her. She knew immediately who they belonged to. Elspeth stopped and inhaled deeply. He had a scent like no other. He smelled of shaving soap and... Ben. It was unique to him, almost a wild scent, and it set her heart to thumping.

Finally she raised her head and met his gaze. "I doona ken what made ye think ye'd be welcome here, Lord Benjamin," she whispered harshly.

His eyes narrowed as he released his hold on her and stood up to his full height. "I came with Alec to bring chairs."

"Ye'll be leavin' when ye're done, I assume?" The words sounded harsh to her own ears, but she couldn't deal with him at the moment.

His fingers reached out to touch her chin, gently but forcefully making her meet his gaze. "No, lass. I'll not be leaving you today. You can hate me all you want. But I'll be staying."

Elspeth couldn't contain the small leap her heart made when he said he wouldn't be leaving.

"Suit yerself." She stepped back, moving out of his grasp. She immediately felt alone. More lonely than she'd ever been.

"Tea is ready," Caitrin called to her from the doorway. Elspeth glanced up at Ben. The annoyance on his face when he looked at her friend would have been funny any other time. She thought she heard him grumble as she turned and went in the house. The other three witches were busy preparing food for the mourners who would visit.

"Why is *he* here?" Caitrin groused.

"He said he came with Mr. MacQuarrie ta bring the chairs, Cait." She sighed, "Just leave it be, please."

"He dinna ken yer grandfather," Cait said quietly.

"Do ye want ta cause a scene and force him ta leave?" Elspeth whispered vehemently. "I would rather have him stay than have ta listen ta all the waggin' tongues. I doona think my grandfather would've wanted that."

"After the service, can I toss him out on his ear?"

"Ye can toss him out on his arse if ye want. I doona care," Elspeth groaned under the weight of a heavy stockpot.

"Here, let me help ye," Caitrin said as she tried to take some of the weight from Elspeth's burden. Suddenly the weight was lifted away.

"Tell me where you want it," Ben said, his hazel eyes twinkling at her. He bore her burden with ease. "I'll be at your beck and call today. So use me as you see fit."

"Ye doona have ta—" El started.

"Just tell me where to put it, Ellie," he said quietly. She pointed to a table across the kitchen. "Over there is fine."

Caitrin suddenly clutched her arm and spun her around. "Did he call ye *Ellie*?"

"I dinna notice," Elspeth lied smoothly as she shrugged her shoulders.

"He's goin' ta ruin ye. I can see it now." She closed her eyes tightly.

"Will ye stop with the theatrics, Cait. He moved a bloody pot," Elspeth said low enough for only her friend to hear. To be caught swearing by anyone else would be terrible for the little bit of reputation she *did* have.

Ben chuckled from across the room. Of course he would have heard her curse. He was party to every nonsensical thing she'd done for the past six days.

Ben could stand in the corner all day and would be perfectly content just to watch her bustle about the kitchen. He tried to appear busy, arranging chairs and helping carry heavy items for the other girls. But he really just wanted to eavesdrop.

He couldn't bite back a chuckle when he'd heard her curse. She was as fiery as her hair. He wanted at that moment to touch his mark and see if she would respond the same way she had the night before, but this wasn't the time or the place. He knew that today was important for her. And he would not detract from her sorrow, nor would he contribute to it.

Alec called from the doorway, "Come and help me, Westfield. There's food to be brought inside."

"*Food?* Where did food come from?" Elspeth asked.

Mrs. Ross lumbered into the kitchen, her girth cumbersome. "I thought ye might need some things for the feast," the woman said as she directed the men to bring in items.

Ben saw the furrow of Elspeth's brow as she looked at the bountiful feast the men carted through the door. They went back and forth and returned time and again.

Ben's heart ached for her when he saw Elspeth approach Mrs. Ross quietly and place her arm on her sleeve. "I'll have ta settle up with ye over all this food. But it may take some time."

The woman squeezed Elspeth's hands before she reached one hand out to cup her face. "No need ta fret, deary. It's been taken care of."

Elspeth spun quickly toward Caitrin. "Did yer father do this?"

Caitrin shook her head. "No, El. I doona believe he did."

Elspeth's gaze searched the other three faces of her friends, and they all denied having set it up.

"Who would have…?" Elspeth's voice trailed off as her gaze finally landed on Ben, who did his best to avoid looking at her. Certainly she wouldn't assume he was responsible for the feast, although he was.

Elspeth raised her hands to her face, and she surprised everyone in the room when sobs started to shake her shoulders. She'd put on a brave face for days. Ben was sorry to see her so upset, but happy to help her ease her burden.

Before she could even take a breath, he was across the room. He pulled her safely and snugly against his chest and stroked his hand over her hair. She settled against him like she belonged there.

"There now, Ellie," he said softly. "No one knows that it was me who paid for the feast. Nor shall they."

Caitrin ushered all the women out of the room, asking for their help outside. She left the door open, but he assumed that Cait would be outside the door, barring anyone else from entering.

"I am very, very angry at ye because of what ye said ta me last night when ye so casually referred ta someone ye had been intimate with as 'just a whore,'" Elspeth sniffled. "I've heard my mother called that horrible word my whole life." She drew in a deep, shaky breath. "Then ye had ta go and do somethin' so kind." She pounded lightly on his chest with one fist. "So I canna be mad at ye right now."

"You can come back to it later, love. I'll expect it."

"Good." She sniffled again.

He lowered his head so that he could speak right beside her ear, wishing more than anything it would reach her heart. "I'm sorry I used a word that's so painful for you. It was a poor choice, and I'll never even use the word again myself. In any circumstance."

He barely felt her nod against his chest, her acquies-
cence was so small. But it was a start. He simply held
her for a moment, enjoying the sensation of her body
pressed against him. But he knew he would have to let
her go or risk ruining her. He brushed the tears from
her cheeks with his thumbs and kissed her lips softly,
gratified when she kissed him back. "I hear footsteps,"
he whispered with a grin, before he stepped back
from her and busied himself with arranging more of
the chairs.

"I'll repay the favor, Lord Benjamin," she said. To
the casual observer, it sounded like she was simply
thanking him for all his help.

"Perhaps I'll take it out in trade, Miss Campbell." His
eyes danced at her, and she couldn't hide the blush that
stained her cheeks. "I could be in need of healing."

∽

Elspeth barely heard the words the vicar, Mr. Crawford,
said in the church. Her mind was too occupied with
reflections of her grandfather. The way he'd tell her
stories when she was a young girl, sitting on his knee.
The way he'd always let her win at loo. The way he'd
draped his arm around her shoulders and tell her that
great things were going to happen in her life.

Since she didn't have a father, her grandfather had
filled that role, until now. It had been hard watching
him wither away over the last year. At least now he
would have the peace that had eluded him since his
illness had set in.

Before Elspeth knew it, Mr. Crawford had finished
his speech and the men from town lined up to take

turns walking the coffin to the churchyard. The women, as always, weren't allowed.

One by one the townspeople filed out of the church, but Elspeth remained in her seat. She should rush back home and make sure everything was ready for the feast. She just couldn't muster the energy to do so.

Then she felt a hand on her shoulder and looked to see Caitrin and the others standing behind her. "Are ye ready, El?"

She nodded, though she didn't really feel ready.

Caitrin linked arms with her on one side while Rhiannon took the other. They stepped out into the bright sunlight, and Elspeth managed a smile. "Did ye have anythin' ta do with the weather?"

Rhiannon looked bashfully away. "Personally, I felt like rain, but Mr. Campbell was always so cheerful. I thought he'd prefer it this way."

"And," Caitrin added, "it would be terribly inconvenient ta host an outdoor feast in a downpour."

Rhiannon giggled. "Aye, that's true as well."

The five of them started back toward Elspeth's cottage.

# Twenty-one

BEN LEANED AGAINST AN OLD OAK TREE, KEEPING Elspeth's cottage in sight. His current position was about as far away as he could get and still hear her voice, though she did very little of the talking.

Sorcha Ferguson chatted nonstop, like a ninny. Ben had the feeling the chit thought if she stopped talking, Elspeth would dissolve into a puddle of tears. Maybe she was right.

"...and he always had butterscotch candies in his pocket. Every time I saw him he'd give me a piece of candy. 'And how are ye feelin' today, Sorcha?' he would ask me. Then he'd sit back in his chair and let me prattle on and on about Mama being overly strict and Wallace no' being fair—"

"*Havers*, Sorcha!" one of the other witches said. Ben wasn't certain which. "Is it possible for ye ta keep yer trap closed for five minutes? I canna even hear myself think."

He heard Elspeth take in a sharp breath and he started forward. What was the matter with these women? They fought like sisters. In just a few strides he was in front of the cottage and knocked lightly on the door.

Naturally it was Miss Macleod who answered, with her perfected sneer. "What a surprise."

Ben wouldn't allow her to bait him; Elspeth didn't need that right now. He looked past her and found his little witch standing in the middle of the room. Her eyes seemed to sparkle when they landed on him.

"Ellie," he said with a smile. "Why don't you come for a walk with me?"

"There's so much ta do," Caitrin Macleod cut in.

The little liar. All the food was out as well as the tables and chairs. Plates, cups, and utensils were simply waiting for the hoard to arrive. Elspeth wouldn't get another break until afterward. "Well, Miss Macleod," he replied smoothly, "I'm certain the four of you won't mind finishing up whatever it is that needs Elspeth's attention, would you?"

There was no other answer she could give other than to nod and, of course, glare at him.

Ben paid her no attention. He outstretched an arm and waited for Elspeth to come to him. The look of relief as she moved toward him was thanks enough.

He tucked her hand around his arm and led her toward the scenic path she'd pointed out earlier.

"Ye canna be gone long," one of the others called after them.

"I'll have her back in plenty of time."

Once they were out of earshot from the others, Elspeth looked up at him and smiled. "How did ye ken I needed an escape?"

Ben squeezed her fingers. "I didn't for sure. But if I'd been in there with those harpies, I would have needed an escape."

"They're no' harpies," she said quietly. "They're tryin' ta help me, and I'm simply worthless today."

They entered the woods at a slow pace, and Ben watched a skylark fly above them. Elspeth noticed it, too. "My grandfather loved birds."

"Did he?"

"Aye. Sometimes he'd sit in the woods just ta watch them."

She was quiet. More wistful than he'd seen her thus far. "Do you want to tell me about him?"

Elspeth smiled. "He was a simple man, and he always wore a smile no matter what went wrong."

"A good quality to have." One Ben did not possess.

"He was my rock. When I was growin' up, children were particularly cruel about my situation. He would sit me down and say, 'Elspeth, I'm no' goin' ta tell ye ye're just as good as those other *tumshie heids.*'"

*Tumshie heids?* "What is that?"

"Loosely translated?" she giggled. "Turnip heads."

"I see. He didn't want you to be a turnip head?" Ben smiled at her.

"He wanted me ta be better than the others. He never let me feel sorry for myself."

"He sounds like a wonderful man."

Elspeth smiled up at him. "He was the best of men. He always pushed me ta do my best."

"Sounds like my brother." Simon's last lecture echoed in his ears.

She stopped walking and faced him. "Ye never speak of yer family."

Ben shrugged. "There's nothing much to tell."

"I doona believe that for a second. Ye come from a family of *Lycans,* and yer oldest brother is a *duke.*"

When she put it that way, he couldn't help but laugh. "I suppose I don't think of them in those terms. They're just my family."

"There are three of ye?"

He nodded and led her deeper into the woods. "Simon is the Duke of Blackmoor, and William is the next in line. I'm off the hook unless they both fail to produce an heir."

"Is neither one of them married?"

Ben laughed again, finding the image of Simon or Will in front of an altar particularly humorous. When she stared at him, he brought his levity under control. "Sorry, it's just hard to imagine. You see, Simon is extremely careful where women are concerned. He keeps them from getting too close, lest they discover our secret."

"And William?" she prodded.

"Is a stubborn mule."

"What do ye mean by that?"

"There's a girl back home—Prisca. Her family is our closest neighbor in Hampshire. She has a hoard of brothers, and we all grew up together. Anyway, she and Will... Well, he should have married her long ago. It's obvious how the two of them feel about each other, but Will walked away from her and never looked back."

"Why?"

In the distance, Ben could hear a large number of people heading their direction. "I think the funeral is over, Ellie. Are you ready to return?"

She faced him and smiled softly. "Ben, thank ye for everythin'."

He wished he could do more. Once he got her to London, he'd do everything he could to make her happy. A strand of her hair had come loose from her wolf clips, and he curled it around his finger. "It was nothing."

"How can ye say that?" she whispered.

"Because," he began and dipped his head down to hers. "I want to give you everything."

Then he touched his lips to hers. The rest of the world vanished for a moment, but not nearly long enough.

The rest of the day was a blur to Elspeth. It seemed as if all of Edinburgh had come out for her grandfather's feast. Neighbors, people she hadn't seen in ages, and some people she'd never met before. But only Ben kept her interest. He never left her. Whenever she was thirsty, he handed her a drink. If she was hungry, he got her a plate. When she was tired, he made her sit.

Caitrin, Sorcha, Rhiannon, and Blaire watched on from a distance, but they never approached her. Somewhere in the back of Elspeth's mind she knew that something had changed in her life.

# Twenty-two

ONCE BEN AND ALL THE TOWNSPEOPLE LEFT, IT TOOK
less than a minute for the five witches to return the
cottage and land to its usual state. After a few simple
spells, no one would ever know that half of Scotland
had been there moments earlier.

Elspeth collapsed onto her settee, ready to fall asleep
as soon as her friends returned to their homes. The
four of them had watched her all afternoon but hadn't
really spoken to her, until now.

"Ye ken I doona like him," Sorcha began.

Elspeth closed her eyes and willed them away.
Were they going to have *this* conversation again?
"Please doona start. No' tonight. Ye can all have a go
at me in the mornin'."

Sorcha flopped down next to her and Elspeth
opened her eyes. The girl was frowning. "I was just
goin' ta say I thought he was real nice ta ye today.
Real attentive."

Rhiannon dropped into a chair across from them.
"Almost as though he knew what ye needed all day
without ye havin' ta tell him."

"Ye really are connected," Blaire added from her spot across the room.

"Aye." They really were connected, in more ways than her friends could understand.

"Well," Sorcha added quietly, "if ye do leave us for him, I could understand it."

"Sorcha!" Caitrin barked from the doorway, arms folded across her chest.

The youngest witch thrust out her chin. "Well, I could, Cait. He's handsome and rich and—"

"A beast," the seer reminded them all.

"There is that," Sorcha replied. "But a well-behaved one. Did ye no' see how he took care of El the whole day?"

"Do ye ken what will happen if Elspeth goes with him? Our circle will fall apart. In six hundred years the circle has *never* been broken."

"What will happen if we separate?" Sorcha asked quietly. "Will we lose our magic?"

"We canna be certain," Caitrin said with a pointed look toward Elspeth. "It has never happened."

"I ken," Sorcha whispered. "I just wish it wasna that way. It seems like he wants ta make El happy, and I think she deserves that."

"We all want Elspeth ta be happy. Just with a decent human. Edinburgh is no' small. There are many men ta choose from."

Elspeth had heard enough. They could go on like this for hours. When she saw them next, they'd probably still be discussing it. She rose from her seat. "I'm goin' ta bed. Once ye've all sorted out my life, let me ken what ye've come up with."

She awoke early the next morning. It felt a bit strange to be in the cottage all alone, but it was something she would get accustomed to in time.

Ben, Ben, Ben. She'd thought about him all night, even dreamed about him. She supposed she should go through her mother's old things looking for something Lycan related. How did one go about healing a werewolf who can't change with the moon?

While an enchanted spoon stirred her oatmeal cooking on the stove, Elspeth removed the rug from the kitchen floor, revealing a hidden door. She hadn't been in her mother's space for years, as she preferred to work on her potions aboveground.

She tugged the door up and peered into the darkness beneath her cottage. Shivers raced down her spine. She'd always hated the stale air and freezing room down below. Her mother had loved the quiet and solitude of the dank quarters. She wasn't afraid of the darkness or the bugs and would sequester herself there for hours at a time, completely engrossed in a new project.

Elspeth tested the top rung of the ladder with her weight. She was surprised when she found it held her with ease. She held a candle aloft and stopped as she descended into the darkness to periodically wipe spider webs from her path. The most stubborn webs clung to her hair and clothing. She fought back revulsion as she pulled the majority of the sticky strands from her hair. When her foot hit the solid earth that was the room's floor, relief flooded her. She lifted the candle and used it to light tapers on the wall. The room was immediately flooded with light. Much better.

Along one wall, her mother had stacked the bottles used for her potions and healing remedies. Elspeth stepped closer to the far wall, which housed a cabinet of small drawers, each no more than three inches in width. She tugged one of the small drawers open and smiled when her nose was assaulted by the smell of mint. She opened another drawer and oregano tickled her nose.

Elspeth went on to find basil and bay leaves. If she couldn't conjure a spell with these, her mother could at least make a decent stew. She laughed lightly to herself at the thought.

A long table was in the center of the room. She recognized her grandfather's handiwork in the piece as she ran a finger longingly across the surface. Atop the table, books were stacked in abandon, some still open to the page her mother had last studied. She felt a tiny catch in her throat as she saw the spell her mother had been writing. It was a spell that would only be used to call a loved one home.

But who would her mother call? As far as she knew, her mother had never loved any man, aside from her father. Elspeth picked up the piece of foolscap and blew the dust from the surface.

That was when she finally knew. She knew who the man was who'd killed her mother. She'd known all along it was her father. But she'd never seen it written in ink the way it was. The foolscap may as well have been marked with her blood, for her mother had poured her heart out on the page. She had finally taken it upon herself to call to him and ask for him to return. To visit her one last time. Obviously, he hadn't come. And her mother had finally died of loneliness.

But she'd left one thing behind. The man had a name—a first one, at least—Des. And Elspeth had to find him.

Ben knew it was much too early to pay a visit to Elspeth, but he'd woken several times thinking of her during the night. He hated the idea of her being all alone in that house. He would take a quick run over to her tiny cottage and see if her friends were around. If so, he wouldn't worry over her.

He jogged through the woods, so intent on his path that he suddenly found himself there and didn't even remember how he'd arrived. Of course, no one was moving about. He glanced at the shrubbery and said quietly, "If you're going to attack me, let's get it over with."

The shrubbery made no response. No leaves trembled. No vines lengthened or entangled him. Perhaps it was safe. He softly knocked on her door. He waited to hear her call out, or at least hear her footsteps as she crossed the floor. His Lycan hearing allowed him to hear the smallest of footsteps, even the ones made by bare feet. He imagined Elspeth climbing out of bed, her feet bare as she padded toward the door.

But no one answered his knock. He tapped a little louder. There were still no signs from inside. What if something was wrong? What if she was hurt?

Ben turned the door handle and poked his head inside. He glanced around the room and saw nothing amiss. But neither did she appear to him. He walked into the kitchen and saw a spoon stirring a pot of oatmeal. All by itself? Surely that wasn't one of her powers. He walked over to the stove and moved the pot from the heat. The spinning spoon immediately stilled. Ben shook his head and called to her again.

He glanced across the kitchen and finally saw the hidden door, which was usually covered by a large rug. The rug had been casually tossed to the side. He stepped to the edge of the hidden door and looked down. And there he finally found her.

"Elspeth?" he called. He could see her there in candlelight, her face glowing as she sat still, thoroughly engrossed in a book in her lap. She didn't look up.

The rungs creaked only slightly as they bore his weight. When he reached the bottom of the ladder, he jumped softly to the hard-packed earth.

He was before her and pulling the book from her grasp before she even realized he was there.

"*Havers*, Ben!" she cried, her hand fluttering to land on her heart, which now beat so loud that Ben could hear it. "Ye nearly scared the life out of me." Her eyes narrowed at him. "What are ye doin' here?"

"I came to check on you. To be sure you're all right." He wiped a smudge of dust from her cheek with the pad of his thumb.

"Oh, I'm fine," she said and pulled the book back into her lap.

Any other woman would be mortified to be caught in her nightrail by a man. And even more so if she knew what she looked like. Back in London, there were chimney sweeps with less dirt on them than she was wearing.

He reached over and tugged the end of a spider web, untangling the mess from her hair, which looked like orange flames in the light of the candle.

"Thank ye," she mumbled. She barely glanced up at him.

"What is this place?" he asked as he took in the sights and scents around him.

Without looking up from her book, she mumbled, "My mother's secret room."

"I can see why she kept it a secret," Ben said quietly. She didn't turn and look at him. He crossed his arms over his chest. "It's filthy."

"Filthy, aye," she murmured, but still didn't raise her head.

"Elspeth, the trees have come alive, and they tried to kill me on my way to your house." Something had to get her attention.

"That's good, Ben," she said quietly as she turned the page.

"I want to make love to you," he said, unable to bite back the small smile and pleasant thoughts that came with that statement. Perhaps he could shock her out of her trance.

"Aye," she nodded.

"Did you say 'aye'?" he cried.

"Mmm... hmm." She nodded. "Whatever ye say."

Ben blew out a frustrated breath as he paced behind her. Then he had an idea. He unbuttoned his trousers and rubbed his fingertips lightly across his birthmark.

"Oh," she cried as she jumped up. The book fell from her hands and thunked to the floor.

"Finally I have your attention," he said as he leaned against a cabinet.

"Doona do that ta me, Ben." Her green eyes flashed in anger. She shook her first finger at him. "That wasna fair."

He chuckled at the look of indignation on her face. "I gave you fair warning, Elspeth."

She bent and picked up the book. "I'm sorry. I was readin' my mother's journal."

"Anything interesting?"

A spark of pain lit in her eye and then quickly died. "Very much that's interestin'. She wrote about my father." She sighed long and loud. Then drew in a deep breath. "Ben, can I ask ye for a favor?"

He stepped closer to her and brushed a lock of hair from her forehead. "You can ask me for anything."

"Can ye take me ta London?"

That came out of nowhere. "I said I would, but what's so urgent?"

"I need ta find my father. Ye said yer major could help me."

Ben nodded. He'd been trying to get her to London, away from the others, anyway. What a stroke of luck to have her change her mind to leave sooner. "I believe he can."

"Good, because I'm goin' ta kill him once I find him."

# Twenty-three

ELSPETH WAS MORTIFIED BY WHAT SHE'D SAID, AND more so by the look of utter shock on Ben's face. Still, she wouldn't take the words back. She was a healer, and she'd never wanted to hurt anyone—except for "Des," whoever the devil he was. Perhaps the loss of a limb would suffice. She scratched her head as she considered her options.

For years she'd heard her grandfather lament the fact that her father had killed her mother. She'd never been sure what he meant by that, since she'd never laid eyes on the man, and her mother had only died five years ago. But now, having read pages and pages of her mother's words, she knew exactly what her grandfather meant. She remembered the day. Elspeth had been sick, so sick that she'd nearly died. She'd been told later that her mother had tried every remedy known to her. And nothing worked. So, in desperation, she'd reached out to El's father for support.

It had taken every bit of power she had, her entire essence, just to reach out to him. And still he hadn't come. The additional stress on her body had weakened her and left her unable to fight when she caught the same illness Elspeth had. It was all because of him. She had called to him, but he hadn't come. He'd put her in the ground, just as sure as if he'd plunged a knife into her heart.

"I must have misheard you," Ben said smoothly.

"Ye heard me correctly. When I find my father, I'm goin' ta kill him."

"You're a healer, Elspeth," he reminded her.

She closed her eyes. It went against everything in her soul to do harm, but how could she let him live peacefully after everything he'd done? "I'll make an exception in his case."

Then she felt Ben's warm fingers brush her cheek, and her eyes rose to meet his. "I don't think you mean that, Ellie. There's not a cruel bone in your body."

She hadn't realized how cold she was in her mother's room, but his touch warmed her in an instant. "I canna just let him roam around out there. No' after what he did ta her." *Not after what he did to me.*

"Are you sure he's even alive?" Ben asked softly.

Elspeth felt the air whoosh out of her. She hadn't considered that. What if he was dead? It would explain why the summoning spell hadn't worked. "I suppose ye have a point. But I need ta find out, Ben. One way or the other."

He flashed her a smile. "We'll find him, one way or another." Then he winked at her. "But you've got to promise me not to kill him, if he is alive."

It should be an easy promise to make. She knew she

could never go through with it, no matter how badly he deserved it or how badly she wished she could. Feeling bitter, she simply shrugged.

"Now, I mean it, Elspeth. I won't have you getting yourself into trouble. As Blackmoor's brother I hold a little clout, but not enough to get authorities to ignore murder charges. That sort of thing is frowned upon in England, you know."

Elspeth heaved a sigh. "All right, I won't kill him." But she wouldn't promise not to maim him. Perhaps she should bring the others with her, as Sorcha's, Blaire's, and Rhiannon's powers could do a bit more damage than hers ever could.

Ben's fingers drifted to her neck and he stroked her gently. "What a relief. I'd hate to see this beautiful neck stretched on the gallows. It would be such a waste."

She frowned at him. "Ye make it very difficult for me ta stay in a foul mood, ye ken?"

His smile brightened the dismal room. "Ah, my sweet little witch, you shouldn't have told me that. I'll hold all sorts of power over you now." His fingers moved lower over her shoulder and down her arm, spreading a tingling warmth all the way to her fingertips. "When do you want to leave? Today?"

He was the kindest man she'd even known, completely ignoring his own ailment. She was embarrassed to realize that she had ignored it as well, and now she knew how to fix him. "Oh, Ben, I'm sorry. I was bein' a bit selfish. I do have wonderful news for ye."

He raised his brow in silent question.

"It's all in there." She pointed to the journal. "We

were right. My father came here for the same reason as
ye did. He couldn't transform either. All of mother's
notes are right here. The potions, oils, spells she used."

She saw pure joy in his eyes. "So you know how
to heal me?"

"I believe so. Mother healed him, anyway."

Ben easily plucked her from her seat and spun her
around in his arms. "Ellie, you don't know how happy
you've made me."

With the room spinning around she had a fairly
good idea. A laugh escaped her. "*Havers*, put me
down, ye silly man."

But he didn't. Though he stopped spinning, he
held her tightly in his arms, her legs dangling off
the ground. Then he pressed his lips to hers. Elspeth
wrapped her arms around his neck and kissed him
back, certain the room still spun.

❧

Ben groaned as his tongue explored Elspeth's sweet
mouth. She tasted like tea and blueberries. She tasted
like Elspeth, which he was discovering was his favorite
flavor in the world. He sat her on the long table before
them and pressed himself between her legs. What he
wouldn't give to sink into her.

The scent of her arousal touched his nose, driving
him to distraction. In her flimsy nightrail, he could
feel her nipples harden against his chest. He gently
pushed her back on the table, never removing his lips
from hers.

He started to put himself above her, but something
fell from the table and crashed to the floor.

Elspeth sat up with a start. She blinked her striking emerald eyes at him and smiled. "I'm certain we'd be more comfortable upstairs."

He wholeheartedly agreed. Her mattress had to be more comfortable than a hard table in a dank room. "Lead the way, love," he growled against her neck. Unable to resist himself, he nipped her lightly and she raked her hands through his hair.

Ben kissed her softly one last time before helping her off the table. She scrambled up the ladder, her perfect little bottom swaying before his eyes. Her nightrail didn't leave much to the imagination, and Ben had to work to keep his hands to himself, at least for the moment.

He thought about riding in his coach with her for a fortnight. He could squeeze that bottom all he wanted, as well as everything else. It would be the most pleasant journey he'd ever take... one that would surely ruin her reputation, should anyone find out about it.

There was only one solution. They'd leave for London right after he married her. He wouldn't make the same mistake her father made. He wouldn't ever let her go, and he would protect her until the end of time, and that meant more than physically. He wouldn't let anyone ever speak ill of her.

Ben climbed the ladder after her. "Ellie, there's something I have to ask—"

Just as his head popped up in the kitchen floor, a blazing ball of light came hurling toward his head. He lost his balance and fell back into the secret room.

"Good God!" he yelped. What was that? And what

was that smell? He touched a hand to his head and realized the ends of his hair had been singed.

He looked above him and found one of her sister witches glaring down at him. The girl's raven hair hung loosely about her shoulders, and her grey eyes flashed with indignation. "Just what do ye think ye're doin' here, Westfield?"

She knew him, but he had no idea which one she was.

"Blaire Lindsay!" Elspeth's panicked voice filtered down to him. "I canna believe ye did that."

A moment later Elspeth peered down at him, concern etched across her lovely brow. "Ben, are ye all right?"

"She burned my hair," he said, at a loss to find other words.

"My aim was off," the vicious witch complained. "I was hopin' for yer handsome face."

"Blaire!" Elspeth admonished. "How dare ye come inta my house and treat my guest in such a fashion?"

Ben leapt to his feet. He was a sitting duck with her standing over him like that. He needed to get to higher ground. He climbed the ladder.

"I dare," Blaire told her in no uncertain terms. "Look at yerself, El. Ye've got next ta nothing on and—"

"My wardrobe is no' yer concern."

Finally aboveground, Ben approached the fighting witches. He stared at the dark-haired Blaire. "What did you throw at me?"

She shrugged, looking completely unrepentant. "A fireball. And I have more, so I'd watch myself if I were ye."

A fireball? That was much worse than the vines that came to life. "Thanks for the warning," he muttered.

"I think ye should leave, Blaire," Elspeth said quietly, though there was a dangerous edge to her voice.

Blaire shook her head. "I dinna come for a social call, El. Caitrin's been hurt. She needs ye."

# *Twenty-four*

"HURT?" ELSPETH ECHOED. HER HEART STOPPED beating. "What happened ta Cait?"

Blaire's eyes flashed to Ben before she replied, "I'd rather explain on the way."

Elspeth grabbed her friend's hand and towed her toward her bedroom. "Explain while I dress. I may need somethin' from my stores."

She shut the door behind them and went straight to her armoire, pulling out the first dress her fingers found. "Speak, Blaire."

"It was Westfield," she whispered.

Elspeth spun on her feet, panic washing over her. "I beg yer pardon."

"She'd gone out for a walk with her maid, and they were both attacked."

Elspeth shook her head. "Ben would never do that."

"Ye doona even ken the man. How do ye ken what he would or wouldna do?"

She didn't know him all that well, but still… "I ken he wouldna hurt anyone." *Except for the "whore" when he had lost control.* Had he lost control again? She shook the thought from her head. Ben's altercation had been during an act of intimacy. He wouldn't attack two women on a walk. There had to be a misunderstanding.

"Ye would believe him over Cait?"

She had a point. She'd known Caitrin all her life and Ben only a week. "What did he do?" Her heart ached as she asked the question.

Blaire took a deep breath and ran her fingers through her dark mane. "He attacked them both, though Cait got the worst of it."

"Attacked them?" Elspeth echoed in horror.

"Aye, the maid said the wolf came out of nowhere and attacked before disappearin' inta the woods. Will ye dress, already?"

Elspeth realized she was clutching her blue muslin in her fists, and she shook her head. "Sorry." She tore off her wrap and nightrail and started to slip into her dress. "It wasna Ben," she said as she slid into her old, worn half boots.

Blaire let go a beleaguered sigh. "Of course it was. Did ye not hear me say it was a wolf?"

"It canna be. He canna change. That's why he's here."

"How do we ken that for certain? Ye're only takin' his word for it."

Elspeth quickly pinned her hair, knowing the effort was futile. "Then why else would he have come, Blaire? I doona believe it was him. There are wolves out there who doona turn inta men, ye ken."

Blaire's grey eyes bore into hers. "Cait has been the most vocal about her dislike of Westfield. So he meant ta silence her. He's come ta destroy the *Còig* one way or the other."

Finished with her hair, Elspeth picked up a small satchel on her dresser, then crossed to her door. "I doona believe it."

She walked out of the room and into her kitchen, where she found Ben's hazel eyes leveled on her. With his ears, he'd heard every word, she knew it.

"I didn't," he whispered.

Elspeth nodded. She wanted to cry. "I ken." Then she went to the cupboard behind him and began tossing corked bottles into her satchel.

"Can I help?" Ben asked from behind her.

"I doona think now is the time, or ye might be attacked by more than a little fireball."

He squeezed her shoulders and dropped a kiss to her cheek. "If you need me, I'll be at Alec's. I'm so sorry, Ellie."

She looked at him over her shoulder. He was so earnest with his light brown hair with singed ends hanging in his eyes. "Be careful, Ben. If any of the others get a chance at ye, I doona ken what they'll do."

Instead of returning to Alec's as he'd said, Ben ran swiftly through the woods toward Caitrin's home. He followed his nose and used it to find the door the two women had used when they started their walk. Then he followed their trail. They'd ventured much farther into the woods than he would expect of two women who were just taking a casual stroll.

But there was a worn path through the area, and it lead to Elspeth's home, so perhaps this was a path much taken. The wind shifted and Ben inhaled deeply.

As usual, he could pick out the scents of animals in the area. But there was a wild scent that was definitely lupine nearby. If anyone knew the scent of a wolf, it was him. Ben crouched behind a boulder at the top of a hill and looked down into the valley. He immediately saw the pups, rustling and tumbling together in the grass. The mother wolf stood sentry nearby, and Ben could smell the father in the area as well.

That explained it. Caitrin and her maid had stumbled upon a wolf den. And wolves protected their young.

Ben heard a low growl behind him, and the hair on the back of his neck stood up. He turned slowly to face the wolf, taking care not to meet his dark stare. If confronted in such a manner, the male wolf would tear him to shreds.

Ben backed away slowly, heading back down the trail as he'd come. He didn't growl or bare his teeth as he would in a normal confrontation. He'd stepped into this wolf's territory, after all. And the male was simply protecting his young. If he'd had children, Ben could imagine doing the same.

The thought brought an immediate image of Elspeth to him, cradling a red-haired wolfling in her arms. Their wolf.

The male wolf continued to watch as Ben turned and jogged back in the direction he'd come. It made Ben feel much better to know there was a valid cause for the attack, if you could consider any cause to be valid.

He circled to the front of Caitrin's house, and the butler opened the door before he could even knock. The man looked down his nose at Ben. It had always amazed him how they could do that.

"If it's not too much trouble, I'd like to check on Miss Macleod," he told the man.

The butler simply nodded and led him to the morning room, where Alec sat, his foot tapping anxiously against the floor as he nibbled his fingernails.

"How is she?" Ben asked, breaking Alec from his fretful fidgeting. He glanced up quickly.

"Elspeth is with her now." Alec stood up to pace. "There was a lot of blood."

"Maybe the wounds are superficial?" No matter what, Elspeth would have to worry about infection.

"She was in a lot of pain." Alec continued his pacing.

"Would you sit down, man? You're making me crazy with all the moving about." Ben knew his voice was a bit too forceful, but the nervous energy in the room was going to send him into a frenzy if it continued.

"She'll be all right, won't she?" Alec's gaze finally met his, and he saw the anguish behind the man's rigid façade.

"You truly care about the girl?"

Alec simply nodded.

Ben motioned to a footman nearby. The man immediately returned with two tumblers of whisky. Ben offered one to Alec. He shook his head.

"You'll be no use to her if you're tied up in knots."

Alec acquiesced and took the glass. He downed it in one swallow. Ben pressed his own glass into the man's shaking hands. He drank that one as well.

Ben clapped him on the shoulder. "She'll be fine, Alec. You told me yourself that everyone in town goes to Elspeth when they need to be healed."

"Aye, it's like she has healing warmth in her finger-tips," Alec said as he finally met Ben's gaze. "She'll be able to heal her. I'm sure of it."

A low murmur of female voices from the corridor reached Ben's ears.

"Ye canna use fireballs on him with MacQuarrie in the room! What's wrong with ye? Are ye daft? Put that thing away."

Ben glanced around the corner and saw Blaire standing with Sorcha. The raven-haired witch balanced a ball of fire over her fingertips, as though testing the weight of it.

"Is that for me?" he asked. Certainly she wouldn't use it in front of Alec.

"Of course it is. Who else would I use it on? If it wasna ye, then it was one of yer kind who hurt her."

"Your kind?" Alec said as he approached the doorway. Blaire rubbed her fingertips together and extinguished the fireball seconds before he looked around the corner. "An Englishman hurt her? Who? I'll kill him."

# Twenty-five

ELSPETH SAT ON THE EDGE OF THE BED AND TRIED TO work quickly and quietly. She was relieved to find that although the wounds still bled profusely, most of them weren't deep.

"Can ye give me a moment, Mr. Macleod?" Elspeth asked, never removing her eyes from an unconscious Caitrin. "I need a bit of privacy."

"Whatever ye need, lass. I'll be right outside the door."

It was a relief not to have to lie to him. She usually had to send loved ones on *special errands* to be alone with the person who needed to be healed. Since his wife and daughter were both members of the *Còig*, there was no need for subterfuge with Angus Macleod.

When she heard him shut the door behind him, Elspeth touched her fingertips to Caitrin's forearms, where most of the defensive wounds were located. She closed her eyes and concentrated, feeling the heat move from her body into Caitrin's. The girl moved, despite the sleeping draught Elspeth had given her when she'd arrived, since healing could be painful.

Elspeth used all the power in her body, transferring every bit of herself to Cait. "Ye will be healed," she crooned softly. "No matter how ornery ye are, I need ye."

The most superficial wounds healed beneath her fingertips. The deepest wounds took more concentration. Elspeth closed her eyes again and imagined the healing power flowing from her touch like a stream of warmth.

Elspeth knew there was a fine line between healing someone else and hurting herself. But at that moment she didn't care. She needed Cait to be healed. She needed to fight with her another day.

Elspeth's arms became heavy and cumbersome. But still she pressed on, because beneath her fingertips the wounds closed and the skin repaired. She tried to open her eyes but found her lids were too heavy. Still, she poured her energy into Caitrin.

She heard voices calling her name, but she was unable to respond. Her tongue refused to move. Her mouth refused to open. Yet the healing powers still flowed freely from her.

Someone caught her when she finally could sit up no longer. Strong arms closed around her body. She wanted to complain about someone moving her away from Caitrin, since her friend needed her help. Her eyes fluttered open.

"What have you gone and done, love?" Ben said before the darkness overtook her.

❧

When Elspeth's body went limp, Ben slid his arm under her legs, lifted her, and cradled her against him. "Ellie!" he said, shaking her just a bit.

A moment earlier he'd been trying to calm Alec's nerves when he sensed Elspeth slipping away. It was as though part of his soul crumbled. He'd raced to Miss Macleod's room just as she slumped forward.

He glanced around the room, unsure what to do. In the doorway, Mr. Macleod looked on. "Is she all right?"

"Does she look bloody all right?" he barked.

Sorcha Ferguson stepped from behind the older gentleman. "Let's get her a room so she can lie down."

Ben shook his head. If he left her with these vultures, he'd never get her back. He could feel it. "I'm taking her home. You can summon a doctor for whatever else Miss Macleod and her maid need."

He stalked toward the door with Elspeth in his arms. Sorcha and Mr. Macleod stepped out of his way, though the young witch followed in his wake. "Ye canna take her from here. There isna anyone at the cottage ta look after her."

"I'll look after her," he growled over his shoulder as he began to descend the steps.

At the bottom of the staircase, Alec gaped at him. "What happened?"

"She collapsed."

Ben reached the bottom and started for the door, but Alec's hand on his arm stopped him. "Where are you going?"

Sorcha's panicked voice came from behind him. "He says he's goin' ta take her home."

"Ben," Alec's voice lowered so that only Ben could hear. "You can't do that. She's better off here."

Ben didn't respond except to glare at his friend.

There was no way in hell he was leaving her with these people. No one would watch after her like he would.

Apparently Alec saw the determination in his eyes, because he released Ben's arm. "Obstinate dolt. In the very least you can't walk her through the woods like this. Take my coach."

"Thank you."

The butler pulled open the large oak door, and Ben stepped out into the bright sunlight. Alec's coach was still out front, and he yelled to the driver, "Open the door."

A moment later they were both safely ensconced inside the carriage, Elspeth still cradled in his arms. Seeing her pale face, he touched her cheek. She was icy cold. He held her tighter, hoping his hot blood would warm her some. "Come on, sweetheart, open your eyes for me."

Before they could rumble off, the coach door opened and Sorcha Ferguson climbed inside the carriage. With a "humph," she flopped onto the bench opposite Ben, a frown etched across her brow.

"What do you think you're doing?" he growled.

The coach moved forward and a look of fear crossed the girl's face, but she bravely met his gaze head-on. "Obviously, I'm goin' with ye."

"I don't need you."

"I'm no' doin' it for ye. Elspeth's my friend, and ye should be nicer ta me. I'm the only one on yer side."

The vines that attacked him were still fresh in his mind. "Indeed? I suppose that ivy took it upon itself to tangle me up, then?"

The chit had the good sense to stare at her hands. "That was Blaire's idea, and at the time, I thought ye were bad for her."

Ben wasn't quite sure what to say to that. He glanced back down at Elspeth, but there was no change in her pallor. He didn't know what he would do if she didn't wake up.

He felt Sorcha's eyes on him and looked across the coach at her. She brushed a tear from her cheek. "She's the sweetest person I ken."

She was the sweetest person Ben knew, too. "How did this happen?" he asked, not sure if she had the answer, but it was worth a try.

Sorcha's gaze fell to Elspeth. "The healer gives her strength ta those who need her. It drains from her inta them."

"And leaves her with nothing?" he whispered in horror. He could never ask her to heal him, not if this would be the end result. It would kill him if he hurt her. How could anyone ask that of her? How could her sister witches ask that of her?

Sorcha shook her head. "I've never seen her respond like this before. But the more attached the healer is ta her subject, the more dangerous it is for her. El and Cait are very close."

Too bloody close. He should have already taken her and left for London. If he had, she wouldn't be lying lifelessly in his arms. He stared at Elspeth, willing her to open her eyes. "Come on, Ellie."

As soon as they reached the cottage, Sorcha leapt out of the coach ahead of him and held open the front door. "Her room is—"

"The one in the back," he finished. "I know." He pushed open her door with his foot. "Pull back the counterpane for me, will you?"

Sorcha scrambled to do his bidding before Ben placed Elspeth on her small mattress. She looked so helpless lying there. He tugged the blankets up around her and dropped to his knees beside her bed.

Behind him, Sorcha cleared her throat. "It isna proper for ye ta be in here, my lord."

"Unless you are capable of dragging me out of here, I'm not leaving her side."

"Well, then," she began, her voice sounding a bit strangled. "I suppose I'll go start some broth."

He touched Elspeth's brow and winced at the icy feel of her skin. If only he could warm her somehow, get her blood moving. He rubbed her skin lightly, trying to generate heat. But she did not warm or wake.

Lycans were known for their body heat. Surely he could warm her with his own body. Ben shrugged out of his coat, lifted the corner of the counterpane and slid beneath it. He pulled her inert form closer to him. But all he felt was her clothing brushing against his. He needed skin-to-skin contact.

The clank of pots and pans he heard from the direction of the kitchen let him know Sorcha was busy preparing the broth she'd mentioned. He quickly and expertly untied the laces at the back of Elspeth's neck and gently tugged her gown from her shoulders. The reason for undressing her was purely medicinal. He tried to convince himself of that fact as he tugged her gown over her hips, leaving her in a thin chemise.

Ben tried not to look at the dusky rose color of her nipples, the shadows of which he could see through the thin fabric. He hurriedly yanked his cravat loose, threw off his waistcoat, and tugged his shirt over his head.

Ben sank beneath the counterpane once more and rolled Elspeth so that the length of her body was pressed along his. He tucked her fiery head under his chin and adjusted her hips to fit nicely against his. She was still too cold.

Ben pulled one of her legs between his so that he could cradle her closely before he pulled the counterpane higher over their shoulders. He waited, stroking her back patiently as he willed her to wake.

He'd never felt such a blinding desire to protect someone as when he'd seen Elspeth collapse. He couldn't get to her fast enough.

She stirred against him, and he took her hand in his, raising it to his cheek. He gently pressed a kiss to her palm. Then he saw the mark she wore, her own mark of the beast. As a last resort, he might use that to reach her. It definitely connected them. He just wasn't sure if the connection was physical or emotional.

For him, she was both. He closed his eyes tightly when he felt a hint of desire. He couldn't hold her nearly naked form so close and feel *nothing*.

The stomp of footsteps met his ears, and he groaned at the very thought of someone seeing such a private scene. He glanced up at Sorcha, who stood still in the threshold, her mouth hanging open, a gasp frozen in the air.

"She was too cold," he said, by way of explanation. "It's the best way to warm her."

"By usin' yer *body*?" she hissed. "I could have warmed some bricks or... *somethin'*!"

"It's really the best way," he started, but a sound cut him off. "Someone is coming," he said quietly.

A knock sounded on the door ten seconds later.

"How did ye ken that?" She crossed her arms over her chest.

Ben rolled his eyes. "I'm Lycan, for God's sake," he growled. "Now, be a good witch and close the bedroom door before you go see who's here."

Sorcha flounced off in a huff, but the soft *snick* of the door closing told him she'd followed his instructions.

Elspeth moved against him and he felt himself harden. He groaned and laid his head against the pillow in defeat. "Sorry, lass. I cannot help it holding you this way," he whispered to himself.

"Canna help what?" she asked quietly from within his arms.

# Twenty-six

ELSPETH'S LIMBS WERE AS WEAK AS WATER, BUT SHE managed to croak out a few words. Strong fingers anxiously pushed at her hair, moving it from her face. An insistent hand cupped her jaw and forced her to look up.

"Where am I?" she croaked. "What happened?"

Elspeth's mind told her to move, but her body really wanted to stay wrapped up in the beautiful heat that was the man next to her.

"You're in your bed," Ben said quietly.

"With ye in it, too?" She couldn't help but giggle. "This is the best dream I've ever had." She slipped her arms around his waist and pressed a cheek to his bare chest. "So warm," she sighed.

"I'm happy to hear that you like me in your bed, lass."

Elspeth tested the huge cocoon that was his body, stretching languidly. Her thigh was trapped between his own. She didn't have the strength to move, so she simply burrowed in closer.

Wiry hair teased her fingertips as she brushed her hands through the hair on his chest. He groaned and captured her hands. "I can only stand so much."

Elspeth raised the counterpane and glanced down. "Where are my clothes?" she whispered.

He chuckled. "I took them off you to warm you up."

"A likely story," she said as she swatted at his chest.

"Do you remember being with Miss Macleod, Ellie?"

"Oh," Elspeth gasped. She did remember. "Is she all right?"

"You healed her." His fingertip touched her chin and forced her to raise her gaze. "At great risk to yourself."

"That's the way it is with healers, Ben." She lifted the edge of the blanket again. "I need ta get up ta go check on Cait. But I canna figure out how ta do so."

"You're not going anywhere," he said as he pulled her tighter against him. "Not until I'm sure you're well."

"Ye canna keep me against my will," she breathed. But her traitorous nipples hardened in response to his closeness, and when she moved they brushed the fabric of her chemise. They may as well have been touching his skin.

"I don't think keeping you would be against your will," he growled. "Are you warm yet?"

"Quite," she gasped as he flipped her onto her back and pressed her into the mattress. The knee that had been so firmly clasped between his was now pushed to the side and he settled firmly between her thighs.

He looked down at her, a curious smile tilting the corner of his mouth. "Against your will, you say?" His head dipped down to touch his lips to hers briefly. It was like the touch of a butterfly on her finger.

That's all she would get? "And here I thought ye were goin' ta devour me," she taunted him.

His eyes narrowed slightly as he quietly regarded her. "Why, thank you for the offer." He smirked. "I believe I'll take you up on your hospitality."

His lips touched hers, more firmly this time, his body pressing her into the mattress. His lower body was still cradled between her thighs. He rocked against her, the movement creating a sudden thumping in her center.

"That wasna an invite ta do that," she gasped as he raised his hand to cup her breast. He lowered his head and touched the aching peak with his tongue through the fabric of her chemise. This time it was her hips that rose to press against his.

"Do I need an invitation?" he teased as he did the same to the other breast. "I know how wet you are. And that you want me. I don't need a better invitation."

"Ye seem mighty sure of yerself," she said, unable to keep from arching her back to bring herself closer to his lips. Her hands tangled in his hair.

Suddenly he stilled. "Someone is coming," he whispered. "And it's not me," he groaned as he rolled from atop her body, slid from beneath her counterpane, and pulled his shirt over his head. He had just finished righting his clothing when the bedroom door was flung open with a bang.

Elspeth groaned to herself when she saw Alec MacQuarrie standing in the threshold and pulled the counterpane up to her chin.

"Why do all the men feel like they need ta crowd my bedroom?" she groaned before she pulled the counterpane over her head.

"Because you don't know how to take care of

yourself, Elspeth. You have no one, save your friends," MacQuarrie ground out.

"I can take care of myself just fine, thank ye very much," she called from beneath the covers. Then she pulled the counterpane down and peeped over it. "It's no' like he's in bed with me."

"Aye, no' now. But he was a moment ago." Sorcha's tiny voice chirped from her safe place behind Alec.

How could Sorcha possibly know that? Elspeth's face warmed.

MacQuarrie turned to the smallest witch. "He was in bed with her?" His face purpled and his hands balled into fists.

"H-he said it was ta w-warm her up," she stuttered, looking at her feet all the while.

"I can just imagine the kind of warming he was doing," MacQuarrie sighed as he pinched the bridge of his nose between his thumb and forefinger. Then he crossed his arms and leveled a stare at his friend.

Ben sat casually in a chair by her bed, his elbows resting on his knees, as though he held court in women's bedrooms all the time. Maybe he did. Why did that thought suddenly make her irrationally jealous? He arched one eyebrow at her, a playful smile hovering about his lips.

MacQuarrie glanced about the room. His face hardened and a muscle twitched by his left eye when he spotted her dress on the floor. "What are you wearing under that counterpane, Elspeth? Please, don't tell me he was in bed with you naked."

"I canna see why that would be any of yer business,

Mr. MacQuarrie," Elspeth snapped. If one more person tried to run her life, she would scream.

"Elspeth, you have no family. I'm trying to stand up for you. Please tell me he didn't take advantage of you. Because then I would have to lay waste to my very best friend."

"You could try," Ben growled under his breath.

Alec MacQuarrie truly did have good intentions, Elspeth believed in her heart. They all did. But she was a grown woman, for heaven's sake.

"Out!" she yelled. "All of ye!" She brought her arms from beneath the counterpane and brushed her hands toward the door when they all stood there like ninnies looking at her. "I plan ta get out of this bed in ten seconds, and unless ye *do* want ta see what I have on—" She raised the edge of the counterpane and looked down. "Or do no'." She shrugged and shook her head in disbelief. "Ye'd better be out of my room by then."

Elspeth sat up and swung her legs to the side of the bed. "Doona say I dinna warn ye." She prepared to drop the counterpane.

The door slammed shut quickly. Elspeth rested her forehead in her hands for a moment before she looked up at Ben. "Why are *ye* still here?"

He shrugged as a wolfish grin crossed his face. "I wanted to see what you wore beneath the counterpane."

≈

"Ye already ken what I'm no' wearin'. Ye undressed me, after all." He'd always known her temper matched her hair. And all the rest of her.

"Oh, yes, I did," he growled, with the sweet

memory of her nearly bare body pressed against his taking over his senses.

"Would ye please leave so I can get dressed, Ben?" she sighed, as though the weight of the world rested on her shoulders.

Ben dropped to crouch before her as she sat on the edge of the bed. "I think I have just well and truly ruined you, Miss Campbell."

"I'm sure ye have, Ben. But worse things have happened."

"What could be worse, Ellie?" he asked. He truly wanted to know what lay in her heart.

"I could be ruined with a bairn on the way, Ben. It seems ta be the way of the Campbell women." She fidgeted with a loose string on the counterpane, which she still clutched to her chest.

"Alec will insist that I marry you now," Ben said quietly, watching her face as he said the words. "Since I *have* been in your bed."

She waved her hand. "That doesna count. It wasna even a pleasure." Her face colored when she realized what she'd said.

Ben chuckled. "It was a pleasure for me."

"Ye ken what I meant ta say!" she cried.

"No. Tell me," he whispered, his voice suddenly straining against his throat, the same way his shaft strained against his pants.

"When ye came ta me under the night sky, and we came together. *That* was pleasure. I canna imagine anythin' more pleasurable."

"I promise that the next time I share your bed, it *will* be more pleasurable."

Elspeth's eyes grew wide, then she looked down at the mark on her wrist. She lifted one hand to stroke across it.

"If you touch that now, lass, I'll have to be inside you."

She lowered her hands. Thank God! He didn't think he could take more torment.

Elspeth leaned forward and touched her forehead to his, her green eyes flashing. "What if I want ye ta be inside me?" A pretty blush crept up her cheeks.

It was the hardest thing Ben had ever done, not to toss her onto her back and surge into her. But he stopped, counted to ten, and then met her eyes. "Then you'll have to marry me first, won't you?"

Elspeth sat back, studying him. "Marriage? That's no' very fair ta ye. I mean ye were only trying ta help me and—"

"I meant to ask you earlier today anyway, Ellie."

She blinked at him. "Ta marry ye?" she asked doubtfully.

It wasn't exactly the way he'd planned to ask her, but a lot had happened between this morning and now. "Yes, before Blaire threw her fireball at me."

She shook her head as though not truly believing his words. "Why would ye want such a thing?"

Ben cupped her jaw. "Because I want *you*. I care about you, Elspeth, and I don't intend to travel with you to London and have you meet my mother and brothers without my ring on your finger." At that he pulled off his pinkie ring and placed it in his palm, offering it for her to examine. "I'm sure it's too big. I'll get you something more appropriate once we arrive in London. A nice, big emerald to match your eyes."

Tentatively, Elspeth picked up the ring, turning it over in her hand. Her gaze flashed back to him. "I like this one. I never noticed the wolf before." She ran her finger over the engraved image and then handed it back to him.

Ben's heart swelled with pride at her words. "It's the Blackmoor crest," he informed her as he slid the ring back on his pinkie. "What do you say, Ellie? Will you marry me?"

"Are ye sure about this?"

She didn't really have a choice. She was ruined, like her mother before her. But saying so wouldn't be the right way to go about convincing her. Besides, he did want her. This situation simply solidified it. "I've never been more sure," he replied with a wink.

Elspeth threw her arms around his neck. "I think ye're mad ta want me for a wife, Ben Westfield. I'm certain most lords doona marry illegitimate—"

He pulled back from her. "I don't think of you like that."

"But it's the truth."

He hated to see the hurt in her eyes, the years of knowing that everyone else thought they were better than her. "It doesn't matter to me," he assured her. "And when you're Lady Elspeth Westfield, no one else will dare say a thing."

She bit her plump bottom lip. Ben could tell she wanted to believe him. "Lady Elspeth Westfield? I do like the sound of that."

Ben grinned at her and pulled her back into his arms. She belonged there, and he wouldn't ever let her go. "Get dressed, love, then we'll go see Mr. Crawford."

"Ye want ta marry me in the church?" she asked, a note of surprise in her voice.

Ben kissed her chin. "My mother will be furious enough that she wasn't invited, Ellie. I can't tell her I married you over an anvil or something like that. She'd have my head."

# Twenty-seven

BEN THOUGHT IT MIGHT BE NICE TO HELP HIS BRIDE-to-be dress, but she promptly tossed him from her room. As soon as he stepped over her threshold, Alec grabbed his coat with both hands and scowled at him. "I can't believe you've done this, Westfield."

Ben shrugged out of his friend's grasp. "It's not the way I planned it, but I can't say I'm unhappy with the outcome."

"She collapsed!" Alec hissed, as if the word meant something more significant. "Fainted."

"You saw that for yourself, MacQuarrie."

"Aye, I just didn't understand what it meant until I found you in her bed."

Ben shook his head, not grasping his friend's meaning.

"Don't play the innocent with me," Alec grumbled. "She's *enceinte*. It was the one thing I asked you not to do. You're the worst sort of blackguard, you—"

A moment later Ben had Alec pressed against the wall of the cottage, his hands wrapped around his friend's throat. "I've told you before, MacQuarrie, I won't let you or anyone else disparage her."

Alec pulled at Ben's hands, grasping for breath. "I'm not the one—"

"I haven't laid a hand on her," Ben hissed. That wasn't entirely true, but true in the way Alec meant.

"You forget, I know you," his friend sputtered, tugging at Ben's hands.

"She's *not* with child," he insisted, wishing he could divulge why she'd collapsed, but revealing the truth behind her healing powers would only hurt her more. So he pushed his friend out the door instead.

On the ground at his feet, Alec rubbed his neck, where Ben had held him.

Glaring down at him, Ben growled, "She's ruined in name only, MacQuarrie. And I'm rectifying that as soon as possible."

"What do you mean by that?"

Ben shook his head in disgust. "What do you think I mean by that? I'm going to marry her."

Alec choked. "You?"

"Of course, me!"

It was quite infuriating that his friend stared at him as though he'd lost his mind. Then Alec's mouth fell open, but no sound escaped.

"What is it?" Ben demanded.

"You don't seem the sort, Westfield. As soon as you bed a lass, you lose all interest in her. I've seen it time and again. I can't imagine you married."

He had been that way. Perhaps he still was, though he didn't want to believe that. Elspeth was different from the others. He shared a connection with her. He couldn't imagine ever losing interest in her. On the contrary, every minute he spent away from her made him want her more. Of course, he hadn't bedded her yet. What if he *did* lose interest?

Ben balled up his fist, wanting to pummel Alec into the ground for even making the suggestion. "Well, I'll thank you to keep your opinions to yourself, MacQuarrie. And I'll expect you to show her the respect due my wife."

Alec pulled himself up from the ground and dusted his hands on his pants. "I've always held Miss Campbell in respect. Just because she marries you, it won't change my opinion of her. And despite our differing opinions, Benjamin, you are my best friend."

"You'll stand up for me then?" Ben asked. Since his family couldn't be present, he hoped Alec would be.

Alec smiled. "I'd be honored."

❧

Elspeth stepped from her room to find Sorcha sitting on the settee, holding her head in her hands. Ben was nowhere to be seen. "Sorcha?"

The young witch's head shot up, and Elspeth could see the tears in her eyes.

"Are ye all right?"

"Oh, El," she said, rising from her seat. "I failed ye. I'm so sorry. I came along ta keep ye out of this sort of trouble."

Only it didn't seem like trouble. It was a bit frightening, the prospect of marrying a man she barely knew, but not trouble. There was something comforting in the fact that she'd be exploring this new role with Ben. If it had been anyone else, she'd have been terrified.

Elspeth wrapped her arms around her friend. "Doona be upset, Sorcha. It'll work out for the best."

"Cait'll be furious with me." She sniffed back tears.

That was definitely true. Elspeth brushed Sorcha's tears away. "Doona let her bully ye. Besides, I think Ben crossin' my path was fated. No' even Caitrin could stop it."

Sorcha nodded sadly. "I was thinkin' that very thing."

"Where is Ben?"

Her friend pointed to the front door. "Fightin' with Alec MacQuarrie in the yard."

"*Mo chreach!*" Elspeth muttered, rushing to the door. She bolted outside, but what she found were the two men huddled together, Ben's arm draped around MacQuarrie's shoulder as if the two were the best of friends.

Both men's eyes flashed to hers when she stepped on the front porch.

"Sorcha said ye were fightin'."

Ben stepped toward her, a charming smile on his lips. "Ah, MacQuarrie and I were just having a lively discussion. Nothing to worry about. Are you ready to go see your vicar?"

Without thinking, she nodded eagerly. Then the world began to spin. She would have collapsed if Ben hadn't caught her against him.

"Ellie!" His voice sounded strangled.

She clutched his waistcoat and smiled what she hoped was a reassuring smile. "I suppose I'm still a little weak. Nothin' ta worry about," she echoed his earlier sentiment.

Ben tilted her chin upward until she met his eyes. His furrowed brow made it obvious he wasn't reassured in the least. "I'll decide what I worry about."

Elspeth stepped away from him. "I'll be fine."

A few feet away she heard Alec MacQuarrie mutter something under his breath, and Ben's eyes shot to his friend. "I warned you about that, Alec. It's not what you think." Then he looked back at Elspeth. "Do you feel up to seeing the vicar, love? I don't think MacQuarrie will rest until I'm legally leg-shackled to you."

Elspeth couldn't hide her smile. "Aye, I'd like that."

Behind her, Sorcha gasped. "Today? The vicar?"

Elspeth glanced over her shoulder. "Ye're welcome ta join us."

When her friend's gaze fell to the ground and her shoulders slumped forward, Elspeth draped her arm around Sorcha. "I wish ye'd come with us."

"Cait'll kill me one way or the other. So I might as well."

Elspeth patted her arm, then looked up to Alec MacQuarrie. "Did ye see Caitrin? How is she?"

He frowned, as though trying to sort out a puzzle. "You'd never know anything had ever happened to her. She looks perfect. Of course, Mr. Macleod won't let her out of bed. That's why I came to check on you. She's worried about you."

Elspeth moved from her spot to slide her arm around Ben's waist. "Well, as ye can see, there's no need ta worry."

❧

They found Mr. Crawford sitting at his desk at the back of the vicarage, flipping through his Bible. His balding pate was tilted down, and he hummed a hymn to himself. How the man failed to notice a hoard of people standing in his doorway, Ben would never know. To get the man's attention, he rapped loudly on the door.

The vicar looked up and smiled at the four of them, but his eyes landed on Elspeth. "Ah, Miss Campbell, are ye here ta settle yer account?"

Before she could reply, Ben drew her close to his side with an arm around her waist. "I'll be taking care of Miss Campbell's accounts, Mr. Crawford." The man's eyes widened at the pronouncement, so Ben stepped forward. "We have another matter that needs your attention, sir."

"Oh?" the vicar asked, rising from his seat. "How can I help you today, my lord?"

Ben smiled at Elspeth, glad she returned the gesture. "I came to visit my dear friend Alec and found something here in Scotland I can't live without."

The vicar inclined his head, waiting patiently.

"I'd like for you to marry—that is, Miss Campbell and I would like for you to marry *us*."

"Indeed?"

Ben nodded. "Can you do so today?"

"I—um—Well, it would be an irregular marriage."

"As long as it's legal," Ben shrugged, "that's all we care about."

The vicar looked from Ben to Elspeth and back again. "I supposed I have the time, but I'm a bit unprepared for such an endeavor. Can ye wait in the church while I gather my things?"

"We'll be happy to."

"Oh!" The vicar's voice stopped them. "Sign my registry first so I have yer names."

Ben watched as Elspeth's hand shakily filled in the vicar's book, then he took the quill from her and did the same. This was one of the ways Scotland was more advanced than England; it might be the only way, now that he thought about it. No waiting three weeks for the banns to post. No spending a small fortune on a special license. Just whisk your intended down to the church, sign your names in a book, and marry her. No need for all the fuss.

As soon as they entered the church, Ben led Elspeth to a pew in the front row and they were quickly followed by Alec and Sorcha.

Thunder clapped overhead and Sorcha gasped. Elspeth turned her head to face her friend.

"Rhiannon," she whispered. "Cait must've seen this."

Elspeth glanced up to meet Ben's gaze. "Doona worry. I'm sure she'd never hit the church."

"Hit the church with what?" Ben asked, looking around the chapel. As if to answer his question, lightning lit up the sky, the flash filtering through the stained-glass windows. "She can make it storm?" he whispered.

"Or stop," Elspeth replied quietly.

Good God! The faster he got her away from these harridans, the better.

Mr. Crawford entered from a door at the front of the chapel. "*Havers!* It looks bad out there. All right, Lord Benjamin, Miss Campbell, are ye ready?"

Ben squeezed Elspeth's arm. "After you, lass."

She stumbled to her feet and met the vicar at the altar, Ben right behind her the whole way. He took her hand in his and lifted it to his lips. Desire raced through his body. It wouldn't be long before she'd be his.

"*Slainte mhor agus a h-uile beannachd duibh,*" Mr. Crawford called over the thunder that continued to boom above them.

"It's just a blessin'," Elspeth whispered, loud enough for only him to hear.

"Have ye got a ring, my lord?"

Ben pulled his pinkie ring from his waistcoat pocket. "Yes, sir."

"Then we'll begin." He read a bit from Galatians, then looked at Ben. "Repeat after me, my lord. I, Benjamin Farrell Jonathan Westfield, take ye, Elspeth Muriel Campbell, ta be my wife before God and these witnesses."

Ben repeated the words, staring into Elspeth's eyes. She was perfect in every way. He couldn't wait to get her back inside her little cottage. They might not come out for days.

Mr. Crawford turned his attention to Elspeth, "And now it's yer turn. I, Elspeth Muriel Campbell, take ye, Benjamin Farrell Jonathan Westfield, ta be my husband before God and these witnesses."

Elspeth swallowed, and Ben squeezed her fingers. Thunder cracked over head, but she ignored it. "I, Elspeth Muriel Campbell, take ye, Benjamin Farrell Jonathan Westfield, ta be my husband before God and these witnesses."

The vicar smiled. "Well, then, my lord, ye may kiss yer bride."

Ben didn't waste one moment doing so. He slid his arm around Elspeth, pulled her against him, and lowered his lips to hers. She giggled against his mouth, "Ye're crushin' me."

"Sorry," he whispered before releasing her.

Ben looked behind them. Alec's mouth hung open, as though he hadn't really thought they'd go through with it, and Sorcha blew her nose, loudly, in a handkerchief.

# Twenty-eight

"IF HE LOOKS AT YE LIKE THAT FOR ONE MORE MINUTE, I'll expect ye ta go up in a puff of smoke," Sorcha mumbled quietly from Elspeth's side, where they stood together in the kitchen.

Elspeth glanced at Ben, who leaned casually against the doorjamb, talking with Alec MacQuarrie. But beneath Ben's outside veneer of calm, there was a storm brewing behind his eyes. He caught her gaze before allowing his eyes to linger slowly over her body.

"What did ye say?" Elspeth asked, fighting the flush of warmth that crept up her cheeks at his gaze.

"Yer new husband," Sorcha said, nodding her head toward Ben. "He looks like he wants ta have ye for dinner."

Elspeth giggled lightly. He did look like he would consume her at any moment. "I suppose it would be terribly offensive ta send everyone home?" Elspeth whispered back.

"Aye, but it would be worse if he lost control and stripped ye down before we're all gone." Sorcha giggled. The hair on Elspeth's arms stood up. What a lovely thought.

She forced herself to stop looking in his direction. "How long do ye think everyone will stay?" she asked as she fought to keep from glancing back in his direction.

"Surely ye can control yerself long enough ta celebrate yer weddin' with friends?" Sorcha gasped, slightly affronted. "We took the time ta be with ye durin' yer nuptials."

"Like ye would have stayed away," Elspeth snorted. Then she bumped Sorcha's shoulder with her own.

Rhiannon, Blaire, and a few friends from town had found their way to Elspeth's cottage as the news had spread. El was sorry to say she wanted nothing more than for them all to leave.

She raised her teacup to her lips and glanced at Ben over the rim. He still leaned against the threshold, talking with Alec. But his regard was completely for her. His eyes narrowed as he took a deep breath, his chest expanding slowly. "You want me," he mouthed in her direction.

Elspeth sputtered in her teacup.

"Are ye all right?" Sorcha asked, clapping her on the back.

She gasped out, "Fine, Sorcha. Ye can stop beatin' me, now."

Sorcha's clapping slowed and came to a stop. Elspeth turned to take a towel from the rack behind her and found Ben blocking her path. How had he moved so fast?

"Speed," he whispered before his lips pressed to her temple. "It's one of our traits."

"Do ye do everythin' that fast?" she asked.

One eyebrow lifted. He smiled as he brushed a lock of hair from her face. "No. There are some things that should be done slowly."

"I've half a mind ta throw a bucket of cold water on the both of ye," Sorcha mumbled as she stepped away. "Pure nauseatin' how much ye want each other."

"She knows nothin' of want," Elspeth said quietly.

"And you do?" Ben asked as he rolled the lock of her hair between his fingertips. "Tell me what you know of it?"

A challenge lit her eyes. "I know I want ye, Lord Benjamin," she said as she lifted on her tiptoes and kissed his chin. The light tickle of her lips along his jaw nearly drove him mad.

"Not nearly as much as I want you, Lady Elspeth." He closed his eyes and inhaled deeply. "I'm glad no other Lycans are here. The scent of you when you are aroused is enough to drive a man to distraction."

"What does desire smell like, Ben?"

"It smells like you, but stronger. Your body warms up and heat radiates from you. The perfume I know you apply between your breasts and behind your ears gets stronger." He wondered how much he should tell her. She was an innocent after all. "And the *other* perfumes get stronger, too."

She colored under his gaze. She did know what he meant. His heart warmed.

"I need to be alone with you."

"We canna ask them ta leave," she whispered back, her brow knit with concern.

"They can stay," he chuckled as he tugged her fingers, pulling her toward the door. "Let's sneak away."

"But they'll know what we're doin'."

Ben really didn't care at that point. He simply wanted to get her beneath him. He could pick her up and carry her from the room. Or he could persuade her. He very lightly brushed across the mark on his lower belly.

Elspeth gasped, her gaze immediately rising to meet his. "Ye doona play fair."

"All's fair in love and war," he chuckled. He tugged her fingertips again. When she didn't follow, he reached to brush his mark. But she deflected his hand from his body and clutched it tightly in hers.

"I'll go with ye. Ye doona have ta tease me." Her eyes glanced around the room. Indeed, everyone was deep in conversation. He pulled her through the doorway and into the night. But they had taken only two steps when he felt her brush across her own mark.

❦

If Ben truly thought she would be an unwary foe, he'd been sorely misled. His jaw clenched before he grabbed her tightly to him. He took her hand in his and pressed it against his hardness.

"I do not need any help becoming aroused by you, Ellie."

"Yet ye thought ta torment me when we were inside," she laughed against his lips.

"You play with fire." His head tilted as he deepened the kiss and grabbed her bottom, pulling her against him. She gasped. Every part of him was hard, from his chest to… everything else.

"Perhaps I want ta be burned." He began to gather her skirts in his hands, inching them up bit by bit. "Come, I ken a place ta go," she said, tapping his chest to get his attention.

"I know where I want to go," he said as he massaged her bottom.

"Ben," she hissed.

He heaved a great sigh when he finally raised his head. "Lead the way, wife." Then he swatted her bottom so hard it stung.

"Ye may regret that," she tossed over her shoulder.

"I doubt it," he joked in response.

His hand engulfed hers as she led the way into the forest. A slow mist began to fall.

Elspeth raised a hand to catch a drop of water. "Rhiannon is sad." Maybe they should go back to the others.

"You are mine," he said softly. He took her face in his hands and kissed her gently. "Your coven sisters will have to accept me. To accept us."

She nodded briefly before she continued into the forest. They finally came to a clearing. This was one of her favorite places. No one knew of it, aside from her mother.

"I should have brought a blanket," Ben said quietly as he watched her.

Before their eyes, the vines on the forest floor mingled with the moss, making a soft mat upon which they could lie.

Ben raised one eyebrow at her. "I suppose we can thank Sorcha for the gift?"

Elspeth couldn't contain her grin. At least one friend wasn't angry at her. Elspeth looked up at the night sky. The clouds moved away, a waxing moon taking their place. The temperature went from frigid to comfortable.

"And Rhiannon?" Ben asked.

"Yes. It appears as though we have their blessin'."

"I need no blessing, lass, aside from yours," he growled as he pulled her into his arms.

She fit against him like she was made to be there. Ben turned her in his arms so that he could untie the laces of her dress. His lips pressed against her shoulder, tasting her skin as he slowly undressed her. She clutched her gown to her breasts when it would have fallen.

"You will hide from me?" he asked, instantly worried for her.

She let the dress fall and stood still and proud under the light of the moon, wearing nothing but her chemise. She tugged it over her own head and shed it, along with her drawers. Then she held out her hands to Ben.

"I hide nothin'," she said, smiling confidently. And she didn't. The dusky rose color of her nipples, the same color as her beautiful lips, taunted him. He quickly peeled off his own clothes and lowered her to the soft earthen mattress.

Ben allowed his gaze to drift over her unhurriedly. He wanted nothing more than to throw her legs over his shoulders and be inside her. But he tempered his lust; she was brand-new to this. She deserved the slow seduction that he wasn't sure he was capable of.

He bent his head and traced his tongue slowly around her nipple, which already stood, turgid and receptive, under the cool night air. Her hands threaded into his hair, her nails raking his scalp as he licked and suckled her nipple. With his free hand, he gently tormented her senses, drawing his fingertips over her skin slowly, until he reached her other nipple. She moved beneath him, gasping and arching into him.

"If you don't stop responding so readily, I'll be done before we get started," he mumbled.

"I'm no' supposed ta make noises?" she asked incredulously, raising her head to look at him.

He laughed against her belly, where he teased her skin before coming up to kiss her softly.

"You know I love the noises you make," he said quietly. "But I'm afraid I'll hurt you. I wanted to pleasure you before I am inside you."

She shook her head wildly. "That's no' what I want," she said, as she wrapped her legs around his waist. "I want ta share the pleasure with ye. Can we no' do it that way?"

"Yes, we can do it that way," he said, breathing deeply. He would spill himself long before he got to be inside her if she kept moving around him.

"Do ye want me ta do it?" she asked, breaking him from his thoughts.

Only Elspeth would ask a question like that. But that was exactly what he needed. He rolled them over, quickly. Elspeth gasped as their positions reversed. She lay on top of him, her soft breasts against his chest, her hair hanging over him. He reached to push it back.

"God, I love your hair," he groaned.

"Has a bit of a mind of its own," she said as she flipped her head, trying to move the locks from her eyes.

Her face shone in the shadows as the moonlight moved across her. "You're so beautiful," he said softly.

Ben moved his hips so that his length pressed against her center. Elspeth gasped above him, then slid down his body a bit farther.

"Ye may have ta tell me what ta do," she said.

"You're doing it, love."

Her heat and wetness slowly overtook him as she sank down on him slowly. It was a exquisite torture.

"You're killing me, lass." He groaned, raising one arm and covering his eyes with it. Perhaps if he didn't look at her face as she was above him, he would be able to last longer.

Elspeth didn't take all of him. She stopped when she met resistance. "I canna," she started, suddenly bewildered.

Ben reversed their positions again, using his hands to cup her face. "Forgive me for being a coward, love." Then he pressed himself home. She cried out, but Ben could not tell if it was from pain or pleasure. "Are you all right?"

"Aye, I'm fine," she said. "And ye?" she asked, as though they were in the parlor talking. Then she giggled.

"Witch," he reprimanded her, before he began to move inside her. He slowly entered and pulled out.

"More," she cried. "Please."

"That's my girl," Ben whispered as he set a rhythm and kept it. She was warm and wet and willing and... wed. To him.

Elspeth cried out when he tilted her hips, taking more of her. "Please," she gasped, reaching for that elusive climax.

Ben reached a hand between their bodies and

touched her center. "Ah!" she cried. If he didn't bring her over soon, he would go without her. But she finally clenched and fluttered around him, crying out his name, just before he spilled himself inside her.

Ben let some of his weight rest on her, his head on her shoulder. As their heartbeats slowed, a blanket of leaves covered their bodies. He smiled against her shoulder. This witch was his.

# Twenty-nine

As they returned through the woods, Elspeth could hear the sounds of her friends and neighbors still celebrating. Ben squeezed her fingers and whispered, "Can we send them all away now?"

She stopped walking and gazed up into his warm hazel eyes, twinkling in the moonlight. "Ye're an abysmal host, Ben Westfield."

He lowered his head and gently kissed her. "They're abysmal guests," he complained. "They shouldn't be standing around in our home the night of our wedding. They should come offer their felicitations in the morning." Then he pulled her to him, and Elspeth sighed, feeling his hardness pressed against her belly. His desire to have her again was very obvious. "On second thought," he growled, "they shouldn't come see us for days."

She giggled. "Or maybe weeks?"

"Months might be best," he decided before kissing her again.

When he raised his head, Elspeth tugged at his hand. "Come along; they're probably wonderin' where we are." Or most of them. Sorcha and Rhiannon had a fairly good idea.

They stepped into the clearing that led to her cottage, and Elspeth stopped in her tracks. Caitrin stood just a few feet away in the darkness, her arms folded across her chest.

"Cait!" She rushed toward her friend. "I am so glad ye're here."

With a pained smile, Caitrin hugged Elspeth to her. "I saw it as soon as I sent MacQuarrie ta check on ye. It was so foolish of me. If I'd just waited a minute longer, ye wouldna be in this situation."

Elspeth pulled away from her friend. "Cait, be happy for me. I like my situation just fine. Please be nice ta Ben for me. I want it more than anythin'."

Caitrin managed a tight nod. "I understand congratulations are in order, Westfield," she bit out. There wasn't an ounce of warmth in her voice, but for Caitrin it was a huge step.

"Thank you, Miss Macleod. I'm sure it means the world to my wife that you've come." His hand touched Elspeth's back, and warmth spread throughout her. "Would you care to join us inside?"

Caitrin shook her head. "I really shouldna let anyone see me. I'm supposed ta be recuperatin'. I doona want ta have ta answer any questions about my miraculous recovery."

Ben trailed his hand up Elspeth's back, to squeeze her shoulder. "I'll leave you for a minute, then. My wife thinks I'm a terrible host. I'll go practice my manners."

Elspeth's heart swelled at his generosity. She

looked back at him and smiled her gratitude. "I'll be along shortly."

When he disappeared into the cottage, Caitrin let go a huge sigh. "Blast him for bein' gracious."

Elspeth couldn't help but laugh. "He's no' as bad as ye think, Cait. He's quite wonderful, really."

Caitrin walked farther into the darkness and kicked a pebble from her path, which skittered across the grass. "I suppose I'm selfish, El. I just dinna want the *Còig* ta fall apart. I hope it's all worth it."

Elspeth shook her head, following her friend. "Cait, who said the *Còig* would fall apart? So I've married Benjamin. He knows who we are. He knows what I am. He doesna mind it, except when fireballs are thrown at his head or he's held captive by vines."

Caitrin stopped walking, and in the moonlight El could see her friend's incredulous stare. "Are ye daft, Elspeth Cam—" She took a deep breath. "Ye canna believe he'll let ye stay here. He's Sassenach. *He's* no' goin' ta stay here. And ye think he'll let his bride stay without him? He'll take ye ta London, and we'll never see ye again. And that'll be it."

Elspeth didn't believe that for a moment. "I am goin' ta London, Cait, but only ta search out my father. Ben says there's a man there who can help me. Ye canna possibly ken what this means ta me."

"And then ye'll return?" Cait snorted in disbelief. "Somehow I doona think that will happen. He wants ta keep ye from us, El. I doona ken why ye canna see it."

"Ye're wrong," Elspeth whispered, though part of her wondered at that. He hadn't mentioned them returning to Edinburgh. But he hadn't mentioned them staying in London either. What were his plans?

"I suppose we'll see, then, won't we?"

∽

Ben couldn't hide his grin from Alec. His friend crossed the floor and removed a small vine of ivy that had somehow gotten wrapped around one of the buttons on his jacket. "Did you not think I'd notice your absence?"

Ben ran a hand through his hair. "I thought you might be gentleman enough not to mention it."

Alec laughed. "You know me better than that, my friend."

Had the situation been reversed, Ben wouldn't miss the opportunity to rib Alec. He clapped his hand on MacQuarrie's back. "Do you have any suggestions on how to get rid of all these people? I'm anxious to have my wife all alone."

Alec glanced around the room at the other well-wishers. "So you haven't lost interest in her, then?" he asked, avoiding Ben's eyes.

He shook his head. "I don't see that ever happening, MacQuarrie. You can rest at ease. She's the one."

"Take care of her, Westfield. She deserves better than her lot so far." Then, without waiting for a response, Alec stepped away from him and spoke loudly to the room. "Tomorrow morning you're all welcome to join me at my home for a wedding breakfast in honor of his lordship's union."

A smattering of applause and a chorus of hurrahs broke out. Alec started toward the cottage door, herding the others out as he went. He threw a glance over his shoulder as the last of the neighbors left, smiling. "You owe me, Westfield."

Ben saluted his friend, just as Elspeth returned to the cottage. Alec dropped a kiss to her cheek. "Congratulations again, Lady Elspeth."

"Thank ye, Mr. MacQuarrie."

As Alec left, Elspeth turned her questioning gaze to Ben. "Everyone streamed out of here as if the place were on fire. I thought ye were goin' ta work on yer hostin' skills, my lord."

Ben stepped across the room and drew her back into his embrace. "I'd much rather host only you, my lady-wife."

A pretty blush stained her cheeks as she rested her hands on his chest. "Did ye ask them all ta leave?"

"Alec," he explained. "Apparently the only way to get hoards of Scots from your home is to promise them another party. I don't know how he'll get rid of them tomorrow."

Elspeth giggled and he scooped her up in his arms. "Benjamin, what are ye doin'?"

"Taking my wife to bed. We have a long day ahead of us tomorrow."

She stared at him quizzically, which wasn't exactly the look he'd wanted. "What's tomorrow?"

"After Alec's impromptu wedding breakfast, we'll start for London."

❧

Elspeth pushed against his hard chest. "Put me down." His hold tightened instead, and her temper began to rise. "Ben, I said put me down," she said more forcefully.

"What's wrong, Ellie?" he asked, allowing her to slide down his body until she was back on her feet.

"We canna start for London tomorrow."

He blinked at her, his hazel eyes shrouded in confusion. "Why not?"

The man seemed so intelligent most of the time. Why had he picked now to play a dolt? "Have ye not heard a word I said, Ben?"

"I hear every word you say. I like the sound of your voice."

So now he was going to try to be charming? Well, Elspeth wasn't going to let him distract her. "I want ta go ta London. I want... no, I *need* ta find my father, livin' or dead, one way or the other. But I canna leave tomorrow."

Ben frowned at her. So he had listened to her; he just didn't remember what she'd said. Well, that seemed like something a wife should know. "Benjamin Westfield, I told ye this very mornin' that I wouldna leave until ye were healed. Everythin' I need is here—"

"About that," he interrupted, and his frown darkened. "There's no need to wait, Elspeth; you won't be healing me."

If he'd sprouted wings or burst into flame she wouldn't have been more surprised. "I willna be healin' ye?"

He shook his head. "And I'd like to get a start on our journey ahead. I'm certain my mother will love you. I'm anxious for you to meet her. And..."

Elspeth stopped listening and she stumbled backward. He didn't have any faith in her. He didn't think she could do it.

A numbness washed over her and she blinked back her tears.

"Ellie," she heard him say, but she shook her head.

She hadn't thought anything through. She'd been so caught up in her feelings for him, she hadn't asked the right questions or heard the right answers. And now she was married to a man who didn't believe in her.

Ben's arm wrapped around her and kept her from falling. His concerned expression pulled at her heart, and she couldn't look in his eyes for fear that she couldn't contain her tears. "Let me go, Ben."

"You don't look well, sweetheart." He directed her to the settee. "Here, sit." Then he sat beside her, clutching her hands in his. "Are you still feeling weak?"

She shook her head, still not meeting his eyes. "I think maybe ye should go ta London without me." Her words surprised her as much as they seemed to surprise him if his gasp was any indication.

"I beg your pardon?"

Elspeth stared at their entwined hands. "Ye can talk ta yer major for me. Ye doona need me." The last bit was especially hard to get out; the truth that he *didn't* need her stung in her throat.

"Elspeth Westfield," he growled near her ear. "I'm not going anywhere without you. Now, tell me what's wrong."

"People here trust me, Ben. They need me."

"Well, they can all hang. You're *my* wife."

She slowly lifted her gaze to meet his. "I was a healer long before today."

A muscle twitched in his jaw and his eyes hardened. "Not anymore, Ellie."

The wind whooshed out of her lungs. Before she could find the words to properly thrash him, he continued.

"I almost lost you today. Do you know what that did to me? Finding you slumped over Caitrin Macleod? And you were so cold, like a lake frozen solid. I could barely make out your heartbeat it was so slow. So no more healing. A doctor could have tended to Miss Macleod, and doing so wouldn't drain his life force."

She gaped at him. He cared about her, even if he had no faith in her abilities. Still, it was disheartening. "I'll have ye ken today was an anomaly. I've been helpin' people for years, Ben. From time ta time I get a little weak, but with Cait... well, we're so close, and—"

"Sorcha explained all of that to me, lass. I won't put you in danger, and neither will anyone else."

And that was why he didn't want her to heal him. It wasn't even the same thing at all. Stubborn man. He should have asked questions before making decisions that affected them both. "Ye told me from the beginnin', Ben, that being a Lycan meant everythin' ta ye. This mornin' when I told ye I knew how ta heal ye, I've never seen yer face light up so. And now ye're willin' ta go through life like a human, turn yer back on who and what ye really are?"

His brow furrowed and he looked at least a decade older than his twenty-six years. "I feel enough like my old self when I'm with you, Ellie. I don't need anything else."

"Ye told me ye needed ta be able ta change with the moon. Ye left yer home and yer family ta seek me out."

He rubbed his hands across his face and rose from his spot. "You're close to Caitrin, Elspeth, and that closeness nearly took you from me today." He stood over her glowering, his hazel eyes dangerously dark. "What we have, you and I, goes beyond closeness. We are connected in a way I don't even understand, a way I didn't even know was possible. So, no, you're not going to heal me. Do you think I would risk losing you, just so I can change to wolf once a month and howl at the moon with my brothers?"

As infuriating as he was, she didn't think anyone had ever cared so much about her. Elspeth reached her hand up and caressed his cheek. "Ben," she said softly.

He closed his eyes and kissed her palm. "I won't let you do it, Ellie."

She heaved a sigh. "It's no' the same sort of thing, Ben. I told ye this mornin' I have my mother's potions and spells. I ken how she fixed him, and if ye'd stop bein' so stubborn and listen ta me, ye'd ken I willna be in any danger."

His eyes narrowed at her. "The extent of your healing will be potions and spells. You will not waste your own energy on me?"

"Silly man. I plan ta spend some of my energy on ye, but not in *that* way." She felt the heat creep up her face as he tipped her chin toward his and chuckled.

He briefly touched his lips to hers before he picked her up and carried her to the bedroom. "You can spend as much of *that* kind of energy on me as you like," he assured her before he tossed her into the middle of the bed and shrugged out of his shirt.

# Thirty

BEN STRETCHED TO HIS FULL HEIGHT IN THE SMALL BED, groaning as his head bumped the headboard and his heels hung off the end of the mattress. He lifted his head and looked around. If he spent any more time in Elspeth's bed, he would have to purchase one made for a fully grown Lycan. Even a normal man would have been uncomfortable in her bed, which was just wide enough for her to sleep comfortably, alone.

He smiled slowly to himself as he remembered adjusting her body during the night to pull her as close to him as he could. He had drawn her into the saddle of his hips, but then her beautiful round bottom taunted him. He had pressed her front to his, but then her nipples teased his chest. Finally he had roused her gently, pulled her atop him, and slid inside her. Then she'd fallen asleep in that position after they'd both found their pleasure, her cheek above his heart, her hair a fiery tangle around them both.

He would love to sleep with her in that position every night for the rest of his life. But they would have to do so in a bigger bed. He added it to his mental to-do list. Right behind *install shutters*.

Her room was awash with offensive sunlight, the kind that forces one to rise even if one doesn't want to. Ben rolled to his side and clutched the edge of the bed to keep from falling off. He pulled the sheet over his hips before he crooked his elbow and rested his head in his overturned palm.

"Ellie," he called. A clatter of pots and pans met his greeting. He groaned. "Ellie!" he called more loudly. The pots and pans ceased their clatter.

But it was Sorcha who stuck her head through the bedroom door. "Ye bellowed, my lord?" the young witch began drolly, then quickly drew her head back when she saw his state of undress. Her gasp was all it took to get him moving.

"Didn't anyone ever tell you witches how *rude* it is to interrupt newlyweds?" Ben called as he swung his legs over the side of the bed and slid into his pants. He tugged his shirt over his head with enough force to rip a seam. "Ugh," he grunted. Between grass stains and tears, his valet would have Ben's head when he saw the state of his employer's wardrobe.

"Did anyone ever tell *ye* how *rude* it is ta call a woman inta a room when ye're undressed?" the little witch shot back.

"I was calling for my wife," Ben said. His voice lowered to a mumble. "Who I'd hoped would be very happy to see my state of undress." And his state of readiness. "Why are you in my kitchen, Sorcha. And where is Ellie?" He pulled on a stocking and stuck his head through the door.

"Doona come out of there unless ye're properly dressed." She pointed a spoon at him in warning.

"Depends on your definition of 'proper,'" Ben grunted as he adjusted the second stocking and padded into the room. He poured warm water for tea. Sorcha stood alone in the kitchen, pots cooking on every warming surface, spoons spinning at random, victims of their witchy powers. He shook his head. "And the word 'proper' should be used very loosely where you all are concerned."

Sorcha pulled his cup from his hand and added something to it. "Elspeth said ye're ta drink nothin' but the blueberry." She handed it back to him. "Careful, it's hot."

Ben nodded absently. "Thank you. Where's Elspeth?"

The witch avoided his gaze. "The blueberry bush is ruled by the moon. As are ye." She shrugged. "Or at least ye should be."

"Sorcha?" he said firmly. "Where is Elspeth?"

The littlest witch hung her head. "They should've sent someone else," she grumbled. Then her eyes met his before skittering away. "She's gone on an errand."

"What kind of errand?"

"The healin' kind?" Was that a question?

"Where?" he barked as he strode back to the bedroom to put on his boots.

"She's gone ta deliver the bairn for Mrs. Kincaid."

"She delivers babies?" Ben was pretty sure that unmarried women were not normally allowed in the birthing room.

"Not really," the girl hedged.

"Sorcha, you *will tell me now*," he growled.

"She only goes if there's healin' needed." She wrung her hands.

"You mean healing like she did with Caitrin?" He shook Sorcha's shoulders. "Don't you?"

She simply nodded.

He had told Elspeth that she was not to heal anyone else. She was not to put herself in danger. It wasn't even possible that she had forgotten from the night before.

He forced Sorcha to tell him where to find her, then he took off at a run toward the Kincaids' small cottage.

As he neared, he slowed and listened intently to the sounds coming from inside. He clearly heard Elspeth's voice, clear and resonant as she encouraged the woman birthing the babe. He heard the frantic pacing of a heavy-footed man, whom he assumed was the father, in the front room of the house.

Ben rapped briefly on the door. It swung open and a man's face met him. He was a bit younger than Ben, and obviously the expectant father, if the way he chewed his fingernails was any indication.

Ben suddenly was at a loss for words. He'd come fully prepared to wrest Elspeth from the clutches of people who would suck the life from her inert body, taking all the healing she had to offer and leaving nothing. Nothing for him.

"My wife is here," he started.

The man stepped back and opened the door widely.

"She's a godsend, she is."

Yes, she was.

"Seamus Kincaid," the man said, offering his hand in greeting.

"Ben Westfield. How are things going?" he asked, although he knew he probably had better information than poor Seamus, since he could hear every word, mumble, and moan from inside the room.

"I doona ken," Kincaid said quietly. "They willna let me in there."

"I hear it's not a place we would want to be."

"Oh, no!" the man gasped. "I want ta be right there, holdin' her hand. This is my fault, ye see."

Ben clapped a hand to Seamus' shoulder. He opened his mouth to speak, and then he heard a whimper. "Ellie?" he asked as he turned toward the birthing room.

Elspeth had never attended such a frightening delivery. The woman had been laboring for hours. If the bairn wasn't delivered soon, there would be nothing Elspeth could do. She couldn't heal the dead. She could only heal the living.

The midwife instructed Mrs. Kincaid, telling her when to push and when to rest. She'd known for some time what powers Elspeth had. She'd used them in her presence on enough occasions. The first time had been an accident. But the woman had just chuckled and said, "Well, that's quite the thing," as though El had just shown her a new pair of earbobs.

The mothers never knew of her powers; they were usually too far gone by the time she intervened to notice what she did. And she'd never asked for any credit. Healing was a gift, and she was meant to share it. To do anything less would go against her very nature.

She heard the door when it opened a crack. "Elspeth," Ben called. "Are you all right?"

Elspeth got up and walked to the door, opening it only enough that he could see her face. "What are ye doin' here, Ben?"

"I had to come and find my wife," he said quietly. "You shouldn't be here."

She nodded to the man over his shoulder. "Tell him that when he loses them both," she whispered. "Because I willna do it."

He'd actually thought to keep her from her life's work? He'd thought to keep her from healing? He would be more likely to get her to stop breathing at his command.

"Ellie," he started.

"Ben, ye willna change my mind."

A muscle in his jaw clenched.

The woman in the bed behind her moaned, and Elspeth closed the door quickly despite his quick protest. She knew the door was a flimsy barrier between the two of them. But it offered some privacy for a moment.

The midwife worked to turn the baby within the mother, as only she knew how to do. With a grunt of satisfaction, she washed her hands quickly in a bowl of water and clapped them together.

"Now we can deliver this babe," she said, her eyes aglow. They wouldn't need Elspeth after all. Within moments, the mother held the bundled baby against her chest, a contented but exhausted smile upon her face.

Elspeth opened the door wide and invited the harried father inside, then quietly took Ben's hand in her own and pulled him out the door.

They walked briefly in silence as he tightened his jaw beside her.

"Ye do a poor imitation of a happy man, Ben," she finally said.

"What were you thinking back there, Elspeth?"

"I was thinkin' that someone needed me." Surely he understood.

"*I* need you." He took her hand and pulled it to his chest, covering it with his own.

"Aye, tell that ta the good people of Edinburgh," she laughed as she pointed toward her own cottage, where three people already stood outside, waiting for her help.

❦

Ben worked beside her for the rest of the day, refusing to leave her side. If he left her, she would probably take it into her head that she needed to heal someone. He couldn't allow that.

She passed out bottles of herbal medicine for coughs, made poultices for wounds, and even gave a child a teaspoon of sugar to help stop her hiccoughs. Everyone received a smile and a treatment for what ailed them.

As the sun finally sank in the sky, she turned to her husband, blew a lock of hair from her eyes, and grinned. "Now it's yer turn."

"My turn?" Ben asked, placing a sarcastic hand upon his chest. "You mean to say that I get some attention from the great healer?" He slid an arm around her waist and pulled her close to him.

"Aye, ye get me all ta yerself." She pulled a large washtub from the corner of the room and placed it

before the fire. Then she began to methodically fill
it with warm water, boiled on the stove. Ben took
over the task, unable to watch her work when she had
shadows beneath her eyes.

"Let's worry about me tomorrow, love," he said softly
as he pulled her down onto his lap. She immediately
curled into him, soft and yielding as she kissed his neck.

"But I want ye naked now," she said, her voice a
little huskier than before, and she began to tug his shirt
from his trousers. He lifted his arms and let her pull it
over his head.

"You want me naked?" he joked. "All you had to
do was say so." His fingers tangled with hers as she
reached for the buttons of his trousers. He left that to
her tender care and started on her clothes.

"What are ye doin'?" she asked as she pressed her
lips to the space beneath his ear.

"Undressing you. What else?"

"But I'm no' in need of a medicinal bath," she
teased, standing up. Her dress fell from her body and
landed in a heap upon the floor. She stood still
and proud before him, nearly naked. He groaned and
reached for her. She slipped from his grasp.

"Inta the tub with ye," she said, pointing her finger
toward the washtub. Ben shrugged out of his clothes
and stepped into the water, sighing softly as the
warmth surrounded him. She stood outside his grasp.
He reached for her.

"No, no," she teased as she dropped dried flower
petals into the water.

Ben sniffed. "You want me to smell like a flower?"
He sniffed again. "Like a gardenia, no less?" Though

he would smell like roses if it made her smile like she smiled at that moment.

"Gardenia is ruled by the moon," she said quietly as she picked up a cloth and began to gently sponge the water onto him.

"Like blueberries?" he asked, laying his head back, happy to simply enjoy her loving ministrations.

"Stronger than the blueberry." She twitched her nose. "The fragrance calls ta the moon. So it canna hurt ye ta wear it."

"Can't *you* wear the fragrance and I'll just keep you with me? I promise not to leave your side."

"I think ye made that quite obvious today," she scolded him gently. He growled at her as her hand brushed over his nipple.

She sat up to pick up a bottle of gardenia oil and poured a few drops into the bath. The oil shimmered on the surface of the water. But nothing shimmered brighter than her smile.

Elspeth sat back to pick up the cloth again, and his eyes trailed down her body. Her chemise was transparent when wet. Her nipples stood hard against the sheer fabric, the triangle between her thighs beckoning to him.

"How long am I expected to endure this torture?" he growled.

"About an hour." She put her hands on her hips. Her breasts shifted. "'Torture' is a mighty strong word for a perfumed bath," she scolded.

"I can't stand an hour." He reached for her hand and pulled it into the water. Her fingers fluttered briefly before they closed around his length. "And even less time if you do that," he snarled.

"Ye're the one who pulled my hand inta the water," she reminded him saucily as her fingertips continued to play across his flesh.

Ben groaned, and with just one arm around her waist, he lifted her from beside the tub and drew her into it.

"Ben!" she squealed as water rolled over the edges of the tub.

"If I have to stay in the bath for an hour, I'll have you with me." He turned her away from him so that her back rested against his chest. Then he cupped her breast in his hand, rolling the nipple with his thumb.

"We both canna fit in this tub," she gasped.

"I think I'll fit just fine," he whispered, the sound no more than a quick brush across her cheek as his hand slid between her thighs and parted her flesh.

"Aye, we both ken ye fit there." Her gasp broke when his fingers rubbed her folds, parting her silky flesh, finding her warm and willing.

"I want to be inside you," he breathed before drawing her earlobe between his teeth.

Ben's hands adjusted her body so that she opened above him. He parted her folds and pressed himself insistently against her center. She settled over him like a warm silken glove. He groaned as she sighed, her head falling back against his shoulder.

Ben lifted her legs over the rim of the tub, parting them so that he could rest his hand in her curls.

"This isna the best position, I'd wager," she said. But then she inhaled deeply when he firmly rubbed around her center.

"It's a perfect position," he groaned. As he began to

stroke her, she arched her hips to meet him, moving along his length in time with his fingers.

Her tiny movements pushed him in farther and farther as his fingers moved faster and faster.

"Watch me," he whispered against her ear.

"No," she gasped, pushing her head into his forearm.

"Watch, or I'll stop." His fingers stilled until she lifted her head and looked down at his hand.

That was all it took to make her erupt around him, the sight of him toying with her, just as he'd known it would. He quickly followed.

# Thirty-one

"ELLIE," BEN BEGAN AS SHE PLACED A BOWL OF hardboiled eggs in front of him. "I never thought to have my wife cook for me. I'm fairly plump in the pockets. Can't I hire someone for you?"

Hire someone to cook for her? Elspeth couldn't help but laugh. Then she slid into a seat across from her husband at the small table. "Eat the eggs, Ben; they're for rejuvenation."

"Rejuvenation," he grumbled. "What I really need is a new bed. *That* would rejuvenate me." Then he rubbed the back of his neck.

Which, of course, she knew. He *did* talk in his sleep. He also had a point. Her bed was rather small, especially for a man his size. "Well, I believe ye'll be happy with what Sorcha has planned for ye then."

"Oh?" he asked warily before plopping one egg into his mouth. After swallowing, he leaned forward. "I don't know that I liked the way you said that."

Elspeth smiled at him. "I think ye'll be pleasantly surprised, my lord."

"Meaning you're not going to tell me." He frowned as he eyed another egg. "How many of these do I have to eat?"

She laughed again. "My, ye're rather grumpy this mornin'. And ye have ta eat all of them, Benjamin. That's why I put them in front of ye."

Finally he smiled at her. "Simon will adore you."

"His Grace?" she asked in surprise. He so rarely spoke of his oldest brother, and then it was generally complaints.

"Hmm. You can take turns barking orders at me."

"Eat yer eggs," Elspeth said, rolling her eyes heavenward.

With a scowl he popped another egg into his mouth, and she slid from her seat to prepare him some more tea.

"I had no idea I married such a moody man, Ben. Ye seemed so sweet up 'til now," she teased.

In a flash he stood behind her, hands on her waist, grinning like a fool. "It's working, Ellie." He glowed like an exuberant child.

She glanced back at the table. "The eggs?"

He shrugged. "I don't know what exactly, but you're right. I *am* moody. I get moody, we all do, in the week leading up to the full moon."

That was good news. She turned in his arms and slid her hands up his chest. "Indeed? Does that mean I can look forward ta a difficult husband one week a month for the rest of my life?"

Ben pulled her flush against him. "We also become more carnal."

"*More* carnal?" she asked, twirling a lock of his hair around her finger. "How will I ever survive?"

Ben nuzzled her shoulder and neck, nipping her lightly. His teeth grazed her sensitive skin, sending frissons of desire straight to her core. Her knees almost buckled, so she wrapped her arms around his waist to keep from falling.

His fingers tugged at the bodice of her gown, then they stilled. "Damn!" Ben grumbled, lifting his head.

"What?" she asked breathlessly, wanting his lips back on her skin.

"A coach just stopped." He rested his forehead against hers, like a man defeated. "Ellie, I'm feeling much more like myself. Can't we leave? A fortnight in a carriage with only you would do wonders for me. No one stopping by unannounced. No one else vying for your attention. Every night a new inn with a decent-sized bed."

Elspeth leaned forward and pressed a kiss to his lips. "Ben," she whispered, "ye should finish yer eggs."

"Rejuvenation, I know," he muttered.

She kissed him again. "My moody wolf." Then she righted her gown as a knock came from the door. She crossed the room, smoothing her skirts one last time before she opened the door.

From the threshold, Alec MacQuarrie winked at her then kissed her cheek. "My lady, you're looking well."

She opened the door wide. "Thank ye, Mr. MacQuarrie. Would ye like ta come in?"

He nodded and stepped into the room, his eyes focused on Ben. "Truly, in all the years I've known you, Westfield, I never thought to see you actually living in a cottage on the outskirts of Edinburgh."

"Me neither," Ben growled. "What do you want, Alec?"

Elspeth ignored her irritable husband and grinned at their guest. "I was just makin' tea, Mr. MacQuarrie. Would ye care for some?"

The man smiled back. "That would be nice, lass."

She started back toward the stove. As she walked past the table, Ben reached an arm out and pulled her onto his lap. She gasped in surprise. "Benjamin!"

He played with a lock of her hair, his hazel eyes twinkling mischievously. "In London, I have staff who will make tea for you, Elspeth. And a cook and more maids than you can count. Then you can focus all of your attention on me."

She scrambled off his lap and planted both hands on her hips. "Do try ta behave. Ye have a guest."

Ben shot an irritated look at his friend. "A guest who should know better than to disturb a newly married man."

MacQuarrie laughed as he took a spot opposite Ben at the table. "Aye, a friend who didn't take it personally when you skipped his wedding celebration in your honor."

How could she have forgotten? Elspeth sucked in a breath. "Oh, Mr. MacQuarrie, I'm so sorry. That was my fault. I got called away." She bustled to the stove and poured two cups of blueberry tea.

"Called away?" MacQuarrie echoed.

"Aye, Greer Kincaid was havin' some difficulties." When she sat a cup in front of them, she noticed a series of looks from one man to the other, a silent communication of some sort. She should let them have their privacy. "Anyway, I'll leave the two of ye alone. Caitrin is expectin' me this mornin'."

"You're leaving?" Ben asked, and started to rise from his seat.

Elspeth smiled at him. "I willna be long, Ben."

～

He watched her, his mouth agape, as she wrapped her plaid around her shoulders and stepped out into the morning light. If she healed anyone along the way, he'd... well, he didn't know what he'd do. Though it seemed obvious he'd have to convince her to leave Scotland soon.

"When you missed my breakfast, I just assumed you overslept." Alec's voice interrupted his thoughts. "Or were still in bed, at the very least."

Ben scowled at him.

Alec gave him a mock toast with his cup. "Blueberry tea?"

"That's how Elspeth makes it."

"It seems to me that Elspeth is the one making all the decisions. Who knew you could be a trained lap dog so easily?"

"Go to hell, MacQuarrie," Ben growled.

His reaction only made his friend laugh. "Not that I'm passing judgment. If I could get Miss Macleod to accept me, I'd drink blueberry tea, and..." He sniffed the air. "You smell like a damned bouquet of flowers, Westfield."

That was the last straw. Ben leapt from his spot and pulled Alec out of his seat. "Go pester someone else. Go pester Miss Macleod, for God's sake." If he did, perhaps Elspeth would come home.

Alec pushed himself free. "Well, I see your temper's returned." Then he straightened his coat and moved across the room to the threadbare settee. "Relax, Ben, I'm on your side. I may be the only one in Edinburgh."

"What do you mean by that?"

Alec shrugged. "Everyone in town is worried you're going to rush her off to London and they'll never see her again."

"That *is* the plan." If only he could get his wife to go along with it.

"Well, it'll never work," Alec said softly.

"She's *my* wife. I can take her any bloody place I want." He dropped into a chair across from his friend.

Alec looked at him as though he'd taken the position of court jester. "Aye, she's *your* wife, but she's one of *them*. And they outnumber you, my friend—" And some of them threw fireballs when he wasn't looking. "—She's been taking care of them since she was a child. She's not like you and me. She hasn't lived a privileged life. This is all she knows."

Ben slumped forward in his seat. "But I want to give her all of that now. I want to give her the world."

"Might I make a suggestion, Westfield?"

Ben shrugged.

"Persephone and the pomegranate seeds."

"I beg your pardon?"

Alec grinned. "You know, Hades and Persephone, the compromise with Demeter. The seasons."

Greek mythology? He had always hated the stuff. "I'm afraid Will is the scholar. Just say whatever it is in plain English, Alec."

"Do you not know the story?"

"Mythology is not a particular interest of mine."

Alec laughed. "Well, then, take a lesson. Persephone was a lovely girl, the daughter of Demeter, the goddess of agriculture. Everyone who saw Persephone fell in love with her. She was beautiful, angelic. Even Hades, from his kingdom, fell for the girl. And he decided to have her for his own.

"One day when Persephone was collecting flowers, Hades appeared in his chariot. He scooped the lass up and drove her into a chasm leading to the underworld.

"Demeter was heartbroken and refused to let anything grow on earth, until finally Zeus had to intervene. He demanded Hades return Persephone to her mother so that the world wouldn't wither away and die.

"Hades grudgingly agreed, but before he let Persephone go, he gave her a pomegranate for nourishment. Now, the lass knew better than to eat food from the underworld, but she was so hungry she ate six seeds from the fruit to tide her over. Her doing so gave Hades a claim on her, as strong as Demeter's.

"So Zeus, in his infinite wisdom, made them agree to a compromise. Persephone would stay with Hades one month for each seed she ate. Half of the year she is with her husband, and the other half she's with her mother.

"When Persephone is with Hades, Demeter is sad and the plants begin to die, until nothing is left alive. To you and me this is autumn and winter. And when she returns to her mother, spring and summer reign once again on earth."

Ben heaved a sigh. "So in your little scenario, I'm Hades, the devil himself. Not terribly complimentary, MacQuarrie."

Alec shook his head. "It figures you'd find some way to take offense."

"So are you suggesting I make Elspeth eat pomegranate seeds? If so, I'll have her eat twelve and not just a measly six," he replied with a smirk.

"And you take offense to my Hades reference?" Alec sat forward in his seat. "It's not the seeds, you dolt. Elspeth is your wife, but she's part of them. All of you care for her, and none of you want to lose her. Split the time, Westfield. I know you're anxious to have your family meet the lass, and that's understandable. But do you truly see her being happy in London?"

She wasn't like the English girls he was used to, that was true. That was one of the things he loved about her.

"Don't rip her from her home," Alec continued. "Live at least part of the year here."

Ben glanced around the tiny cottage. He couldn't live part of the year here. The few days it had been were difficult enough. "This place is not conducive for a man my size."

Alec roared with laughter. "Do you take everything so literal, Benjamin? You don't have to live in *this* cottage. Buy a house, or build one. William has that estate in Dumfriesshire, but I think Elspeth would prefer to stay in Edinburgh, even if it's just a few months a year. I know everyone else would like that."

"Miss Macleod, for instance?" Ben asked, as everything suddenly started to make sense.

"Aye," Alec replied, unrepentantly. "But the others as well. Just think about it, Ben."

# Thirty-two

ELSPETH COULD HAVE KISSED ALEC MACQUARRIE FOR dragging Ben from the cottage, though she wasn't quite sure what they were up to. But now her surprise for her husband could actually *be* a surprise. She stared at the new bed, which took up nearly the entire room. Fashioned out of willow branches, the four-poster bed looked like something fresh out of a fairy tale.

She couldn't wait for Ben to return. She went about the kitchen, putting the finishing touches on dinner. Meat pies, with blueberry cobbler for dessert. She scoffed as she remembered the way he had offered to hire a cook for her. And a maid. She'd never had a servant before and didn't know if she could accept one or not. It would certainly be a change.

Elspeth tugged the tablecloth one last time to remove the wrinkles and smiled as she felt Ben's arm snake around her waist.

His warm breath teased the side of her face as he leaned toward her and said, "I don't know what smells better, my wife or dinner." He spun her slowly in his arms.

She would probably never tire of looking at him. His dark hair hung past his collar, and a wayward lock teased his forehead, as it usually did. She reached up to smooth it into place, and it immediately sprung back.

"Speaking of smells," he started. "All the men I've encountered today have mentioned the fact that I smell like a flower."

"Jealous, are they?" She giggled.

"I don't think 'jealous' is the appropriate word. 'Flummoxed' is more like it."

"They dinna ken about yer feminine side?" she joked.

He growled in her ear and tugged her closer "I don't have a feminine side."

She inhaled deeply. "Ye do now."

He chuckled and swatted her behind as she moved away from him.

"Do ye want ta eat, or do ye want the surprise I have for ye?"

"You have a surprise for me?" His gaze shot toward her as he shrugged out of his jacket. "What kind of surprise?"

"Actually, the surprise isna from me. It's from Sorcha, ta be truthful." His shoulders fell dramatically. "Oh, stop," she scolded him, reaching to take his arm. She tugged it briefly. "C'mon."

"The surprise is in the bedroom?" he asked as he raised one eyebrow. "If not for the witch involved, I might be excited."

"That witch did somethin' very nice for ye, so ye'd better be thankin' her in the mornin'."

"I can hardly wait," he said with a pout, dragging

his feet as he walked toward her, all the enthusiasm gone from his step.

She opened the bedroom door and stepped back, unable to hide her grin as his eyes grew wide with shock. "Where did that come from?" he gasped as he took in the sight of the beautiful new bed.

"Do ye listen to a thing I say, Ben?" she asked, her hands lifting to rest on her hips. "I told ye, Sorcha made it."

"I thought the little witch could only manipulate the plants," he murmured as he walked near the bed and ran his hand lovingly across the willow branches. They'd been bent and manipulated to make a beautiful heart-shaped headboard.

"She does. How else could she get the willow limbs ta behave this way?" Truly, it looked as though she'd told the willow where to put the branches and how to bend them for the proper effect. "Sit," she encouraged him.

He sat down gingerly on the edge of the mattress.

"It's made of stronger stuff than that, Ben," she said. Elspeth sat down beside him and bounced up and down. "And it's as long as ye are tall."

"I don't know what to say," he mumbled. "It's a wonderful gift. I didn't think any of the witches liked me enough to make anything for me."

She still wasn't sure of it. "They'll come ta love ye with time." Maybe.

"I'll thank her as soon as I see her." His eyes traveled lazily down her body.

"Oh, no," she said, scooting across the bed to get away from him. "I've meat pies and blueberry cobbler waitin'."

Nearly effortlessly, he hooked her around the waist

and had her beneath him within seconds. "You're going to turn me into a blueberry."

"I'm tryin' ta turn ye inta a wolf. No' a blueberry," she giggled as he nuzzled her neck, the stubble on his cheeks abrading her skin. She sniffled loudly. "Ye do smell a bit like a flower."

He rested his forehead against hers in a pose of submission. But then he chuckled. "I'll take another bath in flower essence as long as it means I get to pull you in with me."

"Ye're incorrigible."

"Hmm," he agreed, lightly kissing her lips. "One of my better qualities."

"Ben, dinner's gettin' cold."

⤸

After devouring his meat pie, Ben looked at the blueberry cobbler in front of him. Even as tired of blueberries as he was, it smelled wonderful.

Across the table, Elspeth kept her eyes on him, making certain he ate every berry on his plate. She was more vigilant than his old governess, a whole lot prettier, too. "I promise to eat every bite, Ellie." He brought a forkful to his mouth.

She momentarily glanced down at her plate. "Where did ye go with Alec MacQuarrie this afternoon?"

"I might have a surprise of my own," he said, before shoveling in more cobbler.

Her green eyes widened. "A surprise?"

One he would be happy to give her when the time was right. The thoughtful gift from Sorcha went a long way toward a peace offering. Now he was even more convinced that he'd done the right thing when he'd bought the large plot of land outside of town earlier in the day. "But I'm not ready to tell you about it yet."

He still had a few things to work out. Still, it seemed almost preordained when he and Alec *happened* upon architect John Burton on Queen Street later that afternoon. If he didn't know better, he would think his old friend had somehow set up the chance encounter. The meeting turned into lunch, which turned into Mr. Burton promising Ben a set of designs for a large Gothic Revival mansion in the Scottish baronial style. That is, *if* Ben decided to build.

He could almost envision Elspeth in their new home now, standing on a veranda and looking up at the moon. They would be happy there for at least half the year.

"Well, in that case, once ye finish dinner, I'll need ta get ye in bed—"

"I'm done," he said, pushing away from the table.

He'd never tire of her innocent blushes. "*Havers*, Ben! I have an ointment I need ta apply ta ye."

He made no attempt to hide his lascivious grin. "An ointment, you say?"

She nodded.

"And you're going to apply it to my skin?"

Elspeth picked up the dishes from the dinner table and started toward the kitchen. "It's made of aloe and ginger and geranium—"

"More flowers?" he asked with a frown.

She dropped the dishes by the stove and turned to face him. "I canna help it that the healin' properties I need are found in flowers, Ben. The aloe plant is ruled by the moon, and its healin' uses are well known. The ginger is ta increase energy. Also ruled by the moon, the geranium will increase yer confidence."

"My confidence?"

She stepped toward him. "Ye *are* a Lycan, Ben. That hasna changed. Ye need ta believe in yerself, in yer ability ta transform. The willow in the bed should help with that as well. Willow contains the strongest natural properties for shape-shifting."

So Sorcha's gift hadn't really been to help him get a better night's sleep. No matter, he'd still make the best use out of the bed. "So this ointment," he began, tracing her lip with a finger. "Will you apply it for me? Or will you leave me to my own devices?"

Elspeth kissed his finger and wrapped her arms around his middle. "It would be best if ye had a healer rub it inta yer skin."

"What luck," he replied with a wink. "I happen to know a healer."

"Do ye, indeed?" she giggled.

"Hmm. The prettiest girl in all of Scotland." He scooped her up in his arms and started for their new willow bed.

"Ben!" She swatted at his chest. "The ointment."

"We'll get to it later," he growled.

# Thirty-three

ARM IN ARM WITH SORCHA, ELSPETH WALKED THROUGH
the Ferguson orangery. The wonderful scents of
tropical plants and flowering bushes were delightful.
"So do ye think the bed worked?" Sorcha asked.

Elspeth had to look away, knowing her blush
would give her away. "Aye, the bed worked just fine."
It had worked even better than she'd planned, in fact.
With all the extra space, Ben had done things to her
that she'd never imagined were possible.

Sorcha stopped in front of a bush and lovingly ran
her fingers over a bud. Instantly it doubled in size then
opened to reveal a breathtaking white orchid.

"Will ye stop tryin' ta show off?" Rhiannon said
from behind them.

Elspeth couldn't help but laugh as Sorcha puffed
herself up. "What are ye doin' here already?"

Rhiannon shrugged. "Cait said this was when we
were ta meet."

They were meeting? Elspeth hadn't gotten a
summons. "Do ye ken why?" she wondered aloud.
Caitrin had been fairly surly when they'd lunched the

day before, and she had no desire to hear another long list of complaints about her husband.

"She's been so irritable lately, I dinna ask."

Elspeth couldn't blame her. "Rhi, since ye're here, I wanted ta ask ye a favor for tomorrow night."

"The full moon?" Rhiannon questioned, one eyebrow rose in question.

"Aye. Can ye make it a clear night? I'd like ta keep the clouds from interferin'."

Rhiannon grasped her hand. "Ye doona even have to ask, El. I already had it planned. Yer wolf willna have any problems with the weather."

She couldn't quite believe it. They'd all been so opposed to Ben not that long ago. "Have ye had a change in heart about my husband, then?"

"He seems ta make ye happy."

More than she could have ever imagined, his moodiness notwithstanding. "Aye, he does."

"And he was so nice ta me yesterday," Sorcha said with a smile. "And he's so handsome. I'm wonderin' if I can find a Lycan of my own. Dinna ye say he has brothers?"

Before Elspeth could even reply to that, Caitrin called from the door. "There ye are. I should have known Sorcha would be holdin' court in here." She walked farther into the orangery with Blaire following in her wake and turned to Sorcha. "And, no, ye canna have a Lycan of yer very own."

Sorcha's bottom lip poked out.

"Why did ye call us together, Cait?" Elspeth asked, crossing her arms across beneath her breasts. She was a bit unsure of how to respond, since Caitrin hadn't even bothered to call her for the meeting. Had she thought El wouldn't come?

"I had a vision." Cait's gaze rose sharply to meet Elspeth's.

Elspeth raised a hand and forced a sarcastic gasp. "About me? No!" She lowered her arms and moved to walk past them all. "I doona want ta hear it."

Caitrin's hand clutched her arm in a furious grip as she walked by. "Ye have ta hear it. Ye doona have a choice."

"I doona want ta hear ye speak poorly of Ben," Elspeth hissed as she shook Cait loose from her arm. "Ye may no' like it, but he's my husband."

"And ye'd put him before yer own safety, because ye want ta help him. We'll no' let ye do that." Elspeth's eyes searched through the faces of the girls present, surprised to see that none of them, not a single one, would meet her gaze.

"All of ye plan ta interfere? That's the way of it?"

"I wouldna call it interferin'…" Sorcha kicked a clump of dirt in her path.

"We need ta ken what ta expect on the night of the full moon," Caitrin said bluntly.

"I doona ken what ta expect myself!" Elspeth cried. "I have never attempted ta heal a broken Lycan!"

"I can get a clearer vision of it if ye'll let me look inta yer future."

"I'll no' participate," Elspeth said. "Ye can plan my future without me." She stomped past them and toward the door.

Caitrin's voice stopped her. "I did see somethin'."

Elspeth stopped, her hand on the doorknob. She didn't turn to look back at them. "What did ye see?"

Elspeth's heart nearly broke when she heard Caitrin's voice crack. "I saw him hurt ye."

Elspeth didn't turn back. She stepped through the door and closed it behind her. Only when it was firmly shut did she allow herself to rest heavily against the surface and drop her face into her hands.

Ben paced back and forth in front of Elspeth's little cottage. He'd started inside the house but had quickly become overwhelmed by the diminutive size of the dwelling. He felt as though the walls were closing in around him. He'd never felt such a huge desire to be outdoors.

Whatever Elspeth had been doing, it was working. He'd never felt his Lycan side quite as strongly as he did at that moment. He'd worked all day to tamp it down, but he had to admit he loved the feeling. He'd thought he'd lost it forever. He thought that side of himself was gone, but it wasn't.

Elspeth had found it for him. She'd healed him with her silly flower baths, ointments, and blueberries. And she'd healed him with her heart.

He had no doubt that she was his Lycan mate. In his mind's eye he saw himself with her under the light of the full moon. The shadows would part and the moonlight would shine upon her light skin. There he would strip her bare in front of him and take her as his mate. He would pierce her flesh with his teeth and make her his.

Ben grew more and more aroused as his mind wandered. It was physically painful to think about taking Elspeth under the light of the full moon. Twenty-four more hours and he would be one with her; he would press into her body and she would lovingly accept him just as he was.

He imagined her opening her body to him, wrapping her legs around his waist.

The sound of a carriage drew him from his lustful thoughts. He groaned as MacQuarrie's coach rumbled to a stop in the drive. MacQuarrie was the last person he wanted to see. The driver hopped down and opened the door. Ben pressed the heel of his hand against his erection, mentally willing himself to calm down. He buttoned his coat and adjusted the folds to hide the tent of his trousers.

Elspeth's red head popped out of the coach. He would have to thank his old friend for the loan of his carriage. He hated the thought of her walking home when nightfall was approaching.

Then MacQuarrie stepped out behind her. What was she doing alone with Alec?

Elspeth smiled softly and crossed to him, rising on tiptoe to touch her lips to his.

"Where have you been?" he asked. Even he could hear the tone of his voice and knew it was too abrasive, but he couldn't seem to help himself. "With MacQuarrie?"

"No." She smiled, sliding an arm around his waist to turn toward Alec. "Mr. MacQuarrie stopped and offered me a ride home when I left Sorcha's. Thank ye," she said softly to him.

Ben tipped her chin up with a crooked finger. Her beautiful green eyes were rimmed with red, and her nose was abraded, maybe from blowing it. "What happened to you?" he barked. His gaze immediately rose to Alec. "What did you do to her?"

Elspeth's clutch on his arm grew tighter when it appeared he would have charged Alec. "I'll tell ye inside." She turned toward the house. "Thank ye again, Mr. MacQuarrie."

"Any time, Lady Elspeth." The man had the nerve to wink at her. A low growl burned in Ben's throat. With a question in his gaze, Alec asked, "See you tomorrow, Ben?"

Ben ignored him and ushered Elspeth through the door. She disentangled herself from his grasp.

"Why have you been crying?" he growled.

"Oh, it's nothin'," she said and absently waved her hand. It was definitely not *nothing* to him. Anger washed over him and was nearly as potent as his lust. The two emotions warred to determine which would ride the surface of his mind. He raked his hand through his hair.

He crossed the room to her and pulled her into his arms. "It's not *nothing* if it makes you cry." She relaxed against him, which helped to ease his anger a bit, but not the lust that crowded his mind.

His hands moved to her bodice and began to quickly untie her laces.

"Now, Ben?" she laughed. "I'm barely in the door!"

"You're in far enough," he growled.

The red around the corners of his vision should have warned him that he was too far gone. It should have told him that he wasn't himself. It should have told him that he was out of control. But he was too far gone to pay it any heed.

He met a stubborn knot in the laces that held her dress closed and lowered his teeth to it. He bit cleanly through the material with one bite.

"Oh, Ben!" Elspeth cried. "Doona ruin my dress!" Her fingers rose to finish the job he'd started. He batted them away before he simply tore the gown in two. The sound of rendered material hung in the air.

Ben stopped and closed his eyes tightly.

"Are ye all right, Ben?" Her soft hand touched his face. He turned his head and nipped her palm. He closed his eyes tightly.

"I'm all right," he said slowly. Was he?

Ben cupped her face and pressed his lips to hers. He took her mouth with much more force than he'd ever taken another. But she merely met his tongue without complaint. Inside, the beast in him rejoiced.

He drew her bottom lip between his teeth and nipped it.

"Ow!" she cried, raising a hand to her mouth.

"I'm sorry," he immediately confessed, a twinge of guilt making him wince. "I didn't mean to hurt you."

"Slow down a bit, will ye?" she smiled. "I think I need ta catch up."

Slow down? He would sooner chop off a limb. If he didn't have her soon, he would explode. Her dress lay in a heap at her feet while she stood before him in her chemise and drawers. He removed them quickly and efficiently before he lifted her in his arms and walked to the bedroom.

He tossed her into the middle of the bed and climbed atop her. With a quick flip of his thumb, he released himself from his trousers and pressed against her.

"Ben?" She stopped him.

Did she say something? He'd ask her to repeat it later. He was very close to completion. He was close to taking her. He was close to being inside her. He growled as he bent his head and pulled her nipple into his mouth.

"Easy, Ben!" she gasped. "That's a bit rough."

He eased his grasp on her and took her hips in his palms, tipping them so he could slide his full length into her at once.

"Ouch!" she cried from beneath him. She wiggled her body until she slid from beneath him, where she could rest against the headboard, her legs drawn up to her chest, clutching them tightly.

"I want you," he growled as he reached for her.

"Oh, ye remember I'm in the room now, do ye?" she spit at him before she scooted to the edge of the bed and stood up. Light suffused the room. "Look at me," she commanded, her biting tone pulling him from his single-minded objective.

He ran his gaze from her disheveled fiery hair to her breasts, which wore red marks from his rough kisses. He clearly saw the outline of his hands on her hips. Thank God she didn't have bruises.

"What have I done?" he asked as he stood up and raked a frantic hand through his hair.

"It's all right, Ben," she said, her finger trailing down his forearm. "I want ye ta make love ta me. Ye just need ta slow down a bit."

"It's too close to the moon," he snapped. "I can't be in control this close to the moon."

"Ye can, Ben," she encouraged him.

He'd come close to bruising her beautiful flesh, and she still wanted him.

He wasn't nearly good enough for her. Ben buttoned his trousers and turned from her. His voice quavered as he said, "I have to go."

"No!" She walked toward him. He backed up until he tripped over the settee. He crashed to the floor in a disoriented lump. She approached. He couldn't let her touch him. He wasn't deserving.

He scrambled to his feet and rushed toward the door. "Ben," she said. "Doona go."

"I have to," he said as he opened the door and ran out into the night. He ran until he could run no longer, until the air burned his lungs. Until his muscles pleaded for him to cease. Yet he couldn't get far enough away from her. If he could do one thing, he could protect Elspeth from what might hurt her. And today that danger was him.

# Thirty-four

ELSPETH STARED AT HER TATTERED DRESS AND underclothes lying on the floor. What had come over him? She'd never seen him behave in such a way. *We also become more carnal.* Ben's words from days ago echoed in her ears. How could a man such as him become *more* carnal? She hadn't quite believed him until now.

But he was right. He'd not frightened her, but it was almost as though he couldn't hear her words, as though he wasn't in control of himself. She wasn't sure what to make of it, as the memory of the encounter flashed again in her mind. She didn't even recognize this Ben. He reminded her of a wild animal…

Which, of course, he was.

Elspeth's gaze shot to the door he'd flown through. Ben had looked so devastated when he escaped her. That look of pain was just as disconcerting as her own panic. Perhaps if she'd had some notice, been prepared for what he wanted—no, what he *needed*—things would have ended differently.

Her husband had needed something from her, and she hadn't been able to give it to him. Guilt mixed with fear and encompassed her, Caitrin's warning still fresh in her mind. Ben would hurt her, she'd said, but she hadn't mentioned that Elspeth would hurt him in return.

She had to find him, make sure he was all right. With a frown she retrieved a serviceable dress from her armoire and threw it over her head. Why did he have to run off like that? Why couldn't he explain to her what had happened, what he needed from her?

She wrapped the Campbell plaid tightly around her and ran out of the cottage just as the sun was setting and casting a deep crimson across the horizon. "Ben!" she called, not certain at all which direction he'd gone. How would she ever find him?

Elspeth wandered deep into the woods, calling for him until she couldn't yell any longer. Her throat hurt, and she collapsed beside a boulder, exhausted, with tears streaming down her face.

Where was he? Couldn't he hear her? The man had better hearing than anyone else on earth. Then a horrible thought entered her mind. What if he could hear her, but he still wouldn't come? Her heart constricted and ached.

"Ben!" she called again, straining her voice beyond reason. She looked at her wrist. He could ignore her voice, but could he ignore her touch? With a shaking finger she touched her mark, hoping he could feel how much she loved him.

Ben winced when he felt her stroke across him. Why couldn't she just leave him alone? Couldn't she tell he wasn't fit company? He wasn't fit for her?

He pressed deeper into the darkened forest. He would walk all the way to Glasgow if he had to. How far would he have to get from her before he wouldn't feel her touch anymore?

One after another of Simon's old lectures echoed in his mind. *It's too dangerous to be with a woman from the time the moon is nearly full until it starts to wane. You're reckless, Benjamin. You take too many chances. One of these days you'll go too far.*

He'd been reckless, all right, with the one person he was supposed to protect, the one person he'd never wanted to hurt in any way.

He spied a shaft of moonlight in a clearing and looked up into the sky. Hating who he was and what he'd become, he cursed the moon, now nearly full, for the power it had over him.

Ben growled fiercely, until the growl became a scream. He screamed at the moonlit sky until his voice ceased to work. Then he turned and walked back slowly toward Edinburgh. He had no idea how far he'd traveled. But it was far enough that it might take him days to return if he simply walked.

He couldn't go back to her, even though he still felt her tender strokes against his skin. Even though he still felt her touch as she obviously touched her mark, calling to him. He wasn't good for her. It wasn't safe.

The anger and lust no longer raged in his blood. It no longer called to him, and he felt much as he did before he'd sought out Elspeth. He felt empty. He felt less than whole.

Instead of returning to her cottage, he went to the property outside Edinburgh that he'd just bought. There was an old crofter's cabin that seemed reasonably sound. He would go there and wait for the moon to pass him by. Then he'd go back to her and fulfill his obligation.

He passed the rest of the night and day in solitude. When the moon hung high in the sky, he went to a nearby clearing. There, he removed his clothes and stepped from the shadows into the moonlight. He lifted his arms to the sky and felt... nothing. He felt nothing at all. No madness. No shifting. Nothing.

He'd lost his ability to be a Lycan. Feeling nearly dead inside, he walked slowly toward the crofter's cottage, where he remained for six full days.

As the days passed, he hoped the pining for her would gradually decrease. Yet she still called to him, and he imagined her stroking slowly across her mark. It was time to go to her. When he crossed over to her land, he walked casually, knowing he was no longer the person he'd once been. And he just hoped she would accept him as he was.

He knocked softly on her door. Her tiny feet padded across the floor and the heavy wooden door swung inward. There she was. His wife. She held her arms out to him, and he could do nothing more than clutch her to him.

He was shocked that she went to him so easily, but she did. She melted against him and fit into him like she'd been made to be there. Perhaps she was.

She stepped back, took his hand in hers, and pulled him into the cottage as tears pooled in her eyes.

"I—" he started.

She placed a finger to his lips and whispered, "Shhhh..."

"I need to—" he began again. She stopped his words by standing on tiptoe and pressing her lips to his.

He gathered her tenderly in his arms and carried her to the willow bed, where he slowly removed her clothes. She smiled softly as he pulled her nightrail over her head and the wolf combs clattered to the floor.

He bent and picked them up, but she tossed them to a nearby table as though they were nothing. "My wolf," she sighed. "So lost." Her hand stroked the beard stubble on his face.

"Please, help me," he whispered softly, his eyes meeting hers.

"I promise." She kissed him tenderly and unbuttoned his shirt, pulling it from his shoulders. She moved to his trousers and asked quietly, "Did ye miss me?"

"Like a piece of myself was missing," he said as he kissed a slow trail across her bare shoulder.

When she'd fully undressed him, he laid her back on the bed and rose above her. "I didn't mean to hurt you." He proceeded to kiss her softly all over. He kissed her until the scent of her desire reached his nose, and then he settled between her thighs.

"I ken that ye werena yerself, Ben."

"Then who was I?" he asked, looking down into her green eyes.

Who was he? He was her love. He was her life. He was her mate. She had no doubt in her mind that he was the other half to her whole.

"Ye're my wolf," she said as she reached up and brushed the hair from his forehead.

"I'm not," he protested, shaking his head.

"Ye *are*," she repeated, catching his head in her hands. He kept his eyes tightly shut. "Ben," she prodded. "Look at me."

He opened his eyes, but didn't meet her gaze.

"I love ye," she admitted. His eyes immediately caught hers. The intensity in his gaze nearly scared her.

"How could you?" he asked quietly.

She shrugged and laughed. "I doona ken. I just do."

"I am not worthy of your love," he said quietly as his hardness prodded her flesh. She arched to meet him. As he slid into her he said, "But I need you so much."

"And I need ye, too," she gasped as he slowly stroked within her. "I couldna live without ye."

He gently carried her up and over the pinnacle of pleasure, slowly and methodically wringing all the pleasure from her body, then joining her. Finally he rolled to the side and pulled her close to him, clutching her closer than he ever had.

In the back of her mind, she briefly noted he'd never professed to love her back.

# Thirty-five

THE INTRUSIVE AND OBNOXIOUS SUN WOKE BEN THE next morning as it filtered through the bedroom window. He blinked and raised his head, searching for Elspeth with his arm. She was gone. But he heard the clatter of pots and pans in the kitchen again. He groaned and pounded the pillow with his fist.

"Sorcha, if that's you, prepare yourself to be offended," he called loudly. "In fact, I suggest you leave now to avoid the embarrassment."

The clatter ceased. He rose, wrapped the counterpane loosely around his hips, and walked toward the bedroom door on bare feet. Scratching his stubbly face, he wished for his valet. He reached to open the door, but before he could touch the handle it flung open on its own.

"Sorcha?" a familiar male voice asked. "How many women do you have, Benjamin?"

Ben cracked one eye and squinted at the man who stood in the doorway. His brother William looked fit and healthy. His clothes were pressed and his hair combed. "Mornin', Will," Ben muttered.

"You look like hell, Ben."

"Thanks" was the only response he could come up with before he closed the door and prepared to face the day. He sat back on the edge of the willow branch bed.

What the devil was Will doing here? He *was* here, wasn't he? Ben hadn't imagined it, had he? Ben stood up and crossed the floor again. He cracked the door open, peeking one eye through the hole.

No, he hadn't imagined it. Will was sitting at the table, drinking what must be blueberry tea and nibbling at toast, while Elspeth prepared something that smelled dangerously like porridge. Ben groaned; he hated porridge.

Breakfast was the furthest thing from his mind. He hurriedly dressed, wishing for a sharp razor and strop, but more concerned about what would have brought Will all the way from London. He opened the door and padded across the cottage in his now stockinged feet. He wasn't about to stand on ceremony with his brother.

Will glanced up from his tea, a wicked glint in his light blue eyes. "You growing a beard now?"

Before he could tear into his unwelcome sibling, Elspeth caught his eye at the stove. "It's so nice yer brother came for a visit?"

"'Nice' wasn't the word I was thinking," Ben replied as he bent to kiss her quickly before sliding into a seat across from his brother. "What are you doing here, Will?"

His brother drummed his fingers on the table. "Imagine my surprise when I called on you at Alec

MacQuarrie's and was redirected here. What a lovely wife you have."

Ben glowered at him. Will certainly hadn't answered his question. Why was he being evasive? "Yes, she is lovely. The prettiest girl in Scotland."

Elspeth placed a cup of tea in front of Ben, with a shy smile, and he captured her hand. "Sit, love."

"Ye seem ta have things ta discuss. I can leave ye awhile."

After the last week away from her, the idea was like a dagger to his heart. "Don't be silly. You've barely met my brother, and I don't believe he'll be staying long."

Will grinned at Elspeth. "Sadly, he's not even the rudest member of the family."

"Don't try to charm her," Ben said with a scowl. "You want something bad enough to come traipsing after me, so out with it, whatever it is."

"I do *not* traipse." Will frowned. "I do have a question for you, however, Benjamin."

"Indeed?"

His brother's hand stopped tapping out its rhythm, and his icy eyes pierced Ben with a dangerous stare. "Would you care to tell me why you've been writing to Prisca Hawthorne?"

Was *that* what this was about? Ben gaped at his brother, then he shook his head in disbelief. "Do you mean to tell me that you've come all the way from London—"

"Hampshire," Will growled.

Ben squeezed Elspeth's hand. It was that or punch his brother in the face. "Of course it's Hampshire. Prisca isn't in London this time of year, is she?"

"*Why* have you been writing her, Ben?" Will's voice dropped menacingly.

"You could have saved yourself a trip if you'd just asked *her*."

"I've come all this way because *she* begged me to find you and make sure you were all right, since you've not written a word to either her or mother for far too long."

Elspeth's eyes flashed to Ben's. He was sure she'd have questions by the time this conversation ended. He'd have to explain all of it to her later. When Will wasn't around. "I've been occupied, you may have noticed. You'll have to ask them to forgive me."

Will glanced at Elspeth. "Buying property and getting yourself married?"

"Property?" Elspeth echoed.

He was going to kill his brother. Was it possible for Will to keep his bloody mouth closed? Ben tilted his head to one side, looking at his wife. "That might be part of my surprise."

A knock sounded at the door, interrupting the conversation. Elspeth frowned at him but rose from her seat while Ben avoided his brother's questioning gaze.

A gasp sounded at the door, and Ben looked toward Elspeth. Sorcha Ferguson's eyes seared him as she stood on the threshold and looked in. "So ye've come back, have ye? Do ye have any idea—"

"Sorcha!" Elspeth hissed. "No' now. We have a guest."

The young witch's eyes grew wide when they landed on Will. "Oh, I see that." She didn't wait for an invitation, but stepped inside and went straight to the table. "Ye're one of the brothers?"

Will nodded, a look of confusion on his face.

"Will," Ben began, "this is Miss Sorcha Ferguson. Sorcha, this is my brother, Lord William."

With a charming smile, Will rose from his seat. "Ah, Miss Ferguson, I believe my brother mentioned you this morning. It is indeed a pleasure."

Sorcha sighed and Ben cringed. All he needed was the rest of the coven losing their hearts to Will. "Ellie, it appears I do need to have a conversation alone with my brother after all. Do you mind terribly?"

His wife shook her head, though a look of worry marred her brow. "Will ye be here when I get back?"

He pressed a kiss to her cheek. "I'm not going anywhere without you, love." Though she deserved much better than him, he wasn't about to let her go.

Elspeth's hands settled on his chest. "Good. I'm no' through with ye, Ben Westfield."

"Sorcha," Ben called, "Ellie needs your help with some *plant* thing."

"Some *plant* thing?" the dark-haired witch echoed. "Are ye tryin' ta get rid of me, my lord?"

He couldn't resist winking at the lass. "Pretty *and* smart, Sorcha."

"Come along," Elspeth said, draping her plaid around her shoulders and towing her friend toward the door. "I *do* need yer help with somethin'."

As soon as the women were gone, Ben noticed the look of dismay on his brother's face. "What have you gotten yourself into, Benjamin? I admit when mother and Prisca were worried about you, I thought this was a fool's errand. But now—"

"But now?" Ben asked, sinking onto the old settee.

"Are you honestly married to that girl?"

Ben felt anger roil inside him. He didn't like the arrogant tone of Will's voice. "Yes, she's wonderful," he snarled.

"She's lovely," Will agreed, taking a seat opposite him. "But, Ben, MacQuarrie says you bought property here. You're talking to John Burton about building a house?"

"Elspeth wants to stay here. It's all she knows." And with everything he'd done to her, giving her that happiness was the least he could do.

Will shook his head in disbelief. "I can't believe you're serious. At least the two of you would get a fresh start in London, where no one knows the circumstances of her birth."

He was going to kill Alec MacQuarrie at the first available opportunity. "Her father was a Lycan, Will. It's not Ellie's fault he abandoned her mother before she was born."

"A Lycan?" Will echoed. "Are you certain?"

"She has the mark."

Will seemed to think about that and rubbed his brow. "Who was he?"

Ben shrugged. "She's not sure. But we intend to find out."

"So, then, she knows about you? About us?"

More than Ben liked. She knew all about what Lycan men were capable of. Yet she *loved* him anyway. The idea warmed him from the inside out. "Yes, she knows everything."

"Well, you're more fortunate than Simon, then."

"Simon?"

Will took a sip of tea. "Blueberry?"

"Don't ask. What about Simon?"

"I left his wedding breakfast to seek you out."

Ben sat up quickly. Wedding breakfast? Simon? He didn't believe it. Not for a minute. "You're joking."

Will shrugged. "Heard the vows myself."

"Simon?" Ben repeated, dumbfounded. "Our brother who keeps respectable women at arm's length? Our brother who would never let a woman near him during a full moon? *That* Simon?"

Will chuckled. "He didn't plan it. He sort of got tangled up in one of Prissy's machinations."

"Not Prisca?" Ben couldn't think of two people less suited than his oldest brother and their pretty young neighbor.

Will scowled at him. "Lily Rutledge. Now, Benjamin, I am waiting for you to tell me the nature of your letters to Prisca."

Which he wouldn't get from Ben. He was not about to admit to keeping the girl appraised of Will's exploits. His brother would kill him on the spot. "You can bare your teeth at me all you want. I won't break her confidence. If she wants you to know, she'll tell you herself."

Will's frown darkened. "Does your wife know the nature of your relationship with Prisca?"

His brother was definitely reaching. "The only woman in my life is Elspeth."

"I have half a mind to tear your head off, you disloyal mutt."

He might welcome the punishment at the moment. "If you spent half of that energy talking to Prissy, you might be a whole lot happier, Will."

"Go to hell."

"You first, brother." Ben rose from his seat and started toward the stove. He looked in the abandoned pot. It *was* porridge. Yuck.

"So what is your plan, Ben?" Will called from his seat. "You just going to stay in Edinburgh and play house? Forget you have family and a life in England?"

He didn't have anything to return home to. "When I want your advice, William, I will ask you for it."

Will scoffed. "As well thought out as always, I see." He rose from his seat. "I'll be at Alec's if you decide your older and wiser brother may actually be of help."

Elspeth groaned and stuck her fingers in her ears as she walked down the lane beside Sorcha. She said loudly, "I'll no' hear another word about Lord William, Sorcha. No' one more word." Then she hummed a tune to block the rest of her friend's gushing.

Sorcha finally tugged violently on her arm. She removed her fingers from her ears and said, "Aye, Sorcha?"

"Nothin'," the youngest witch sighed. "I'll find out for myself." Her eyes lit with mischief.

Elspeth shook a finger at the girl. "Ye'll no' find out anythin' about that man. Ye're much too young for him." The girl just skipped along. "Keep it up and I'll tell yer papa that ye've set yer sights on him."

That finally got the young witch's attention. "Ye wouldna dare!" she gasped.

"Aye, I would."

"Marriage doesna set well with ye, Elspeth. It makes

ye grumpy," the girl muttered. "What did ye want with me this mornin'? I'm sure ye dinna need me for a walk in the woods."

Elspeth reached into her pocket and pulled out a folded piece of foolscap. Inside lay several small seeds. "I need ye ta make these grow for me. Right away."

Sorcha shook the seeds into her hand and brought them to her nose to smell them. "Hyssop?" she asked. When Elspeth just nodded, she continued. "What need do ye have for hyssop? Ye have nothin' ta be sorry for."

"It's no' for me, Sorcha. It's for someone else."

"It's pretty powerful," Sorcha hedged.

"I ken that it's powerful. That's why I need it."

"What does Ben have ta be sorry for?" Her gaze rose sharply. "He dinna hurt ye, did he?" She clutched Elspeth's arm, her nails digging into the skin.

Elspeth winced. "No, he dinna hurt me," she groaned. "I wish I could say the same for ye."

"Sorry," the girl mumbled.

"So can ye grow the flowers?"

"Aye, the seeds are alive. Did ye get these from yer mum's collection?"

She simply nodded. "How quickly can ye do it?"

"Today," Sorcha said, shrugging her shoulders. "Why the rush?"

"They're the flower of forgiveness. And I may need forgiveness for what I plan ta do."

"Elspeth Campbell, ye *will* tell me what ye're speakin' of. And stop the riddles."

Elspeth closed her eyes tightly and spit it all out in one breath. "I'm going ta London ta find my father. I'm leavin' Edinburgh."

The girl blew out a relieved breath. "Is that all? *Havers*, I thought ye were goin' ta kill someone or do somethin' despicable."

"Ye doona think leavin' the coven is despicable?"

"No. Because I ken ye'll be back."

But Elspeth wasn't so sure.

# Thirty-six

BEN HUFFED PAST ALEC MACQUARRIE'S HARRIED BUTLER and called up the stairs, "Will, where the devil are you?"

Alec's head popped out of the study doorway, one eyebrow arched. "For God's sake, Ben, have you suddenly lost all your manners? You don't walk into a gentleman's house and bellow."

The butler sniffed loudly from behind Ben as though to say, *Next time, remember that.*

"Alec, I don't have time for manners. Where's Will?"

"Your lovely wife came for him awhile ago." Alec shrugged. "She said something about blueberry pie."

"It's a wonder I don't bleed blueberry juice," Ben muttered as he dashed back toward the door.

He didn't even stop when Alec called, "Nice to see you, too, Ben. Do come again when you can stay longer. And have better manners!"

Over his shoulder, Ben made an obscene gesture in response. He heard Alec chuckle as he closed the door behind himself.

Ben jogged back to the cottage he shared with Elspeth. As he neared the house, he slowed and finally came to a stop outside the door, where he could listen to the voices of his wife and brother.

"I'm quite glad ye've come, William," Elspeth said softly. "I've been worried about him."

Of course she'd been worried. He'd nearly mauled her like the wild animal he was right before the moonful.

"Understandable," Will replied. "Ben has always been a bit odd."

*Odd?* What a nice way to speak of one's brother. He snorted.

"Elspeth, what are you doing with him? You could do so much better."

"Better?" she echoed.

"Hmm. Me, for example. I'd love to get you naked," Will said huskily.

Elspeth gasped as Ben flung the door open.

He had Will pushed up against the wall within seconds. "How dare you speak to my wife that way?" he growled.

Will smiled, a sparkle in his blue eyes. Elspeth giggled from behind him. She patted his shoulder. "He was but teasin' ye, Ben. He heard ye as ye came down the walk."

"I believe you forget that I have the same senses you do. And you shouldn't eavesdrop, little brother. It's ill-mannered."

First Alec and now Will. Ben was in no mood for a reprimand about his manners. He grunted and removed his arm from beneath Will's throat. He turned and kissed Elspeth quickly. "I missed you," he said as he tucked a loose curl behind her ear.

"I have good things in store for ye later," she said

quietly. "After ye tell me about the land ye purchased."
She raised one eyebrow and he nodded.

"I look forward to it."

Elspeth began to set the table and smiled at his
brother. "Will ye join us for dinner, Lord William?"

"I would love to, but I have an appointment in
town with a lovely young woman I met at the Thistle
and Thorn."

"An appointment?" Elspeth asked innocently as she
sat down beside Ben. "At the inn? But I thought ye
were stayin' with Mr. MacQuarrie."

"Love, I don't think you want to know the nature
of Will's *appointment*." She colored prettily as Ben
caressed her knee beneath the table.

"Oh," she replied quietly, realization dawning in
her eyes.

Will laughed. "Well, I can't stay around you two for
long anyway, or I'll get singed by the sparks." He bowed
slightly toward Elspeth then glanced toward Ben. "See
you tomorrow. We've some things to discuss."

Ben nodded, avoiding his gaze.

After finishing their cock-a-leekie soup, Elspeth cut
a slice of blueberry pie and placed it in front of Ben.
Dinner had been a rather muted affair, as her husband
seemed consumed in his own thoughts. "What's it
like havin' brothers?" she wondered aloud. All her life
she'd wanted siblings, and though Ben and William
had done nothing but bicker since Will had arrived,
there was a comfort in their exchanges.

"Irritating," he growled.

She reached out her hand to him. "Ye doona mean that."

He nodded. "I do, but I suppose it's nice, too. They do come in handy at times. Like when you're in the middle of a brawl in a rowdy pub." He chuckled at her expression and chucked her chin. "Don't worry, love. No more rowdy pubs for me."

"Tell me about the land ye purchased. What's yer intention with it?"

"I thought you might want to stay here." He looked everywhere but at her.

Had he really planned to stay in Edinburgh? "But what about London? Ye promised ye'd take me."

"Oh, I will. I want to take you to meet my mother, though she's not in London this time of year. She resides at her family's ancestral home, Hampton Meadows, in Surrey; but it's not far. I know she'll love you."

"But my father. The Society," she prompted.

"Oh, we'll see Major Forster and have him search the records for any clues to your father. But after all that you'll want to come back here. And I want nothing more than to make you happy, Ellie."

Though he hadn't spoken of his own happiness. "And what about what *ye* want? It's no' all about me, ye ken."

"I bought the land so that we could build a home and start a family. And my thought at the time was that it's fairly secluded, so I would have the privacy I'd need when the moon is full. But I'm no longer Lycan. So it's not a problem anymore."

"No longer Lycan?" She stood up swiftly. "What do ye mean no longer Lycan?"

"I mean I didn't change. So the moon means very little to me now." He tried to hide it, though there was pain in his eyes when they met hers. "But I have you, so it's all right."

"It most definitely is no' all right." She pushed the blueberry pie toward him. "Eat up, because I will find the Lycan in ye if it's the last thing I ever do."

"Maybe it's better this way. You won't have to worry about my hurting you again."

Elspeth's heart ached as he said the words; his weeklong isolation had left her worried and fractured while he was away. It hurt all the more knowing how he must have blamed himself. She knew the loss of his confidence wasn't good for him. "Benjamin, ye dinna mean ta hurt me, I ken that. And truly, if I'd known what ta expect, I doona think I'd have reacted the way I did. I'll be better prepared for next time."

"There won't be a next time, Ellie. I'd rather cut off my own arm than ever hurt you again."

She rose from her seat and brushed the hair from his brow. "Please doona say such things. Seeing ye miserable is more painful ta me than a few bruises."

He looked so forlorn, it nearly broke her heart.

"Will ye do anythin' I ask of ye?"

"You know I will."

She kissed his brow. "Eat yer pie, Ben."

He groaned, but picked up his fork.

❧

Ben nuzzled against Elspeth's neck. She slept so soundly, and her rhythmic breathing calmed him in a way he hadn't felt for days. There was something about the woman in his arms. She brought him such peace and harmony. All he'd given her in return was scaring the hell out of her and turning her life upside down.

If he had it to do over, he never would have tangled her life with his. She was kindness, compassion, and purity all rolled into one, and she deserved so much better than him. But the die was cast. He was her husband in every sense, and nothing anyone could do would change that.

So he'd have to make it up to her. If she wanted the moon, he'd find a way to catch it in a net and offer it to her. If she wanted jewels or silks, he'd keep her supplied in them for life. If she wanted to go to London… well, he supposed, they'd leave as soon as possible.

Elspeth rolled in her sleep and pressed a kiss to his chest. "I love ye, Ben," she whispered against his skin, and he felt the words deep in his soul.

He caressed her back and tangled his hands in her fiery hair. "Rest well, Ellie."

# *Thirty-seven*

ELSPETH GRINNED WHEN SORCHA ENTERED THE COTTAGE carrying a full-grown hyssop plant. "Sorry I dinna make it back yesterday, El. I got a bit caught up," her friend explained as she put the potted plant on the kitchen table.

Stepping forward, Elspeth ran her fingers over one of the pretty blue flowers. "Doona fash yerself, Sorcha. It's just fine."

The young witch glanced around the cottage. "Is Lord William no' here?"

Elspeth raised one brow. "Oh, I understand perfectly now, ye goose. Ye wanted to wait 'til ye thought his lordship was here ta bring me my hyssop."

Sorcha blushed. "He is rather handsome."

"Oh, doona start again."

Her friend giggled. "Ye're a mean witch, El. Ye have yer very own Lycan; why shouldn't I have one, too?"

"In the first place, I already told ye, Lord William is too old for ye. And secondly, from what Ben says, some English lass has hold of his heart." Though Elspeth wasn't so sure if that was true. Why would William make an *appointment* with some lass at the Thistle and Thorn if this Prisca Hawthorne woman held the strings to his heart? If Ben Westfield ever thought to do such a thing, she'd... well, what would she do? The answer hit her and she bit back a laugh. She'd turn him into a frog, like any other proper witch, of course.

"What are ye smilin' about?" Sorcha asked sourly. "I doona think it's amusin' at all."

Elspeth hugged the girl tightly. "Doona fret, dear. I'm sure Cait'll eventually tell ye who yer true love is."

Sorcha grinned. "Perhaps I should ask her specifically about Lord William."

"Aye." Elspeth rolled her eyes. "That'll go over real well. Ye ken how fond she is of Ben. I'd love ta hear ye ask her about Lord William. Just give me time ta get ta Aberdeen before ye question her, so the screaming willna hurt my ears."

At that moment, Ben walked out of the bedroom, a devilish smile across his lips. He'd obviously heard every word, and Elspeth turned away from him to hide her blush.

"Sorcha," Ben began playfully. "You're too sweet a girl to lose your heart to my scoundrel of a brother."

She didn't even have the good sense to be embarrassed that he'd caught their entire conversation. "Is there really a lass in England?" Sorcha asked, stepping closer to Ben.

He patted the top of her head. "Yes, and a wonderful lass she is, too. He broke her heart, and I won't let him do the same to you."

Sorcha furrowed her brow and twisted her lips in contemplation. "Is she very pretty?"

"*Havers!* Sorcha," Elspeth groaned, "the man is nearly twice yer age. It doesna matter if the lass is Helen of Troy or Helen of the trolls."

Her friend slumped into a seat at the table, touching one flower of the hyssop and causing it to turn brown and fall off the stem. Elspeth snatched the pot away from Sorcha and scowled. "Doona hurt my plant with yer dark mood."

Sorcha sighed. "Bring it back, I'll fix it."

Elspeth shook her head. "It's fine. Doona worry about it. And honestly, Sorch, ye just turned sixteen. There's no rush."

The girl shrugged and muttered something under her breath, though Elspeth couldn't quite make it out. Then she rose from her spot. "Well, then, I've got lots to keep me busy." She started for the door.

"Thanks," Elspeth called, "for the hyssop."

Sorcha waved her hand in acknowledgment then shut the door behind her.

Elspeth noticed Ben wore an amused look. "What is lady's mantle?" he asked.

She sucked in a breath. "Where did ye hear that?"

"Sorcha mumbled it on her way out."

Elspeth rubbed her face in frustration. "The little sneak!"

"What is it?" he asked again, but this time concern laced his voice.

"It's used in love potions. Ye'd better warn yer brother no' ta eat or drink anythin' in Sorcha's presence."

Ben threw back his head and roared with laughter.

She punched her hands to her hips. "I hardly think it's funny. It's a very powerful plant. And she could make it more potent than anyone else."

He dropped down to the settee and pulled Elspeth with him. She landed on his lap, and her mouth fell open in surprise. "Ben!"

"It's hard to imagine anyone wanting Will that badly."

"Well, he's yer brother. I imagine ye doona see him the way women do."

Ben's muscles tensed beneath her. "Oh, and how do you see him?" he growled.

Elspeth leaned forward and kissed his jaw. "As my brother-in-law."

He held her tighter and kissed her brow. "It's no matter anyway. Will can breathe easy, since we'll all be on our way soon."

"Ye mean ta London?"

He nodded. "Can you tie up your loose ends so we can leave in the morning?"

She'd already talked to Rhiannon about watching the cottage for her and helping those who needed her. The weather-channeling witch didn't have the same healing powers, but she could mix potions. Most people didn't need the sort of healing Elspeth was capable of, and Rhiannon could fill the void for a while.

"I think that can be arranged."

Alec MacQuarrie's persnickety butler pointed Ben toward the library. There were a couple of people Ben would miss when he left Scotland, but this particular servant wasn't one of them.

He sighed when his eyes landed on his old friend, who frowned with concentration and turned the pages of an old tome. "Looking for something in particular?"

Alec closed his book with a thud. "Ah, Ben, just doing a little light reading."

Light reading? The volume looked to be thicker than the betting book at White's. Ben couldn't read the spine or cover before his friend dropped it to the floor beside his chair.

"Care to join me?" Alec asked, sitting forward in his seat and gesturing to a matching overstuffed leather chair across from him.

Ben obliged him and raked a hand through his hair. Alec didn't seem quite right, but he'd worry about that later. He had more important things on his mind at the moment. "I was hoping to find my brother here."

Alec smiled. "He's still abed. Poor fellow raced from England without stopping, as though the fires of hell chased after him."

"How do you know this?"

"I'm housing not one but *two* of his drivers. They apparently traded off the whole way, switching with the horses. He didn't rest at even one inn along the way, always moving forward."

Good God! All because Will found out that Ben had been writing Prisca? He shook his head. "I do believe my brother is more complicated than I originally thought."

Alec laughed. "I could say the same about you, my friend."

"Complicated" didn't even begin to describe Ben's life at the moment. He shrugged. "I also came to say good-bye. I've decided to take Elspeth to London."

At that, Alec winced.

"We'll be back, MacQuarrie," Ben teased. "It's only

for a while. I intend to have my new home here, like we discussed. With the most modern conveniences, a jewel in the Westfield crown."

Alec's grimace deepened. "About that..." He scratched his head. "There's been a slight problem with your traveling coach, Ben. I was hoping to have it repaired before you needed it."

"What sort of problem?" he asked as a feeling of dread washed over him.

"Strangest thing, really. The day we had that awful storm, the day Miss Ferguson and I accompanied you to the vicarage..." Alec shifted uncomfortably in his seat. "When you married Elspeth."

Ben's dread increased. "Get on with it, already."

"Well, my groomsman said a bolt of lightning flashed across the sky and... well, it struck the top of your coach—"

Ben fell against the back of his chair. Rhiannon's storm. That little witch purposely ruined his coach! And ever since then she'd been as sweet as could be.

"—There's a gaping hole in the top from where it caught ablaze."

"Good God!" Ben muttered. "Why didn't you tell me before now?"

Alec scoffed. "Well, you took off for a week and no one could find you, and before that you'd been a little preoccupied with your wife. I just thought I'd have it taken care of for you. Sort of a wedding present."

"How am I to take Ellie to London now?"

"Will brought his own carriage. You could go back with him," Alec suggested.

Ben groaned. He'd envisioned spending a fortnight

with Elspeth inside his carriage. William had *never* entered those fantasies, and he'd rather not put him there. Maybe they could delay going until his carriage was travel-ready. Then he thought of the way her smile had lit up in the cottage when he told her they were leaving. She was already getting things in order for them to depart.

A fortnight with Will. He cringed at the thought, but he didn't really have a choice. "I suppose I'd better go wake the blackguard."

He left Alec to search out his brother's room. Dear God, he hated the idea of traveling with Will! Even Simon would be better. Simon wouldn't chat his ear off or try to charm Elspeth right from under his nose.

Ben tossed open Will's door and didn't even bother to knock. He supposed he shouldn't have been surprised to find a naked maid draped across his sleeping brother's form, but he did suck in a startled breath.

The sound woke the poor lass, who squealed and pulled the counterpane up to cover herself. Will blinked open his eyes, a lazy smile on his lips. "It is customary to knock, little brother."

Ben scowled at him. "I'll wait in the hallway." Then he stalked out and shut the door behind him. He could hear Will trying to soothe the lass while she dressed, promising her that his brother knew how to be discreet.

Finally the girl opened the door and scurried past Ben, her face the color of over-ripened strawberries. Inside the chamber, Will pulled his trousers up around his hips and grinned unrepentantly. "I suppose you need something, Benjamin."

He stepped inside the room and closed the door. "Have you no care for your reputation, Will?"

One dark eyebrow rose in question. "Since when do such things matter to you?"

He sighed. Will was right. Not that long ago he would have done the same sort of thing. "But one of Alec's maids?" He hated that he sounded like a prude.

Will chuckled as he pulled a fresh shirt over his head and began to tuck it into his trousers. "I'm certain my little brother didn't leave his quaint cottage to chastise me about my bed partners. What do you want, Benjamin?"

"I suppose you're heading back to London soon?"

"No reason to stay here." Will slipped into a shiny grey waistcoat.

"Ah, well, I was hoping you'd consider taking Elspeth and me with you."

Will's hand stilled on one of his buttons. "You want to travel with me?"

Not particularly, though he didn't have much of a choice. He shrugged. "You can get to know Ellie better."

Will's brow rose in amusement.

"Not that much better," Ben growled. "Keep your hands off her."

Will laughed again, shrugging into his jacket. "Didn't you come here in your own coach?"

Ben sighed. It would have been so much easier with Simon. A simple yes or no would have sufficed. "My coach had a bit of an accident."

"Oh?"

Then it hit Ben. He was going to have to tell his

brother everything. Well, almost. He still had no desire for Will or Simon or anyone else to know he was broken, but the general brushstrokes would have to work. "Elspeth's a witch, Will."

"Not a very complimentary thing to say about one's wife, Benjamin." Will reached into the armoire, retrieving a snowy white cravat.

His brother always made everything more difficult. "Not like that. I mean she's a *real* witch. Can you stop moving for a bloody minute and listen to me?"

Will dropped the cravat on the bed and faced Ben, surprise reflecting in his light eyes. "A *real* witch?"

"Yes, and her coven hasn't exactly welcomed me with open arms. I just found out that one of them sent a bolt of lightning straight through the roof of my coach."

"Sent a bolt of lightning?" Will echoed. "They have those sorts of powers?"

Actually, it was a relief to say the words aloud to someone else who wouldn't think he was mad. "And then some. I've been attacked by fireballs and plants intent on cutting off my circulation. Which reminds me, Elspeth wanted me to warn you not to eat or drink anything in Miss Ferguson's presence."

"Why not?"

"She thinks the girl is creating a love potion with you in mind."

Will smirked. "The chit doesn't have to go to all that trouble. She's quite a pretty little thing."

"You're old enough to be her father," Ben barked.

His brother's smile faded immediately. "How old is she?"

"Sixteen."

Will's smile returned. "I hardly think I was fathering children at twelve, Benjamin."

Ben resisted the urge to growl. "Just stay away from the girl. She's like a little sister to Ellie."

"Very well. So you need a ride to London?"

Ben nodded. "If you don't mind. We'd like to leave tomorrow."

"Before lightning can strike *my* coach?" Will joked.

"Go ahead and laugh. They're a formidable force."

# Thirty-eight

BEN ROLLED OVER IN THE BIG WILLOW BED AND REACHED for Elspeth as soon as the sun came up over the green hills of Edinburgh. He smiled to himself when his hand stroked over her hip. He loved waking up beside her in the morning. This was the first morning he'd actually been able to do so. She usually woke with the chickens, but he was much more used to Town hours.

Without opening her eyes, she rolled toward him and placed a hand over his heart. Fiery locks of hair covered her face, disheveled beautifully from sleep. He brushed them back with the tips of his fingers, lingering to draw his finger teasingly down her nose. She twitched it and smiled a sleepy smile.

She moved to stretch, rolling onto her back. "Time to get up?" she asked, her voice crackly from sleep.

"Not yet," he said as he began to unbutton her nightrail. He moved down her chest and placed a kiss on the skin he'd exposed. "We have time."

But then he lifted his head when he heard footsteps on the walk. Dainty footsteps. Feminine footsteps. Witchy footsteps. He groaned and laid his head on her belly. "Sorcha's here," he mumbled against her skin.

Elspeth giggled, causing the muscles of her stomach to ripple under his head. "Are ye hearin' things again?" she laughed.

"In three… two… one…" he whispered, counting down on his fingers. Then a gentle knock sounded on the door. Elspeth slipped from beneath him and buttoned her nightrail as she stood up.

"I'll never get used ta that hearin' ye have," she laughed as she went to the door.

"I'll never get used to the coven, love, so we're even."

"I heard that!" she called back.

"Of course you did," he replied, unable to keep the smile from his face.

He quickly washed and dressed while his wife talked with Sorcha in the kitchen. Elspeth came in when he was nearly dressed, looking so cute in her frilly white nightrail that he simply stood and looked at her. Her hair tumbled over her shoulders in disarray. He wondered what she'd look like in fifty years. Still just as beautiful, he'd wager.

"Will's here already?" he asked.

She nodded. "Why else would Sorcha be here? I doona ken what I'll do with the girl."

"I know what Will would do with her, so keep her far, far away from him, love." He kissed the top of her head as he walked by her and hefted her heavy chest of clothes with ease.

"There's another by the door," she said, pointing to a small bag full of bottles and pages with notes.

"Are you sure you need to take all this with you? Might not be much need for healing in London." What he really wanted to say was that people didn't readily seek out her kind of healing unless they couldn't afford a doctor. And he'd not have all the miscreants and vagrants knocking on his door to summon his wife.

"There's always need for healin', Ben." She simply smiled at him, so he loaded the bag along with the chest.

As they prepared to leave, Rhiannon and Blaire arrived. He chuckled under his breath when Blaire said, "Ye hurt her, Lord Benjamin, and I'll do the same ta ye." She glanced toward Will. "Or someone ye care about. Ye ken?"

"I wouldna laugh at her, Lord Benjamin. She has power like ye've never seen," Sorcha said as she walked by a plant in the front yard. She touched it and it immediately flowered. She plucked it, smiled softly, and held it out to Ben, who just shook his head. Would he ever grow used to women with powers?

"You do not have to worry about Elspeth. I would protect her with my life."

"But who will protect her from ye?" a voice called from the other side of the carriage. Then Caitrin stepped into view.

She took Elspeth's hands in her own and squeezed so hard that Elspeth winced.

Ben moved toward the two young witches, but Will's hand suddenly hit the center of his chest, stalling him. "Let them work this out," he said quietly. "I'd rather not see an example of their powers firsthand."

Ben just grumbled to himself as he finished helping his coachman load the bags onto the carriage.

"I canna see yer future, El, " Caitrin admitted.

Good. That suited Ben just fine. He liked having some surprises in life.

Caitrin continued quietly. "I think it's because ye're already separatin' yerself from us, with yer mind."

"But never with my heart," Elspeth said vehemently before she dropped Caitrin's hands. "I will see ye all very soon." Then she addressed each sister in her coven separately before stepping inside the coach.

It wasn't until he closed the door and pulled her into his lap that she finally broke. She turned to his shoulder and sobbed. When her tears subsided, he passed her his handkerchief and stroked her hair. It nearly broke his heart to see her so upset.

"We can stay here if you'd rather," he offered. Though in the back of his mind, he really liked the idea of having her to himself for a bit.

"No. I need ta find my father." She sniffed loudly. "I need ta understand why he left my mother." She sniffed again. "And me." Then she tucked herself into him again.

"We'll get the answers you seek. I'm sure of it." But he truly wasn't. And he was fearful that she wouldn't like the answers they *did* find.

"Where is yer brother?" she asked.

"He's riding alongside until we reach the first coaching inn. I wanted to be alone with you. I feel like we haven't had any time together."

"My coven," she started.

But he cut her off by tipping her chin up and kissing her softly. "They're not with us now. It's just you and me."

"Tell me why ye came lookin' for my mother, Ben," she said as she slid from his lap into the seat beside him. He instantly felt the loss.

He scrubbed a hand over his face and thought. Then he let out a sigh. "You know why. Because I was broken."

"Ye're no' broken," she said as she reached up to brush the hair from his forehead.

"I've lost a part of myself, Ellie. And I'd hoped your mother could help me find that part."

"I can help ye, Ben. I ken that I will be able ta do it."

"If you can't, I'll be all right without it. I have you."

"Ben Westfield! Doona ever say that! I couldna take the place of yer wolf. Nor would I try." She batted at his hands as he tried to pull her near.

Maybe a kiss would take her mind off his problems.

She narrowed her eyes at him. "Ye willna take my attention from this topic. No matter how sweet yer kisses."

He smiled. "You think my kisses are sweet?"

"Ye ken I do," she giggled as his questing fingers traced the line of her bodice. "Stop that."

"I can be even sweeter," he teased.

"Ben, yer brother is outside the carriage, and he has the same hearin' ye do!" she reminded him.

He pulled her atop him, despite her halfhearted protests. "I can be quiet," he whispered as he tugged her dress off her shoulder. Her breast popped free, and he immediately took her nipple in his mouth. Her head fell back. He loved how responsive she was. "Can you?" he asked, catching her gaze with his.

❦

Elspeth seriously doubted she could be quiet, not as quiet as she needed to be. If Will's hearing was anything like Ben's, he'd hear every gasp and sigh.

She drew her bottom lip between her teeth to keep from crying out as he uncovered her other breast and pressed them together so that all he had to do was turn his head back and forth, giving more and more pleasure with each turn of his head.

"Quiet, now," he laughed when she couldn't contain her gasp as his fingers slipped beneath her skirts and tiptoed up her leg to touch her heat.

"Ye beast," she whispered.

"Not so much anymore," he said, a sad look crossing his face.

"Aye, ye are," she affirmed as she let him move her to the seat beside him. He threw her skirts up to kiss her inner thigh and then pulled her drawers off and bent to kiss her center.

"You bring it out in me." He opened her with his fingertips and licked slowly across her center. She squirmed, hoping he would touch the place she needed most. Then he did. She couldn't contain her groan as her hands moved into his hair.

"Shhhh," he said, his breath blowing softly against her tender flesh. He pressed a finger to her lips to silence her. She drew it into her mouth and sucked, then nipped the pad of his finger. He groaned that time.

"Shhhh," she said with a light laugh.

"Witch," he remarked as he went back beneath her skirts.

"Aye, and ye're my beast." She threw her head

back as he licked her to new heights, then he finally pushed her over. But he caught her when she fell. Before she'd even come back down, he picked her up and opened her legs to straddle his lap. Then he lowered her slowly onto him.

She took him carefully, her gaze never leaving his as she settled around him. He gently helped her rise and fall, riding him until her body fluttered, and then he joined her in pleasure.

"We were no' very quiet," she whispered as she lay against his chest, her breasts bare and her skirts around her waist. It felt perfectly decadent to be so free and open with him.

"Yes, I know. My brother will be ready to do bodily harm to me by the time we get to the coaching inn."

"Why?" She didn't understand.

"'Cause I plan to take you again. At least once more. And I plan to make lots of noise," he laughed.

# Thirty-nine

THE COACH FINALLY STOPPED, AND BEN STEPPED FROM its confines, eager to stretch his legs a bit. Again, he thought to himself how coaches weren't made for men his size. He stepped out and asked the coachman, "Where is his lordship?" as he looked around for Will.

"He went ahead as soon as we left Edinburgh, my lord."

"Do you know where he was going?"

"Permission to speak frankly, my lord?"

"Of course," Ben said, waving his hand impatiently as he glanced at Elspeth to be sure she wasn't listening.

"He said he was going to find a whore." The man shrugged and smiled. "Not sure what put him in such a hurry."

As though Will needed an excuse.

Ben offered his arm to Elspeth and escorted her through the inn yard. "Where is yer brother?"

He shook his head. "I have no idea, apparently he rode on ahead."

Elspeth breathed a sigh of relief. "Thank heavens. I was so sure he would have heard us. I doona think I could ever look at him again."

"Ellie," he laughed. "You are my wife. I'm certain he has some idea of what happens between us." He pulled open the door to the taproom and directed her over the threshold.

As soon as Ben's eyes adjusted to the darkened room, he noticed his brother, relaxed and clearly sated, enjoying a pint in the far corner. With a rakish grin, Will lifted his mug in a mock toast.

"Found him," Ben muttered, though he wasn't sure if he was happy about that or not.

"Ah, Benjamin," Will called. "I've already acquired rooms for us. The beds are rather comfortable."

After more than a fortnight of travel, Elspeth had decided that even though her brother-in-law was an unrepentant rogue, she liked him quite a bit. William had a charming personality, though he seemed to irritate Ben to no end.

He knew about her healing powers, but not why Ben had sought her out. As London came into view, she stared across the coach at Lord William. Once they arrived in Town, she was sure she wouldn't see much of him. She had been wondering something about him ever since they met.

As Ben was sleeping, she knew this was her last chance to find out. "Will," she began quietly, "doona ye tire of yer debauched life?"

He winked at her. "My life is wonderful as it is."

"But Ben says there's a girl, a neighbor, who owns yer heart."

Will took a deep breath, his eyebrows knitting together. "Ben says more than he should."

"Who is she? And if ye care for her, why do ye…?" She waved her hand to encompass his entire person. After all, the man hadn't spent one night alone since their journey began. It had taken only one day for her to be glad he wasn't still in Scotland near Sorcha.

"Things with Miss Hawthorne will never come to fruition, no matter how badly I may want otherwise." His gaze flashed to Ben, she assumed to make certain his brother was truly asleep. "Since that's the case, there's no reason I should stop living my life, Elspeth."

"Why do ye say things willna come ta fruition?" He seemed so sad about the situation.

Will shrugged. "You haven't met her. Once she's made up her mind about something, there's no changing it. Prisca is the most stubborn woman I know."

She reached across the coach and squeezed his hand. "I am sorry."

"It wasn't meant to be." He pulled back the curtain and stared out at the ever-approaching skyline and let out a world-weary sigh. "So what is the plan, Elspeth? How do you and Ben plan to discover your father's identity?"

She leaned against her husband's shoulder. With him she always felt so safe. "Ben says we'll go see Major Forster, that there are records in yer Society that can be of help."

"It's a start. If you don't end up with your desired results, we'll think of something else."

*We.* How nice to be part of a family. Her coven sisters were one thing, but now that she was part of the Westfield family, she realized how much she'd been missing. "Thanks." Then she cleared her throat. "Yer mother... Ben seems ta think she'll like me, but I'm a bit nervous."

Will dragged his eyes from the window and smiled at her. "Ben's right. She will love you, but if I were you, I'd wait to inundate yourself with the Westfields. Mother will demand your time. Simon's wife is a bit of a mother hen, though I must admit I don't know her well. Find your father, then step into our fray."

"He's right, love," Ben mumbled from beside her, stretching his arms above his head and groaning as he woke from his nap. "Steer a clear path away from the Westfield women, or they'll drag you down like a hare caught in a trap."

She punched his shoulder. "I thought ye were asleep."

"I was for a bit," he said, then shot an uncomfortable glance toward Will. "I only heard you when you began to talk about Mother."

"That's because you're a mama's boy," Will said, his voice dripping with sarcasm.

"There's nothing wrong with a grown man loving his mother, is there, dear?" he asked playfully as he dropped one arm behind Elspeth. "You should try it sometime, Will."

"Aye, I heard it said once that you can learn a lot from a man by the way he treats his mother. If he treats her like a prized possession, he's capable of lovin' with all his heart," Elspeth said, watching Ben's face as she said the last. He turned from her with an uncomfortable look on his face, as though he was suddenly ready to change the subject.

"You two know how to turn a man's stomach, don't you," Will broke in. "All this talk of love. It's all fluff and nonsense."

"Ye ken that's no' true," Elspeth scolded as the coach came to a stop.

"Ah, home at last," Ben sighed. He opened the door and stepped out of the coach. And out of her conversation about love.

# Forty

BEN WAS QUITE HAPPY TO STAND OUTSIDE OF HIS townhome in Mayfair and direct the servants instead of being swept inside with Elspeth and the household staff after introductions were made. In truth, his presence wasn't needed. His staff was competent, and he would be much more of a hindrance than a help.

"If I didn't know you better, I would accuse you of avoiding your new bride and her discussion of love," Will said from behind him. Ben groaned and turned.

"Can't a man get five minutes to himself to think about things?" Ben bit out. "You're too bloody nosy for your own good."

Ben stepped into the entryway of their home and glanced left and right.

"Playing hide-and-go-seek, now, are we?"

"Go to hell," Ben snarled as he walked toward the study. He cringed when he heard the clop of Will's shoes as he followed him. "Now you've taken to stalking me?"

"I believe you've forgotten that I live here, too," Will reminded him. He turned and poured two tumblers of whisky and then handed one to Ben. "You've a perfectly lovely wife, Ben. Congratulations."

Ben harrumphed and downed his liquor in one swallow.

Will would not be set off his path, evidently. "She's easy on the eyes."

"She's bloody gorgeous," Ben grunted as he tried to occupy himself with rifling through his correspondence and ignoring his brother.

"She's smart." Will filled Ben's glass again. He tossed it back. The bite of liquor soothed the bile that rose up in his throat like fear.

"Brilliant." Ben nodded absently.

"And head over heels in love. With you."

Ben glanced up quickly. There was no teasing glint in Will's eyes. There was no sarcastic twist to his mouth. Just a stare that searched him, reaching all the way to his gut.

"And you, my brother, are a fool," Ben growled.

"I am a fool about a lot of things." Will blinked once, obviously thinking about something. "A goddamn bloody fool." There was no doubt in Ben's mind that he referred to Prisca. Will placed his glass so hard on the table that it made a knocking noise. "But *that* woman is in love with you."

"And what am I supposed to do?" Ben said as he stood up to pace.

"Why did you marry her if you don't love her back?" Will asked.

Ben shrugged. "It seemed like the right thing to do at the time." He knew he sounded like a complete idiot. He rubbed his eyes with the heels of his fists in frustration. "She didn't have anyone. Her grandfather had just died. And I wanted her."

"You still want her."

Ben's head shot up. "Of course I do. I'm simply not sure I'm capable of... loving her." His eyes rose to meet Will's. He saw no censure in his gaze, thank heavens. No judgment. "I really fouled things up in Brighton."

"Yes, you did."

Will's eyes narrowed, but Ben continued. "I didn't mean to hurt her."

"No one thinks you did. You mustn't blame yourself for being too much of a Lycan. There's no such thing. You simply chose to go to a whore too close to the full moon." He shrugged, as though he'd just solved the riddle to how the universe was created.

"I hurt her," Ben said quietly.

"It wasn't something she didn't recover from. You scraped up her back with your fingernails and got too rough with her. I'm sure she's had worse happen in her line of work. Simon settled a tidy sum on her, by the way, so she's quite happy with the way things turned out."

"I didn't mean her." Ben let his voice trail off and refused to look up at Will.

"Then who the bloody hell did you hurt?" The dawning of recognition passed over his face. "You hurt *Elspeth*?" Will gasped.

Ben nodded as he picked at a fingernail.

"What. Did. You. Do?" Will bit out, syllable by syllable.

"I got too rough with her," Ben said as he buried

his head in his hands. "If I allow myself to love her, it will mean nothing but trouble for her."

"Something tells me she's not going to settle for that. You'll work it out. The two of you, together. Talk to her. She'll understand and will probably welcome you with open arms, no matter how *stupid* you are."

Ben picked up a heavy wolf paperweight and threw it at Will's head. It was a shame the man moved so quickly to avoid it.

"Charming as ever," Will laughed. "May I offer a suggestion?"

As though he could stop him. Ben shrugged, having a go at another fingernail.

"Let nature take its course."

"We can have a good life." Ben nodded his head. "Can't we?" he asked as he looked toward Will. "I can still make her happy. Even though I can't love her."

"Are you trying to convince me? Or yourself?" Will asked. He squeezed Ben's shoulder once and walked from the room.

Elspeth wasn't spying. She really wasn't. She just wanted to hear what they were talking about. She would wait one minute longer and then let them know that she stood outside the door to the study.

But then they began to talk about her. Elspeth's heart soared. She had so much love in her heart that she felt like it would burst. He thought she was brilliant. And beautiful.

Her heart suddenly plummeted to the floor. It felt

like someone had pulled it from her chest and dropped it at her feet, where it went splat.

He didn't love her. She pressed her hand against her lips to keep from crying aloud. The pain of hearing that was nearly unbearable. Tears formed in her eyes and began to trail down her cheeks.

She heard every word he said and heard Will's responses. Ben planned to settle for her, even though he didn't love her. She couldn't let him waste his life when he could be out looking for his true love.

Elspeth's life had never been easy. She didn't know why she'd ever expected to meet a nice man, fall in love, and marry. She was too much like her mother.

She knew what she had to do. She had to give him his freedom. He'd brought her to London, and she owed him a great deal for his trouble. It would break her heart, but she wouldn't keep him trapped.

Elspeth turned to walk away from the door and heard the hiss of a whisper. "Tsk, tsk. Listening at doorways is so unladylike," Will said.

She brushed her hands across her cheeks and squared her stance. "I wasna eavesdroppin'."

"Sure you were," Will said, pulling her into the front sitting room. "And you probably heard more than you wanted." He handed her a handkerchief and motioned toward a chair. "Sit, please."

She paced across the room.

"Or not," he mumbled. "Look, Ben doesn't know what he's saying. Give him a little time."

She'd never known Ben to say something untruthful. He knew exactly what he had told his brother. He didn't love her. And he never would—not if he didn't now, after all they'd been through together. And she couldn't stand around and watch him, knowing what wasn't in his heart.

"Elspeth," Will began softly.

She turned to face him quickly. "Do ye ken Major Forster?"

Will's eyes narrowed. "Yes, he's an old friend of our father's, and I help him out with the Society."

Perfect. She wouldn't have to see Ben, then. "Can *ye* take me ta him?"

"I think this is something Ben should be discussing with you." Will turned to walk away.

"Please, Will," she begged, following after him.

"I can't," he said, holding up his hands. "It's not my place."

"If ye doona take me, I'll simply go by myself," she threatened, though she didn't know how to go about doing so.

"I hate it when women do that."

"Do what?"

"Manipulate us," Will bit out.

"Doona consider it ta be manipulation," she argued. "Just a bit of assistance gettin' ye ta where ye should be." She smiled at him.

He had the nerve to roll his eyes at her. "I can go in two hours. Can you be ready by then?"

"Of course." She would need to leave a few things for Ben and write a note. She'd leave the aloe and the blueberry tea. And she would instruct his cook to make blueberry pies, tarts, and cobblers. There were a lot of things she had to do. She'd also leave the final potion. The one he'd need if he didn't change with the next moon. According to her mother's notes, she'd used the same and it had worked.

She had to leave Ben well prepared for the moonful. Because when she left, she wouldn't be coming back.

# Forty-one

WILL POUNDED ON BEN'S DOOR. IF HIS IDIOT BROTHER didn't come to his senses soon, he'd lose his wife. And that was a loss Will doubted Ben would ever recover from. Personal experience had taught him that.

He'd watched Ben and Elspeth the fortnight they traveled together, and it would be obvious to the simplest of simpletons that the two of them loved each other deeply. But apparently Benjamin was completely inept.

When there was no answer to his banging, Will pushed the door open and found Ben lying on his bed, staring at the ceiling. "You obviously can't take a hint. Go away."

"Stop being obstinate, Benjamin. I need to talk to you about Elspeth."

Ben winced. "I'm not taking advice from you, so you can save your breath."

Will heaved a sigh. Why did he even bother? Ben was as stubborn as all the Westfields before him. He'd always had to learn things the hard way and never did listen to reason. "When you've lost her, don't come running to me."

Ben scoffed. "Nothing can change the fact that she's my wife, William. Melodrama doesn't suit you."

The hard way it was, then. Will rubbed his brow. This would be painful for all involved. Poor Elspeth. How could she even care for the bloody dolt? "Don't say I didn't warn you."

❦

Canis House was in the middle of nowhere. Elspeth and Will had taken horses from the Westfield stables and ridden quite a way from Town into a heavily forested area. Only a small path led to a large Tudor mansion that stood proudly in the distance. A great stone wolf guarded the entrance. It was a bit awe-inspiring.

"That's it?" Elspeth asked, knowing the answer in her heart.

Will nodded. "You're not supposed to go in. It's a gentleman's club. Wait just inside the entrance, and I'll go find the major."

"Are ye sure he's here?"

"He's always here." Will urged his horse toward the stables around the back, and Elspeth followed.

Her pulse raced as her anticipation intensified. She'd never been so close to finding her sire. It had never been a possibility until now. And it gave her something to focus on instead of her broken heart. Why were the Campbell women so unlovable? What was it about them that prevented the men they loved from returning the feeling? Perhaps her father could answer that when she found him. Perhaps then she could understand why Ben was unable to love her.

After dismounting his stallion, Will helped her off her filly. "You should really wait and do this with Ben," he said.

Elspeth forced away her tears. She wouldn't be doing anything else with Ben, and she needed answers to a lifetime of questions. "Please, Will. We've come this far."

"And my brother will never forgive me," he mumbled.

Major Desmond Forster rubbed his brow, looking at the file in front of him. Poor Captain Redding. He was a good soldier and a better man. Matthew Redding had served under Desmond's command all throughout the Peninsular Wars; returned the previous year, after Waterloo; and sold his commission. Within weeks he had married his childhood sweetheart, and last night the lass had gone into labor. Neither the girl nor the babe survived the event.

Redding was nearly out of his mind and rejected all the assistance the Society had offered. It broke Desmond's heart. But he couldn't help someone who refused to let him. He closed the file and rose from his desk. He started to descend the steps from his office, but stopped midway down the stairs.

His foot nearly slid out from under him as his knees gave way. *Rose?* It couldn't be. He blinked in astonishment. At the foot of the steps, a young, red-haired lass stood quietly, fidgeting with her hands. Dear God, she was the spitting image of Rosewyth Campbell. The same compassionate green eyes, alabaster skin, fiery hair.

Just as he made up his mind to turn around and go back to his office, the girl's eyes flashed up the staircase. She smiled tentatively, and his feet dragged him the rest of the way down the stairs. "Miss, are you lost?"

She shook her head. "I've come with Lord William, he asked me ta wait here."

The girl's Scottish lilt nearly knocked Desmond to the ground. She not only looked like Rose, but she sounded like her, too. Why would Will bring a girl here? He knew the rules. Desmond scratched his head. "The thing is, lass, ladies aren't allowed here. Would you like to wait for Lord William in my office?"

She bit her lower lip. "I suppose that would be all right. Can ye get word ta his lordship?"

The lass wasn't Will's usual sort of conquest. Desmond found himself smiling at her. "Of course. My office is at the top of the stairs, first door on the right. What's your name, lass, so I can tell Will?"

"Elspeth. Lady Elspeth Westfield."

Desmond's mouth fell open. He'd known the Westfields for more than three decades. There wasn't a Scot in the mix. But *he* had sent Benjamin to Edinburgh to find Rose.

An uneasy feeling washed over him. He knew instantly that this girl was Rose's daughter. There wasn't a doubt in his mind. Rose had obviously gone on with her life while he'd mourned her loss every day.

"Top of the stairs, first door on the right," he repeated numbly. Then he stepped into the drawing room and caught sight of Will in the far corner.

Why the devil had the scoundrel brought Rose's

daughter here? Desmond stalked across the room, ready to tear into the lad, but as he approached, Will seemed to sigh with relief. "Major, I was just looking for you."

Desmond frowned at the overgrown pup. "Would you care to tell me why you've brought a woman here, William?"

"You've seen her?" Will frowned. "She's Ben's wife."

"I figured she belonged to one of you. That doesn't explain why she's *here*, William."

Will gestured to a seat in the corner and collapsed into one himself. "She's here to see you, Major. Ben told her he thought you could help her find her father."

Her father? The last person he'd want to find was Rose's husband. "How the devil would I know where to find the man?"

"He's a Lycan. One of us. She bears the mark. Ben thought you could help her figure out who he is."

The air whooshed out of Desmond, and his mouth went dry. The odds that Rose knew another Lycan were minuscule. He did the math in his head. The girl looked to be about twenty. He stumbled into the seat Will had indicated earlier.

It wasn't every day a man learned he had a grown daughter.

"She doesn't know who he is?" Desmond managed to ask. Why had Rose kept the girl in the dark? Why had she kept *him* in the dark?

Will shook his head. "Scoundrel apparently abandoned her mother before she was born."

He hadn't known Rose was with child. He never

would have left if she'd told him. He would have made Rose come with him. Damn Fiona Macleod and her vision to hell. "What does she want with him?"

"Ben says she wanted to kill him, but I can't imagine that. She's really the sweetest girl. Compassionate. She actually loves Ben, for God's sake, if you can believe it—though that's a whole other matter."

Desmond's mind was awhirl. His *daughter* sat in his office, and he didn't have a clue what to say or do with her. But he had to see her again, to look at her with his eyes. His daughter.

He was rocked to his core.

Elspeth fidgeted in her seat. What was taking Will so long? He said the major was always here. Then the door opened and the gentleman she had met earlier walked into the office, a look of confusion marring his brow. "My dear, William says you are here to see me. I am Major Forster."

"Oh." She rose from her seat. "Major, it's so nice ta meet ye. My hus— Benjamin speaks so fondly of ye. Did Will tell ye why I've come?"

"I told him, Elspeth," Will replied from the door. "He thinks he can help."

She smiled at the older gentleman. He raked a hand through his dark hair, sprinkled with bits of grey. His brown eyes seemed so distant, not filled with the warmth she had noted earlier. "Oh, that's such a relief. I'm sorry ta barge in here without any notice."

The major locked eyes with hers. "It's no trouble, Lady Elspeth."

Will glanced at Forster. "You'll see her home tonight?"

The old officer agreed with a curt nod. Elspeth had no intention of returning, but neither of these men needed to know that. Once she had a name and a direction, she'd be off.

Will bent and kissed her forehead, just as he would a sister. "Good luck. I'll see you later, Elspeth." She avoided meeting his eyes as she nodded. If he looked too closely, he would see her planned subterfuge written all over her face, as she was a terrible liar.

The major motioned toward a chair and encouraged her to sit again. "May I get you some tea?" he asked politely.

Elspeth shook her head. "I really just want information about my father. Then I'll take my leave. I willna trouble ye for long."

"You're no trouble at all, my dear," he said, his gaze lingering at her hair. A flash of pain crossed his face.

"Are ye all right, Major?" She scooted forward in her chair, ready to jump up and help him if he needed it.

"I think my eyes are fooling me, Lady Elspeth. Because you look just like her. The memories are painful."

"I'm sorry, but I'm no' sure what ye speak of. Do I remind ye of someone ye once knew?"

He simply nodded and sat back in his chair, his fingers steepled in front of him. He breathed out the words with a long sigh. "I knew your mother, lass, and you look so much like her that it nearly takes my breath away." Then he smiled softly at her.

She pressed a hand to her chest. So close to solving the mystery of her parentage. "Oh? What was her name?" she asked, still skeptical about all the developments.

"When I knew her it was Rosewyth Campbell. Her friends called her Rosie. To me, she was Rose." His eyes narrowed. "How is she?"

"Dead," Elspeth said softly. She watched his face for a reaction, but he gave none. Aside from the look of sheer misery he'd worn since he walked in the door.

"How did she die?" he asked as he crossed to the sideboard and poured himself a drink. His hand visibly shook as he raised the glass to his mouth.

"She took a fever. Nearly the whole town was sick. I became very ill. Mother *nursed* me back ta health, then she died." There was no need to go into too much detail until she found her sire. "So do ye think ye can help me find my father?" she asked.

He nodded. "Aye, lass, I believe I can."

Relief washed over Elspeth. "How did ye ken her?" she asked. Thousands of questions ran through her mind, and she couldn't pick which to ask first.

"I went to her to be healed."

"Ye look hearty and hale. What was yer ailment?"

"I had lost a part of myself. And needed to find it again. Your mother helped me." She could tell, even as he spoke, that he had memories running through his mind. Fond ones, if she had to judge.

"I feel like we're speakin' in riddles here. So pardon me for speakin' bluntly. But what do ye ken of my father?"

His eyes narrowed as though he concentrated hard to find the right thing to say. Then the words tumbled from his mouth like water from a spout. "I went to Scotland to find your mother, because I knew of her powers. The *Còig* is an ancient entity, and I'd been raised on the stories of their legend when I was a boy in Glasgow. I knew their healer was the only one who could help me find myself."

Elspeth swallowed anxiously as she listened to him. The *Còig* was an ancient entity, and she'd left her sister witches for a man who didn't love her.

The major leaned forward. "Would it surprise you if I told you I'm a Lycan?" he asked, one eyebrow arched.

Not particularly, since they were sitting in Canis House. Elspeth shook her head. "Would it surprise ye if I told ye that I'm half Lycan?" she asked as she removed her glove to show him the mark of the beast on her wrist.

"No." His dark eyes captured hers. "It wouldn't surprise me at all." The major smiled a gentle smile.

"Was she able ta help ye?" Elspeth asked.

"Oh, she did more than help me. She made me fall in love with her. Then she broke my heart and made me leave her in Scotland to return to my troops."

Elspeth's heart jumped in her chest. Did he mean *he* was the one? She jumped to her feet. "Ye!" she gasped.

He leapt up as quickly as she did and was around the desk in a flash. "I believe so." He pointed to the pewter wolves that held her hair back. "The combs you wear, they were hers?"

"Aye, they were." Elspeth nodded as her eyes met his again. She wasn't quite sure what to say. She had imagined that she would get a name and directions to her father and would have time to figure out what to say. But here she was, staring right at him.

"I gave them to her," he said quietly. "I wanted her to remember me when I was gone."

"She wore them every day."

"That brings me some comfort." He smiled softly. "As does knowing about you."

He made it sound as though she were a new discovery. Surely her mother had told him, hadn't she? And he'd chosen to ignore all the letters and the spells she'd used to call to him. And now he would pretend to be happy about having a daughter?

"Why did ye never come for us?" She couldn't keep the bitterness out of her voice.

"I tried." She opened her mouth to protest, but he held up a hand. "I came back through Scotland a few years later and went straight to the Campbell cottage. Your grandfather wouldn't even let me in. But I'm of stubborn stock and planted myself on his porch. It didn't matter. I could have waited a lifetime, since Rose didn't live there anymore."

Elspeth frowned. Her mother had lived in the cottage every day of her life.

He continued quietly, "Then Fiona Macleod came out of the woods. She told me I was making a fool of myself. That your mother had gone on with her life, married a nice man from the other side of town, and had a daughter. That seeing her wouldn't do me a bit of good." He shrugged.

Why would Cait's mother do such a thing? Why would she keep her mother from happiness? But she knew the answer, or thought she did. After all, Cait had tried to keep Ben from Elspeth. "She hated ye," Elspeth said, shaking her head.

"Aye, she didn't like that a beast had tried to steal her healer away." The major rubbed his brow, as though the memories caused him pain. "I was so stunned by her words, I didn't even have the presence of mind to tell her that Rose's new marriage wasn't valid, since she was still my wife."

"Yer wife?" she gasped, stepping backward. "My mother was *never* married ta anyone. I was born out of wedlock." She still bore the scars of that.

The major leaned forward and touched her cheek. "Oh, no, my dear. I loved her too much to ruin her. We were married in Ormiston. When we came back the next day, Rose didn't want to tell her coven or your grandfather just yet. I needed to prove myself to them, your mother said. To be worthy."

"So the courtship would come *after* the marriage?"

"That's what it felt like. Only Bonnie Ferguson ever warmed up to me. And your grandfather wouldn't accept me, no matter what. When I asked for her hand, which was already *mine*"—he bit the last out in a growl—"he said no. Then I was called back to my regiment. I told Rose to pack her things. That she'd be coming with me."

None of that made sense, and Elspeth shook her head. "And she refused?"

"Aye, it was all foretold. A beast would come for Rose and try to take her from the coven, but she would resist him. Fiona's prophesy was correct. In the end, your mother loved the *Còig* more than she loved me."

Elspeth didn't believe that for a moment, and she stepped away from the major. "She never stopped lovin' ye. My grandfather said ye killed her. Ye broke her heart and it just took her fifteen years ta die of it. When she got sick, she didn't have the strength ta fight the fever. She even summoned ye, and ye didn't come."

"Summoned me?" The major frowned. "My dear, I never received word from Rose. Not one letter. If she had told me about you, I'd have never let her stay in Edinburgh, no matter what Fiona Macleod saw."

Elspeth's mind was awhirl. Nothing seemed to make sense. Then the room began to spin, right before her world went black.

# Forty-two

BEN STALKED THROUGH THE HOUSE, BARKING AT ALL THE servants, which made the maids skitter into corners and the footmen wince as he walked by. It wasn't like him to act so boorish. Even Polack, the unflappable butler, simply raised his nose and regarded him with surprise.

"Elspeth!" he called again. Where the devil was she? He'd been looking for her for hours. The sun was falling in the sky, and he couldn't find her anywhere. He'd entered every room in the house at least three times.

Finally Ben retreated into the study and sat down behind his desk. There he found a folded note on the center of the desk and picked it up. The feminine scrawl immediately caught his attention.

He unfolded the foolscap and couldn't hold back a gasp as he read the contents.

> *My Dearest Ben,*
> *I have left specific instructions with the cook as to your diet in the days leading up to the moonful. Please do not be as difficult for her as you have*

been for me. Also, there are some potions with
labels in the top drawer of your desk. The largest
should be used as a last resort, if you do not feel
the beast within you on the night when the moon
is at its best.

You deserve a wife who loves you, as I deserve
to have a husband who loves me. I am aware that
you do not, and cannot be that man. So I think it
is best for us to sever our ties at this point. For what
it is worth, I do love you.

*Always,*
*Ellie*

Ben's heart lurched in his chest. She'd left him?
Just like that? He could hardly believe it. Ellie was
patient and compassionate. She wouldn't destroy him
like this.

What was it that Will had said earlier? *When you've
lost her, don't come running to me.* Will knew she meant
to leave and hadn't told him?

Fury replaced his emptiness, and he strode from the
room with the intent to kill his brother. "William!" he
bellowed through the house. "William!"

Polack approached him cautiously in the main hallway.
"My lord, your brother is not here at the moment."

"Where the devil is he?" Ben barked.

"I'm sure I don't know, sir."

"What about my wife? Do you know where *she* is?"

Polack looked at his shoes. "I have inquired about her
ladyship's whereabouts, as you seemed intent on locating
her. Clarke says she left this afternoon on horseback."

Horseback? She could be anywhere. "And he just

let her go?" he asked, mortified. He would sack the groomsman this instant.

As he started toward the back exit, Polack cleared his throat, stopping him. "She was with Lord William, sir. I'm certain Clarke would have had no reason to deny her a mount."

A red haze filled Ben's vision, and anger bubbled in his veins. He'd find the blackguard if it was the last thing he did.

After a half dozen bawdy houses, Will's usual haunts, Ben finally found his brother at a hell, sitting at a hazard table, seemingly foxed. The last several hours he'd spent chasing after Will hadn't dimmed Ben's anger in the least. He stalked up behind his brother and yanked him out of his seat.

Will fell to the floor with a thud. "Ben?"

If anyone noticed the interaction, they hid it well. The other fellows spread out at the hazard table, absorbing Will's vacated spot.

"I am going to kill you," Ben hissed. "Where is she?"

His brother's eyes narrowed, as though he was trying to focus on Ben. Then Will shook his head and scrambled back to his feet. "Elspeth?"

Who else would he be asking about? "Where did you take her? And how dare you tell her I don't love her! What did you do, Will? Sweet-talk her with your damned irresistible charm? Did you console her? Did you touch *my* wife?"

A number of men who had been ignoring them suddenly became interested and shifted their attention from the tables to watch the Westfield brothers' interaction. Will simply gaped at him. "Have you lost your mind?"

"Where is she?" Ben pushed Will with both hands, sending him crashing against a hazard table. Money and markers tumbled to the floor while players protested the interruption of their game.

"Hey," one of the burly footmen called loudly. "You two, out of here."

Will dusted himself off and glared at Ben. "I was winning, you lout."

Winning! Ben would see to it that the only thing Will would *win* was a broken nose. He rose to his full height, then marched out the door, with Will following in his wake.

As soon as they were out on the dimly lit street, Ben grasped Will's jacket and forced him up against the stone façade of the hell. "Did you put her on a coach headed back to Edinburgh? Tell me, or I'll snap your neck."

Will's light blue eyes glared daggers at him. "You have three seconds, little brother, to remove your hands from my person."

"Where is she?" Ben hissed again.

Will twisted from his grasp and pushed him with such force that Ben stumbled into the street. He looked up just in time to see a carriage led by matched greys about to trample him. He leapt out of the way, but the coach clipped his arm and spun him back to the ground.

"Agh!" he howled.

The pain from his shoulder spiked down his arm and across his back. He rolled out of the street back to the safety of the walk, groaning and grasping his bad arm with his good one. He wasn't unaccustomed to pain, but as a Lycan, it never lasted long. Not until now.

Will stood above him, glowering. "Don't be a baby, Benjamin. You brought this fight."

He winced when he felt a sticky wetness through his jacket. Still, the pain in his arm was dull in comparison to the loss of Elspeth. "Tell me what you did with her, William."

Will heaved a sigh. "I'm sure she's patiently awaiting your pathetic hide at home, though I have no idea why she puts up with you."

Ben shook his head. "No, she's gone. And you took her from me. Clarke said you rode off together."

Will scoffed. "I took her to Canis House. Forster was going to return her home after they looked through some records."

His heart ached as her letter echoed in his mind. "She left me, Will. She left a note. She's not coming back."

"What?" Will asked, surprise in his voice. "I knew she was upset, but I didn't think she'd take it that far, not without giving you the chance to come to your senses." He looked down at Ben with a mix of sympathy and disgust.

"Why was she upset?"

Will heaved a sigh and pulled Ben back to his feet. He couldn't hide the painful grunt that escaped him. Will's expression turned to confusion. "You're not healed yet?"

Ben shook his head. He wasn't healed. Not his arm. Not the Lycan in him. Not his heart. "Why was she upset?"

"Why haven't you healed?" He heard the panic in his brother's voice.

Ben didn't have it in him to hide from the truth anymore. "Because I'm broken, Will. I can't transform, and I can't heal myself." His eyes dropped to the ground, escaping the look of pity that must be in his brother's eyes. "Why was Ellie upset?"

"I tried to tell you this afternoon. She heard us talking, you and me. She heard you say you couldn't love her."

What had he done? His poor Ellie! He'd never meant to hurt her. If Will had plunged a knife into Ben's chest, it would have been less painful. "Oh, dear God."

"I told her you didn't know what you were talking about," Will explained. "I told her to give you time."

Ben glowered. "Don't speak for me, William. I know exactly what I'm talking about. I just wish she hadn't heard." Ellie was the kindest soul he knew. He would never have inflicted such pain. It was the reason he kept himself from giving her his heart, to keep from hurting her.

"You're an even bigger fool than I've always thought."

No matter what, she was still his wife, and Ben wouldn't let her leave him. He turned his back on his brother and hailed a hack, still clasping his arm, which he was certain was broken. He barked out an address. Perhaps Major Forster knew where she was headed.

# *Forty-three*

ELSPETH BLINKED HER EYES OPEN, LIGHT FROM THE HALF–moon filtered in through the window. Where was she? After rubbing her eyes, she yawned.

"Awake, dear?" the major's voice asked from the darkness.

She sucked in a surprised breath and managed to sit up in the bed. "Major Forster?"

He stepped out of the shadows and sat on the edge of her bed. "You gave me quite the scare."

"Where am I?"

"In my apartments at Canis House. Would you like some tea?"

She nodded. Her throat was a bit parched.

"I sent word to Benjamin so he wouldn't worry." He walked to the corner of the room and tugged the bell pull.

A lump formed in her throat and tears streamed down her cheeks. Now Ben would know where to find her. "I-I wish ye hadna done that."

The major turned back to her and noticed her distress. "What is it, Lady Elspeth?"

She choked on a strangled laugh. The major was her father and yet he called her Lady Elspeth. Ben was her husband and yet he didn't love her. How had her life become such a tangled mess?

He rushed forward and pounded on her back, a bit more forcefully than was needed. "Are you all right?"

Elspeth nodded, though tears poured from her eyes.

The major seemed at a complete loss, as though women crying in his presence were a new experience for him. "What can I do?" he asked, offering her his handkerchief.

"I–I doona want ta see Ben," she managed to get out.

"All right," he agreed quickly. "Just please stop crying."

Elspeth blew her nose in the handkerchief and tried to bring her sobs under control. Thinking about Ben would only make her cry harder. "Tell me about yerself."

Even in the dark room she could tell that his dark eyes warmed a bit. "What do you want to know, dear?"

She dabbed the tears on her cheeks. "I doona ken. Anythin', everythin'. I doona ken the first thing about ye."

Again the major sat at the edge of her bed. "I don't even know where to begin."

"Ye said ye were from Glasgow?"

He nodded. "Aye, but most of my life has been spent in England or on one battlefield or another."

She listened quietly as he talked, not wanting to miss one detail.

"I went off to Harrow as a young lad. My mother's family had a tidy sum and wanted me educated in England's finest schools. They wanted me to go on to Cambridge, but I bought my commission instead. I was stationed in Canada, then on the Continent. After Waterloo I sold my commission. I've been heading up the Lycanian Society ever since."

"In Glasgow ye'd heard tales of the *Còig*?"

His answer was interrupted when a scratch sounded at the door. "Come," he called.

A young girl in a mop cap pushed open the door, carrying a tea service, and placed it on a bedside table. When she left, the major rose from his seat and started to pour. "How do you take it?"

"Two sugars, please."

He returned to the bed and handed her a cup. "Just like Rose. I should have known."

The mention of her mother made Elspeth frown. "Did ye say Mama never summoned ye? Her journal said otherwise."

The major sighed and settled his large frame in a seat near the bed. "How would she have even known how to get in touch with me, lass? I didn't have a permanent address. If she sent me letters, I never received them."

"But she used a summoning spell. I–it drained what was left of her strength." As soon as the words left her mouth, she wished she hadn't said them. He looked as if she'd struck him.

"Trying to find me?" he whispered in horror. "Oh, my poor Rose."

His anguish brought fresh tears to her eyes, and she didn't try to stop them as they trailed down her cheeks. Even here and now in a dimly lit room, she could see the love and pain reflected in his eyes. "I'm sorry," she offered numbly.

"It's my fault. I shouldn't have left her."

"She resisted the vision ta stay with the coven." It was a strong pull. One that Elspeth could understand, one that she should have followed herself.

"Resisted the vision?" he echoed. "No, lass. She wasn't supposed to go with me. That vision was why she wouldn't budge."

That didn't make any sense. Elspeth sat up straight. "But that's no' what Cait said."

"Cait?"

"Our seer. Caitrin Macleod. She said her mother saw ye come for Mama and that ye'd take her away. It was the same vision Cait saw about... Ben."

It was painful even to say his name, and Elspeth swallowed the ache that formed in her throat. Did the major—her father—remember the past differently?

He shook his head, and his eyes darkened. "No. Fiona Macleod said that I would come for Rose but that she would stay with the *Còig* and resist the temptation. I've heard it echoed in my heart every night since, Elspeth."

An awful thought entered her mind. Mrs. Macleod wouldn't...? But it was the only thing that made sense. "Why would she lie?" she muttered under her breath.

But with his Lycan hearing, her father heard her. "To keep Rose. To keep their coven intact."

Even Cait wouldn't do such a terribly selfish thing.

Elspeth's heart plummeted. All those years she and her mother had been alone. All those years that her mother spent mourning him, he'd apparently spent mourning her, too. She'd grown up with a stigma that she could never live down, no matter how many people came to her for help. All those years they could have been together. It was a waste.

"Did ye really marry her?" she asked softly.

His eyes met hers and he nodded. "I still have the license."

Another scratch came at the door. The major's eyes never left hers, and another wave of sadness washed over Elspeth. All the years they'd lost weren't his fault. All the years she'd spent blaming him were in vain.

"Come," her father called.

The same little maid pushed the door open. "Major, Lord Benjamin would like to see Lady Elspeth."

She drew in a breath and shook her head. "I canna see him."

"What did he do to you?" her father asked, his brow furrowed.

Elspeth simply shook her head. "Please."

He glanced at the maid. "Tell Lord Benjamin I'll be there shortly."

When she shut the door, he turned his attention back to Elspeth. "Did he hurt you?"

She closed her eyes and shook her head. "Not in the way you mean. He… he doesna care for me. Please, I doona want ta see him."

"Then he won't bother you." The major rose from his spot and left her alone.

Ben paced around the private drawing room, thanking God once again that he'd received the note from Forster. Ellie was safe. He could still make things right.

How could he explain things to her so that she'd

understand? That question had plagued him the entire ride to Canis House, which wasn't terribly easy with a broken arm. Though now that he was here, he no longer noticed the throb in his arm. All he wanted was the opportunity to see his wife.

"Benjamin," Major Forster said from behind him.

He spun around. "Oh, Major. Thank you so much for the note. I was half out of my mind with worry."

The major frowned at him. "She's not up to seeing you right now, Ben."

"What do you mean? Is she all right?" Ben growled.

"No need to show your teeth, pup. She's fine." The major didn't growl, but his voice held a subtle warning nonetheless. A gust of wind blew as the door flew open behind them and Will burst through. "Nice to see you, too, William." The major shook his head.

"Why did you come here?" Ben snarled.

"Because you left a trail of blood in your wake that a blind wolf could follow. I don't care how much you hate me right now. I'll not leave you when you're injured."

"Injured?" the major scoffed. "His heart is not involved with my daughter, from what she tells me. So I doubt Elspeth's leaving has caused him any injury."

"Your daughter?" Will and Ben asked in chorus.

The major ignored their question and turned to pour a drink.

Ben weaved a bit unsteadily on his feet as he moved toward the major, a growl stuck in his throat.

"Look at you, Ben," Will said. "You can't even walk." Then he turned to the major. "Why isn't his injury healing?"

"Injury?" the major echoed. The sound of Will's

teeth as they ground together was the only noise in the room. The major looked down at the floor, where a steady drip of blood ran from beneath the sleeve of Ben's jacket to hit the rug at his feet. "You're truly injured? And have not healed?"

Ben nodded weakly.

"You should have told me," he said.

"You were having such a grand time bringing me to heel, I didn't want to ruin your fun," Ben breathed out, gasping in pain as the men pulled his jacket from his shoulders to get a better look at the wound.

Darkness clouded the corners of his vision. Thankfully, Will hooked one foot around the leg of a chair and drew it near, just before Ben would have swooned and hit the ground.

"Honestly, Ben," Will chided, his eyes clouded with worry. "I would think you were wearing garters if you didn't have all that blood dripping from your body." As they finally removed his jacket, Will whistled softly when he saw the way Ben's shirt was stained with blood, his arm twisted at an unnatural angle.

"The day I wear garters is the day you'll marry Prisca Hawthorne."

"Not bloody likely," Will whispered.

"Exactly," Ben hissed as they adjusted his broken arm. Will finally gave up and ripped the shirt cleanly from his body. Why hadn't they thought of that earlier? It was much less painful.

"It's worse than I thought," Will said as he tested the edges of the deep wound.

The major called to a maid in the corridor. "Have one of the men fetch the doctor, will you?"

But then Ben was called from his weak stupor as he heard a voice with a lilting Scottish brogue say, "No need. I can heal him myself."

She looked so beautiful there in the doorway that Ben could barely get his breath. She'd removed her combs, and her hair hung wildly about her shoulders. Her image swam before his eyes. "Elspeth," he breathed. "You will *not* heal me."

"No man has ever told me what ta do, Benjamin Westfield. And I'll no' start with ye." She walked toward him slowly. Her image split into two. He shook his head.

"I'll not let you put yourself at risk," he said quietly. "I've seen how it affects you."

"I'll no' let ye be injured when I can help ye." She gestured toward the settee. "Can ye move him so he can lie down, please? He's about ta fall from the chair."

Will moved to help and barely caught him as he did just that. Then darkness was all Ben knew from that moment forward.

# *Forty-four*

ELSPETH DID HER BEST TO FIGHT THE PANIC AS SHE descended the stairs. She'd already known something was wrong with him; she'd felt it in her soul. She didn't understand the connection they had, since he professed not to love her, but they were tied to each other, regardless.

When they'd settled his big body on the settee, Ben was so deeply unconscious that he'd not uttered a sound.

"Ye say a Lycan can normally heal his own self?" she asked the men.

"Yes, we heal almost immediately. I've never known anyone who is unable to heal. Have you?" Will asked the major.

Major Forster got a faraway look in his eye before he shook it off and said, "Yes. I have seen it. It's rare, but it happens."

"What causes it?" Will asked as she gently probed the wound. Ben didn't even move beneath her fingers. She halfheartedly listened to the response.

"Usually an imbalance. Some unrest within the soul. Or the heart, as the case may be. It's often an event that tests a Lycan's confidence and weakens him. It's not in a corporeal sense. It's internal. And it can be deadly to one of our kind if we can't find a healer."

"Can you heal him, Elspeth?" Will asked.

"Aye, I can." There was no doubt in her mind. She could heal him and make him whole, in body and in spirit. She wished she'd realized it before. The answer could not be found in blueberries, flower-scented baths, or potions. All she had to do was love him. And make him believe it. "Can ye give me a moment alone with him?"

"Why?" Will wanted to know.

She smiled a gentle smile at him. "Because I need ye ta leave us be. And let me do my work."

"We'll be a few steps outside, Elspeth. So call if you need us."

"Aye, I can already imagine ye passin' each other in the corridor as ye pace in opposite directions. Go on, now. Out." She pushed her hands at them impatiently.

When they were gone, Elspeth took a moment to look at Ben's sleeping form. She brushed the hair back from his forehead. He looked as peaceful as a child.

Then she touched her hands to the area of his wound, bringing the edges of the gaping cut together with her fingertips. She closed her eyes and focused all of her power on the job she had to do. His flesh warmed and slowly knitted together. The edges of the wound went from red and jagged to being completely healed. She lifted her hands and was quite content with what she saw.

Ben still slept peacefully. She touched his arm above the break with one hand and below it with the other. When it was completely healed, she tested his arm by bending it at the elbow. She stopped to smile at her own work.

But she wasn't done. There was more that needed to be healed. She didn't know why she hadn't seen it before. She placed her hand above his heart. Her power immediately flowed into him, as though this was what his body waited for, what his soul yearned for. Her palm heated against him as her power flowed into him, and she imagined it moving through his body, nourishing his soul and feeding his needs.

Elspeth tried to open her eyes so that she could gaze upon him as she fixed him, fixed her broken wolf. But her lids refused to lift. Her power continued to wash into him, now pulsing through his entire being. She felt the pieces of him that were broken unfurl. She felt the insecurity vanish. She felt the doubts and fears about himself and his ability to control his Lycan side replaced by her healing warmth.

Elspeth found she could no longer support her weight and sank down slowly onto his chest until her face rested against his skin. Her hand fell off his chest and hung limply toward the floor. And there she finally gave in to the need for sleep that so clutched at her.

❦

Ben woke slowly, wrapping his arms around Elspeth's body as she slept on his chest. He could wake like this every day for the rest of his life. Why did he have his shirt off while she was clothed? He raised his head and looked around the room. They weren't at her cottage. Or his house in London.

He ran his hand down her back and cooed gently

into her ear. "Ellie, wake up, love." She didn't move. He jostled her slightly, but she didn't raise her head. "Ellie?" he said more loudly, panic taking over.

Will and Major Forster bolted into the room. "What happened?"

"I have no idea. I woke up and she was sleeping on my chest." He turned her hand over and gasped when he saw blood. "Is she injured?" he croaked.

"No, it was you who was injured, Ben."

It slowly dawned on him. "You let her *heal* me?" he cried. He sat up and adjusted her body so that she was cradled in his arms. Her head hung back limply. "Ellie! Ellie!" he called to her. He brought a hand up to touch her face. "She's freezing! What have you done?" He glowered at the men.

"She said she could heal you—" Will started.

"And put herself in jeopardy!" Ben cried.

Will glanced frantically toward the major.

"We didn't know that she would be injured in the process. I would have let you die before I'd let you hurt my daughter," the major bit out as he moved to take Elspeth from Ben's arms.

Ben stood up quickly and moved out of reach. "You'll not take her from me."

The major put his hand under Elspeth's nose. "She breathes, Ben."

"Yes, I can hear her heart beating. But it's much too slow. And she's so cold." He moved toward the stairs. "Where is the bedroom?" he barked.

"Top of the stairs."

Ben ran up the stairs, taking two steps at a time. He burst into the nearest bedroom, slammed the door shut, and pulled back the counterpane. If this was like the time she'd healed Caitrin, she would need warmth from his body. Quickly he undressed her and himself and laid her on a pillow before he pulled her frigid body close to his and raised the counterpane, tucking it tightly around her.

A knock sounded at the door.

"What?" he barked.

"I'm coming in," Will said.

Ben didn't respond. He just ran his hands up and down Elspeth's cold body, trying to use the friction of his touch to warm her.

"What can I do?" Will asked softly.

"She needs to be warmed."

Will stepped into the hallway and directed the servants to light a fire in the grate. They scurried to do his bidding.

"Why did you let her do it?" Ben cried softly as he held her close to him.

"We didn't know."

Servants began to pour into the room. One stoked the fire while another added layers of counterpanes until the room was filled with a radiant heat. Then they were all alone again.

Ben held her like that for what seemed like hours. She slowly warmed against him, but didn't wake. Her eyelids never fluttered. The slow, even cadence of her breathing never changed. Her heartbeat never quickened. What he would have paid at that moment to hear her heartbeat speed up. He didn't care if it was in anger, in fear, in passion. He simply wanted her to be healthy.

Why had he said those stupid things that drove her away from him? Of course he loved her. How could he not? He just hadn't wanted to admit it to himself. He'd wanted to protect her, but instead he put her in danger. If she didn't wake, he'd never forgive himself.

When morning came, Will tried to get Ben to take a break. But he stoically refused. He needed to be with her. If she drew her last breath, he would be there.

"You need your strength," Will reminded him. "Go and take a walk. Get something to eat. I'll sit with her."

He looked down at her sleeping form. His Elspeth was warm. Her lips were no longer blue. Her cheeks were a rosy red. But she refused to wake.

"Trust me. If she wakes, I'll call you," Will said. "I'll not leave her."

Ben rose, dressed, and stepped out the front door. He walked into the yard and kicked the stone wolf in his path. He didn't even feel the pain. He wanted to vent his frustration. He wanted to hurt someone. He walked down the winding path into the woods, a heavy rain immediately soaking him. Had it been raining when he'd stepped outside? He couldn't remember.

He took a few more steps. The rain stopped and the sun shone. Then, within moments, it poured again.

"Rhiannon?" he asked quietly. He must be losing his mind. He scrubbed his hand across his forehead.

A few feet before him, a small plant emerged from the ground. It flowered prettily. Ben bent and looked at the plant offering. Only Sorcha could present such an item.

"What do I do?" he asked. Another blossom appeared, as if to say *Pick me, you idiot.*

He picked the purple blossom. A pinecone dropped from a nearby tree and hit the top of his head. What else could go wrong? He kicked the cone from his path. Four more dropped from the sky. He raised his arms above his head to block more falling objects. "I get the idea," he growled as he picked up a pinecone. A ginger root tugged at the toe of his shoe. He looked up at the sky and said, "That's for me, too?" A pinecone hit his head.

He shook his head with wonder and dug up the ginger root. "You know I have no idea what to do with these things or how much of each to use," he called. He hoped no one was watching him, but he really didn't care. The root and the flower immediately shriveled into dried bits in his hand. Then a gentle wind blew. The majority of the dried leaves left his palm, leaving only a small bit behind.

He raised his eyebrows and said, "Now we're getting somewhere." He held up the pinecone. It fell apart in his hand and left four tiny seeds.

"What do I mix them with?" Thunder crashed in the sky and rain poured from the heavens, soaking him immediately. He closed his fist to keep his precious ingredients safe. When the water stopped, he stood with his eyes closed, a bemused look on his face as he blew water from his face and shook his head like a dog. "I assume that means water." He nearly chuckled. "Is that all?" The sun shone brightly.

He turned and jogged back into the house, stopping to make a fresh pot of tea, and steeped the ingredients in his hands, adding them to the brew. When it was done, he carried the tea upstairs on a tray.

Will sat on the edge of the bed, rubbing the tips of his fingers across Elspeth's lifeless hand. "What do you have there?" he asked.

"A brew from the witches."

"In Scotland?" Will looked befuddled.

"In Scotland," Ben confirmed.

"Why are you all wet?"

"It was one of the clues." He shrugged as he raised a small spoonful of the brew to Elspeth's lips. She took it in without gasping or choking and swallowed slowly. It was the first movement she'd made since she'd passed out.

"When you get yourself in a mess, you really know how to do it, don't you, Ben?" Will asked.

"This isn't a mess, William. This is love."

# *Forty-five*

ELSPETH BLINKED HER EYES OPEN AS LATE AFTERNOON light poured into the room. Weak, she tried to turn to her side, but she couldn't gather up the strength. She looked to her side and found Will flipping through *The Times*. Her heart sank when she realized it wasn't Ben.

Not that she should have been surprised. Though she loved him with all her heart, nothing had changed. She must have made some sort of sound, because Will dropped the paper and sat forward. He smiled with relief. "Thank God. We were so worried."

She tried to sit up but couldn't manage to make her limbs do anything. "Water," she whispered.

"Of course." He leapt from his seat and poured some from a pitcher, sloshing most of it on the floor in his haste to bring it to her.

He helped her sit and brought the cup to her mouth. It was like nectar from the gods, and she drank her fill. Only when she finished did she realize that the counterpane was down around her waist and she had nothing on.

Elspeth gasped and Will's eyes widened. Apparently he didn't realize it either. Quickly, he pulled the blankets up to her neck and tucked them around her. "Ben doesn't need to know about that," he said quietly. Then he added with a wink, "He'll accuse me of trying to seduce you in your weakened state."

Just hearing his name tore at her heart. It was best to think of other things. She shook her head. "My father," she managed, her voice sounded raspy.

Will started for the door. "I've got to wake Ben first."

"Just my father."

He glanced over his shoulder at her but didn't say a word as he stepped over the threshold.

&

When Ben heard a soft knock, he bolted off the bed he was napping on, rushed across the room, and opened the door. Will stood before him, frowning.

"Is she awake?" he asked.

Will nodded. "She's asking for the major."

Ben took a step backward, realization dawning on him. "But not me."

Will winced. "Forster has a claim on her, but she's *your* wife. I think you should go to her anyway. She can talk to him later."

It wouldn't do any good. She was a stubborn lass when she wanted to be. Apparently, in her eyes he hadn't yet paid for his sins. He certainly didn't want to fight with her, not when she was in a weakened state. Ben sighed. "How is she?"

"She looks frail, but her color is back. She's said a few words, but her voice is scratchy."

"Make sure she drinks the tea."

Will stepped closer to him, so there was only an inch between them. "You should go to her, Ben."

He had every intention of going to her, when she was stronger and he could make her understand. Or when she asked for him. Whichever came first. "In good time. Get Forster. Make sure she drinks the tea."

"She loves you."

Ben knew that. He could feel her inside him, in his heart, his soul, his very essence. She'd healed more than his broken arm. "It won't be good to upset her right now, and I think my presence would do so."

With a curt nod, Will left him and started for the staircase.

Ben rested his forehead against the wall. How could he make things right? There had to be something he could do.

❧

The little maid from the night before bustled into Elspeth's room. It looked as though the young girl was blushing. "Lord William said you needed help getting dressed."

The reason for the blush was obvious now. Elspeth cleared her throat. "Thank ye."

The girl retrieved Elspeth's dress from the day before and shook out the wrinkles. Then she pulled back the counterpane and slid the gown over Elspeth's head. How awkward for someone else to dress her! She felt like a rag doll being pushed and pulled in odd directions.

"The major is so relieved you're awake, milady," the maid said as she smoothed the dress over Elspeth's body.

"How long have ye worked for the major?"

She shrugged. "A little more than a year now. Ever since he returned from the Continent."

"Is he a good employer?"

"The best, milady." The girl tugged the gown down around Elspeth's ankles. Then she pulled the counterpane back up to her waist.

"And honest? Does he seem honest ta ye?" Did she dare believe all that he'd told her? Did he really not know about her? Had her mother really not been in contact with him?

Clearly affronted, the maid raised herself up to her full height, which wasn't all that tall. "Who said otherwise? Major Forster is the most honorable of men!"

"That's quite all right, Molly," the major said from the doorway. "I'm certain my daughter was just curious."

"I—um…" Elspeth felt her face heat and was certain her cheeks were the color of her hair. She really must be more careful around Lycans, with their superior hearing.

The major laughed. "You remind me so much of her. It'll take some getting used to. For both of us, I imagine." He crossed the floor and took the seat Will had vacated earlier. Then he leaned forward, took her hand in his, and squeezed. "How are you feeling, my dear?"

"Fine," she replied softly.

One of the major's dark eyebrows rose disbelievingly. "Fine?"

She shrugged. "Just a little weak. I'll be fine in no time."

Her father pursed his lips. "You knew what would happen, didn't you? That you'd collapse?"

Elspeth's eyes dropped to the counterpane. She hadn't known for sure, but she'd had a pretty good idea. "I couldna let him suffer."

"He was furious with us for letting you put yourself in danger. If I'd known…"

"Ye wouldna have stopped me." She raised her gaze to his. "I ken he doesna feel the same about me that I do about him, but I could never let him be in pain."

Her father's features softened, and he smiled wistfully at her. "So much like Rose."

She hoped not. She didn't want to spend the rest of her life mourning Ben the way her mother had mourned her father. It was an awful way to live. "How did you go on without her?"

He snorted. "Badly. I was fortunate there was always a battlefield that required my attention. But at night there was nothing to distract me from my memories of her. Was she happy?"

"She missed ye. But she had me and my grandfather and the coven…" Her voice trailed off when she saw his countenance fall.

"I'll never forgive myself for listening to Fiona Macleod. I should have seen Rose with my own eyes. At the time, I didn't think I could bear to see her as another man's wife. I was a coward."

Elspeth's heart ached for him, and she understood completely. When Ben went on to find his happiness with another, she didn't think she could ever see him again. She couldn't imagine anything more painful. "I doona think ye're a coward."

He sighed and she noticed tears in his dark eyes. "You have a compassionate nature, my dear."

"Where do we go from here, Major?"

Her father shook his head. "Wherever you want, lass. I'm your humble servant."

"No' a servant," she choked on a laugh. "Ye're my father."

"I don't know how to make up for lost time, but I'll do whatever you need, help you anyway possible."

"Thank ye for that." She sat up straight and fought back the tears that threatened to spill down her cheeks. "I'd like ta stay here with ye for a while. I'd like ta get ta ken ye."

A smile spread across his face, and he scratched his whiskered jaw. "I'd like that, lass." Then his brow furrowed as he regarded her. "But Benjamin?"

"Is free ta do whatever he wants."

"I'm fairly certain he wants to be with you, Elspeth. He guarded you with his life last night."

She shook her head. "I canna go with him." It would kill her to do so, to see him every day and know he didn't love her. She was safer here, where she could focus on her father and, hopefully, figure out how to go on without Ben.

# *Forty-six*

AFTER MORE THAN A FORTNIGHT OF TRAVEL, ELSPETH took her father's hand in her own as she stepped from the coach in front of her small cottage and took in the sight. A comforting breeze caressed her face. The witches knew she was home. They'd probably known she was coming long before she did.

"Are you all right?" the major asked. It was still hard to think of him as "Father," since they'd spent so little time together, but they had definitely grown closer as they traveled from London to Edinburgh. She'd learned all about her grandparents in Glasgow and hoped to meet them very soon. She also had several distant cousins and one spinster aunt, whom the major said would dote on her.

Elspeth closed her eyes and inhaled. It smelled like home, so much sweeter than the thick London air. "Aye, I'm all right." Then she looked over at her father. "Ye didna have ta come all this way just ta see me home, Major."

He chucked her beneath her chin. "I finally find out I have a daughter, and you want me to let you run off to Scotland alone? What kind of father do you think I am?" He chuckled. "Honestly, I have no idea what kind of father I'll be."

"And I've no idea what kind of daughter I am," she said, smiling in his direction. "We'll learn together." His eyebrows pushed together as his eyes took in the sight of the old cottage. "Does this bring back good or bad memories, Major? If it's too painful, we can go straight ta the Thistle and Thorn, and ye willna have ta spend time here."

"Actually, Elspeth, I'd like to go and pay my respects to your mother." He avoided her gaze, and her heart ached for him.

"Down the lane. In the church cemetery." She nodded her head in the right direction. Part of her wanted to go with him, but she knew he needed to do this alone.

"Will you be all right?" he asked.

Elspeth grinned at him. "I've lived here my whole life. I'll be just fine. Besides, I've got some things ta tend ta."

He caressed her cheek then loped off slowly down the lane, his gaze pointed toward the ground. It had to be hard coming back to Edinburgh after all this time. After all they had been through.

A coach rattled down the drive and stopped in front of her. Elspeth smiled as she recognized the crest. The door flung open with a bang; the inhabitant didn't even wait for the driver to dismount and open the door. Sorcha tumbled out, a vision in white with a coronet of white flowers in her dark hair. "Welcome home!" she cried, nearly knocking Elspeth to the ground with her exuberance.

"*Havers*, Sorcha! Ye act like I've been gone for years!" Elspeth said as she hugged the girl back.

"That's what it's felt like. Like ye disappeared from the face of the earth."

Elspeth laughed and tugged the girl's arms from around her neck, setting her back so that she could look at her.

"Somethin' is different about ye," Sorcha said, touching a fingertip to her chin as she regarded Elspeth from head to toe. "But I canna determine what it is."

"Aside from the loss of the wolf that was hangin' on her arm when she left us?" a voice called from behind the coach. Caitrin appeared, with Blaire and Rhiannon in her wake.

"Doona start with me, Cait," Elspeth bit out. "I've only just come home. Let me settle in before I have ta start battlin' with ye."

Caitrin crossed her arms and leaned against the side of the coach. "Where's yer dog? He's no' nippin' around yer skirts."

Elspeth turned to go inside. She held the door open and raised her eyebrows. "Anyone who can keep a civil tongue in their head can join me. Otherwise I have a lot of work ta do."

Blaire, Sorcha, and Rhiannon went in and made themselves comfortable on the settee while Caitrin lingered in the doorway.

"Do I need ta ply ye with hyssop, Cait?" Elspeth asked, gesturing to the plant that still thrived on her tabletop.

Caitrin sighed and stepped into the room.

Elspeth's voice finally broke when she said, "I miss him…"

Caitrin flew across the room in a flash. She pulled Elspeth into her arms and cooed softly as she let her cry it out. "I ken that ye miss him. I'm sorry for bein' so cruel."

Elspeth wiped her cheeks with her fingertips. "I doona ken what's wrong with me. I am usually no' so emotional." All four of the girls suddenly avoided her gaze.

"What's wrong?" Elspeth barked. "What is it that keeps ye from lookin' me in the eye?"

"It's no' our place ta tell ye—" Caitrin began.

"Ye've seen my future, then?"

"Aye, I've seen yers. And that of the bairn ye carry," Caitrin said softly as she brushed a tendril of hair from Elspeth's brow. Then she turned and walked out the door.

"Doona go!" Elspeth called. "Ye canna leave me without knowin'."

"Yer future waits," Caitrin called back, smiling. Then all four girls started down the lane, their heads pressed closely together as though they were telling secrets she wasn't privy to. The coach Sorcha had arrived in was abandoned, as the women apparently thought a long walk would be better for their scheming. Elspeth directed the coachman back to the Fergusons'.

She shook her head with dismay as she walked back into the house and sank heavily into a chair, placing a hand on her belly. *A bairn.* She smiled softly. Then it hit her what Caitrin said. It wasn't like her to start to speak and then end in a riddle. "Yer future waits?"

"Do you think I'm the future of which she spoke?" a deep voice said from the doorway.

"Ben!" Elspeth cried as she jumped to her feet.

It had been weeks since he'd seen her last. He allowed his gaze to travel slowly over her body. He smiled when he heard her heart start to beat faster. He did still affect her. He'd hoped so. And prayed. And wished.

"May I come in?" he asked.

"We've only just arrived."

"Where's Major Forster?"

"He went ta the church cemetery."

"Oh." Ben understood completely. If anything ever happened to Elspeth, he would probably die with her. Or die a million deaths as the days passed before he could join her.

"How are ye?" Her hands fluttered nervously until she finally clutched them before her.

"Hale and whole. Thanks to a lovely Scottish witch who gave me the healing I needed."

"So with the moonful ye did change?" she asked as her eyebrows knit together.

"Yes, I did." He nodded. "I'm back to my old self."

She smiled slowly at him. "I'm truly happy ta ken I could help ye, Ben."

"I'm in need of one more bit of healing, though," he said softly as he walked slowly toward her. She stood still and quiet, but the flowery scent of her became stronger as her body warmed beneath his gaze.

"What seems ta be wrong with ye?"

He took her hand in his and pressed it to the center of his chest. "I think I've a problem with my heart."

Elspeth gasped. "What kind of problem? I have potions for the heart. I can heal ye," she said frantically.

He placed a finger to her lips. "It's not that kind of heart problem." Her confused gaze rose to his. "I'm afraid my heart is broken."

"That's no' humorous," she said, trying to pull her hand back. But he held tightly. He'd not allow her to mistake his intentions. Her green eyes flashed. "Ye'd have ta love me before yer heart could break."

He bent his head to touch his lips softly to hers. "I know." He pulled her closer to him, until her body pressed against his in the most delightful way. He'd missed holding her, the feel of her in his arms. He breathed beside her ear. "Fix my heart, Ellie." Then he loosened his hold and stepped away from her.

She shook her head. "Ye shouldna have come."

His stubborn, beautiful, intoxicating wife. "Come now, love. You heal everyone else."

Elspeth dropped onto her old threadbare settee. "I've given ye all I have, Ben. I doona have anythin' else."

Which was why it was time for him to take care of her. Something he would do for the rest of his days. He just had to win her back first. "Come to dinner with me tonight, Ellie."

"Ben," she groaned.

"I won't take no for an answer." He sunk to his haunches before her. "It's just dinner. You have to eat anyway."

She shook her head. "But my father—"

"—has been eating camp rations most of his life. I'm sure he can manage one night at the Thistle and Thorn."

The corner of her mouth twitched, and for a moment he thought she was going to smile at him, but she quickly schooled her features back in place.

Ben tucked a curl behind her ear. "I promise not to bite."

"Just dinner?"

"Just dinner." *For now.*

"All right," she finally agreed.

# Forty-seven

"WHATEVER YE DO, DOONA SAY ANYTHIN' STUPID,"
Caitrin warned Ben. Then she thrust a picnic basket
into his arms.

He almost stumbled backward against the Macleods'
grand staircase. A footman snickered, but quickly
adopted a stoic expression when Ben glowered at the
man. "Findlay," Caitrin replied waspishly, "ye may
leave us."

Once the servant was gone, Ben turned his attention back to the pretty seer, whom he still couldn't
quite believe was helping him. "Thank you for your
confidence," he grumbled.

Caitrin raised one arrogant brow. "I believe that's
why ye're in this situation, Westfield. I'm simply sayin'
doona make the same mistake again."

"Well, that goes without saying."

She ignored him, then handed him a folded-up
plaid he'd come to recognize as belonging to the
Campbells. "I've put some red candles in there, too."

"Why red?"

She frowned at him. "Do ye want my help or no'?"

To be honest, he wasn't sure. He knew he could trust Sorcha, but Caitrin was another matter. "Why *are* you helping me?"

At once she looked remorseful, which was a change from her usual haughtiness. "My mother was so consumed with keepin' the *Còig* intact, she dinna see what she was doin' ta Elspeth's mother. At least that's what I've been tellin' myself." She took a deep breath and met his eyes. "I canna fathom lyin' about a vision, Westfield. It goes against my very nature. Her fear and selfishness cost El a lifetime's worth of happiness. It's a little late, but if I can bring some ta her, I'll even help the likes of ye."

Even when she was helping him, it still came off as an insult. "A truce, then?" he asked.

Caitrin cocked her head to one side, assessing him. "Are ye really goin' ta split her time between London and Edinburgh? Like Hades and Persephone?"

Ben couldn't help but laugh. "*You* whispered that little myth in MacQuarrie's ear?"

A wicked smile played on her lips. "I'm a bit selfish myself, Westfield. And ye dinna answer my question."

Ben sighed. He'd never thought he'd have to get approval for his time allotted to him by this particular witch. "Yes, Miss Macleod."

She winked at him and smiled. "What a good wolf ye've turned out ta be. And ye can call me Cait."

"Cait?" He raised his brow in amusement.

"Well, I'm goin' ta be the godmother of yer children, after all."

"Are you, indeed?" He couldn't resist smiling.

"If ye can win her back. I doona trust my visions

completely anymore. And El can be more stubborn than most."

But she saw them together. Ben released a sigh. He would take all the help he could get.

"Now, El's favorites are in there, and Rhiannon has guaranteed nice weather for ye tonight. But the rest falls ta ye. Doona say anythin' stupid."

"Yes, you said that already."

Ben helped Elspeth out of his coach, and her eyes swept over the land—a beautiful heather-covered meadow that edged the forest. The warmth of his hand holding hers sent tingles racing to Elspeth's soul.

She sucked in a steadying breath as her eyes darted back to her husband. Ever since she'd agreed to this outing, she'd worried it was a mistake. Spending time with him would only make things more painful when he left.

Ben scooped up a picnic basket and plaid in one hand, then offered his free arm to her.

"Where are we?" she asked.

"Home," he answered, with a smile in his voice. "Do you like it?"

"Home?"

"This is the land I bought, Ellie," he said, gesturing to the open space. "We'll have the grandest home in Edinburgh, save the castle. Society will be lining up to attend your parties. And out back by the woods you can have your own wing to tend to as many sick Scots as you want. Just say you'll come back to me." He brushed his fingers across her cheek.

She closed her eyes at his touch, momentarily lost

in a happier time when she thought they were in love. "Ye doona have ta do this, Ben. I doona blame ye for anythin', ye ken."

Ben looked away from her and spread the Campbell plaid on the ground.

"We just weren't meant ta be," Elspeth continued softly, though her heart protested.

She remembered when Will had uttered the same words about his Prisca and the sadness that emanated from him. The sentiment hadn't made much sense to her back then. Now she understood it too well.

"We *were* meant to be. We're connected, lass, in more ways than one."

Distance and time would solve those problems. Elspeth stepped away from him and took a spot on the corner of the plaid. She smiled, hoping he wouldn't see the tears in her eyes. "What have ye got in yer basket?"

He sat beside her; his warm hazel eyes raking across her seemed so sad. "I'm told that roasted pheasant with currants is your favorite."

Elspeth grinned at him. Who had he been talking to? "No blueberries?" She couldn't help but ask.

Ben groaned and squished up his nose. "I don't think I can ever look another blueberry in the face."

Elspeth laughed. "They're really very good for ye."

"I'll survive," he replied, leaning back on his elbows.

She glanced at him, relaxed on the plaid and staring out at his land, his hair hanging rakishly across his brow. Elspeth didn't think it was possible for her to ever stop loving him. Why was he intent on making this harder for her? "Ben, sell the land. Go back ta

London. Yer life is waitin' for ye. The right girl is out there somewhere waitin' for ye."

In the blink of an eye he pulled her onto his lap and wrapped his arms around her waist. "The right girl is here, Ellie. I'm not going anywhere without you."

"Ben," she sighed, staring at his neckcloth to avoid his eyes. "I ken ye care about me. But—"

"I do care about you. I love you, Elspeth Westfield. And I was a fool not to realize it sooner. I'll spend the rest of my life trying to make that up to you."

Elspeth's eyes slowly rose to meet his, and her heart leapt at his words. She wanted to believe him. She wanted it more than anything.

"Tell me the right thing to say, Ellie. Everyone seems to think I'll say something stupid and you'll bolt."

She couldn't help but laugh at that. "Everyone thinks that, do they?"

"Caitrin pounded it into my head." He nodded, his eyes searching hers.

"Cait?" she asked in amazement. Her friend was the very last person she would expect to aid Ben in this quest. She wasn't quite sure what that meant.

He smiled at her. "She said she was going to be our children's godmother."

Elspeth's hand flew to her belly. This was about the bairn. He didn't want her to raise their child alone. Her heart plummeted again, and she scrambled from his lap.

"I doona need yer help, ye ken. I'll manage just fine on my own."

Ben's eyes widened and he shook his head. "What did I say?"

"She never should have told ye," Elspeth snapped

as she crossed her arms beneath her breasts. *How could she?* Elspeth had planned to tell him in her own time, in her own way.

"Told me what?" he asked, his eyebrows drawing together as he reached for her.

# Forty-eight

ELSPETH AVOIDED HIS TOUCH AND HIS GAZE. THEY'D immediately gone from having a casual, comfortable conversation to her pulling away from him.

"What did I say? Please tell me so I can avoid saying it in the future." He recognized the bite of sarcasm in his own voice and chastised himself. This wasn't the time to show her his bruised ego. Caitrin told him not to say anything stupid, and he'd somehow done so anyway.

Elspeth sighed and raised her knees to wrap her arms around them. Then she dipped her head to rest on her knees. Her voice was muffled when she finally spoke. "Nothin'."

"I seem to have a way of putting my foot in my mouth, Ellie. I'm still learning, though. And I'm a quick study."

"I ken ye are," she said, her voice still muffled as she refused to raise her head.

What could he do to bring her back to him? He reached into the picnic basket and started to unload it. "Can you tolerate my presence long enough to eat with me?" He tried not to sound defeated, but it was difficult.

"Aye, I can tolerate ye." She finally raised her head and looked at him. "Her cook makes the best pheasant."

If he couldn't win her with his personality, at least he could win her with food. But when he unwrapped the roasted bird, Elspeth's hand immediately flew to her mouth. Her eyes grew round. And she turned a most horrid shade of green.

"Are you all right?" he asked.

She stood up quickly and ran to the bushes. He closed his eyes and pounded his forehead with his fist when he heard her cast up her accounts. Now his very presence made her sick. The situation was beginning to look hopeless. Instead of Caitrin telling him not to say anything stupid, she should have told him specifically what *not* to say.

A few minutes later she returned. Thankfully, the greenish tint to her skin had receded. "I'm sorry," she started.

He held up a hand. "That's quite all right. You can't help it if being with me makes you ill."

"It's no' that," she said as he passed her a cup of water to rinse her mouth out. "It was the smell of pheasant. I havena been feelin' my best lately." She looked toward the dish and shuddered. "I appreciate ye havin' it prepared for me, though."

Her hand lifted as though to caress his face, and he was so happy he nearly bumped his nose to her hand like a pup who wanted to be petted. But then she pulled back.

"So how do ye feel about what Caitrin told ye?"

"I was quite put out by it at first." Wouldn't anyone who'd been called an idiot be a little upset by it?

Elspeth gasped and pursed her lips.

"What did I do now?" he groaned.

Tears filled her green eyes and welled up behind her lashes but threatened to spill over at any moment. "I'd like ta go home, now."

Ben took Elspeth back to her cottage, his heart breaking the entire journey as she sniffed back tears. Her breathing was labored, and he felt like the biggest cad. If only he knew what stupid thing he'd said.

Once at her cottage, Ben walked her to the door, where he kissed her forehead softly and watched her as she brushed past him into the house. Her stance, which was usually so proud and erect, seemed almost defeated.

He stayed outside until she blew out the candles. Then he went to the Thistle and Thorn to get properly foxed. He could have gone back to MacQuarrie's, but the man would only try to talk to him, and Ben wasn't in the mood to converse with anyone.

He entered the taproom and found Major Forster at a corner table with a glass of whisky, talking amicably with the townspeople. He should have realized the major would still be there. After years of traveling with his regiment, the man naturally made friends wherever he went.

Ben sighed. The major *was* his father-in-law; perhaps he had some insight into Elspeth. As Ben approached him, the major kicked a chair from beneath the table by bumping it with his boot. Ben sank heavily into it.

"Aren't you supposed to be enjoying dinner with my daughter?" the major asked, pulling out his pocket watch to glance at the time.

"I was. She asked me to take her home. It appears as though my presence makes her physically ill."

The major chuckled and motioned for another whisky for Ben. "You turn her stomach, now, do you?"

"Obviously. She was sick in the bushes as soon as I brought the food out." Ben threw back his whisky and motioned for another.

"You mean she's *truly* sick?" The major's eyebrows shot upward. "I should go check on her."

Ben shook his head. "I stayed until she turned out the light. She's fine."

"I wonder what's wrong. Maybe she ate something bad?"

"She didn't eat a thing. She got sick as soon as I uncovered the food!" he cried out, then rested his chin on the heel of his hand in disgust. "And she cries at the smallest things."

"You made her cry?" the major asked, frowning.

"I didn't mean to," Ben defended himself. "But it didn't seem to matter what I said. I've never seen her so emotional, not even when her grandfather died, and she was plenty upset then."

Recognition dawned in the major's eyes. "I'm a fool not to have seen it earlier."

"Seen what?"

With a toothy grin, the major slid his whisky toward Ben. "Congratulations, pup."

"For turning my wife's stomach?" Ben grumbled and looked down at the amber liquid in front of him.

"I believe you may have made me a grandfather!" The major rose from his seat and cackled all the way out the door.

Ben's mouth fell open. Then he picked up the whisky in front of him and downed it in one gulp.

A child? Dear God! He replayed his last conversation with Elspeth over in his mind, under that context, and winced. If she was with child, it was no wonder she was furious with him.

He was going to be a father! Ben signaled the bar maid that he didn't need the next glass of whisky. If he was going to work this out, he needed a clear head. He *would* find a way to make it work.

Elspeth enchanted a spoon to stir some porridge and then collapsed into a seat at her table and laid her head across her folded arms. She'd slept restlessly all night and this morning wasn't feeling her best.

Her father emerged from his room, whistling an old Scottish lullaby. When he spotted her, he grinned widely. "Morning, lass."

"Ye seem awfully cheerful today," she grumbled.

"Many things to be cheerful about," he replied and dropped into a seat across from her. "How was your dinner with Benjamin?"

Elspeth shook her head, then realized her eyes were watering again. She brushed her tears away with the back of her hand. "It could have gone better."

"I gathered that when I saw him last night. Poor fellow looked as if he'd lost his best friend."

"Ye saw him?" Her gaze shot to her father's.

"Hmm. The taproom at the inn. He seemed intent on getting deep in his cups."

Elspeth snorted and rose from her seat to check on her porridge. Of course he was intent on getting drunk. He didn't love her and felt stuck because of the bairn. She peered down into the pot, but it was too soupy.

She didn't feel like eating anyway. She leaned heavily against the far wall and rubbed her face with both hands. How had she gotten herself into this situation?

"Elspeth," her father's voice caused her to jump and drop her hands.

"Yes?"

"You need to sit down and have a conversation with the lad."

"I wouldna even ken what ta say." She stepped forward and slumped back down in her seat at the table.

His warm brown eyes seemed to twinkle. "I'm sure something will come to mind, dear. You can't go on like this. Both of you are completely miserable."

"Aye," she admitted, but for different reasons. There was no solution that would make them both happy.

A knock sounded at the door, and the major crossed the room to open it. "Benjamin," he said in greeting.

Elspeth couldn't keep her gaze from shooting across the cottage to her husband. His hair seemed to sparkle where the morning sunlight hit him. And he was more handsome than ever, though at the moment his hazel eyes looked angry, as did the stubborn tilt of his jaw.

"Major," he replied tightly. "I'd like a word with my wife."

"Ben," her father began with a placating tone.

But he paid no attention to the major and pushed past him into the cottage. "Ellie, this has gone on quite long enough. At first I let you have space, because I thought you needed it and I felt awful for hurting you. And I am sorry for that."

He continued into the room until he stood before her. "But you're my wife and I've put up with all of this that I intend to. I stayed up all night thinking everything through, and I cannot believe that you thought to keep this from me. Living separately, keeping secrets—it's over. All of it. Do you hear me?"

Anger and hurt coursed through her, and Elspeth raised herself up to her full height. Still, she only reached his shoulders. "Ye willna dictate ta me, Benjamin Westfield. I was runnin' my own life before ye came along, and—"

He hauled her into his arms and kissed her. He pulled her flush against him and took her breath away. She'd nearly forgotten how wonderful it felt to be wrapped in his strength. When she sighed against his mouth, Ben's tongue slipped inside hers, tangling with her own.

His hold on her softened, and his hands caressed her back and stroked her arms. Elspeth pressed herself against him and intertwined her fingers in his hair. Time and place lost all meaning, and only the sound of Ben's breathing echoed in her ears… until her father, clearing his throat, broke through to her senses.

Elspeth pulled back away from Ben and gaped at him. He seemed as affected by the kiss as she had been. "Why did ye do that?" she asked, trying to catch her breath.

"I intend to do it again," he warned her. "Every time you even think of disagreeing with me."

"Then ye'll be doin' it a lot," she mumbled under her breath.

He raised his eyebrows meaningfully. "It's been far too long since I kissed you, Ellie. Don't tempt me." He looked over his shoulder at her father and nodded. "Major, a moment, if you don't mind."

He winked at Ben. "Good luck, my boy."

As soon as the major retired to his room, Elspeth glared at her husband. "Why did ye come here, Ben?"

"Because I love you, and if you don't believe it, I'll say it over and over until you do."

"This is about the bairn," she said as she stepped out of his reach and made her way to her old settee.

"This is about us. You. Me. Our family," he called after her. "I was a fool, Elspeth. Do you want me to yell it through the streets of Edinburgh? If it will make you believe me, I'll do so." He followed her to the other side of the room and dropped into a chair across from her.

"Ben, ye doona have ta do all this."

His jaw stiffened. "I'm doing this because I love you. I've never met a more stubborn woman, lass. Maybe I'm going about this the wrong way." He leaned forward in his seat, so close his knees were almost touching hers. "Do you still love *me*, Ellie? Or have I destroyed that, too?"

It hurt to look at him, the emotion on his face, so Elspeth stared at her own hands. "Benjamin, I'll never stop lovin' ye. No matter where ye go or who ye're with."

"There's only you."

She lifted her gaze to him. He seemed so sincere, so concerned. Yet she hated to get her hopes up. Her heart couldn't take being broken again. "What changed?"

"Nothing," he said quietly. "I always loved you, Ellie. I just didn't want to. I didn't want to admit it."

"Why?"

He leaned back in his seat and raked a hand through his hair. "I didn't want to hurt you, and I didn't trust myself not to do so. I cannot control the beast within me. Not when it's close to the full moon. I thought if I kept a bit of distance between us, I could keep you safe."

His anguish was apparent and Elspeth's heart ached for him. She could never watch anyone in pain without feeling it herself, but that was especially true with Ben. "I'm safe with ye."

He scoffed and raised his eyes heavenward. "I don't know if you are or not, Ellie. I hurt you once, and I hurt the girl in Brighton. But I can't live without you, I've learned that much. So I'll just have to be diligent. More careful."

Elspeth swiped at the tears that began to trail down her cheeks. "You willna hurt me."

When he heard her voice tremble, Ben lowered his head to look at her. Then he reached his hand out to her. Elspeth moved to his side and he pulled her to his lap. "Oh, love. I've needed you."

"I need ye, too." She allowed herself to nuzzle against him, feeling the first bit of contentment she'd felt in weeks. He still didn't trust himself, but it was a start.

Ben traced a circle on her belly. "You were going to tell me, weren't you?"

"Of course. But I could kill Cait for tellin' ye first."

Ben shook his head, his hazel eyes boring into her.

"She didn't tell me anything, Ellie. The major figured it out last night in the taproom."

Elspeth blinked at him. She'd been certain he knew. "Oh. Well, what do ye think about it?" she asked, afraid of his answer.

His smile warmed her from the inside out. "I do wish the little fellow had waited a bit. I'd like to have you all to myself for a while, but I couldn't be happier, Ellie. And I want this one to be the first of many. I want us to build that sprawling house and fill every room with children."

Elspeth rested her head against his shoulder and sighed. "I suppose ye'll make me hire maids and footmen and a cook and—"

"You can do whatever you want, love. Whatever will make you happy."

"Ye make me happy." She slid her hand inside his waistcoat.

Ben groaned as though in agony. "Unfortunately, the full moon is approaching. It's only a few days away. So I can't be close with you right now." He cupped her chin in his hands and kissed her softly. "Though I want nothing more than to be with you in every way possible."

Elspeth shifted in his lap and felt him hard against her thigh.

"Don't look at me like that, Ellie," he growled as he set her away from him. "I am not sure I can trust myself."

"I'm no' made of glass, Ben. I willna break," she reminded him.

"I won't take that chance, love." He lifted her off his lap and to her feet, where he drew her close to him as his hands skimmed over her body. Finally he groaned and gently pushed away from her. "I'll see you in a few days."

"Must we wait that long? Will we have ta separate when the moon is full for the rest of our lives?"

"If that's what it takes to keep you safe, then that's what we'll do." He kissed her once more, his lips touching her cheeks, her eyelids, and finally her forehead, where he lingered. Then he turned and walked out the door.

&

Ben had been craving Elspeth for days. Forcing himself to separate from her was the hardest thing he'd ever done. But he'd gladly die a thousand deaths before he allowed himself to hurt her again.

Typically, at this time of the month he would be craving a woman to the point of distraction. Any woman would do, anyone who would stroke the beast within him. But he found himself disinterested in other women. The only woman on his mind was Elspeth. She was the only one he wanted to stroke. To hold. To love. To take. To… claim. He wanted her desperately.

Avoiding Elspeth was like avoiding a piece of himself. He knew now he could not live without her. How he'd been such a fool before, he wasn't sure. But he would spend every day making it up to her.

A voice broke him from his reverie. "I received word from Simon today." Will walked from the forest into view.

"Just how is our big brother doing?" Ben asked as he put down the ax he was using to clear his land and wiped his brow with his forearm. Nothing better than manual labor to take one's mind off a woman.

"He says life with Lily is wonderful. And that he's extremely happy."

"That doesn't sound like the Duke of Blackmoor." His brother Simon didn't have a romantic notion in his body.

"All right." Will shrugged. "It's Mother's translation. But she assures me it's the way Simon feels when he's with Lily."

"I'm sure they're blissfully happy, aside from those few days a month when he has to leave her side and hide out in exile, like a dog that's too dangerous to tether near home." The ax arched through the air and straight through a log, with much more force than was necessary.

"Mother says that he took Lily to the forest with him last month."

Ben's ax struck sideways when he lost his concentration. The mistake trembled up his arm until he dropped the quivering handle. "You're such a poor liar, Will."

"I'm not lying."

"And just how would Mother know this?"

"She's staying with them for a time. And Mother knows *everything*." Will spoke the truth. Their mother *did* know everything. And what she didn't know, she found out.

Ben met Will's eyes. "Would you put Prisca at risk like that?"

"My relationship with Prisca is not what we're discussing," Will hedged.

"Would you?" Ben said. Will glanced away. "That's what I thought." Will could never lie about Prisca.

Suddenly Will reached over and clutched Ben's shirt in his hands, raising him onto his tiptoes. He pushed and clawed to get free, but then Ben saw the desperation in Will's eyes and stilled. "If Prisca loved me the way Elspeth loves you, I would let *nothing* stand in my way. So quit being a goddamn fool."

Will released him and stepped away, then walked back into the forest with nothing more than a shake of his head.

Ben took a deep breath and raised his ax again. But before he could mangle the tree trunk before him, another masculine voice called out.

"I see you've done a lot of work here," Major Forster called as he approached.

"I had a great opportunity to work on the land. Since I'm not fit company for anyone else at this time." Ben pointed to the sky, where the sun was just about to drop below the horizon.

"You look like great company to me," the major said as he sat down on a log.

"That's because you grow hairy and drool at the sight of the moon, the same way I do. To everyone else, I'm dishonorable and untrustworthy. And I bite."

The major picked at a string on the leg of his trousers. "Did Elspeth tell you that?"

The ax struck wood. "No."

"But that's what you believe?"

"It's what I know." He slung the ax again.

"I'm not going to talk to you about my daughter." Ben moved to interrupt. He really didn't want to discuss Elspeth at that moment anyway. But the major held up two hands to stop him. "So I want to tell you about the love of my life. If you're of a mind to listen, that is."

Ben sighed and tried not to grumble as he laid the ax on the ground.

"Thank you."

"It's getting dark." Maybe he'd leave if he realized night was approaching.

The major just smiled. "I can run into the forest as quickly as you can."

"At your age?"

The major chuckled. "At least you still have your sense of humor."

"I have a lot of things. Just not my wife. You said you had a story?"

"Aye. You know I've only had one love in my life. Rosewyth. Elspeth's mother. She was my one and only."

"And why does this involve me?"

The major frowned at him. And Ben felt as though he'd been picked up by the scruff of his neck and shaken, like any bad dog should.

"I'm sorry. Continue. Please." Ben took a seat across from him.

"I just need to tell you that when it's right, it's really right."

Ben just stared at him. That was his story? Forster could use a little practice in telling a decent tale.

"A Lycan has one true mate. If you're with that person, even under the light of a full moon, it can be beautiful."

"But not safe."

"Do you doubt Elspeth is the other half that can make you whole?"

"It's not that," Ben started.

But the major raised a hand and stopped him again.

"It *is* that."

Ben nearly hung his head in defeat.

"I have regrets, Ben. And I don't want you, when you're old and grey, to *wish* you had done things differently."

# Forty-nine

ELSPETH WALKED SLOWLY THROUGH THE WOODS ON the well-worn trail away from Caitrin's house. She had never been as lonesome as she'd been the last few days without Ben. She'd spent plenty of time alone before, but never had she *ached* for someone. Not just someone—*her* someone.

Caitrin had been quiet the whole day. She had avoided having any conversation at all. She usually avoided talking with people if she'd had visions about them. She preferred to let people live their own lives and have their own surprises. The things she did reveal were for fun. Or to help someone through a bad time.

Blaire had offered to enchant Ben with a potion so that he wouldn't be able to resist the love Elspeth had for him. But Elspeth preferred Ben coming to her on his own.

Rhiannon and Sorcha wanted to tie him up with vines again and make him listen to reason. She smiled at the thought.

As Elspeth topped the hill, she heard a low growl from within the bushes. She stilled completely. That wasn't Ben. It was too menacing and too scary. She froze. After a few minutes, the bushes rustled and a dark animal skittered from them and down the hill. Elspeth took two tentative steps forward.

From her vantage point she could see her way to the bottom of the hill. A solitary wolf stood there, as though standing sentinel over its pups. The growl sounded again from close by. This wolf was slightly larger than the one at the bottom of the hill. The smaller was probably the female, and Elspeth imagined that she was guarding her den. And the male kept a watchful eye on Elspeth.

A cloud moved across the sky and finally uncovered the full moon. The male wolf looked up at it in a pose very similar to the one on her combs. He raised his snout to the air and howled.

"I'll no' hurt yer pups," she whispered.

The male wolf still stood, his body rigid and ready to move if Elspeth took even one hesitant step toward his family. But then the mother wolf ran to him, licked his face, and nipped his ear. The male turned to her. She licked the ear she'd just nipped, as though to soothe him. He growled and playfully nipped her back.

That was when Elspeth knew what she had to do. If Ben wouldn't come to her, she'd have to go to him. The female wolf in a pair held a noticeable place of power. Now it was time for Elspeth to display some of that power herself.

She smiled the whole way back to her cottage.

Ben ran through the forest in his Lycan form, feeling the freedom that came with the change, but this time there was a sadness with it as well. It was a gnawing feeling that chewed at his very soul. He wanted Elspeth. He wanted her more with every step he took.

Ben's ears perked up as he heard the cry of a wolf. It wasn't Will—he'd heard that howl since adolescence. And he doubted it was the major—it seemed a bit more feral than what he'd expect from the softened old soldier. Then he remembered the wolf with pups that he'd seen. Of course, both those wolves would be out, basking in the rays of the moon as well.

Ben clenched his eyes shut tightly. It was almost painful to think of the pair of wolves. He would never be part of a pair.

He walked a bit farther and stopped. Then he felt it. It hit him harder than the carriage that had broken his arm. It hit him harder than an anvil thrown from a great height.

Elspeth had stroked her mark.

Ben gritted his teeth as lust swamped him. He fought the urge to run to her. Perhaps she'd simply grazed it when she was bathing. But that brought him to thoughts of her naked in the tub, and he ground his teeth together again.

His front legs shook with a desire to run. His whole body quivered. Then two minutes later, she stroked her mark again. He lifted his snout and cried out. It was the longest and darkest howl of his life. If any of his kind heard it, they would surely think he was dying from pain.

*Stop, Elspeth!*

She touched him again. He could no longer fight it. He tore through the forest as fast as he could to her cottage. He brushed through brambles and briers, thanking his heavy coat for keeping him safe from them or he would be a bloody mess by the time he reached her.

He ran toward the cottage, but the windows were dark. He stood up on his hind legs and looked through the bedroom window. Thankfully, he had never installed those shutters. She wasn't home? Where would she be in the middle of the night?

Then she stroked him again. His flesh quivered. It felt as though her hands dug deeply through his fur to reach his skin, where she scratched her fingernails against him. He stood still and tried to absorb it. He wasn't able to fight it. Not anymore.

*Where are you, Elspeth?*

Then the wind shifted and he picked up her scent. The beautiful scent of magnolia met him, and he ran in her direction. He finally saw her, in the clearing where they'd made love for the first time. She lay in the middle of the area, on her plaid, completely and totally naked.

The moonlight glinted off her alabaster skin, making her shine. Her breasts were full and crowned with rose-colored nipples. Even from where he stood, he could see that they were erect. He wanted to cup them in his hands and bring his mouth down to taste her. But he couldn't. Not in this form. He stood and watched her.

"I ken ye're there," she called. "Come out and let me see ye."

❧

Elspeth knew she was taking a chance. It could be disastrous for them both. If he hurt her, he'd never forgive himself. But she had faith in his love for her.

He stepped into the clearing. Her breath caught as she sat up to look at him. He was beautiful. There were no more adequate words to say. The moonlight glinted off his shiny brown fur. She nearly ached to touch it.

He tipped his head as though to ask a question.

"I couldna howl," she said, shrugging her shoulders. "So I called ta ye the only way I knew how."

His head straightened.

She held up her arm and was about to stroke across the mark again, but he suddenly raced across the clearing and stood before her. One corner of his mouth lifted in a fierce snarl.

She held up two hands in surrender. "I willna touch it anymore." He turned to leave. "As long as ye stay with me!" she called to his retreating form.

He stopped, but did not turn his head.

"Look at me!" she cried, frustration nearly ready to take over. He turned and walked back to her, his eyes half closed. She reached out a hand, but he skittered back out of her reach. "I want ta touch ye."

He didn't move.

"Ye willna let me do that, will ye?"

He still didn't move. She reached out a hand and stroked the silky fur on the top of his head. His eyes closed. Then she ran her fingernails down his back, scratching him gently.

Then, before her very eyes, he changed. His

features shifted. He changed from beast to man. To man with a beast within.

Before she could blink, he shoved her back to the ground and spread her thighs forcefully so that he could settle between them. He covered her completely. A wild thing, hoping to dominate.

"What games do you play, Ellie?" he snarled against her lips as his hands slid into her hair and tugged.

"No games, Ben. I simply want ta love ye."

He dipped his head at her shoulder and gently abraded the skin with his teeth.

Heat pooled in her body where he insistently pressed his length against her.

"In me," she said, adjusting her body to lie directly beneath him.

"I cannot claim you." He closed his eyes. "You don't know how much this hurts me," he growled. "If you did, you would let me be."

"I'll never let ye be, Ben. I plan ta claim ye as my Lycan mate this night. And every day from this moment on."

Ben was startled when Elspeth pushed his shoulder, shoving him from atop her body. *Finally!* She saw reason. She recognized the danger. But she just pushed him onto his back then climbed her naked body atop him, straddling his hips.

Ben covered his eyes with his forearm. He growled and grabbed her hips to lift her off him.

"I am half Lycan, Ben," she said, pointing to the mark of the beast she wore on her wrist. "Just as ye are. And this night I plan ta claim ye as *my* Lycan mate." She smiled at him, but there was suddenly something wild in her gaze. Something *wanting*.

Ben moved to slide from beneath her. "Ye canna leave me," she said as she covered her body with his. She lay along his length, her thighs parted to straddle him. Then her teeth touched the tender place where his shoulder met his neck.

"Ah, God. I cannot fight you." He wanted to scream.

"Then doona try." She licked across the sensitive skin and then moved to kiss his lips. Then she sat up and took him into her body, sliding down on him like warm silk, tight and soft.

He grabbed her hips and clutched her tightly. Then he remembered how he'd bruised her the last time and took his hands down. She lifted them, putting them on her hips. "Help me. I doona ken what ta do."

So he clutched her hips and set the rhythm, then she took over. The beast in him was content to let her ride him. And he reveled in the way she took him fully within her body with every stroke. He'd never have believed it.

Her breaths grew shorter and shorter. He knew she was close to reaching her peak. And the beast wanted to please her. He sat up to reach her breasts and drew her nipple into his mouth. All gentleness had left his body. He was afraid he'd hurt her when she cried out. But then she led him on when she said, "More," and pulled his head toward her breast.

While his mouth pleasured her breasts, his hand dove between her thighs and circled her center. As she cried out, she removed her breast from his mouth and bent her head to his neck. Then she exploded around him, and at the same time her teeth nipped the tender flesh of his shoulder. He stilled and threw his head back, growling as he enjoyed the supreme satisfaction he felt to have her claim him as her own.

When she stilled, he held her face in his hands and looked into her green eyes. "I love you," he said.

"Then take me," she laughed.

Ben wasn't gentle with her at all as he lifted her from him and set her on the plaid. He was rough and demanding. And she loved it. On his knees, he pulled her back against his front, rubbing his length along her slit. She spread her legs to give him entrance. The tip of him touched her but didn't slide inside. She wanted to shout to the heavens.

"Don't be so impatient," he growled as he cupped her breasts and teased her into a frenzy.

Sliding one arm around her waist, he pushed her shoulders down toward the blanket. "On your hands and knees, love."

"We've never," she started.

"Now we are," he growled.

She smiled. Maybe, finally, he would take her. Make her his in every way.

When he slid into her in one hard stroke, she cried out. The pleasure of it was nearly overwhelming. He commanded her body as his hips thrust into her, forward and back. She moved to meet his thrusts and he went harder.

Then he bent over her back to talk low in her ear. "I love being inside you. I love to feel you squeeze me, so wet and warm." He had never before talked to her about what they were doing. But it excited her even more. He continued to mumble in her ear as he took her to new heights. Then when she was ready, they came together, just as he pierced the skin of her shoulder with the most gentle of bites.

He sank to the ground atop her, and rolled to the side, taking her with him to cuddle against his chest. "That's all ye have for me, wolf? A teeny, tiny bite?"

"Yes, I found that I could control the beast more than I thought." He absently brought his hand to his own shoulder. "I think you bit me harder than I bit you." He chuckled and slapped her bottom so hard it stung.

"I wasna worried, even if I'd broken the skin. Because I ken I can heal ye."

"Heart and soul, witch."

# *Epilogue*

"Good morning, William," Elspeth said brightly as she held open the door for her brother-in-law to enter the cottage.

His eyes swept across her, landing on the exposed skin of her neck and shoulders. His light blue eyes twinkled. "Found Ben last night, I see."

She couldn't hide the blush that warmed her cheeks. "I doona think he'd appreciate that."

Will laughed. "My dear sister, Ben rarely appreciates me. It's one of his flaws."

Elspeth shook her head and started back toward her small kitchen. "Would ye care for some tea?"

"No. I've just come to say good-bye."

"Ye're leavin'?" She stopped in her tracks to turn back and look at him. Will hadn't been in town all that long, and the journey was tiresome, as she well knew.

He shrugged. "I only came along because I didn't trust Benjamin to return my coach in one piece. I'd prefer it not be set aflame by your well-meaning friends in a fit of pique."

She couldn't help but laugh. "They'd never do such a thing. Ye've charmed them all."

"Ah," he agreed with a roguish grin. "It's a curse I have."

Elspeth gestured to the old threadbare settee. "Ben's asleep, let me wake him for ye."

"In a minute, lass," he replied with a smile. "Sit down."

Curious, she took the spot beside him. "Ye want ta talk ta me?"

Will nodded. "You're good for him, you know. I'm glad he has you."

"He's good for me, too."

"I'd tell you that if he starts behaving foolishly to let me know. Knocking sense into him has become a bit of a habit of mine, but somehow I don't think you'll need my help."

Neither did Elspeth. She and Ben were more connected than ever, and she knew in her heart that they'd turned a corner the night before. Nothing to come between them again.

"My wife is capable of bringing me to heel on her own, William," Ben said from the bedroom doorway.

Will winked at Elspeth. "Take care of yourself, lass." He rose from his seat, striding toward his brother. "And you, little brother, I'll miss you. Will I see either of you in England anytime soon?"

Ben ambled into the great room and shrugged. "I suppose I'll bring Ellie to Westfield Hall for the holidays. Mother will be dying to meet her, as will Simon, I'm sure."

"The holidays it is, then." Will embraced Ben, then stepped away from him. "Take care of her, Benjamin. You don't know how lucky you are."

"I know exactly how fortunate I am." Ben crossed the room and slid his arm around Elspeth's waist. "Besides, she's stuck with me now."

She laughed. "Travel safe, Will."

Her brother-in-law saluted her. "I always do."

"Ye could always stay a couple more days."

Will shook his head. "Alas, I have my debauched lifestyle to return to." And with that he winked at her and then left them alone.

Elspeth turned in Ben's arms. "How are ye, my handsome wolf?"

His hazel eyes darkened seductively. "Missing my witch."

"Are ye?" she giggled.

"Hmm," he growled. "I don't think the beast is completely sated, Ellie. You better climb back into bed."

His suggestion sent a jolt of anticipation straight to her core. "But breakfast."

"I think I'll just have you instead."

❦

Ben glowed with pride as he led Elspeth into Alec MacQuarrie's drawing room and a footman announced their entrance. "Lord Benjamin Westfield and Lady Elspeth Westfield."

The finest families in Edinburgh were present, and the people who'd once looked down on his wife now smiled at her with acceptance. When Elspeth spotted Caitrin on the other side of the room, she squeezed Ben's hand. "I'll be back soon."

"Take your time, lass," he replied. Months ago he

had hated Cait's interference, but she'd come to grow on him. And Elspeth did love the chit like a sister.

He watched his wife walk across the room with a regal confidence she'd lacked when he first met her before the Fergusons' ball those many months before. She had blossomed since finding the major. He never would have guessed that meeting her sire would have helped her come to terms with her past.

A hand clapped him on the back, and he turned to find Alec regarding him curiously. "If you can drag your eyes off your wife for a minute, I'd like to have your ear."

Ben smiled. "Of course."

He had been so caught up with Elspeth, he hadn't noticed until now that Alec seemed different somehow. Solemn. Distressed.

Ben followed his friend to a far corner of the room. Whatever this was must be serious. "What is it, Alec?"

"I'm afraid you'll think I've lost my mind." He began, as his eyes flashed toward Elspeth and Caitrin. Then he rubbed his brow. "There's an old Scottish lore about a group of fabled witches—"

Ben swallowed uncomfortably. "Witches?"

"Aye," Alec breathed out slowly. "I always thought it was nonsense, but…"

"Well, of course it is. A group of *fabled* witches?" Ben chuckled. "You're right, MacQuarrie. I do think you've lost your mind."

Alec met his eyes. "The thing is, Westfield, Miss Macleod… well, I think she might be a witch."

Ben laughed even louder. "Alec, that has to be the most ridiculous thing I've ever heard. The woman is at my house every day. She's haughty and full of herself, but a witch?"

Alec shook his head. "I'm sure you're right." He sighed. "I suppose I should return to London, where my mind doesna play tricks on me and women actually want my attention."

"You're leaving Edinburgh?"

Alec shrugged. "I've been chasing the lass so hard, and she hasn't budged a bit. I suppose I was hoping maybe she was a witch, because that would explain things. I think I need a change of scenery. I'll be off in a few days."

That was probably for the best, at least for the time being. If Alec discovered the truth about Cait, it would only be a matter of time before Elspeth would be figured out as well. Ben tried not to feel guilty about misleading his best friend, but he'd never risk his wife's secret. "We won't be too far behind you. I promised we'd go to Hampshire for the holidays. You're more than welcome to visit us there."

Across the room, Elspeth found his eyes and she touched her belly. She wasn't showing yet. Very few people knew she was expecting. His family, the major, and her coven. But her glow was hard for him not to bask in. "Excuse me, Alec."

His friend laughed. "Well, I had your attention for a few minutes. Go on."

Ben wasted no time doing so and crossed the floor, sliding his arm around Elspeth's waist. "How are you feeling, love?"

Caitrin rolled her eyes. "Ye're as bad as a mother hen, Westfield."

He winked at her. "You should be thanking me. MacQuarrie was just telling me he thought you were a fabled witch."

Her mouth fell open. "He was?"

"I talked him out of it."

She bit her bottom lip and furrowed her brow. "I, um, should talk ta him."

"I don't know, Cait. He's headed for London. You may want to leave him be."

But she paid him no attention and started off toward their host. Ben looked down at his wife. "What was that about?"

She shrugged.

"Jonathan," Ben suggested, his mind now back to his wife as he moved his hand to her belly. "My father's name."

"It's a fine name," she said, grinning up at him. "Though we have months ta find just the right one."

"Or Desmond," he offered, with less enthusiasm.

Elspeth laughed at him, her emerald eyes dancing with mirth. "I doona think my father would appreciate the way ye said that, Benjamin."

True, the major would surely blast him if he thought Ben were serious, which he wasn't. Any name would be fine, as long as the child was healthy. His lips twisted to a grin. "Your grandfather was Liam. Liam Westfield has a nice ring to it."

"Ye ken," she began, smoothing her palm across his chest, "it might be a *girl.*"

He rolled his eyes playfully. "Heaven help me from living in a house with more than one witch."

Elspeth giggled. "With the size of that monstrosity

ye're buildin', I could have my entire coven move in with us and ye'd never notice."

"Ha!" he snorted. "Don't even think about it. I'd sooner send myself off to Bedlam." But there was something glinting in her eyes, something that made him wonder. "Caitrin told you! *Is* it a girl?"

Elspeth's smile brightened the room. "Ye'll just have ta wait and see."

# About the Author

**Lydia Dare** is an active member of the Heart of Carolina Romance Writers and sits on the board of directors. She lives in a house filled with boys and an animal or two (or ten) near Raleigh, North Carolina.

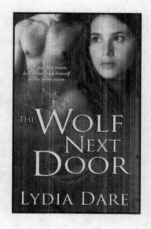

FROM

# A CERTAIN
# WOLFISH
# CHARM

*Maberley Hall, Essex*
*August 1816*

LILY RUTLEDGE HAD NEVER CONTEMPLATED MURDER
before, though she was warming to the idea. The most
recent column in the *Mayfair Society Paper* taunted
her at the breakfast table. The Duke of Blackmoor
seemed to have plenty of time to gamble away his
funds in one hell or another, race his phaeton along
the old Bath road for sport, and spend every other
waking hour enjoying the entertainments of one
Mrs. Teresa Hamilton or visiting fashionable bawdy
houses throughout Town. Not that Lily was terribly
surprised. They were the same sorts of things he'd
done for years, though she hadn't cared until now.

"Aunt Lily," called her twelve-year-old nephew,
Oliver York, the Earl of Maberley, from a few seats
away. "Your face is turning purple again."

Purple indeed. Lily sighed, looking at the boy.
What was she to do with him? Especially when she
couldn't get Blackmoor to even respond to one of

her letters. Of course, he sent funds every time she wrote him, though that was not what she asked for. Infuriating man! Did he even read her letters?

The Maberley estate was not terribly far from London. Visiting Oliver would only interrupt his debauched lifestyle for a day or two at the most. Was that truly too much to ask of her nephew's guardian? After all, he hadn't seen the boy in years.

"Finish your breakfast, Oliver," she directed, glancing again at the maddening society rag. There must be some way to get His Grace's attention. Perhaps if she picked up and went to London—

"I'm through," the young earl responded. "May I be excused?"

*Through*? Food had been piled high in front of him just moments ago. Lily's eyes flashed to Oliver's plate, only to find it completely empty, as was the sideboard behind him. Not a crumb was left uneaten. Where had he gotten this appetite? It wasn't natural. And how could he possibly have devoured all the food in the room so quickly and quietly? It was another one of the unexplained transformations she'd noticed in her nephew over the last month. "Yes, of course. You would do well to go over your Latin before Mr. Craven arrives."

Oliver scowled as he pushed away from the table. "I'd rather not."

He never wanted to go over his Latin, which was a problem. According to Mr. Craven, his tutor, Oliver was far behind in that particular subject. When he began his first term at Harrow in October, he'd need to do better. That was assuming Lily sent him off to school, and, at the moment, she didn't know if she could do so. It was one of the many things she needed to discuss with that scoundrel Blackmoor.

Lily shook her head. "Mr. Craven says you need to practice, Oliver. Please do so."

The young earl stomped from the room in a manner she was getting unfortunately accustomed to. Just a month ago, Oliver had had the sweetest disposition. Now she barely recognized him. His shoulders were suddenly broad enough to fill a doorway, and he almost had to duck to cross the threshold as he left the breakfast room. Gone was the little boy in short pants. The young earl's valet had replaced Oliver's clothing twice in as many months and had sent more than one pair of trousers to the seamstress to have the seams reinforced.

To make it even worse, Oliver had developed a terrible temper, with the smallest annoyances setting him off. He seemed to rumble more than talk, his singsong voice replaced by a gravely growl. Entry into adulthood was hard, but Lily had never expected it to come on so suddenly and with such force.

Perhaps things would be different if Oliver's parents were still alive. Perhaps things would be different if Blackmoor showed even the slightest interest in the lad. Perhaps if she'd ever raised an adolescent boy before, she'd know if Oliver's *changes* were normal—though she couldn't imagine they were. Lily knew in her heart that something was drastically wrong with her nephew, and she was at a complete loss for what to do.

Blast Blackmoor for ignoring her letters!

An idea occurred to her. If *he* couldn't be troubled

to visit Oliver, she'd simply have to pay *him* a visit instead. His Grace would have an impossible time ignoring her in person. She was hard to miss.

Lily picked up the society rag, rereading it. Everything was there. Everything she needed to know. Where he spent his time and with whom. The Duke of Blackmoor would regret shirking his duties, if making him do so was the last thing she ever did.

The only thing Simon Westfield, the Duke of Blackmoor, regretted was purchasing the services of one whore instead of two. Two would have been a great deal more fun and would have helped ease some of the restlessness that seemed to be his constant companion of late. He could count on the disquiet seeping into the dark recesses of his mind the same way he'd learned to expect the fullness of the moon with each lunar cycle. It just happened. It wasn't something he thought about. He simply began to feel an anxious flutter, a *want*.

To ease the discomfort and restlessness, the duke began his infamous prowl. He'd spent so much time and money perfecting his routine that he'd even been written about in the society pages. He supposed he should feel some shame at being reviewed so harshly. One paper even said that he'd lost more than he had to spend, but that was rubbish. He had a lot more to lose. A lot more to enjoy. He usually won at the gaming tables, even when he had a wench settled upon his knee waiting for him, like now.

He reached around the plump brunette, seated

solidly on his groin, to tap the table, asking for another card. The doxy squirmed in his lap, giggling as he lifted her bottom to put more of her weight on his thigh. "Sit still," he mumbled at her. She squirmed again, becoming more impatient. He sighed and laid his cards on the table, as he lost the hand. "You don't listen very well, do you?" he drawled slowly.

"I follow directions very well, Your Grace," she snickered as she boldly whispered a suggestion in his ear. He dipped his head and kissed the swell of her bosom. She arched toward his mouth, reflexively. If he remembered correctly, this particular woman could arch various parts of her body, because he'd enjoyed her flexibility in the past.

With his cards on the table, he was able to put his hands on her hips and turn her toward him. Her breasts pushed at the top of her bodice, so much skin displayed that she threatened to topple out at any minute.

It wasn't enough. He was past the point where he could take solace in the body of a willing woman. Sadly, the thought of holding those fleshy orbs didn't titillate him. She wasn't going to ease any of the restlessness in him. He knew it. He knew that nothing would satisfy him at this point, nothing that wouldn't scare the wench off. They even scared him, the things he wanted to do when he got to this point.

He forced the beast within him to subside. Reaching into his jacket, he withdrew a guinea and tucked it between her breasts. The tiny jostle caused the creamy flesh to tremble, and the edge of a dark areola peeked over the top of her bodice. The beast reared its ugly head.

What he felt wasn't an attractive desire. It was an overwhelming need to copulate. To force submission. To cover a body with his and *own* it. It was more than he could control. He stood up and placed her solidly on her feet. She put her hands on her hips and stomped a slippered foot.

He laughed and flicked her nose gently with the tip of his finger. "Don't pout, love. I'll be back in a week." It would take a week before he would feel safe enough to be in polite company. Or impolite company, as the case may be.

Simon strolled out of the hell and walked toward the street where his ducal coach waited. His crest, a lone wolf—gold emblazoned against blue—mocked him. He ignored it. His coachman opened the carriage door, and Simon slipped inside, the springs groaning under his weight. He sank heavily into the seat and reached up to loosen his cravat. He hadn't been careful enough. He'd almost gone too far and taken that wench above stairs, even though he knew how close he was to losing control. That could have been disastrous.

This time, he couldn't go to his townhouse. It was time to head for Westfield Hall in Hampshire. He needed a secluded area where he could relax and calm himself. He needed to be locked up for a sennight. But no one was able to do that for him, for his brothers would be suffering the same curse. He would take himself out of harm's way, as he normally did. Of course, the prison was one of his choosing and lacked the cells of Newgate, which is where he would most assuredly be sent should anyone discover his terrible secret. The isolation of the quiet countryside was what he sought. He would go where he could walk the hills at night under the full moon, safe from the intrusion of others. And they would be safe from him.

He slept a fitful sleep the remaining hours of the night, the rocking of the coach his only comfort. He tried to straighten his clothes as he stepped from the coach onto his own cobblestone path, but he knew he still looked disheveled. It was a completely unrespectable way for a duke to present himself to his household. Thank heaven he wasn't a stuffy old member of the peerage. And his staff didn't expect him to be. Of course, they'd also seen him in worse shape.

Not even bothering to tie his cravat or fasten the top buttons of his shirt, he turned toward the front door and drew in a deep breath. It felt good to be home. He was safe again, until nightfall. Thankfully, the desire had dissipated with the darkness. If only the darkness of his soul could be lifted as easily as the sun in the sky.

Simon passed through the doorway with a nod to his butler.

"Welcome home, Your Grace."

Simon immediately knew something was wrong when he saw the normally unshakeable man wipe his sweaty brow. "Is something amiss, Billings?" he asked.

"You have a visitor." The butler gestured toward the closest sitting room.

From his spot in the corridor, Simon had a clear view of the room. The last person he'd ever expected to see here was Lily Rutledge. But there she was, sitting on his settee as though she belonged. With the moonful quickly approaching, that wasn't in her best interest. Simon glared at his butler. Had the man lost his mind? Miss Rutledge could be injured in his presence. "What is she doing here?"

Billings shrugged. "The London staff told her you were here."

Damn! Fight or retreat? He sighed.

Retreat. He couldn't see her. There was no telling what the beast would do.

"Ready the coach to take Miss Rutledge home, Billings." He turned and hastened toward his study.

Simon leaned heavily against the door once he was safely ensconced inside and turned the key. He took deep breaths to try to calm his racing heartbeat. She shouldn't have come. Not when he wasn't fully in control. He couldn't hide from the fullness of the moon. It would take him whether he wanted it or not. Sure, she was reasonably safe during the day, but when the sun sank behind the horizon, the danger would become more and more real.

He knew Lily Rutledge was a strong woman. She was nearly as tall as the average man, standing well above most females. But he wasn't an average man. She only reached his shoulder. He bet that he could tuck her under his chin and still have room to look down at her. He imagined himself doing just that, having her close enough to feel her body against his. He groaned and shifted his trousers.

No matter how strong she was, Simon would still hurt her. He slumped down in the seat behind his desk. As long as Lily remained safely on the other side, all was well.

But then he heard her voice.

"I know he's here, Billings," he heard her cry from the hallway. Simon flinched when her fist hit the door.

"You *will* see me, Your Grace," she called.

What other woman, he wondered, could make "Your Grace" sound so much like an insult?

**Now Available**

FROM

# THE WOLF NEXT DOOR

*Langley Downs, Hampshire*
*December 1816*

PRISCA HAWTHORNE WAS FAIRLY CERTAIN BEDLAM WAS in her future. Still, she couldn't help herself. She had to leave, to see if her wolf had returned. It was a foolish thing to do, Prisca well knew. How many nights had she gone in search of him, only to return home tired and disappointed? Still, something in her soul told her she'd be successful tonight. And she never questioned that feeling; it had always been correct in the past.

She slipped into her long, wool coat as she padded across the cold marble floor. After all, it would be simply foolish to traipse around her property in the middle of night in only her flimsy nightrail. More foolish than searching for an elusive wolf.

Prisca pushed open the double glass doors that led to the veranda. The frosty winter wind swirled around her, lifting the edge of her coat and making her shiver. This was surely madness.

She quietly closed the doors behind her and rushed across the veranda, down the stone steps, and out toward her garden. The moon was full tonight, lighting her way, which made her smile. He only came to her when the moon was full. She sped up her pace.

The garden was not in bloom this time of year, but the hedgerows and topiaries still kept their form. Prisca pressed forward down the path, first around one hedge and then around another.

She spotted him and stopped in her tracks.

He *had* come.

Standing in a shaft of moonlight, the wolf seemed to be waiting for her. Prisca's heart pounded out a familiar beat, and anticipation coursed through her veins. He was still the most magnificent creature she'd ever seen, with his regal black coat, icy blue eyes, and proud stature.

If anyone else had seen her approach the dangerous creature, her conveyance to Bedlam would have been summoned immediately. But she knew from their past encounters that he was, if not tame, of no risk to her.

She was the only one who'd ever seen the wolf. At times, she doubted he was real. In fact, it seemed like a lifetime since she'd seem him last.

Prisca smiled at the beast and stepped forward. "There you are. I didn't know if I'd see you again."

She sat on a stone bench and patted the space beside her.

The wolf appeared to heave a sigh, though that seemed an odd thing for him to do. Then he slowly walked toward her. He stopped before her feet, peered up at her with his cool blue eyes, and rested his head in her lap.

Prisca stroked his coarse black fur and closed her eyes, reveling in the feel of him. There was something so familiar, so comforting in the animal. Which was why she could never tell anyone about him; they'd all think she had lost her mind.

The wolf pressed closer to her, and Prisca laughed. "I missed you, too. You should visit me more often. You could even stay here," she suggested. Wouldn't all of Hampshire faint if they discovered she kept a wolf for a pet? "I'd take good care of you."

The wolf closed his eyes, and Prisca scratched behind his ears. She told him all about her brothers and the goings-on around their village, just like she always had whenever he visited her. All the while, the wolf enjoyed her ministrations and seemed content to stay there forever.

Suddenly, he lifted his head with a jolt, looked her straight in the eyes, and ran out of the garden and into a copse of trees at the edge of the property as though he'd been summoned by some invisible force. It happened so fast that Prisca couldn't even call out for him to wait.

She sighed in defeat, wondering how long it would be until she saw him again.

Emory Hawthorne sank down into a chair at the breakfast table and stifled a yawn. He glanced around at the other places at the table and discovered the eyes of his four younger brothers all focused on him, which was a bit unnerving. How unusual for any one thing to capture the interest of each Hawthorne brother at the same time. Emory scrubbed a hand across his face. Had he neglected to shave this morning? Or were his eyes red-rimmed? Or his cravat uncharacteristically wrinkled?

What the hell were they looking at?

"Well?" Pierce began, his dark brow raised in question.

Emory frowned at the brother closest to his own age. What the devil was going on? "I beg your pardon."

"You're the only one who still lives here," Garrick informed him, as though Emory might be unaware of the circumstances of his own residence.

"And by God, you were supposed to keep the rest of us informed." Darius folded his arms across his chest.

No question about it, Emory was definitely missing something. Had the others been this mysterious when they'd all lived together? He couldn't quite remember that far back, at least not this early in the morning. Life was fairly peaceful without his brothers, however. As it was, only their father and Prisca still remained at Langley Downs...

Then it hit him. *Prisca.* This inquisition was about their sister.

"Ah, the light finally dawns." Garrick, the vicar, leaned forward in his seat. "What *is* Prissy's status?"

Emory groaned. He wished he knew the answer to that question. He really, truly did. He'd labored over such ponderings on too many sleepless nights. "You know as much as I do," he admitted, then winced a bit when four sets of brotherly eyes narrowed on him. But what was he to say? Lying won't do any good.

"Oh, for the love of God, Emory!" Darius growled.

"Don't blame me," he insisted. "You know how stubborn she is. I've tried a million times over to get her to consider a suitor, any suitor. I haven't been picky."

"But she *said* she was husband hunting." Pierce, the merchant, raked a hand through his dark hair.

Emory rose from his seat. "She may have said that—"

Garrick cleared his throat. It was hell having a man of the cloth at his very own table to keep him honest, Emory thought.

He shook his head. "All right, she *did* say that. But I don't think she meant it."

"What's wrong with her?" Garrick complained. "Most chits want to get married. I've performed enough weddings to know the truth behind that. They always have starry eyes. Every last one of them."

Prisca's eyes were never starry. Emory shrugged his answer. If he knew what was wrong with their sister, he'd have done his best to fix it long before now.

"It's William Westfield," Blaine, the youngest and furthest down the table, finally spoke.

A hush fell across the room and lasted until Darius chuckled. "God help her if that's true."

"Do you think," Garrick began, glaring at the recently returned army lieutenant, "that you can keep the Lord's name out of this, Dari? That's the third time in as many minutes."

Darius ignored the vicar and focused on their youngest brother. "I know she fancied herself in love with him when she was in leading strings, but you don't think she still does, do you?"

Blaine sighed. "She still looks at him like a mooncalf."

Did she? How had Emory missed that? He'd

always thought she looked at Will with barely concealed disgust.

"It was just an infatuation," Pierce muttered. "At least I thought it was."

Emory sank back down in his seat. Will and Prissy bickered like an old married couple. They'd done that for more years than he could remember. In fact, Prissy saved her most vicious barbs for his old friend. Did she truly fancy herself in love with the scoundrel? It seemed far-fetched.

"Well, if Westfield is what she wants," Pierce began, "I say we get him for her."

Garrick dropped his cup of coffee back to the table, sloshing the contents on either side. "Have you lost your mind? *William* Westfield?"

Pierce shrugged. "Well, of course, Will. Simon and Benjamin already have wives. Besides, she has her heart set on him."

"At one time or another, each of you has caroused with the man," the pious vicar complained. "I hardly think William Westfield would make a suitable match for our sister."

Darius broke out into a fit of laughter. "Would you rather thrust her at some unsuspecting man who thought he was gaining a malleable wife?"

*Malleable* didn't begin to describe Prisca. Emory couldn't believe he actually agreed with the army lieutenant. But Will was one of the few men of their acquaintance who could actually handle their baby sister. "I say we do it."

"And just how do you propose that?" Garrick gaped at him, as though he'd grown a horn and sprouted a tail. "The man is far from the marrying sort."

At this pronouncement, Blaine rose from his seat. "I think I have the solution."

As Blaine was fresh from Cambridge and still wet behind the ears, Emory doubted that his youngest brother had the answer to their problem. Still, he had no ideas himself about how to proceed. "And?"

Blaine shrugged. "Will plans to spend the holiday at The Hall. He's going to be around for a while, and we're all in residence here at the moment. We can finagle reasons and opportunities to thrust her in his path. There are five of us and only one of him. Besides, he has a hard time avoiding pretty women as it is."

"For a tumble!" Garrick's face resembled an outraged tomato. "Do you want Prissy ruined?"

"No, not ruined—married." Emory shook his head. Despite whatever character flaws Will possessed, he was honorable. "Perhaps we can trick him into compromising her. Will would do the right thing in that *unfortunate* circumstance."

The air escaped from Garrick's lungs, and he sunk back in his seat like a deflated hot-air balloon. "You want William Westfield to compromise her?"

Darius grinned and nodded with enthusiasm. "Brilliant! Think about it, Gar. How many times have you said the ends justify the means?"

Pierce raised his hand as though he were a schoolboy and had the answer the instructor wanted. "Wrong brother, Dari. That was me. Business is business, after all."

"Never mind." Emory rose from his spot at the table, and though he hadn't eaten a bite, he felt more rejuvenated than he had in quite a while. Together, they could pull off this charade and see their sister finally walk down the aisle. Of course, if they failed, she'd probably kill each and every one of them. Still, one needed to take chances in life as often as one did at the hazard table. "I say we do it."

"Put it to a vote," Pierce suggested.

"Very well. It has been proposed that we will seek out ways to thrust Prisca and Will together at every conceivable opportunity. And if there are no opportunities, we will create them ourselves. All in favor, raise your hand."

Three arms shot up in the air. Emory smiled as he raised his own and sent a meaningful glare in Garrick's direction. "If you don't join us in this, you may not be happy with how we go about it."

Grudgingly, the vicar raised one finger in assent. "You're still a bully, Emory."

Emory shrugged. "We all have our talents."

Darius leapt to his feet. "We need a campaign."

"A campaign for what?" Prisca asked from behind them.

Emory turned and bowed slightly to their sister and smiled. His mind raced, hoping to come up with a plausible response. "A, um, campaign for Father."

"For Papa?" She raised one delicately arched brow.

"Yes," Pierce answered, coming to stand beside Emory and clapping him on the back. "I've been looking at a piece of property in South Hampton, but Father doesn't think it's sound. Darius suggests we put a campaign together to change his mind."

She looked from one brother to the next, finally settling her gaze on Garrick. "Is that true?"

The blasted vicar squirmed in his seat. "Father can be difficult at times. You know that."

Emory bit back a smile at Garrick's evasion. Still, if questioned again, his pious brother would break. He stepped toward Prisca. "Speaking of difficult, I was at Westfield Hall yesterday and the dowager has taken a bit ill. Perhaps you should pay her a call. You know how your visits always cheer her up."

Prisca sighed. "A bit ill?"

"I do think you should visit," Emory pressed.

"I'll go this morning."

This morning would be perfect. Will was due to arrive at any time.

**Available June 2010**

# A CERTAIN
# WOLFISH
# CHARM

## BY LYDIA DARE

## REGENCY ENGLAND HAS
## GONE TO THE WOLVES!

*The rules of Society can be beastly...*

...especially when you're a werewolf and it's that irritating time of the month. Simon Westfield, the Duke of Blackmoor, is rich, powerful, and sinfully handsome, and has spent his entire life creating scandal and mayhem. It doesn't help his wolfish temper at all that Miss Lily Rutledge seems to be as untamable as he is. When Lily's beloved nephew's behavior becomes inexplicably wild, she turns to Simon for help. But they both may have bitten off more than they can chew when each begins to discover the other's darkest secrets...

**"*A Certain Wolfish Charm* has bite!"**

—SABRINA JEFFRIES, *NEW YORK TIMES* BESTSELLING
AUTHOR OF *WED HIM BEFORE YOU BED HIM*

978-1-4022-3694-5 • $6.99 U.S./$8.99 CAN/£3.99 UK